DANGEROUS DECEPTION

SUSAN HUNTER

SEVERN RIVER PUBLISHING

Severn River Publishing
www.SevernRiverBooks.com

ISBN: 978-1-64875-461-6 (Paperback)

ALSO BY SUSAN HUNTER

Leah Nash Mysteries

Dangerous Habits

Dangerous Mistakes

Dangerous Places

Dangerous Secrets

Dangerous Flaws

Dangerous Ground

Dangerous Pursuits

Dangerous Waters

Dangerous Deception

Dangerous Choices

To find out more about Susan Hunter and her books, visit

severnriverbooks.com/authors/susan-hunter

For Polly

"We are all travelers in the wilderness of this world, and the best we can find in our travels is an honest friend." ~R.L. Stevenson

PROLOGUE

Monday, June 1

If today is any indication, Police Captain Rob Porter is going to have a very good week. He smiles as he watches the sun sinking on the horizon, feels the light breeze on his face, hears the slap of small waves as they gently rock the fishing boat moored to the dock he's standing on. Life is good. He's had to do a lot to get here, but it's all his—the cabin, the woods, this little lake. It's true he doesn't own it outright, but it won't be long before he can mark that mortgage paid in full— provided his plans work out. And there's no reason why they shouldn't. He's played his hand extremely well.

Just yesterday, things weren't looking so rosy, but like they say, what a difference a day makes. Now, his Erin Harper problem is over. There won't be any more threats, no attempts to undermine him, no "Me, Too," bull coming from her either. He'll be able to glide right into the Himmel police chief position when Mick Riley retires in the fall. He can't help grinning when he thinks about his confrontation with Erin. She thought she had the upper hand, but Rob was ready for her. The look on her face was priceless.

And as if that wasn't enough, he's got Spencer Karr and GO News firmly in his back pocket. Sure, Rob caught a lucky break, but he knew what to do with it.

Exploiting opportunities is one of Rob's special talents. There's only one thing he hasn't taken care of yet, but her day is coming. The Himmel Times is still a pain in the ass. They're always digging around, always putting a negative spin on his department. That bitch Leah Nash thinks she and her stupid newspaper are out of his reach because she's best buddies with the sheriff. Let her think that. Rob will find a way to shut her up. He just has to be smart about it. And if there's one thing Rob is sure of, it's that he's a hell of a smart guy.

Before he lowers the beer cooler into his boat, he bends down and opens it, checking to see if his wife Bethany remembered to put in a six pack. Damn! Just four cans of Bud. He told her six. And she forgot to tuck some jerky in, too, like he told her to. He shakes his head. It's like she's not even listening to him when he talks to her. Well, that's going to stop. He's got his professional life running smooth, now it's time to get the support he needs at home. She's gotten away too long with teary apologies and promises to do better.

He straightens up and reaches for his life vest. Lots of guys don't wear them, especially on a small lake like this, but Rob can't swim. Not even a dog paddle. He blames it on being raised on a farm in Nebraska. No lakes or ponds for miles. Not like Wisconsin where you practically can't turn around without falling into one. He knows he should learn, as much as he's out on his boat. But he doesn't want to admit that he doesn't know how.

He pulls the life vest over his head, but the straps get caught up with his shoulder holster somehow. Rob doesn't go anywhere without his gun, not even fishing. He untangles the vest and sets it down. Then he takes his gun and shoulder holster off and puts it on the dock before trying the vest again. As he's adjusting it, he hears a footstep on the dock and looks up.

"What are you doing here?" He's surprised and irritated when he sees who's standing there.

"You know why I'm here," his unwelcome guest says.

"You know what? I don't have time for this. And I'm not all that interested, either. You can see I'm busy, right? I'm about to go fishing. Try me tomorrow."

"I'm here now."

"And I said I don't have time. You're lucky I'm in a good mood. Otherwise, I'd arrest you for trespassing. I don't know what's got your undies in a bunch, and frankly, I don't care. Quit wasting my time. We're done."

Rob's voice is full of contempt as he turns his back and begins lowering items for his night fishing excursion into his boat.

"We're not done yet, Rob! I say when we're done!"

The words startle Rob with their force and anger. He straightens up and turns to see that his visitor is shaking with rage—and holding Rob's gun. Rob takes a step forward. The gun fires, but the shot is wild, and the bullet goes wide over the lake. Rob reassesses the situation.

"Okay, okay," *he says, holding his hands up in a placating gesture.* "You've got my attention. Put the gun down before you hurt somebody. Tell me what you want."

"What I want? I want you to know I won't let you do it. I won't let you destroy me." *The unblinking eyes staring at him are shiny and hard, radiating barely controlled fury. Rob is no longer irritated. He's afraid.*

"All right, take it easy now. Calm down. We can work something out. Be rational about this. You don't want to do anything foolish. If you think you're scaring me, you're not."

Rob's words are brave, but his throat is so dry he can barely get them out.

His visitor laughs, but there's no humor in it.

"Calm down? You take what you want, you ruin lives, and you just go on like it's nothing. Don't tell me to calm down. I could kill you right now."

His visitor speaks the violent words in a flat, steady tone that is somehow more frightening than an angry shout.

Rob's eyes dart from side to side, looking for a way to escape. If he rushes ahead, he'll get shot. If he jumps into the water, he'll drown, or get shot, or both.

"Listen, you don't want to kill me. You're in for a world of hurt if you do. I'm warning you."

"It's too late for a warning. I'm already there. And you're the one who put me there, because you think you can do anything you want and never face consequences. Getting rid of you would be doing myself, and the world, a favor."

"Come on, let's just talk about things. Put the gun down."

But Rob's words have the opposite effect from the one he intends.

"That's why I came—to talk. But I don't feel like it anymore. All I feel looking at you is hatred. I hate who you are, what you did, what you're trying to do now. I hate everything about you, Rob."

Rob can't wait any longer. He has to make his move. He lunges forward. A flash of light explodes from the gun as a bullet leaves the barrel. Rob feels a fierce blow as white-hot pain explodes in his chest. He stumbles, falls off the dock and into the boat. His eyes close. He feels the boat rock from the weight of his killer stepping in beside him. Rob can't breathe, he can't speak, but he can still hear. And the last words he hears in this world are whispered in his ear.

"Now we're done, Rob."

1

I woke up to the sun streaming through the windows and looked over at the man next to me in bed. Coop in sleep looked very different from his daytime persona as the Grantland County Sheriff. His dark hair was tousled, his normally clean-shaven face was stubbily with whiskers, and he had a crease-line on one cheek from his pillow. I couldn't resist the urge to reach out and brush a piece of hair off his forehead. He didn't stir.

David Cooper has been my best friend for 20 years. He'd been my secret lover for two months. It wasn't a secret because neither of us was cheating on a partner or spouse. We'd been keeping our relationship quiet because it had been a long time coming, and we wanted to enjoy it for a little, just the two of us—without jokes, and teasing, and I-told-you-so's from family and friends.

Coop must have felt me staring at him, because one eye opened and he said, "Hey, you. What's for breakfast?"

"Cheerios, toast, eggs, or any combination thereof are on the menu at the *On Your Own* restaurant this morning. I'm grabbing a quick shower, then I've got some work to do on my manuscript, and I've got a therapy appointment with Claire Montgomery at 11:30. My last one, I think. You need to get up, too, so you can be gone before people start coming in to work at the paper."

My name is Leah Nash. I'm a writer, and I also co-own the *Himmel Times Weekly* in my hometown, Himmel, Wisconsin. I'm not involved much in the daily operations anymore—at least I'm not supposed to be. My focus is on making a switch from the true crime writing I've been doing to help keep the paper afloat to fiction writing.

Both of us—my newspaper and me—live in the same renovated historic building in downtown Himmel. My apartment is on the third floor, and the *Times* is on the ground floor. I like being close to the action, but it can be a little tricky keeping my private life private, when most of the people I care about are just two floors down.

Coop rubbed his eyes and yawned as he sat up in bed.

"How much longer are we going to keep this up, Leah? I think it's time we let our secret out. It would make life less complicated. And I wouldn't have to get up so early."

I threw aside the covers and stood as I answered.

"I know. You're right. It's probably time. I just dread all the fuss that you know people are going to make."

"You might be surprised. Everyone is dealing with their own lives. The fact that we're together now may not figure all that large in their worlds. You're worried about a big to-do that may not even happen."

"If Miguel wasn't in the mix, maybe. But there's nothing he loves better than generating hoopla," I said. Miguel Santos is the senior reporter at the *Times,* and one of my favorite friends. He loves romance, and any excuse for a party.

"Hoopla, is it? I think my grandpa used to say that. Next thing I know, you'll be asking me why in tarnation I'm still in bed."

"Oh, be quiet. And get up."

He did and began making his side of the bed.

"It's not just fear-of-fuss that's holding me back, Coop. I still haven't told Gabe. Now you and I are all happy, and he doesn't have anyone. I don't want to rub it in," I said as we both tugged the bedspread into place and fluffed the pillows.

"Gabe's a good guy, and I don't want to make him feel worse, either. But you broke up with him months ago. He'll be all right."

"Maybe, but he was really hurt. What about Kristin?"

Kristin Norcross is the assistant prosecutor Coop was seeing before he and I stumbled our way to each other.

"I don't expect her to take it too hard. She's the one who kicked me to the curb, remember? Gabe has to know sometime, why not now?"

"Yeah, I guess . . . I just . . ."

"Leah, why is this so hard for you? This is a happy secret. It's not like you killed anybody."

He stopped abruptly, aware of what he'd unintentionally said.

"Damn! I'm sorry, that was pretty insensitive. I—"

"It's all right. It's not like if no one mentions it I can forget I shot someone to death. I'm okay talking about it now. And that's because of Claire."

"I know the therapy's been hard, I'm proud of you for sticking with it. And you're doing so much better."

"Yeah. I guess a night with me isn't quite the emotional roller coaster it once was, is it? No more nightmares, no more daytime panic attacks. Now I'm just your ordinary, run-of-the-mill girlfriend. I'll have to find some other way to keep your attention, I suppose."

I tried to make light of it, but I'm here to tell you that the aftermath of killing someone, even in self-defense, can mess with your head pretty good.

"You always have my attention, and there's nothing run-of-the-mill about you. I'll be happy when everyone else knows how I feel about you. It doesn't bother me like it does you."

"It's not the knowing part that bothers me. It's the finding out part and all the commotion surrounding my—our—personal life that comes with it that I'm not looking forward to. Are you?"

Coop shrugged. "I wouldn't say I'm looking forward to it, but I don't mind either. It'll be kind of nice to just be together, without worrying about whether someone sees me leaving in the morning, or your car in my driveway in the middle of the night. You'd think we were two married people cheating on our spouses. Let's just tell everyone already. Please."

"All right, all right. Just give me a couple more days to brace myself for the big announcement, okay?"

He walked around the bed to where I was standing and tilted my chin up with his finger, then leaned down and kissed me.

"Okay," he said. "I'll just be happy when everyone knows that the ace reporter, true crime writer, and soon-to-be best-selling fiction author Leah Nash is not only my best friend, she's my best girl, too."

––––––––––––

Coop came into the kitchen as I finished my bowl of Honey Nut Cheerios.

"You've got just about enough time to grab some cereal. It's almost seven o'clock. People will be coming in to work pretty soon. You'd better hurry."

"I want something a little more substantial this morning. I'll pick up a breakfast burrito and some coffee on the way to work. But before you throw me bodily down the stairs, I have something for you."

He reached in his jacket pocket and brought out a small velvet jeweler's box. I felt a flutter of apprehension ripple through my body. Before I could say anything, he did.

"Take it easy. It's not an engagement ring. I just got hold of you. I'm not about to scare you away."

"What is it?"

"Open it and see."

I undid the fancy ribbon and lifted the hinged top of the box. Inside nestled a gold pendant with a small diamond in the center, threaded on a fine gold chain.

"Coop, it's beautiful!"

"I had a friend who's an artisan jeweler in Door County make it for me. It's unique, Leah, like you. It's a Celtic love knot—it stands for eternal love. I know it's kind of sentimental. But I feel sentimental about you, about us."

My eyes filled with tears that I had to blink away.

"I think this is the loveliest thing I've ever received. And that includes the trophy I won when I beat Spencer Karr in the regional Lincoln-Douglas Debate. And you remember how much I loved that trophy," I said.

"I do. I'm glad you like it."

"Like it? I love it. Here, help me put it on, will you?"

He stepped behind me and fumbled with the small clasp for a few seconds before getting it hooked. Then he stepped away as I turned around to show it to him.

"Beautiful. Just like you."

The expression in his dark gray eyes made my heart turn over.

But I'm not very good at receiving compliments—or at giving them. Instead of responding in kind, I fell back on my usual awkward deflection.

"The necklace is beautiful, it's true. But I'm not. Reddish-brown hair that's almost always messy, hazel eyes that can't decide if they're green or brown, a mouth that's too wide . . . and some would say too big. My eyelashes are pretty good, and my dimples are kind of cute. But me, beautiful? I don't think . . ."

He stepped closer, put his hands on my shoulders, and looked down at my face.

"Leah, stop. You're beautiful to me. You always have been. You always will be."

If ever there was an emotional occasion that called for me to rise to the moment, this was it. I took a deep breath and let it out slowly before I answered.

"Thank you for saying that and thank you for the necklace. I love it. And I love you."

"There, that wasn't so hard, was it? One of these days you're not going to feel like letting yourself be happy and showing it is risky. But what are you going to do when someone sees you wearing the necklace and asks where it came from? Our cover will be blown."

"I didn't say I was going to wear it on the *outside* of my clothes. It will tuck very nicely under my T-shirt. Anyway, I told you, just give me a couple more days while I work myself up to the big reveal. Then it won't matter who sees it or asks about it."

"All right. I'll hold you to that."

2

Although I hated going there, my therapist's office was actually a warm and welcoming place. The walls are painted a soothing blue-gray, the wood flooring is dark, and the large second-floor window overlooks a park.

Claire Montgomery, my therapist, was seated in a comfortable leather chair that faced the loveseat where I always sat. I liked the spot because it gave me a clear line of sight over her shoulder to a mesmerizing photograph on the opposite wall—the constellation Virgo shining brightly in a sky full of stars. It gave me a place to focus my gaze during sessions when the guilt or the anxiety I felt was so great I had a hard time looking directly at Claire. But that morning I didn't need it. I was ready to end my treatment and thank Claire, because she had done her work well.

When I started, I wasn't sure she was the right therapist for me. Claire is flat-out movie star beautiful. Her thick, shiny, dark brown hair is the kind rarely seen outside of a shampoo commercial. Her brown eyes are large and wide-set, and her style sense is classic and understated. In addition to resembling Audrey Hepburn, she also projects warmth and confidence. That amount of perfection can be off-putting, at least to those of us who are significantly less well put together.

But I soon got over my doubts that someone as gorgeous as Claire could also be exceptionally good at her job. She had metaphorically, and sometimes literally, held my hand as she helped me come to terms with the fact that I had killed someone. In self-defense, yes, but it had still haunted my dreams.

"How've you been doing since your last appointment?"

"Good. Great, actually. I'm sleeping well, no nightmares, no flashbacks. I can even listen to the recording we made for the Prolonged Exposure work without my hands sweating or my heart racing. I admit I was a little skeptical about the EMDR when you started it, but I think it really helped."

"A little skeptical? I think you called it "woo-woo" therapy when I described it to you the first time."

"Yeah, well, I'm not an early adopter, okay? Who would think shifting my eyes back and forth could cure my PTSD? But it did."

"There's a little more to Eye Movement Desensitization and Reprocessing than that, Leah. Following my finger movement with your eyes helped bring buried emotions to the surface. Guiding you through them while you kept the memory in focus lowered their intensity, so they don't cause you deep pain anymore. EMDR is a good adjunct to the Prolonged Exposure work you've done."

"Now that I've used them both, EMDR is a piece of cake compared to Prolonged Exposure. Going through the afternoon of the shooting step-by-step for the first time here in your office was excruciating. Then later, listening to the recording you made of me, hearing the fear and panic in my voice, not being able to shove the memory away and distract myself with something else ... That was really, really tough."

"It takes courage, Leah, and you've got plenty of that. You've put in the work, and I'm so glad that you're reaping the benefits."

"Thanks, Claire. Along those lines, there's something I want to tell you today."

"What's that?"

Suddenly I was reluctant to tell her that I was ready to stop our sessions. Was I really? Could I go it on my own without having the nightmares return? I felt a ball of anxiety forming in the pit of my stomach. I began babbling about the photo on the wall instead of saying what I'd intended to.

"You know, that's a great photo. Where did you get it? It really draws you in. Is that why you got it for your office? I'd like to get a print for myself."

"It was a birthday gift from a college friend years ago. We were both born in September, on the same day. The constellation Virgo is our astrological sign. I don't know where she bought it."

"Oh, really? Well, it's a great photo. Maybe I can do a Google image search and find somewhere to get it."

Claire watched as I jumped up and took a picture of the photo with my phone, then sat back down.

"Leah, we can discuss my wall art, or I can watch you do a Google image search on your phone to find it, if you like. This is your session and your time. But is that really how you want to spend it?"

I looked directly at her, embarrassed.

"No, it isn't. I don't know why I'm being so weird about it. I planned to say that I'm ready for you to cut me loose. But then I started feeling nervous at the idea of not having you, this office, this weekly appointment, as an anchor, or a safe harbor, or whatever."

"It's natural to feel a little separation anxiety when you move away from a safe space. I'm glad my office feels that way to you. But I agree with you. You're ready to move on. I have confidence in you."

A deep sigh I didn't realize I had been holding in escaped then as a feeling of relief washed over me.

"Wow. I feel like I just passed my driver's test."

She smiled.

"In a way, you did. You're ready to drive solo as far as your PTSD is concerned. But I'm here as a safety net if you need it. And, if you'd ever like to address any of the other things that we touched on outside of the immediate PTSD issue, you can always come back."

"Sure, thanks. But I don't really have anything else that I need help working out," I said, shrinking back a little on my chair. Unconsciously my fingers had found the necklace hidden by my shirt and pulled it out. I began sliding the pendant up and down on the chain as I spoke.

"That's a beautiful necklace. Why are you wearing it inside your shirt instead of outside where people can see it?"

"Coop gave it to me," I said.

"Ah."

I realized that I'd given her an opening. I tried to close it by deflecting her attention.

"That gold cross you're wearing today is really lovely. You have some beautiful jewelry, Claire."

"Thank you. But I'd like to talk about why you're hiding your necklace."

"I think you know the answer," I said.

"I think I do, too, but it may be good for you to say it out loud."

"Fine. I'm wearing it inside because yes, I still haven't told anyone about Coop and me."

"And that's because . . . "

"Because I don't want all the hoopla," I said, repeating the old-fashioned word Coop had teased me about. "And because putting it out there means, well, oh, I don't know . . . " My words trailed off.

"Don't stop there, Leah. Finish your thought."

"I don't really know what I was going to say. Besides, I don't want to run over my time."

She laughed at that.

"Given that we're less than 10 minutes into a scheduled 90-minute session, and we've already established that we've done all we need to with your PTSD, I don't think we have to worry about going into overtime. I have a feeling that you've got something you'd like to talk about."

"I don't know where you're picking up that vibe."

"Can I pose a question to you? You don't have to answer now."

Short of leaping from my chair and running out of the office, there didn't seem to be a way to cut this conversation short.

"Okay, sure, fine. Ask."

"Knowing you as I've come to over our sessions, I can easily accept that you wouldn't enjoy the 'hoopla,' as you called it, when your friends learn the news. But I think there might be something more than just reluctance to have a fuss made over you."

"What are you saying?"

"What do you think I'm saying?"

There was no sense sparring with her.

"That as long as my relationship with Coop is in our little bubble, I feel like it's safe. But once we tell, and everyone knows, we won't be able to keep it safe."

"Safe from what?"

"From all the things that can happen to your dreams when you put them out into the world. I don't want to lose what it took me so long to find."

"Why would you?"

"Why do people lose anything? I don't know. Fate, misunderstanding, disappointment, deception, deceit, malice, jealousy, envy, anger—all kinds of things can take happiness away from you."

"Leah, I can't fault you for feeling like that. You've lost a lot in your life. But you and Coop have a very solid base for a relationship. You've been close friends for years, you know each other's strengths and weaknesses, each other's fears and foibles. You're both young, healthy, and you're in love, right?"

I nodded.

"So, you have every reason to look forward to a wonderful future and to share your happiness with others, don't you? Talking about it won't destroy things for you and Coop. In fact, I think that when you decide to let the news out, you'll feel like a burden has lifted. It's hard to carry secrets, even happy ones."

"When you say it like that, it sounds sensible and easy. But it isn't."

"Can you tell me why?"

"I just don't trust the future, I guess. It feels like I'm tempting Fate by saying 'Look at us! See how happy we are!' And then it will be taken away from us. I don't like taking leaps into the unknown."

"But you do that all the time, don't you? When you're investigating a story, you don't know how it's going to end, you don't know which sources to trust, you don't know if your conclusions will be correct, do you? But there comes a time when in order to move ahead, you have to take that leap, even though you may not land in a safe place."

"That's different."

"Is it?"

"Yes. When I start looking into a story, I don't have the option of choosing. Something inside compels me to go on. Like when you run down a hill and gravity takes over and pulls you along faster and faster until you can't stop, you have to keep going. It's not the same at all as choosing to leap off an emotional cliff. I don't want to crash and lose everything. I have before. It's not fun."

"But you're still here, aren't you? You've loved, and lost, and loved again. Leah, your intractable fear of loss, the feeling you have that it's dangerous to love, is rooted deep in your childhood. You suffered two major losses—your sister and your father—back-to-back. Later your youngest sister died. But—"

"Claire, I appreciate that you're trying to help me be a more well-adjusted person. I really do. But I think I'll take a cue from my sister Lacey. When she was really little, she ran into this cubby hole under the stairs at our neighbor's house. She ran right back out and said, 'Lee-lee, it's dark and 'pooky in there!' That's how I feel about taking a deep dive into the hidden depths of my psyche—it's dark and 'pooky in there. Maybe some things should be buried."

She gave a small shake of her head, then smiled and said, "Leah. I know you'll do well with your PTSD. But you can always call me if you ever feel the need for a little help to work through anything else."

3

When I got back home, I stopped in at the *Times* office to see if anything was happening. My mother, who does the books and manages the office, was in her office just off the newsroom.

"Hey, Mom. Are you here alone?"

"Almost. Miguel is on the move. He started out at the Himmel Police Department early, then he had to drive to Omico for the city hall ground-breaking. He should be back soon. Troy is coming in after lunch. Maggie had a meeting at the library. Allie is off today. Courtnee is at the front desk, but she's busy entering herself in the Grantland County's Favorite Receptionist contest."

Troy Patterson is the junior reporter on our two-person reporting staff, which we supplement with stringers. Maggie is the editor. Allie is a high school kid with a lot of promise who works part-time in the office doing anything she's asked. Her dad is a detective with the sheriff's office. Courtnee Fensterman is the reluctant receptionist at the *Times*.

"Isn't *GO News* sponsoring that? And also, isn't someone else supposed to do the nominating, not the person who is hoping to win?"

Grantland County Online News, better known as *GO News,* is our county's digital-only "news" site. I always pair the word news with air quotes when I'm using it to reference the sketchily sourced online site owned by my nemesis Spencer Karr. To my constant anxiety and frequent dismay, *GO News* beats us in both subscription numbers and advertising on a regular basis.

"Yes, to the first question. *GO News* is sponsoring it, but Courtnee isn't about to let loyalty and a paycheck stand between her and the chance of winning a $200 gift card."

"Based on her performance, I would have to rank that chance pretty low."

"Don't place any bets. The Fensterman family is a large voting bloc. What've you been up to this morning?"

"I had an appointment with Claire. My last one."

"Is that because you're tired of going, or because Claire thinks you've made enough progress? Are you sure it's the right time to stop?"

Her dark blue eyes reflected the concern I heard in her voice.

"Yes, I'm sure, Mom. Therapy isn't supposed to last forever, you know. I'm doing fine now. Seriously."

"Well, I can tell by your eyes that you're sleeping much better, and you do seem happier. And if Claire agrees . . ."

"She does," I said firmly. "Let's talk about something else now, okay?"

"Okay. How about your book, how's that going?"

"Not that well."

"Why? What's wrong?"

"I just can't get it to hang together. I've changed the opening three times and it's still not what I want it to be. I'm getting worried that maybe I just can't write fiction."

"Oh, you're always too hard on yourself. What does Clinton say?"

Clinton Barnes is my agent and the one who talked me into making a switch from true crime writing to fiction. He's a true believer in my abilities, a tireless advocate for my work, and also a harsh taskmaster—which I sometimes need.

"To quit second-guessing, to stop revising as I go, to just keep writing and things will come into focus. He also suggested that I remember that I'm not the editor of the paper, I don't work at the paper, and the newspaper is not my primary responsibility."

"And you're going to do that?"

"I signed the contract, I took the advance, and now I'm committed. So, I'm sure going to keep trying. I can't let my worst nightmare come true."

"Which is what?"

"That I'll fail miserably, and Spencer Karr will have gloating privileges which he will exploit in the most public way on his 'news' site. You know, if he wasn't Paul's son, I'd seriously consider hiring a hit man to take him out."

"I appreciate your restraint."

Paul Karr has been our family dentist forever, and my mother's significant other for several years. He's a very nice man who married a not very nice woman, and then the fairies stole their human baby and replaced him with a changeling who grew up to be Spencer. That explanation is the only one I can think of for why Spencer is the way he is.

"Maybe you should cover your ears for this part, then. I'm feeling a Spencer rant coming on. I've had three people ask me why *GO News* had a 'great' story on Harley Granger and we didn't. I don't get why some people can't see the difference between a puff piece like that and real reporting. *GO News* is starting to make me feel like you *can* fool all of the people all of the time. Otherwise, how could Spencer be so successful? He's self-centered, entitled, and casually cruel. He's wasted space on this earth, and that's all there is to it. Thank you for coming to my TED Talk."

"Are you still crying because *GO News* beat us on the Harley Granger story, Leah?"

We both turned in response to the question from Maggie McConnell as she walked into the newsroom.

"I'm not crying, Maggie, but I'd be lying if I said it didn't still annoy me that Spencer got the jump on us on that one. Although, with Spencer and Harley being best buds in high school, he had the advantage."

"Well, we didn't get it first, but at least we got it right. The way *GO News* wrote it, Harley Granger is a misunderstood victim of circumstance. He's seen the light after 10 years in prison and now he's starting over. That'll be the day," Maggie said, her eyes snapping behind tortoise shell glasses that for once she was wearing on her nose instead of on top of her thick, gray bob.

"Harley was a friend of Spencer's in high school? It's hard to imagine Marilyn Karr approving of that," my mother said.

"Is there anything Marilyn approves of? Yeah, they were friends. Well, maybe friends is a bit of a stretch. Their relationship was more transactional than that. Spencer used Harley because he had easy access to weed —what with the Granger family's main business at the time being small-time drug dealing."

"You said transactional. What did Harley use Spencer for?" Maggie asked.

"Access to a cool car, to money, to the pool at his house, to the high-end booze in the Karrs' liquor cabinet. Spencer gave Harley a taste of the good life. Maybe that's why Harley ramped things up after high school and went into making meth instead of just selling it. It was his play to get that kind of cash for himself."

"That sure blew up in his face."

"Good one, Maggie, given that his meth lab literally did blow up," I said, standing up to go. "I can't put it off any longer. I have to get down to work on my book, and I know you don't need my help putting out a newspaper, so I'll leave you guys to it. See, Maggie," I said, turning to her. "I can walk away anytime. Anytime."

As I moved past her in the doorway to prove my point, she shook her head, but she let it pass. Maggie knows, and I know, and anyone who's ever waited for their story to drop online or hit the newsstand knows, you can take a reporter out of the newsroom, but you can't take the newsroom out of a reporter.

4

"Chica! Where have you been? I haven't seen you in forever."

Miguel Santos had come through the back door of the *Times* as I was walking down the hall, heading for the backstairs to my place. He smiled, flashing a row of white teeth that would set a dental hygienist's heart aflutter. Actually, all of Miguel sets hearts aflutter. He's in his early 20s, tall, has great hair, dark brown eyes, and skin the color of a perfect latte. Alas, those hearts that belong to females are destined to be broken because Miguel is also gay. He's ten years younger than me, and I have long thought that the universe put him in my world to make up for the little brother I never had.

He's also a great photographer and a very good reporter. My secret worry is that one day he's going to take his skills and his sweet, smart, funny self to another publication that offers more money and more scope for his talent.

"I just got back from Claire's office. She gave me a clean bill of mental health—more or less," I amended.

"Oh, I'm so happy!" he said, giving me a hug. "No more nightmares for you? I hope no more guilt too. You had no choice and you saved Coop's life. And yours, too!"

"Yeah, well, I guess. At least Claire helped me put the guilt to bed.

Moving on, Mom said you were at HPD this morning. I thought Troy was doing the police beat. Anything going on?"

"He is. I wasn't there for the paper. I had a seven a.m. appointment to take photos for my side hustle."

"Which is?"

"Chief Riley wants a big annual report for the department this year. It's his last one before he retires. I'm picking up a little *dinero* taking some pictures and doing the layout for it. But something interesting is happening there."

"Oh? Do tell."

"I took the chief's photo and Erin Harper's early this morning before work. But when I went back at noon to shoot Rob Porter's picture, he wasn't there. While I was waiting, I tried to talk Erin into doing an interview for my podcast. Then she got a phone call and asked me to step out of her office for a minute. When she finished, she said she didn't know when Rob would be in, and I should plan on rescheduling for another day."

"No offense, Miguel, but that doesn't really qualify as the 'interesting' you promised me."

"That's because I'm doing a feature lead, not hard news. Now comes the interesting part. I talked to Dale Darmody on my way out."

"Sorry, my friend, you're losing your audience here, feature lead or not. Interesting and Darmody rarely go together."

Dale Darmody is the longest-serving member of the department. He could—and probably should—have retired several years ago, but he loves the job. I'm not saying he's as bad as Barney Fife, but he's not a lot better. On the plus side for the paper, he never heard a secret he didn't want to share. In fact, "on the QT" is his favorite phrase. But on the negative side, his propensity for blabbing is well known and he's not usually trusted with anything really juicy.

"No, listen! He told me Rob Porter is missing!"

"Okay, you've got my attention now. Missing? As in disappeared?"

"I'm not sure. Dale said Rob was supposed to meet his dad for an early lunch at 11. He didn't show up. Rob's dad tried his cell, but he didn't answer. He called Rob's wife to check. She said Rob told her he was going night fishing and staying the night at his cabin. After that, his dad tried HPD, but no one had seen him since yesterday afternoon. They tried to get him on the radio, but he's not answering."

"Hmm. That doesn't sound good. Did you confirm it with someone other than Darmody?"

"Yes. Melanie told me it's true, no one knows where Rob is. But that's all she'd say."

Melanie Olson is the department secretary. She usually knows what's going on, but she rarely shares.

I tried Coop to see if he knew anything, but my call went to voicemail. Then Miguel and I heard the sound of sirens that seemed to be coming down our street. I raced to the front of the building. Maggie, my mother, and Courtnee were watching out the window as three cop cars, an ambulance, and a fire truck barreled out of town, heading in the direction of Police Captain Rob Porter's hunting land.

"I think they may have found Rob," I said.

Troy Patterson came in through the front door as the wails of the sirens died out. Miguel began filling the others in, and I forced myself to walk away, repeating to myself, "This is not your job, Leah. This is not your job."

When I got back upstairs, I called Coop, but still no answer. Then I tried to work.

When my phone rang, I grabbed it.

"Coop, what's going on? Is Rob hurt? Is he dead?"

"Let me take a guess. You're working on something for your newspaper, not something for the book you're allegedly writing."

"Oh. Clinton. Hi. I forgot you were going to call. No, I'm not reporting the story, I'm just an interested bystander. The local police captain is missing."

"Is he a friend of yours?"

"No."

"Then too bad, so sad, I hope it turns out all right," he said in a voice that didn't hold much sincerity. "Now, tell me about something we both really care about. Are you doing what I suggested—pushing through without second-guessing?"

"I'm trying, I really am. But it still feels like my descriptive writing is too detailed and my character descriptions aren't detailed enough. I've been thinking maybe I should toss everything out and start all over again."

"No. Don't start over. Just keep going. Leah, you can do this. You've just got the jitters."

"I know I do but knowing doesn't take them away."

"You know what does? Doing the work. Stop trying for perfection as you go. That's what revising is for. If you're telling a great story to a friend, you don't keep going back and changing what you just said, do you?"

He didn't wait for my answer.

"No, you don't. You just tell it. That's what you have to do here. It will come together. Now, go forth and write and I'll be waiting to see what shows up in my Dropbox folder. Promise me you'll do that."

"I promise you I'll try very hard."

"Don't try. Do. Write that book. Don't get distracted by your newspaper, or your missing police captain, either."

And he was gone. Clinton doesn't waste time on goodbyes.

I looked at my watch. It had been more than two hours since the cop cars raced through town. Coop must know something by now. Or Maggie must have an update from Miguel or Troy. I started to call her, then forced myself to stop. It wasn't my job. I had plenty on my plate. Someone would call me when there was news to share.

I got up and made some coffee, put some music on, and took my laptop over to the window seat. I had just started making a list of key plot points I needed to hit to reach the midpoint of my book when my phone rang. Coop.

"Leah, I don't have much time. Just wanted to let you know. We found Rob. He's dead."

"Dead? Did he drown? Have a heart attack?"

"He was shot in the chest. Rob was murdered."

"Who? Why? What happened?" I asked.

"Sorry, no time for even just the three W's right now. Miguel and Troy are here, so's *GO News*. You can read all about it online shortly, I'm sure. I've got to go. It's our jurisdiction. Owen just got here. I need to brief him."

"Wait, is Al there? How's he doing?"

Al Porter is the fire chief, and Rob's father. I've always really liked him, even though I puzzle over the father/son mix there, the same way I do over Paul Karr and Spencer. Al's a good guy, too, like Paul. But Rob is an ambitious backstabber and as phony as they come. He can turn on the charm and come across as a nice, friendly guy. But that runs about an inch deep. Thwart him, or be someone he can't use, and look out.

"Al's about as good as can be expected—which is not good at all. I've got to go. I'll talk to you later."

I ran downstairs to check in with Maggie but found my mother instead.

"Mom, did you hear?"

"About Rob? Yes. Maggie told me. She's out taking a photo that Miguel was supposed to shoot at the city pool. He and Troy are still out at Rob's property. I can't believe Rob was murdered! It's such a shock!"

"Yes and no," I said.

"How can you say it's not shocking that a man was killed? And not just any man, the police captain."

"I didn't mean it's not a shock that a man was killed. Murder is always shocking. I meant that Rob was such an ass, if someone was going to get killed it's not that surprising that it was him."

She frowned.

"I know you didn't like him much. I can't say that I did, either. But the man is dead, Leah. Murdered. Can't you summon up a little compassion?"

"Sure, I can. For his dad, and his wife, and anyone else that may have cared about him. But it doesn't change the fact that he wasn't a very good person."

"Not meeting your personal standards for a good person doesn't mean Rob deserved to be killed."

"Hey, I didn't say that. I don't think he 'deserved' to be murdered. I'm just saying maybe he was nasty to the wrong person. Or, okay, I'll be more charitable here. Maybe someone was mad enough at him for doing his job to kill him. If that's the case, I'd put Harley Granger at the top of the list. Rob is the one who arrested him and got him sent away for 10 years. Now that he's out, maybe Harley took some payback."

"That could be," my mother said. "I was in the courtroom when Harley was sentenced. He said he was framed, and someone was going to pay. Maybe that someone was Rob. Well, I'm sure Coop and his office will figure it out. I'm glad about one thing, though."

"What's that?"

"At least this time you don't have any reason to be involved, so that's one worry I don't have."

Or so it seemed at the time.

5

"That was a seriously long day. Are you hungry? I can make you something," I said.

It was 8:30 and Coop had just walked into my apartment.

"No, thanks. I had some pizza at the office."

"Well, sit down on the couch. You look really tired. I'll bring you a beer and you can tell me about your day."

"Ah, now it's coming clear."

"What's that?" I asked.

"My favorite Lucinda Williams playlist is on. You're willing to cook for me, and you're offering to bring me a cold beer. You're plying me with music, food, and drinks to get me to reveal details of a police investigation."

"You have a suspicious mind. I'm not trying to pump you for information. I'm trying to help you unwind from your day."

"Uh-huh," he said as he took his shoes off and stretched out on the couch.

"No, really. I already know from the excellent reporting of Miguel and Troy that Owen Fike is leading the investigation, that Rob was shot at his property, and that you and Al found his body in his fishing boat, which was caught up in some weeds on the other side of his lake. I also know that Al called you after he couldn't locate Rob and asked you to go with him to

Rob's hunting land. And that the sheriff's office, with assistance from several local law enforcement agencies, including HPD, searched and processed the crime scene."

"Sounds like you're up-to-date. Nothing I can add to that."

"Nothing you can add, or nothing you will add? Never mind, I already know the answer. But Harley Granger is a person of interest, right? I mean because Rob sent him to prison."

"The investigation is just getting underway. We don't even have the medical examiner's report yet."

"But you're going to be questioning Harley, right?"

"We're talking to everyone who had a relationship with Rob, and we'll see where that leads us. How's your book coming? Did you get much done today?"

"Very subtle. All right. I give up. For now, anyway. And no, I didn't get much done today."

"Maybe letting my team investigate and your staff report on Rob's murder would free you up to focus more on your writing."

"Have you been tag-teaming with Clinton? Because that's basically what he said, too. For the record, I'm not getting involved in either the investigation or the reporting. I'm just interested, that's all. It's not a crime to be interested."

"Leah, it's even more important than it was before to make sure there's a clear line that we don't cross between my office and your newspaper. You know that us being together doesn't mean that you've got a pipeline into the sheriff's office. "

"Oh, no worries there. I don't even have a fiber optic thread into the sheriff's office with you there, let alone a pipeline. I used to get more from Art Lamey when he was sheriff than I do from you," I said.

"Really? Did Art Lamey give you this?"

He leaned over and kissed me.

"Are you trying to distract me?"

"Yes. Is it working?"

"Try harder and I'll let you know."

Coop had temporarily succeeded in taking my eyes off the prize the night before. However, when I woke up in the morning the first thing I thought about was whether or not Harley Granger was connected to Rob's death. The second thing I thought about was that I needed to stop thinking about real-life murder and get to work on my pretend murder world. I nudged Coop awake and he smiled at me sleepily.

"Good morning. How did you sleep?" he asked.

"Good, thanks. I'm going to take a quick shower, and you probably should get going before anyone gets here. And before you complain about being tired of sneaking out so early in the morning, you should know that I'm meeting Gabe at the Elite today to tell him about us. That's our agreed-upon first step before we tell everyone else. How's that for being responsive to your wishes?"

"I like it," he said.

"Don't forget that I promised Miguel I'd ride the new bike trail with him this evening. He has to do some photos for a spread in next week's paper. We're riding to Duckpool and back, so I probably won't get home until eight or so."

"Have fun. I imagine I'll be getting back late myself."

I stayed in the shower longer than I'd intended. Being in that small enclosure, the pressure of the water massaging my muscles, the sound of it blocking out the world, soothes me. It's like a cut-rate sensory deprivation tank. I expected Coop to be gone when I finally got out, but as I toweled off, I heard his voice. I figured he was on his phone. I picked mine up to check the time. When I saw the text that had come in while I was in my personal Zen zone, I threw on my robe and bolted to my bedroom. Too late. Coop was sitting on the bed, still in his T-shirt and underwear. Miguel was standing next to him with a very big smile on his face.

"Oh! I am so happy," he said, running up to give me a hug. "Dr. Love is never wrong. But you were so, 'No, no, don't go there, Miguel. It's not going to happen.' Of course, it was going to. How long has Coop been your boo? You should have told me. I can keep a secret. I can't wait to tell everyone!"

I looked at Coop. He held out his arms, palms extended upward in the universal what-can-you-do gesture. It was too late to put a finger in the dike to stem Miguel's flood of excitement.

"It's not your fault, Coop. It's mine," I said to him. "Miguel texted, but I didn't hear it come in because I was in the shower."

I looked down at the phone in my hand and read the text out loud.

" 'I'm downstairs. Unlock your office door. I'm coming up to help you accessorize for the party.' Though you could have pretended no one was home when he knocked."

"He was too fast. I heard a tap, looked up, and then there he was, staring at me from the doorway. You must have left the stairway door unlocked," Coop said.

"What are you doing here so early, Miguel? I know you don't trust me to outfit myself but picking out my accessories for the Himmel Players fundraiser could have waited."

"It's going to be a busy day. I came in early, just for you."

"Thanks. I guess."

"Also, too, I didn't just walk in. When I tapped the door and tried the handle, it opened. I thought you got my text. Then I came through your office, and here we are."

"Yes. Aren't we."

I sighed, resigned to answering Miguel's storm of questions about the who, what, when, where, and why of Coop and I coming together. However, this exchange was filled with more expressions of delight and editorializing than would normally occur in an interview. When he was done at last, I said, "Just please, don't make such a big deal out of this, okay?"

"Oh, but it is a big deal. Two of my favorite people, together at last. Everyone will be excited, not just me. Why aren't you so, so happy?"

"I am. This is my so, so happy face. I just don't like a big fuss, you know that. But I guess you might as well go forth and spread the news. Oh, except wait a minute—"

"Wait for what?" Miguel asked.

"I want a chance to talk to Gabe, and Coop needs to talk to Kristin. Can you keep a lid on it until the Players fundraiser on Friday night? That'll make sure we have time to get with both of them. Also, everyone we know will be at the fundraiser, so we can rip the bandage off with one yank and get this over with."

"That is not a very sexy metaphor for romance, *chica*. But yes, of course I can wait until they know. Poor Gabe. Poor Kristin. I love a happy ending, but not when it makes a sad one for someone else," he said, his voice full of sympathy. Then his face brightened. "But maybe Gabe and Kristin will fall in love with each other. They're both lawyers, they're both nice. They're both single. I can plant a little idea out there and—"

"Whoa, slow down, 'Dr. Love.' I'm feeling a strong *Hello, Dolly!* vibe coming from you now."

"I'm a full-service love expert," he said. "I diagnose, and I prescribe. If I see a match to be made, I'm professionally obliged to encourage it. Like I did with you. And look how that turned out."

His voice was so ecstatic it made me wonder if he'd be able to hold true to his nondisclosure agreement for the next several days.

6

After Coop left, Miguel wanted to get down to his original mission—ensuring I was presentable for the upcoming cocktail fundraiser for the Himmel Community Players. I pulled out the dress my mother had found for me in the clearance rack at Nordstrom.

"Will this meet your standards?"

"Carol has such good fashion sense. That will be perfect. The floral print is very nice and summery, and I like that it's fitted. You always wear things that are so, so . . . " He searched for a word to describe my taste in clothes.

"Comfortable?" I supplied.

"No, baggy. And I like the length. You have nice legs. You should show them off more. What about the shoes?"

"These?" I asked, holding up a pair of plain black pumps with a low heel.

"No, no, no. Not even close."

"But they're—"

"Comfortable? Don't say that word to me again. It's about the look, the look, not the comfort."

"Can't it be both? Also, I thought black goes with everything," I grumbled.

He shook his head and didn't deign to respond.

"Fine, how about these?" I dragged a pair of flip-flops from the back of the closet to mess with him.

"You are giving me a heart attack," he said, moving me aside so he could rummage in my closet for himself. A few seconds later, he backed out and then stood holding a pair of tangerine-colored, open-toe, ankle-strap, high-heeled sandals aloft.

"Here, these. Remember, we bought these for you in Milwaukee last spring? You haven't even worn them once yet, have you?" he asked, examining the pristine soles and perfectly smooth uppers.

"Well, I don't go to a lot of fancy parties, you know."

"But you are going on Friday. The cocktail party fundraiser will be very fancy. Your flirty dress with the V-neck is just right. I cannot let you ruin the look by wearing a pair of shoes you must have stolen from a nun. No."

I objected again on the grounds of comfort.

"It is for what, two hours maybe, at the most? You can do it. These shoes, that dress, you will be straight fire! Now, what about the earrings? Gold, I think."

He zeroed in on a pair of medium gold hoops with a hammered finish from my jewelry box. "These, yes. Now a necklace." He began to look in the box again.

"No, wait, I've got the perfect one."

I picked up the necklace Coop had given me and showed it to him.

"Will this do?"

"Ah, that is just right! But I haven't seen you wear this before. When did you get it?"

"Coop gave it to me. Yesterday."

"It's beautiful. The pendant, it's a Celtic love knot. It means eternal love."

"Yes, Coop told me. It is pretty nice, isn't it?"

"It's perfect."

Before he got into more detailed fashion advice, a topic which is of limited interest to me, I changed the subject to something else we both enjoy talking about, crime reporting.

"What's going on with Rob's murder?"

"Coop must have given very strict no-leak orders to everyone on the investigation team. Troy and I have both been making calls, but not getting very much. I'm going to stop by HPD and see if Erin will tell me anything."

"Erin? I wouldn't count on it. If anybody is by the book it's her. If the word is out not to talk to the press, she won't do it, even off the record."

Erin Harper is the only female senior officer in the Himmel Police Department, and she's made no secret of wanting to climb the ranks. It wouldn't surprise me if she went after the captain's spot with Rob gone now. She'd be pretty good at it if she loosened up just a bit. She's a stickler for the rules and wound pretty tight. We've had drinks together a few times and helped each other out once or twice. But every time I think we might be heading toward an actual friendship, she always pulls back.

"I know. But maybe I'll catch her in a weak moment. You know, I think Erin isn't so reserved as she seems. I think she might be lonely. You know who else is lonely? Charlie Ross."

"Miguel, I know you're riding the high of correctly predicting romance for me and Coop, but I think you should stand down on this one. Let Erin and Ross find their own ways to love—or not. I highly doubt they'll be going in a direction that leads them to each other. Also, I was serious before. Please don't be the town crier on this whole me and Coop thing. On Friday at the fundraiser you can tell a few people and the word will gradually spread out. Hopefully everyone that wants to say something about it will, and that will be that."

"People that like you will be happy. What's wrong with that?"

"Nothing. I'm just not that comfortable having my love life be the center of attention. Can you please try to keep things low key, just this once?"

"I am not a low-key person, but for you, about this, I'll try."

He looked so earnest, and he was so willing to try to accommodate his ebullient personality to my crabby one, that I had to laugh.

"Listen, this new thing with Coop, it's the best thing ever. That's why I don't want to jinx it. In my experience when things start going really well, and you relax, that's what brings the bad juju. You have to trick Fate by pretending you don't care."

He stepped forward and hugged me then.

"Sometimes you think too much. Just relax and enjoy and be positive. It's the law of attraction. You bring into your life what you focus on. No more negative. Nothing is going to go wrong."

7

Gabe was already seated in the Elite Cafe and Bakery when I arrived. He saw me and waved, then pointed to the cup sitting across from him to indicate I didn't need to stop up front to order.

Before I could move in his direction, I was waylaid by the sudden appearance of the cafe's owner, Clara Schimelman.

"Leah! Where you been? I don't see you for weeks. Are you ghosting the Elite?" she asked in her cheerful and heavily German-accented voice.

She wasn't wrong that I hadn't been to the Elite much lately. The unassuming little eatery with its sloping wooden floor, round tables circled by rickety ladder-back chairs, and assorted sad-looking plants placed randomly around the large room is a favorite of mine.

I'd been staying away because it's a favorite of Gabe Hoffman's, too. I wanted to minimize the number of times I ran into him. It had seemed kinder to give him some space and time. But it would be extremely unkind not to tell him about me and Coop before the rest of the world found out.

"No, Mrs. Schimelman. I haven't been ghosting you. I've just been pretty busy lately. How have you been?"

"Oh, good, always good, you know me. So," she said in a conspiratorial whisper with a yank of her head in Gabe's direction, "what's the story with you two? I never see you together no more. I heard you canceled him. Is true?"

Mrs. Schimelman likes to pepper her speech with the slang she picks up from the high school kids who stop in on their way to and from school for one of her brownies, or *rugelach*, or a *döner kebab*.

"We just agreed we make better friends, that's all."

"Okay, I get it. Hey, I bring you a cranberry orange muffin to your table. It's to die for."

"Sounds great, but I just ate, really. I'll get one next time I'm in," I said as I hurried away. This was going to be a hard enough conversation without Mrs. Schimelman popping in to join it.

"You look great. I like your bangs," Gabe said as I sat down at the table.

"Oh, thanks. Miguel talked me into it. I'm not sure about them yet," I said with a nervous laugh that made me cringe inwardly.

"You look good, too," I said.

Gabe has black hair and intense, dark eyes under thick, straight eyebrows.

"I like your Jason Isbell T-shirt," I said.

"Yeah? I got it when we went to hear him that time in Madison. That was fun, wasn't it?"

"Yes, it was. So, how's Dominic doing?" I asked, to stop a trip down memory lane that wouldn't make this conversation easier for either of us.

"He's great. I just got back from taking him to Lucy's in New York. He's really missed his mom. They should have a great time together."

"I'll bet your place is quiet without him," I said.

Gabe's son Dominic is five, but Gabe had only found out he was a father in the past year. Long story short, he and Lucy had been casually dating in an on-again, off-again way for a while. It ended with no bad feelings when Lucy announced she'd met her dream man. She and Gabe didn't keep in touch. The marriage went bad, and during a nasty divorce her husband insisted on a paternity test. Surprise, surprise, Gabe was her son's biological father. He'd been stunned, but happy to step up to the role.

"I miss him already. But I'll be going out a few times over the summer for some long weekends. Actually, Lucy and I decided that it's best for Dom to spend the school year with me, and summers with her. He loves his school here and he's made lots of friends."

"That's great! I'll be glad when he gets back. I picked up a new dinosaur book for him at Buy the Book that I think he'll really like."

A heavy silence fell between us then as I cast about for the right words to say. I stared down into my chai as though I would find an Oprah-level message floating on the foamy top that would supply them. I did not. Finally, I looked up and plunged ahead.

"Gabe, I need to tell you something. I'm acting so awkward about this because, well, because I feel awkward. Coop and I are seeing each other. Romantically, I mean. We're in a relationship now. We have been for a while—but never when you and I were together—and we're about to go public with it."

"Ah. I thought it might be something like that. Don't look so sad and worried. I knew when we broke up it was final for you. You were straight with me when you ended things. Now I guess you're finally being straight with yourself, too."

"What do you mean?"

"Come on, Leah. It was always Coop for you. I'm doing all right if that's what you're worried about. Sometimes the one you love doesn't love you back. It hurts, but there it is."

"Gabe, I am so sorry that I hurt you. I really am. Stop being so nice about it. It's making me feel even worse."

He reached across the table and touched my hand lightly.

"You don't need to feel bad. I'm fine, really. And I'm sorry that I ever said I didn't want you as a friend if we weren't together anymore. I didn't mean it. I was just lashing out. I miss you being my friend. The clumsy interactions we've had since the breakup suck. I want to get back to the place where we can be real and have fun with each other again. Do you think we can do that?"

"You're making this way too easy. Yes, I know we can do that. I've missed you, too."

"All right then. Our post-break-up relationship reset conversation is done. I feel good. How about you?"

"Yes," I said, smiling. "I hope this means you'll still call when you think I can help. With me writing fiction now, I'll have to get my true crime fix where I can, I guess."

"The biggest case I'm handling is a bar fight arrest for one of the Grangers. I don't think we'll be needing any investigative help on that one. But I'll hold you to the offer. Now, tell me how writing is going for your new series."

"Not great. But if you've got the time to let me whine, I'll tell you all about it."

"I do. Whine away."

8

"Slow down, Miguel. Remember, I don't have any gears to shift. I'm making this trek with pedal power alone. We've still got what, a hundred miles before we get home? My legs are killing me. We should have driven out and biked from the parking lot up ahead instead of from all the way in town. Then the end would be in sight."

I puffed the words out rather than said them as I struggled to keep up with Miguel on the bike trail Wednesday evening.

My 10-speed, which has served me well for years, was at the Mr. Bike Shop for repairs. I was using an old single speed that my mother had in her garage. I'd forgotten how much work it can be to ride without gears. As I grew progressively sweatier and more out of breath, I was getting a touch irritable as well.

"The whole trip is only 12 miles. We're over halfway home. You can do it. Come on, make Troy proud," Miguel said over his shoulder as he moved effortlessly down the trail.

Troy runs a cycling group that he's invited me to join several times, but I've always declined. However now, with my breathing labored and my leg muscles rebelling, I was rethinking my refusal.

I put my head down and pedaled. When I looked up, I saw that Miguel had stopped. I assumed he'd taken pity on me and was giving me a rest break. As I got closer, I realized he wasn't waiting for me, but for the car I could hear coming up fast at the spot where the trail crossed a gravel road. I pulled up next to him just as it zoomed past at far above the 45-mph speed limit. But I had time to read the vanity plate on the red SUV that roared by. SPENCER.

"Where is Spencer going? There's nothing up that way except . . . " My voice trailed off as my brain kicked in.

"Except what?" Miguel prompted.

"We're in Granger country here. They own the property to the north, on the other side of the bike trail. I know for a fact there aren't any houses out here. And it's a dead-end road. Come on," I said as I turned in the direction the car had taken. "Let's find out where he goes."

———

"You said there was nothing down the road. So, what are we looking for?"

"The fact that there's nothing down that way is kind of the point, Miguel. Where is Spencer headed, and why? I'm curious."

Trees hedged us in on either side as we pedaled on. Although twilight was just starting to fall, the road was already heavily shadowed and a little spooky. Up ahead, I spotted an opening in the dense tree line. As we approached, we saw a two-track lane leading into the woods.

We braked and hopped off our bikes, leaning them against a tree.

"The trail is too rough for our bikes. Let's just walk in a little way and see what we can."

"That doesn't sound like a good idea. This is private property. Granger property. What happens if Harley Granger jumps out of the bushes with his rifle?" Miguel asked.

"I'll greet him like the old high school pals we never were and tell him we were out riding and just stopped by on the off-chance he might be around, so I could wish him well on his re-entry into society."

He shook his head, but I was already starting down the path.

"You don't have to follow me, stay here and wait if you like. I just want to see—"

I stopped abruptly and waved him to come forward. I pointed to an opening off to the side. Spencer's SUV was parked back among the trees, but he wasn't in it.

"That settles it. He's got to be meeting someone. But why?" I asked.

"Don't you mean who?"

"Well, both really. It's got to be something important to drag Spencer out into the mosquito-filled woods," I said as I swatted at one of the little vampires buzzing near my ear. "Maybe Harley has some info to sell Spencer—*GO News* isn't as fastidious as we are about not paying sources. Or maybe he and Harley are plotting some kind of trouble for Coop—neither one of them are fans. I think I know where they might be meeting. Come on."

I began walking quickly up the track.

The path was uneven and covered with enough moldy, muddy vegetation and loose rocks to dismay Miguel, whose shoes were meant for biking, not walking. He grumbled under his breath and said a few words in Spanish. It wasn't hard to guess what they were.

I turned my head to look at him as we rounded a curve in the trail.

"You really don't have to follow me and ruin your cute cycling look."

Miguel had appeared for our bike ride dressed in a lime-green zip-up jersey, black biking shorts, and the lime-green shoes he was so distressed about. He was perfectly attired for a bike ride on a paved trail. However, he was not suitably dressed for where our ride had taken us. My jeans and sneakers were faring much better than his ensemble so far, and it was probably going to get worse.

"Why don't you wait here? If memory serves, it's just beyond this curve and—"

"Oh-oh, look!" Miguel said. I turned and saw that he was pointing at a high gate topped with barbed wire stretching across the trail. It was attached to a barbed wire fence on either side that disappeared into the dense mix of trees.

"Oh, come on. Seriously?"

I walked up to the gate, but it was locked, and I couldn't see a way of either climbing over it or getting around it. But what I did see a few hundred feet beyond the gate was a weathered wooden building with a light gleaming out from a window on the side.

"Yes! I thought that might still be here. Come on, let's go," I said, turning and heading back down the trail to where we'd left our bikes.

"But where are we going now?" Miguel asked, surrendering all attempts to protect his shoes and apparel as he hurried to keep up with me.

"I'll tell you when we get there. Follow me."

"""""""""""""""""

Despite my inferior bike, my eagerness combined with Miguel's reluctance put me in the lead as we rode back to the point where the bike trail met the gravel road. When we turned onto it, Miguel said, "No. You have to tell me where we're going now."

He slowed his bike and put his feet firmly on the ground, leaning forward on the handlebars.

"Don't you always say you'll follow me anywhere?" I asked as I, too, came to a stop.

"I will follow you anywhere, that is true. But I want to know where is 'anywhere' this time."

"Okay, okay. The Grangers have a sugar shack—"

"Wait, what is a sugar shack?"

"I forget you were a city boy before you came to Himmel. A sugar shack is a place where you take sap from maple trees and turn it into maple syrup. At one time, the Grangers had one out here. It's the building we saw past the gate. I think that's where Spencer is meeting Harley—or whoever."

"But why are we back on the bike trail now?"

"Because that fence can't run all around their property. It's way too big. This bike path runs right next to the Granger land. That means all I have to do is ride up it a little way, and I should be right across from the shack. Then I'll just push through the line of trees and brush separating the Grangers' land from the trail and zip on over to the sugar shack. There's enough cover there to let me get close. You can wait for me here while I go check it out."

"I'm coming with you."

"What about your shoes?"

He sighed. I knew the stained state of them was paining him. "You need me more than I need my shoes. Let's do it."

I felt pretty sure that Miguel had some serious regrets about his show of solidarity as we pushed our way through the brambly undergrowth and trees along the edge of the trail. Small branches smacked our heads, poky twigs scratched our arms, and little crawly things found their way down our necks. But when we popped through on the other side, it was worth it.

The sugar shack was maybe two hundred yards away. A monster pickup truck was parked next to it, confirmation that Spencer was not alone. I motioned to Miguel, and we moved forward at an angle toward the building, using the sparse trees and bushes in what had once been a clearing to cover us. As we got closer, we could see that the window on the side was nearly obscured by a dappled willow bush. When we reached the edge of the shack, we both dropped to the ground and slithered into the narrow space between the bush and the building, just under the window. Once situated, we cautiously raised our heads just high enough to look through the smudged and cloudy glass.

Across the room, two men sat at a rough-hewn wooden table opposite each other. Fortunately, neither was facing the window Miguel and I were peering through. An overhead bulb provided enough light to recognize Spencer easily. He looked frightened.

Harley, on the other hand, was clearly in command of the situation. He leaned in toward Spencer in a menacing posture. The lower half of his face was covered with a bushy beard that obscured the small mouth and receding chin I remembered from high school. But there was no mistaking his beady, close-set Granger eyes, or the large ears that stood out almost at right angles from his head.

I couldn't resist a slight arching of my eyebrow and a small I-told-you-so smile as I glanced at Miguel. We could hear the low growl emanating from Harley but weren't able to distinguish what he said. It couldn't have been good news for Spencer because his head kept dropping lower and lower.

Suddenly, Harley pushed back from the table, stood, reached across it, and pulled Spencer off his chair. He held him by the collar of his shirt, which was bunched up in Harley's big fist. I had my hand on my cell phone, ready to call 911 if Harley started getting more physical.

He didn't. Instead, he said something that made Spencer nod his head multiple times in agreement. Harley loosened his grip then, and flicked Spencer back onto the chair the way you'd toss a used Kleenex into a wastebasket. Spencer tried to recover some of his dignity, smoothing down his hair and straightening his collar. Then he rose cautiously. He began moving around the table and toward the door. Then Harley placed one of his massive paws on his shoulder and Spencer involuntarily shrank back. Harley laughed and began steering Spencer toward the door like a host saying goodnight to a guest at a party.

As the door handle turned, Miguel and I dropped out of sight behind the bush. Our breathing was so shallow we were in danger of hyperventilating.

"You just remember, Spence. You can't go back now," Harley said.

"You can trust me. I came through like I promised, didn't I?"

"You did, but we gotta see how this plays out. Let's say you made a down payment on trust. We'll leave it at that."

Spencer began walking rapidly down the track toward his vehicle. Harley watched him for a minute, then went back inside and closed the door. I peeked up over the edge of the window. He was on his phone. I nodded my head in the direction of the bike path and we began slowly crawling backward out of the shelter of the willow.

Once we were clear of the shack, we began walking quickly toward the bike path. Miguel was in the lead this time. He turned his head to say something to me. I shushed him to keep silent until we were back on the bike path again. He nodded, turned around, and let out a yell.

9

A lot of things happened at once. The door of the shack burst open, and Harley came out shouting. Miguel put a hand to the back of his head, and it came away bloody. As I looked up, an owl glided away with a screech that was no match for Harley's roar.

I grabbed Miguel's hand and we ran with the heavy thud of Harley's tread behind us.

"Don't look back! Just keep running!"

"*Dios mío*! I thought I was shot."

"Hurry, or we might be." Fortunately, Harley isn't one of those guys who muscle up in prison. He's big all right, but it's mostly fat. I could hear his tortured breathing over my own ragged gasps, then the sound began to fade as he fell farther behind us.

"Don't slow down!" I urged Miguel. "We don't know what he's doing back there!"

A number of scary scenarios ran through my mind as I pushed my legs to move faster. Harley could be jumping into his pickup to track us down. He could be calling for reinforcements. He could be grabbing a gun.

When we got to the border of trees and bushes separating the Granger land from the bike trail, Miguel and I put our heads down and pushed through the tangle of branches, briars, and malevolent roots all attempting to maim or impede us. We ignored the scratches and the sound of fabric ripping and burst onto the bike path. Neither of us said a word as we hopped on our bikes and took off. Adrenalin is an amazing thing. Despite the bone-tired weariness I'd felt just a short while earlier, I pedaled faster than I ever had.

We didn't stop until we were within the city limits of Himmel, where we coasted until we reached the park, got off our bikes, and flopped down on a park bench. Miguel reached over and pulled the water bottle from his bike, took a big swig, and passed it to me. I drank long and hard before looking over at him.

"Miguel, you've got blood all down your neck! Turn around. Scooch over a little so you're more under the light."

He slid a few inches over and I stood up so I could look down at the top of his head. I gently moved his hair around until I found the source of the bleeding. He had a gash maybe an inch long, but the blood had begun to coagulate.

"Whoa! No wonder you yelled. It's a good thing your hair is so thick, or you might've had a serious problem. It's not bleeding anymore, though; that's good. Does it hurt bad?"

"No, no, it's all right. I just yelled because he surprised me. Why did he do that?"

"I don't know. Maybe it was a female owl protecting her nest, or a male protecting his territory. I'm not too up on my ornithology. We should go to the emergency room and get you checked over."

"No, my tetanus shot is still good. But oh, look!" He pointed down at his feet in horror. His shoes that would never see another bike trip. "And also, my shirt has a big hole in it," he said.

"I'm sorry."

"I told you we shouldn't go. I said it was private property. But no. 'I just want to take a look,' you said."

"Miguel, I said I'm sorry. I really am. I did tell you to stay behind. You're the one who insisted on coming with me."

"I've told you this before. Does Robin let Batman work alone? Does Benson leave Stabler behind? You need me. And I think you should also listen to me sometimes."

"Okay, yes, I need you. And yes, I probably should listen to you more often. I'll work on it," I said. Miguel was a touch cranky, unusual for him, and he deserved a bit of placating. "I'm totally prepared to listen right now. In fact, I need you to help me think. What the heck was going on between Spencer and Harley? I mean, it was obvious that Spencer was scared out of his mind. I might be too if Harley had me by the throat, but why did he?"

"I have no idea. But an idea I *do* have is making me a little nervous."

"What's that?"

"What if Harley recognized us? What will he do?"

"I doubt he did. It was getting pretty dusky. He wouldn't have been able to see that well. What would he do, even if he had recognized us? Report us for trespassing? The land wasn't posted. I don't think that's a big worry. We should let Maggie know something's afoot, though."

"Hey, you. It's about time. Where did you guys bike to—Milwaukee and back?"

Coop asked the question without looking up from his phone as I walked into my place. When he finished texting and glanced at me, his eyes widened in surprise as he took in my filthy sneakers, the tear in my T-shirt, and my scratched and bleeding arms. He jumped up and came quickly over.

"Leah, are you okay?"

"Yeah, I'm fine. You should see the other guy."

"What happened? Did you fall off your bike?"

"No, I'm fine, really. Seriously, though, you should see the other guy—or guys, I should say. For real. Harley Granger and Spencer Karr. Come on in the living room with me. After riding 10,000 miles with Miguel tonight, I'd like to sit on a soft couch instead of a hard bicycle seat. I'll tell you all about it."

I recounted the night's adventure and then I peppered him with questions.

"Why were Harley and Spencer meeting? And why in such an out-of-the-way spot? And why did Harley threaten him?"

I waited a few seconds for him to speak, but not much more than that.

"Come on, you're thinking something, what is it? Wait a minute, do you already *know* something?"

"I know a lot of things, but nothing specifically about why Spencer and Harley were meeting."

"What kind of things, then?"

"We've got some information we're checking out, that's all. It might touch on what you saw tonight, or it might not. It's at the preliminary stage, definitely nothing for the paper, especially because it may not be good intel."

"Something about Harley, or something about Spencer? Come on, off the record, just give me the bare minimum. It's something to do with drugs, right? Is Harley dealing again? But how would that connect to Spencer?"

"You're reading too much into what I said. When I can tell you something, I will. Is that good enough?"

"I guess it will have to be. For now. How's the investigation into Rob's murder going? Anything new?"

"It's going fine. Let's stop talking about work. Did you see Gabe today?"

"I did."

"How did it go?"

"Pretty well, I think. He was really nice about it, actually. Did you talk to Kristin?"

"Yes. She was fine. In fact, she said she expected that we'd come to our senses sooner or later, and she was happy for us."

"Really? I've always liked Kristin. Maybe Miguel's right. Maybe Kristin and Gabe should get together."

"Maybe so. But you're not going to change the subject on me. The two people we agreed who needed to know first about us, now do. So, Friday night is when it happens, right? The Himmel Players fundraiser is our coming out party. We're on the same page there, aren't we?"

"Yes. Even if I tried to back out, Miguel wouldn't let me. Friday night it is."

10

I was lying in bed on Friday morning, thinking about how glad I'd be when the evening was over, when a sudden realization made me sit up with a start. My mother! How could I have forgotten that she, of all people, needed to hear about me and Coop before the Players fundraiser? She'd never forgive me if she found out the same time everybody else did. I showered, dressed, and ran downstairs to catch her before anyone else was in.

She was in the break room making coffee and setting out a tray of apple bread she'd brought in for a treat. From the back, her trim figure made her look much younger than 60. Actually, when she turned around, she still didn't look her age.

"Good morning! You're up and about early. Did you smell the apple bread?"

"I didn't, but it looks great. Seriously, Mom, how do you stay so fit when you're always baking things?"

"The secret is sharing them, Leah. I like to bake. It soothes me. Also, I run most days, and that helps, too. Want to take a couple of slices upstairs to sustain you while you're writing?"

"I do, thanks," I said as I grabbed a napkin and wrapped up two pieces. "But that's not what I came down for. I need to talk to you."

"Oh? Do you want to go in my office?"

"Yeah, we probably should, in case anyone comes in. What I've got to say isn't for general consumption."

Her eyebrows drew together in a worried frown, but as we walked to her office, I said, "No, it's not anything bad. Don't worry. It's just, well, I'll wait until you sit down."

"Now I really am worried," she said as we reached her office. She turned the two visitor chairs around so they faced each other, and we each took a seat.

"Don't be. I just want to tell you that you were right."

"An admission like that is always music to my ears. Right about what?"

Her expression had changed from wary to interested and she looked at me expectantly.

"About me and Coop. I did what you said. I took a chance. I told him that I loved him—well, I cheated a little. I thought he was unconscious when I said it. Turned out he wasn't. But it worked out. We've been together ever since he got shot, but we—I—needed some time to get used to it without everyone knowing and weighing in and saying things. But then Miguel found out this week, and there was no going back from that. Tonight at the fundraiser, we're going to let people know."

She jumped up from her chair and hugged me hard.

"Hon, I'm so happy for you both! So happy that I relinquish my right to say, 'I told you so,' even though I did. A couple of times lately I wondered. It's felt like I've been running into Coop around here more than usual. And one morning when I got here extra early, I thought I saw his car pulling out of the parking lot. I didn't ask you, because I am not a sitcom mother who always has to know everything. Even though you sometimes act like I am."

"Well, sometimes you kind of are, but I still love you."

"Me, or my apple bread?"

"Both, Mom. And thanks for pushing me. I might never have done it. You were right. Some things are worth taking a risk for. You're the best. I mean it."

This time, I was the one who hugged her.

"Leah, you look great in that dress. And the necklace looks even better when it's out of hiding," Coop said as I walked into the living room where he was waiting.

"Thank you. It's my good luck charm to get me through the evening. I can't wait until this is over and the fact that we're together is just a regular thing, not something to ooh and ahh about."

"The way you look tonight, all anyone's going to be talking about is how beautiful you are."

I smiled and shook my head, but I liked hearing it.

"It feels kind of strange when you say things like that. Mind you, I enjoy it. But I'm still not used to the 'us' that includes romance and compliments. I'm sure we'll settle down after a while."

"I hope I never get so used to 'us' that I don't tell you when you look amazing."

"You clean up pretty nice yourself."

Instead of his off-duty jeans and T-shirt, Coop wore a gray suit with a white shirt and patterned blue tie. His dark hair was parted on the side and still slightly damp from his shower.

"I have to try and keep up with you, don't I? Come on, let's do this."

"I get that you're not looking forward to this," Coop said as he pulled into the nearly full parking lot outside the community theater building. "But I have to be honest. I am. I'm happy about it."

"Oh, I guess I'm not unhappy, exactly. But let's just get in there and get it over with so I can enjoy the rest of my life."

As we walked up to the door, he gave my hand a squeeze. Then he pushed on the handle, and we went inside.

The Himmel Community Players building used to be a fraternal lodge years ago. It closed after its membership declined along with Himmel's shrinking population. The Players had transformed it into a theater with a stage, lighting, sound system, and seating that any community would be proud of. And they have plenty of space to host events like the fundraiser tonight.

There had been some discussion about canceling the event because of Rob Porter's death. But tickets were already sold, catering was arranged, and liquor was ordered. So, the members of the board had decided that Rob would have wanted the show to go on.

Coop and I paused just inside the doorway to survey the scene. Clusters of people were talking, laughing, drinking, and happily socializing while smooth jazz played in the background. But as soon as Miguel spotted us, my worst fears came true.

He made an adjustment to the sound system, and the music changed to Bonnie Raitt singing "Nick of Time." I caught his eye and made a cut-the-mike gesture with my hand at my throat, but he just grinned. His voice came over the microphone loud and clear as he said, "Ladies and gentlemen, I give you what most of their friends have been waiting a long time to see. Leah and Coop, together at last. And I mean together together!"

So much for low key.

I leaned in so I could whisper to Coop.

"I am going to kill Miguel."

"Try to smile and be nice. It will be over quicker that way," he said, though I noticed he didn't seem at all distressed.

As I looked up, first one, then two, then a wave of people began heading our way, including Miguel who was beaming. The first to reach us was Charlie Ross. His work as a detective in the sheriff's office and mine as a journalist sometimes causes friction, but we've got a pretty decent friendship going.

"Ross! Where's Allie?"

"She's too young for a shindig like this. She won't be happy that she missed the big announcement, though. She's still packing and unpacking, tryin' to decide what to take. You'd think we were gonna be gone for three years, not three weeks. I'm still not sure how she talked me into this."

"Stop it. I know you're thrilled that she got into the creative writing academy at Georgetown."

"Yeah, I guess I'm pretty proud of her," he said, unable to keep a smile from forming. "I'm kinda proud of you, too. I think you finally got this romance thing figured out. I'm real happy for you, Leah."

Ross and I usually converse in a style that leans more toward snark than sincerity, and we almost always call each other by our last names. I'm not sure why. It just kind of evolved into our thing. His heartfelt response and the use of my first name took me by surprise. I was even more taken aback when he gave me a hug.

"Thanks, Charlie," I said, feeling a bit verklempt.

Not one to belabor an emotional moment, he stepped away from the hug quickly and turned to Coop.

"You sure about this, Coop? Nash can be pretty high-maintenance."

"I've been sure for years, Charlie," Coop said. "It just took a while for Leah to catch on. She's not as quick as I am."

Ross laughed and then said to me, "Nash, you got a good one there."

Before I could answer, he was more or less pushed out of the way by other people coming up to greet us. One of whom was my friend since kindergarten, Jennifer Pilarski, a warm, cuddly, and tender-hearted person who is pretty much my exact opposite. Maybe that's why we get along so well. Although we'd had a pretty serious falling out a few months earlier over something I did. I didn't have any choice, but it took Jennifer a while to accept that. We were still walking a little gingerly around the friendship we were rebuilding.

"Leah! I can't believe you didn't tell me! It's about time. No wonder Coop's been in such a good mood." She hugged me then, hard. Jen's a good hugger, she doesn't hold back.

"Thanks, Jen. I would have but . . ."

"But I was being such an idiot you didn't think you could. Go ahead, you can say it."

"No, that's not what I was going to say. It's just, well, it didn't feel right. It seemed almost like rubbing your face in it. 'Hey, Jen, look at me, I'm super happy!!!' "

I did an exaggerated pump of my arm and a few hops up and down. I'd forgotten I was wearing heels. Jennifer reached out with a steadying arm that kept me from falling.

"Yeah, things haven't been that great for me, but what kind of a friend do you think I am? You can't be happy because I'm not? Don't be crazy. Besides, I'm doing a lot better. And I have soooo much to tell you."

"Tell away, what's the news?"

"No, not here. This is an epic story that should be accompanied by several glasses of wine. But it'll have to be when I get back from Florida with the twins. I'm taking them to Disney World—my parents are treating. We're leaving Sunday morning."

"The boys must be wild with excitement."

"You have no idea. I'm glad. They've been through a lot lately. At least this trip will give them something happy to remember about this year. I'll call you when we get back. Well, I can feel the people behind me boring holes into the back of my head, waiting for their turn. Love you, love Coop, love you guys together!"

After she left, people continued to approach to congratulate us, tease us, and tell us they always knew we'd get together. My face was starting to hurt from smiling and saying thank you. When the first lull came, I turned to Coop.

"You know, I think I'm going to clock the next person who tells *me* how lucky I am, and *you* how much trouble I'm going to be as a girlfriend. I'm going to get a Jameson. I think I deserve it. I'll be back in a minute. Or thirty."

11

On my way to the bar, I saw Claire and veered in her direction.

"Leah! I was hoping to get a chance to talk to you."

"Hi, Claire. Well, I did it. Finally."

"So I see. How do you feel about it?"

"I feel like I'm in the chair at the dentist office. He's started to drill and it's too late to leave, so I'm just surrendering to the inevitable and hoping it ends soon."

"Well, you look like you're holding up fine."

"Yeah, I guess. I mean, I still hate all the fuss, and I definitely could have done without Miguel's big announcement, but Coop seems to be enjoying it."

"You've made it this far with a smile on your face. I think it's safe for you to relax and enjoy the evening, too, don't you?"

Claire's husband William joined us then. He handed Claire the glass of wine he held in his hand before turning to me. At that moment, Claire was approached by someone on her left. Rats. There was no hope of avoiding a one-on-one with William. He can get a little intense when he gets talking about his faith. Which I guess is a good quality in a minister, but not one I look for in casual party chit-chat.

"Hello, Leah," he said.

At first glance, you might wonder how a fairly ordinary-looking man like William attracted someone like Claire. He's in his early 40s, average height, light brown hair, ears a bit on the large side, light blue eyes on the small side. However, once he begins speaking it's clear his secret weapon is his voice. Think Gregory Peck in *To Kill a Mockingbird*. William's voice has that same deep, rich, almost mesmerizing quality. If the Sirens were trying to lure women to their destruction, instead of Ulysses and his men, that's the kind of voice they'd use.

"Hi, William. How are you doing?"

"Well, thank you, Leah. Congratulations on your engagement."

"Oh, no, no. This isn't that. Coop and I aren't engaged."

"Oh? With all the hoop—"

"William," I interrupted him. "Were you about to say 'hoopla?' Because if you were, I salute you in solidarity and appreciation."

He looked at me with a puzzled expression.

"Yes, I was going to say hoopla. Why does that warrant a salute?"

"Because I've been dragged by both Coop and your wife recently for using that very word. I'll stipulate that it's fallen out of use, but I'm glad to know that you agree it's the perfect word for this evening. Much ado about nothing. Well, not nothing. But Coop and I aren't engaged or anywhere close to it. We just recently realized that we're more than friends, and now that everyone else knows it, too, the hoopla has ensued. That's life in Himmel, I guess."

"I see," he said, though it was obvious that he didn't. However, I didn't feel like getting into the whole backstory of me and Coop with him, so I moved onto another topic.

"Speaking of life in Himmel, how are things going at your church?"

"Fairly well, I think. We're seeing an increase in numbers, not only at our Sunday services but also in our youth groups and family activities."

"That's great. It must be hard work, though. I mean, people have so many distractions it can't be easy to get them into church."

"It's a challenge, but one that I enjoy. Bringing people to God is what gives my life purpose—that and my family, of course. I feel very lucky that God called me to serve him."

"Well, I've heard some good things about your way with a sermon."

"Thank you. You should stop by for our Sunday service one day, Leah. Our church is a very welcoming place."

"I'm sure it is. But I'm not really one for organized religion. No offense intended," I added.

"None taken. But I'll pray that God opens your heart to his Word. He has a special love for lost sheep, you know."

"I don't think I'm lost, William. I'm just on a different path. One that I don't think has much chance of crossing yours."

"Don't be so sure. As the old hymn goes, 'God moves in a mysterious way

His wonders to perform.' My prayer will be that he moves you onto a path that leads to our church door," he said.

I was beginning to feel a little cornered. But it was hard to get annoyed when he was so obviously sincere. Instead, I looked to Claire to rescue me. But when I turned to draw her in, I saw that she was deep in conversation with someone. I did a double take when I realized who it was—Erin Harper, but a different Erin than I'd ever seen before.

She had abandoned the blazer, blouse, trousers, and sensible shoes that made up her daily wear as a lieutenant in the Himmel Police Department. Instead, she wore a pale-blue dress of some soft material that draped nicely on her slender body. The toes peeking out of her high-heeled sandals were painted a bright coral. Her light brown hair, normally scraped back into a tight French braid, hung in loose waves to her shoulders.

However, despite her off-duty ensemble and softened hairstyle, her posture was, as always, ramrod straight. Her expression was serious bordering on stern. It's not that Erin doesn't have a sense of humor, she does. But I've found that it takes a couple of after-work beers to find it beneath her professional drive.

"Erin, hi!"

I tried to keep my surprise at her glam appearance out of my voice.

"You look fantastic. I see you already know Claire. Have you met her husband William?"

"Yes."

She gave a quick nod in William's direction. Then she looked back at me. In her usual clipped voice she said, "I'm happy for you and Coop."

"Thanks, I know it's—"

She cut me off.

"Excuse me. I see someone I need to talk to."

Then she left.

I'm used to Erin's abruptness, but people who aren't can be taken aback.

"I'm sorry, Erin's always a little brusque. It's just her way. She doesn't mean anything by it," I said to William and Claire.

"No need to apologize. I know Erin from the workshops I've been doing for the police department. I'm used to her communication style," Claire said.

"Good. Then you know she's not as crabby as she seems at times."

"I wouldn't characterize Erin as 'crabby.' Just not very skilled socially."

"It's nicer the way you say it. Well, I think I've let Coop face the crowd on his own long enough. I better join him in his mingling."

"Yes, of course. Good to see you," Claire said.

"Nice to see you both," I said. William nodded as he took Claire by the elbow, and they moved away together.

I was musing about the odd-coupleness of them as I made my way across the room toward Coop when I bumped into my mother. Literally.

"Oops, sorry, Mom. I wasn't paying attention. I was thinking," I said.

"About what?"

"About Claire and William Montgomery. Claire is so calm and low key. William is so intense, at least about his religion. I assume Claire must have a strong faith because she's married to a minister, but I've never heard her talk about it. Every conversation with William seems to circle back to God talk. Besides that, Claire is next-level gorgeous and William, is, well, kind of ordinary looking."

"I think you're being too hard on William. He has intelligence, and passion, and that wonderful voice. Claire might view his 'God talk' as a plus, not the minus you feel it is."

"Hey, I've got nothing against God."

"I'm sure He'll be relieved to hear that."

"I'm just saying I'm surprised at Claire's choice. I'm not judging, just making an observation."

She just looked at me.

"Okay, so I'm judging a little. But I will absolutely concede that William's voice has a mesmerizing quality that could have bewitched Claire. And he's obviously smart, too. But passion and William? I don't think so."

"I'm not talking about sexual passion. I mean passion for the things he cares about—his faith, his family, his calling. He can be very charismatic. He spoke at the Interfaith Council lunch last week. He made me think of Reverend Dimmesdale—very eloquent and yes, passionate about his faith."

"Is Reverend Dimmesdale the one who was the minister at the Church of God years ago?"

I know that Reverend Dimmesdale is the sensitive, intellectual minister character in *The Scarlet Letter,* whose passion for his religion equals his passion for Hester Prynne. But I like to yank on my mother's English major chain once in a while.

"Leah, I despair of you sometimes. I know that you read *The Scarlet Letter* in high school. I—"

She suddenly realized that I was teasing her and shook her head.

"You're not as funny as you think you are."

"Oh, come on, yes I am."

"I think you—"

Over her shoulder I spotted Spencer Karr.

"Excuse me, Mom. There's someone I need to see," I said, touching her lightly on the shoulder as I moved quickly in Spencer's direction. Maybe with a little cautious probing I could learn something about his meeting with Harley on Wednesday night.

"Hello, Spencer. I'm surprised to see you here."

"Why? I'm a patron of the arts, Leah, and *GO News* is a big community booster, you know that," he said. His eyes were slightly bloodshot behind his trendy clear-framed glasses.

"You look more like a closing time patron of McClain's than the arts. Rough time last night?"

"No. It's allergies," he said, sniffing a little. "That and the smoke from burning your little has-been paper with our daily scoops. But I'm glad I came tonight, so I can wish you and Coop my very best."

"I'm sure."

"No, I'm sincere. Well played. You just slept your way into all the inside information you need from the sheriff's office to try and compete with *GO News*."

He had put special emphasis on the word try.

"Do you have to practice to be so obnoxious, or does it just come naturally?"

"Oh! I struck a nerve, didn't I? Are you still mad that Andrea got a great, in-depth feature story on Harley Granger's return from prison? We got a lot of traffic on our site from that. Maybe you need a shake-up in your reporting staff. Someone with Andrea's drive might help you."

"We fired Andrea, remember?"

"That's right, I forgot. You didn't like the competition from a younger, hotter reporter than you, wasn't that it?"

"No. We fired her because she did the kind of sloppy reporting that you specialize in at *GO News*. That makeover piece she did painting Harley as a reformed citizen was bad journalism even by the low bar you set at *GO News*. But I guess that's because you and Harley are still besties, right? Is that why you were meeting with him the other night?"

Not exactly the cautious probing I'd planned, but Spencer has a way of getting under my skin. However, I'd be lying if I said I didn't enjoy watching his face turn white and lose its smirk.

"Now who struck a nerve, Spence? What's going on with you two?"

Though I'd shaken him, he recovered quickly.

"Harley's an old friend. He wants to turn over a new leaf. He's had some hard times. I want to be there for him."

"Yes, of course. I know how compassionate you've always been when someone needs a helping hand." I shook my head. "You're lying, Spencer, and you just made me really curious to find out why."

"You know what they say about curiosity, Leah?"

"It has nine lives? No, wait, that's cats, isn't it?"

"The trouble with you is that you think you're smarter than you are. Harassing a man like Harley, a private citizen who paid his dues to society and is just trying to get back on his feet, might not come out so well for you."

"How's that?"

"I'll let you figure that out for yourself."

12

"Well, that wasn't so bad, was it?"

Coop sat on one end of my sofa rubbing my feet, which were throbbing after several hours of standing in high heels.

"It could have been worse," I conceded. "I wish Father Lindstrom wasn't visiting his sister. I think he would have enjoyed being there tonight."

"You didn't tell him already?"

"No! We had a deal. The only ones besides Gabe and Kristin to know ahead of time were my mom and your dad. Why? Did you tell someone else in advance?"

"No. I promised. But it was hard not to, because I'm happy."

I leaned over and kissed him lightly.

"What was that for?"

"Because you're reliable, and I know I can trust you."

"That's not a very sexy description of me. It makes me sound like a Volvo."

"Oh, believe me, reliability and trust are *very* sexy to me. Plus, you have some other very nice attributes. I like your hair. I love your eyes and your smile. I like how smart you are, and how kind you can be. In fact, I'm pretty much in love with you. Is that better?"

"Much. Speaking of telling, I saw you talking to Spencer tonight. You didn't look very happy. Neither did he. Do you want to tell me what that was about?"

"No, but I will."

I explained that I had talked too much when Spencer goaded me, and that he knew I'd seen him with Harley.

"You can be sure it's going from Spencer straight to Harley. And they'll probably figure out it was Miguel with you," he said.

"I know. It's not a great turn of events, but if I start digging a little into Spencer's life, he'd find out anyway."

"And is that what you're going to do?"

"Yes. And don't even say it. I'm going to work on my book too. I can handle more than one thing at a time, you know. Besides, I'm just going to poke around a little in Spencer's background. If there's anything there, I'll pass it on to Maggie."

He shrugged. "All right. It's your call."

"It is indeed. Do you think Harley and Spencer's meeting could have anything to do with Rob's murder?"

"How did you get there?"

"You said Harley was a suspect, because of his past with Rob."

"No. You suggested him as a suspect, and I said we were talking to people who had a relationship with Rob. I didn't say Harley was a suspect."

"But he must be. And if he is, do you think Spencer is connected somehow?"

"Leah, I know it would be a dream come true for you to see Spencer sent to prison for murder, but at this point I don't see any way to link him to Rob's death. What's his motive?"

"I haven't worked that out yet."

"Could be there's nothing to work out."

"Maybe, but I hope your team finds Rob's killer soon. Otherwise, it won't be long before *GO News* comes after you. Spencer might even imply that you had something to do with Rob's death, because you hated him."

"I didn't hate Rob," Coop said.

"I know that. It was the other way around. Rob hated you because he knew he was second choice after you turned down the captain's job. His ego couldn't handle it. But that won't matter to Spencer. If he sees an opening, he'll come after you. He lives to make trouble for other people."

"Well, that's not something I have time to worry about. We've got too much going on at the sheriff's office."

"That's true—there's Rob's murder and the drug investigation you said you're doing, right? Maybe Harley's involved in both."

"I didn't say we were doing a drug investigation. You inferred it. I can neither confirm nor deny your conclusion."

"Fine. But I'll tell you something, Spencer had it even more wrong than usual."

"How's that?"

"He said that now that I'm sleeping with you, I'd get all the information I want from the sheriff's office. If I'd known you were going to be so tight-lipped, I might have had second thoughts about this whole romance thing."

"Oh, is that right?"

"No, it isn't. But it is kind of frustrating."

"I'm sure. But I can't give you details of investigations no matter how much I might want to."

"Well, you get credit for saying that you 'might want to.' So, I'll drop it for now. But don't think that means I'm not still thinking."

"Oh, I never think that you're not thinking. Here's something for you to consider. Spencer *will* go to Harley and let him know you saw them together. How do you plan to handle that?"

"If Harley comes to me, I'll just say that Miguel and I were biking, I remembered the sugar shack and we took a small side trip to see it. We left as soon as we realized someone was there, but we panicked when Harley came roaring out after us and we ran. No harm intended. No harm done."

"I hope that works for you. Harley can be a pretty unpleasant guy to deal with."

13

On Monday I spent the morning and the early part of the afternoon trying to write, but I had a hard time sticking with the plan to just keep plowing forward. Finally, around one, I went downstairs for a break and a chat with whoever was around.

Troy was there alone, finishing a healthy home-packed lunch.

"Hey, Troy. I haven't seen much of you lately. How are things going on the police beat? Morale must be pretty low at HPD. Is everyone upset that the sheriff's office has the investigation instead of them?"

"They're upset about Captain Porter, for sure. But I picked up something else from a source I've been trying to develop there."

"You did? That's great. What is it?"

With freckles, large brown eyes behind corrective lenses, and his ever-present backpack, Troy looks far younger than he is. Sometimes it works to his advantage because people don't take him seriously. When that happens, he often gets more information than a more seasoned reporter would.

"I got it from Shane Jennings, he's a patrol officer at HPD. Do you know him?"

"Just to say hi to. He's your source?"

"He's getting to be. See, he's a cyclist too, and we ride together sometimes."

"Sounds promising."

"Yeah. Anyway, I had a couple of beers with him at McClain's last night. He told me something pretty interesting."

He hesitated for a second before going on.

"Don't leave me hanging. What is it?"

"Well, it's off the record . . . "

"Troy, I'm the publisher at the *Times*. You can tell me off-the-record things."

"Shane said there's a rumor around that Captain Porter and Lieutenant Harper had a thing going, and then he broke it off, but she wouldn't let go."

"Rob and Erin? No way. Those are the last two people who would ever get together. Who started the rumor?"

"Officer Darmody told Shane about it."

I couldn't stop myself from a head shake at Darmody's name.

"I know, he isn't always reliable. But he told Shane that he heard it from the captain himself. He said that the captain was worried because he made a bad mistake. He had an affair with Lieutenant Harper, but when he broke it off because he loved his wife, she threatened to tell her, and to file a sexual harassment complaint against him—even though she's the one who came on to him."

"Wait a minute. Why would Rob choose Darmody of all people to confide in? Everyone knows that telling him anything is the equivalent of posting it on social media."

"Maybe he wanted it out there, to make Lieutenant Harper's complaint seem like revenge, not real."

I considered the idea.

"Excellent point, Troy. Rob casts himself as the victim of a revenge-seeking woman who couldn't take rejection. Like *Fatal Attraction* without the boiling water and the pet bunny."

"But there's a little more, too, that maybe makes Captain Porter's story sound true. Shane was alone in the squad room working on a report the day Captain Porter was killed. The captain was in his office with Lieutenant Harper. The door was closed, but after a few minutes, Shane heard loud voices. Then Lieutenant Harper came out. As she was leaving, she told Captain Porter something like, 'You can't treat me like this.' Then she left."

"Did Shane say anything to Rob?"

"No. He didn't want to get involved in anything between the two of them. Especially when he's trying for a promotion."

"Has he talked to Owen Fike?"

"Yeah, sure. Once he knew Rob was murdered, he knew he had to tell the investigating team."

"Well done, Troy. Though I really can't wrap my head around the idea of Erin and Rob together. Although sometimes people pair off in surprising ways," I said, thinking of William and Claire.

"They do, don't they? I was surprised when I heard about you and Coop."

As soon as the words were out, his face flushed and he began to stammer.

"I wasn't comparing you to Lieutenant Harper or Coop to Captain Porter. I didn't mean you two don't go together. I just meant—I was trying to say—"

I put him out of his misery.

"Yes, Troy. I know what you meant," I said, and smiled.

The shy and relieved smile he gave back to me made me think that I should try being nice more often. Realistically, though, I knew I probably wouldn't.

Back upstairs after talking to Troy, I poured a glass of iced tea and took it over to the window seat. I felt the need for some mindless staring-out-the-window time. But before the staring could commence, my phone rang.

I didn't recognize the number, but I picked up anyway. I'm always handing out business cards to possible sources and sometimes the best calls come from people I don't know.

"You get involved in my business and I will mess you up, bad!"

Apparently, this wasn't going to be one of those times.

"Who is this?"

"You know damn well who it is. I don't know what you were doing on my property, but you better never be there again. You were a nosy bitch in school, and you caused me a lot of grief. That's not happening again. I'm warning you."

"Oh, hello, Harley! Now I recognize your voice. You're not still angry at me, are you? Come on now, we were just wild and crazy kids in high school, right?"

"You stay away from my place, and out of my business, or you'll be sorry."

"Don't be like that. I just wanted to show my friend your sugar shack. He's never seen one. Are you mad because I didn't poke my head in to say hi? I didn't want to disturb you when I saw you were in a meeting."

"Don't push me, I'm warning you. You won't be the one laughing if I ever catch you there again. Or if I hear you're poking around in my business!"

Since we no longer have handsets that allow a satisfying slamming down of the phone to end a conversation, Harley contented himself with calling me a very unpleasant name and pressing (very forcefully, I'm sure) the hang-up button on his cell phone.

That's when something outside caught my eye. Cole Granger, Harley's younger brother, was jaywalking across the street toward my building.

Cole had dated my youngest sister Lacey when she was in high school and in a bad place emotionally. He was exactly what she didn't need at the time. Or ever, really. For a while, I blamed him for the trouble she'd gotten into. But it had turned out to be a betrayal more devastating than anything Cole could have done to her that had caused her downward spiral. He's not as bad as Harley, but he's bad enough.

14

"Cole, what are you doing here?"

He stood on the landing at the top of my front stairs. The short-sleeved T-shirt he wore over his jeans allowed him to display the dragon tattoo that runs from his wrist all the way up his forearm. His small eyes, a yellow-flecked green, looked amused by my irritation.

"Well now, is that any way to greet a friend that come all the way into town to see you?"

"We're not friends, Cole."

"You are cuttin' me to the core, Leah. 'Specially seein' as how I got somethin' to say I think you're gonna find real interestin'."

Cole had spent some of his childhood in Kentucky, the origin of his drawling accent. Though it's interesting to me that his older brother Harley's accent is straight up Wisconsin, without a trace of the south in his words. On the other hand, Cole's accent has become more pronounced over the years. I suspect that it's a ploy to fool people into assuming that his brain is a little slow, like his speech pattern. But I've learned that underneath his fake "aw shucks" demeanor, Cole is quite bright and a little dangerous.

"I'm not going to let you in unless you tell me more than that."

"I'll give you a little preview. I got somethin' I could share about a couple old friends of yours. Now, are you gonna invite me in?"

Although I was tempted to respond with, "Not by the hair of my chinny-chin-chin," I restrained myself. He had to be referring to Harley and Spencer.

"All right, fine. Come in."

I opened the door wider and gestured for him to follow me as I led him through to the living room and kitchen area. He looked around with an assessing eye at the polished wooden floors, exposed brick walls, gleaming stainless-steel appliances, and the granite-topped island that separated the kitchen from the living room.

"You got a real nice place here, Leah. That book business must pay pretty good. Maybe I should try my hand at it. I got a lotta stories I could tell. How come you didn't ask me over before now?"

"Because I didn't want you here. I don't want you here now. I let you in to hear your 'interesting information.' Sit down," I said, pointing to a stool next to the island. "Do you want water or something?"

"If you got some Mountain Dew, I wouldn't say no."

"Sorry, water, iced tea, or Diet Coke," I said as I checked the inventory in my fridge.

"Don't I see a bottle of Leinie in there? Or is that Coop's special reserve? I heard about you two. I can't say as I think it'll last. When you get ready to dump him, you give me a call."

"Knock it off, Cole."

Making the beverage decision for him, I handed him a bottle of water and took the stool across from him. "Just tell me what you came to say."

"No need to get so uppity. I'm just tryin' to make some friendly conversation. But as this ain't exactly a social call, I guess I could get down to it."

"Go with that thought."

"Fine. First off, you need to know that you and your gay friend are busted. We know you two were on our family property the other night. That's trespassin'. I could report you to the sheriff—though what with you sleepin' with him and all, that probably wouldn't do me much good."

"I already got the word from Harley. Your big brother called me just before you got here."

"Yeah, well, you're lucky you only got a phone call. Harley was real, real mad when his business associate told him you were spyin' on them the other night. He was gonna come and see you personally. I convinced him it wasn't a good idea to rough up the sheriff's girlfriend. So, you're welcome for that."

"Wait a minute. Spencer Karr is in business with Harley? What kind of business?"

"I don't know as I said anything about Spencer, did I?"

I ignored his non-denial denial.

"What are your brother and Spencer up to?"

He took a drink from his bottle of water and then wiped his mouth with the back of his hand.

"Can we get off these hard barstools and move into your living room? Or is that only for fancy guests, not for workin' men like me?"

"If that will help you get to the point, yes."

He sat down on the couch. I took the rocking chair and pulled it over so I was sitting across from him.

"What's the matter? Too scared of the heat to sit next to me? Me and you've always had a lot of sexual chemistry, that's true."

"It's easier to tell when you're lying if I can see you straight on."

He shook his head and assumed a downcast look.

"I'm not even gonna address that hurtful comment. And if you don't wanta hear my story, then maybe I should just leave."

"What you should do is get to the point. I invited you in. I gave you water. You're sitting on my sofa. Now, tell me why you're here within the next 10 seconds, or leave."

It's best to take a tough approach with Cole, otherwise he doesn't respect you. It's not that I crave his respect. I just don't want him to think I'm afraid of him. Even though a small corner of my mind is, a little.

"All right, all right. Don't get all cranky on me. You're a lot better off with me here than Harley."

I recalled the way Harley had grabbed Spencer by his shirt, and the scared look on Spencer's face, and couldn't disagree with him.

"But you're not here as Harley's messenger boy. Why are you here?"

"I got somethin' of a problem. And I want you to help me with it."

15

"Why would I help *you*?"

"Because there's somethin' in it for you. It's a win-win for both of us," he said.

"Go on."

"When Harley got sent to prison, I stepped up as head of the family. He left things in a right mess. I took care of it all, expanded our business interests—we got the Ride EZ car service now, and a little handyman business goin', a few other things. But now Harley's back and he's takin' over again. And he's gonna wreck everything again with his big ideas."

"What kind of ideas?"

"He's got a business deal goin' with some friends he met in prison. They're big boys outta Milwaukee and they're into some big-time drug trafficking. I told Harley they are outta his league. But Harley, he doesn't want to hear it. He's all set up to be sorta like their first franchise holder."

"How's that going to work?"

"They got good access to the product. It comes in from across the lake, and up from Chicago, and down through the Upper Peninsula. Now they wanta expand their operations to out here in the sticks. Harley's gonna be their distribution system. And Harley is gonna mess it up. And even though most of the family ain't directly involved, we'll suffer when Harley blows it. But he's got veto power over me."

"Okay, you and Harley are having a family feud over who runs the show. How could I help even if I wanted to? Which I don't."

"You could do what I'm tryin' to ask you if you let me finish a thought. There's somethin' in it for you. A big story, if you follow me."

"Cole, the day I'm not smart enough to follow you, I'll turn in my reporter's notebook. You don't think Harley is bright enough to manage an expanded drug distribution network without getting caught. I'm with you on that, by the way. You'd rather stick to your small-time crime-ing—lower return but a lot lower risk. You're also jealous that Harley took back the top spot in the family. You want me to help you take him down, and then the *Times* gets the story on it as my prize. Is that right?"

"That is mostly correct, but it ain't right," he said. "Harley can't be trusted to run the family again. But Mama, she's stubborn. She just says the eldest son should be head of the family. It's what Daddy would want, and it's what she wants."

"Why don't you just go straight to Coop with the information?"

"I'm no fool. Harley would not take kindly to that. I need to keep outta the line of fire. Harley already knows you're nosy as hell, and he knows you saw him with Spencer. And he knows you're the sheriff's girl. If he gets busted, he'll think it was you who set the law on him. When he goes back to prison, I get restored to my rightful place in the family, with nobody thinkin' I turned against my own kin."

"Oh, okay. I make myself a target for Harley so you can get back on top in your family. That doesn't look like a win for me."

"That's 'cause you're not lookin' at it clear. You got issues with Spencer, right? This could make them all go away."

"You're saying that Spencer is in the drug dealing business with Harley?"

"There you go again. I never said Spencer and Harley was in business together."

"You said Harley was having a business meeting with an associate. I saw Spencer meeting with Harley. It's not hard to connect the dots."

"Spencer's not in business with Harley as such. Let's just say he's providin' a little help to an old friend."

That was almost exactly how Spencer had explained his meeting with Harley to me.

"What kind of help?"

"I believe I'm gonna have to withhold that information for right now."

"Why would Spencer do anything for Harley? Is Harley blackmailing him?"

"I'm not sayin' he is. I'll just say I might have a little more information for you, if you was to partner with me on this. What do you say?"

"I say you have lost your mind if you think I'd ever partner with you on anything. Or take your word as fact on any lead."

"You got a sharp tongue, Leah. But your harsh words don't bother me none. I made a fair offer to you. Truth to tell, I already got what I come for. But if you was to be a little nicer to me, I still might be persuaded to help you out."

"How did you get what you came for? I told you no."

"But I got you to listen to me. You're gonna go straight to your boyfriend Coop and tell him everything I said about Harley. I know you. Without me havin' to go near him."

He was right. There was no way I wasn't going to pass this on to Coop.

"Then the way I see it, you owe me one. Tell me what Spencer's involvement with Harley is, if it's not about the drugs?"

"Hold on there. You and me, we don't see this the same way. From my point of view, you owe *me*. I saved you from a personal visit from Harley, which would not have been near as pleasant as this little chat we just had. And I gave you some real interestin' information to share with the sheriff. I don't appreciate your tone."

I knew he wanted me to beg him for whatever he had on Spencer. And that there was a good chance it was just a tease anyway. That he was just trying to get one over on me again.

"Then I'd say we're done. You know where the door is."

After Cole left, I sat down in the window seat again, this time to think. Most of what Cole had said rang true. Periodically a dealer with an operation in Madison, or Milwaukee, or Green Bay, or Chicago will get the bright idea to expand their territory outside of their metro area. A couple of years ago we'd had a big multi-county drug bust that involved a local doctor who was a lot smarter than Harley.

Cole's story also fit in with my suspicion, which Coop had refused to confirm, that the sheriff's office was involved in an investigation into drug trafficking in the area. So, did he actually have something useful to tell me about Spencer?

Maybe I shouldn't have dismissed him so abruptly. There was no way he'd give me anything now unless I begged him for it. I wasn't reduced to that yet. I'd try some other ways to find out what Spencer was up to before I went crawling to Cole.

16

"Mmm, that smells really good," I said as I came through the kitchen door at Coop's. He was standing at the stove stirring something, and as I walked over, he turned and smiled.

"It's Dad's spaghetti sauce recipe. Or you could be smelling the garlic bread in the oven. Could you drain the pasta?"

"Sure. I'll set the table, too."

We moved around his small kitchen with the ease of long practice and within a short while were sitting down across from each other at the table.

"I had a surprise phone call today," I said.

"Yeah? From who?"

"Harley Granger."

"Harley! What did he have to say?"

"That I'd better stay off his property and out of his business or I'd be sorry. Then, I was blessed with a personal visit from his brother Cole."

"And what did he want?"

"He just stopped to say hi. And to tell me his brother is gearing up to get back into dealing drugs in a big way, and Spencer Karr is involved."

It's very hard to ruffle Coop's calm demeanor. That's why I find it so satisfying when I do. He started choking on the sip of water he'd just taken.

When he regained control, he said, "Cole told you the Grangers are getting into major league drug dealing again?"

"Not if Cole has his way."

I explained Cole's frustration at being demoted from leader of the Granger pack, and his fear that Harley's plans would bring a lot of problems for the whole family.

"Why would he tell you all that?"

"So that I'd go running to you because he doesn't dare to. He wants Harley to go down, but he doesn't want to be fingered as the one who caused it. And there's more."

I then explained the little I knew about the Spencer side of things.

"It seems to me that Harley has a hold over Spencer, which means that Spencer has done, or is doing, something he shouldn't. But what? Maybe he wasn't really in Chicago all those years being the great success his mother claims he was."

"Then where was he?"

"I don't know. Maybe that's what Harley is holding over him. Maybe he was in prison. Or he's a bigamist with three wives. Or maybe he writes *Gilmore Girls* fan fiction. What do you think?"

"I think that you're going to dig into Spencer no matter what I say."

"That's true, but I still want to know what you think. Could whatever Spencer is hiding have anything to do with Harley and the drug investigation you're already doing?"

"Nope. Not going there. I told you—"

"I know you did. I'm just checking to see if you changed your mind."

"The only thing I can say is that I need you—"

"You need me to not get in the way of your investigation, I know, I know. I don't intend to mix it up with Harley. I'll stay in my lane, which Spencer is definitely in. Of course, we could avoid any problems if you just tell me what you're doing, so I can be sure I don't get in your way by accident."

He shook his head.

"Nice try. Let's move on. What's the update on the book?"

"There isn't one. Next topic."

"Did you see anyone interesting today?"

"Outside of Cole, nope. Oh, wait, has the investigation into Rob's murder picked up anything about him and Erin Harper?"

"What do you mean by anything?"

"You know, sometimes you're not very good at this obfuscating game. You would have just said no if you hadn't, and you would have said yes if it wasn't anything relevant to your investigation. Therefore, my dear Watson, I infer that you know about the rumor that he and Erin had a fling."

"What do you know about it?"

"Even though you are withholding information—which, since the rumor is out there already, you really could have given to me—I will be the bigger person and tell you what I've heard."

I gave him the story Troy had given me.

"I'm having a hard time seeing Erin being dumb enough to hook up with Rob. How does that jibe with what Owen Fike has turned up?"

"We're following every lead."

"Does that mean you think there's something to it?"

"The investigation is moving ahead."

"I hate when you talk press briefing talk to me. This is off the record. I know you have to be looking at Harley, and you must have already interviewed Rob's wife Bethany, and no doubt some other possibilities, but are you also investigating Erin? Is it true, did she file a sexual harassment complaint against Rob?"

"No comment, on or off the record at this stage. And do you really have time to poke around in Rob's murder? Don't you have enough on your plate with your book?"

"I'm not poking around in Rob's murder. I'm just interested. And yes, I have plenty to do, and that includes digging into Spencer's background. You need to get over thinking that every answer to every question I ask you is going on the front page of the *Times*. Can't you just think that I'm being supportive about your work? Isn't that what builds a good relationship?"

"I don't think everything I tell you is headed for the front page. But I have an obligation to the integrity of an investigation. Look, I know you want to be sure that the *Times* beats *GO News* on this story. I don't have an issue with that, or with you or your reporters asking questions. But that doesn't mean I'm going to answer them—at least not in the detail or the time frame you like. I'll treat Andrea Novak or anyone else from *GO News* the same way."

"Seriously? I get *no* girlfriend privileges?"

"Regarding an active investigation, that's correct."

"All right. But I'm still going to keep asking questions."

"I never doubted it."

17

I got up early the next morning and settled down in my office with my laptop and a cup of coffee. I hadn't spent the night at Coop's. Lots of times we don't stay over with each other. Both of us enjoy our own space. And to be honest, I think I'm a bit too messy for him. My place is fairly clean, but not always picked up. And if he hits his head on one more kitchen cupboard door I left open, it could be the deal breaker in this relationship. Just kidding. Maybe.

Although I hadn't conceded it the night before, Coop was right. Rob's murder wasn't my job, and Spencer's secrets weren't my job. I still planned to look into them, but fulfilling my commitment to write a decent murder mystery was my main task at the moment.

Feeling very virtuous, I buckled down, and I held to that determination. I made writing the chief occupation of my days for the next week. I followed the investigation of Rob's murder, but it was from a distance. I read the autopsy report findings in the *Times,* but I didn't call Connie Crowley, the medical examiner, for more details. I asked Coop how things were going in a general way, but I didn't push on anything he didn't want to answer. I didn't quiz Troy, or Maggie, or Miguel for details on other leads. In fact, I stayed away from the newsroom so diligently that my mother came up to see if I was feeling well, and Miguel asked if I was mad at him. I think Maggie enjoyed the break, though.

I was feeling pretty proud about sticking to my plan. Until Tuesday came around again, and I got a phone call from Gabe.

"Leah, hi, have you got a minute?"

"Gabe, yes, sure. I just finished my lunch break, but I haven't started writing yet. What do you need?"

"Well, maybe I should have asked have you got a *few* minutes. I need to ask you something, but it'll be easier to explain in person. Can I come over? Right now?"

"Sure," I said.

"Great, I'm on my way."

"Hey, Gabe, just a second. Everything's okay with Dominic, isn't it? He isn't sick or—"

"What? No. He's great. We ate breakfast together over FaceTime this morning. This isn't anything to do with Dominic."

"All right, good to know. See you in a few."

Gabe had brought me a fountain Diet Coke with extra ice, one of my favorite beverages, and a coffee for himself. He put them both down on the kitchen island while I pulled up a stool. Out of habit he went to my refrigerator to get the creamer he likes but came away empty-handed.

"Sorry, I don't keep the hazelnut stuff anymore. I never use it and Coop —" I faltered as it hit me that not having the creamer I'd always kept on hand for him underscored the change in our relationship.

"Hey, don't look so stricken. I'm a little disappointed that you don't have a container of it in your fridge labeled *In Memory of Gabe*, but I'll get over it. I shouldn't have just dived into your refrigerator anyway. That's a boyfriend privilege. Which I'm not."

"You're still my friend. My very good friend. And if it will keep you coming around now that we've established that, I'll be happy to start stocking hazelnut creamer again. Deal?"

"Yes. Deal."

He sat down across from me and took a sip of his coffee before he spoke.

"I've got a real problem, Leah."

"What is it?"

"I'm trying to help a client who doesn't want to be helped. But she needs it in a big way."

"Who?"

"It's Erin. Erin Harper. She's been arrested for Rob Porter's murder."

"Erin? Why? When?"

"It happened this morning. Coop didn't tell you?"

"No, I've been trying to stay out of things, and he's been very okay with that. I didn't know they'd zeroed in on Erin. Why is Harley Granger out of the picture? And Rob's wife?"

"They both have good alibis from 8:30 p.m. to midnight. That's the time-of-death window. Bethany Porter was at a book club and then at home. A neighbor confirms. Harley's is actually better than good. It's very detailed and it all checks out. He was out of town at a Brewers night game with his mother and his aunt. He's got witnesses and receipts including one from the gas station stop he made outside of Lake Mills at one a.m."

"Sounds too good to be true."

"It checked out, Leah."

"Yeah, well, it seems made-to-order to keep Harley from being a suspect. Almost like it was planned in advance. What about Erin's alibi?"

"She started out saying she was home all night, never left the house. But unlike Harley's alibi, hers doesn't hold up. She lied."

"Where was she?"

"Phone records put her at Rob's hunting land the night he died. Now her story is that she went to talk to Rob, but he wasn't there. Says she knew it wouldn't look good, so she didn't mention it until Owen questioned her about it."

"What made Owen suspect her in the first place?"

"Witnesses at HPD who said that things weren't good between Erin and Rob."

"You mean the rumor that Erin and Rob had an affair and Erin couldn't let go when he cut her loose?"

"Owen Fike doesn't think it's a rumor. And he's got more."

"Like what?"

"She had at least two run-ins with Rob that other people witnessed, one of them pretty heated on the day he died. And an earring that's a match for a pair Erin has was found at the crime scene. Most damning of all is a letter from Erin to Rob."

"Those last two sound pretty bad."

"They are. They couldn't get DNA off the earring, so it's not conclusive, but it's pretty suggestive. Multiple people in the department say it matches a pair Erin wore. Erin says it's not hers, that she lost one of them weeks ago, and when she couldn't find it, she tossed the other one in the trash. But the earring the cops have is physical evidence. Juries love physical evidence."

"Why couldn't they get any DNA from the earring?"

"The cops won't say this, but I got it from a friend in the prosecutor's office. Dale Darmody was the searcher who found the earring. He mishandled it."

"He wasn't wearing gloves, right?"

"No, he had gloves on. But he had a full-on coughing/sneezing fit while he was holding the earring. Let's just say some gross bodily fluids got all over it, and then he wiped it off on his sleeve."

"Oh, boy."

"Yeah. It can be hard to lift DNA off a metal surface anyway. Because of Dale, whatever they might have been able to get is thoroughly contaminated."

"Tell me about the letter."

"It's in Erin's handwriting, and it was found in Rob's office. She doesn't deny writing it, but says it wasn't to Rob and she insists that she never had an affair with Rob. She says she doesn't know how Rob got it, unless he was snooping in her office."

"What does the letter say?"

"She begs this guy—whoever he is—to reconsider their break-up. She can't live without him, that kind of stuff. But absolutely refuses to say who the guy is, so the cops think she's straight up lying."

"Do you?"

"I don't want to think so. But she's making it hard for me to defend her. It's almost like she wants to get convicted."

"It could be that her secret lover has a lot to lose if his identity comes out, and she's trying to protect him. That makes more sense to me than the idea that Rob Porter inspired so much passion in Erin that she couldn't quit him. Also, I think if Erin had killed Rob, she'd do one of two things."

"Such as?"

"Either she'd own it, and face the consequences, or she'd have an alibi that would be hard to break. She's smart, and she's an experienced investigator. She'd be prepared for the questions Owen had, and not get trapped in her own lies."

"Good points. But the case against Erin is strong. I'm not sure I can dig her out of this. I need your help, Leah."

"It doesn't sound like Erin wants my help, or yours either."

"Maybe not, but she's dead in the water without it. Right now, she's got no one in her corner but me, and I can't do this alone. There's no money for a private investigator, no way to develop other suspects or an alternate theory of the crime. Defending her is going to be a lost cause without you."

I stared at him for a minute, well aware of what he was doing but unable to resist.

"No wonder you're such a good lawyer. You know exactly which buttons to push."

"I don't know what you mean," he said in a pretend puzzled tone.

"Oh, come on. You know you had me at 'I need your help.' I'm a sucker for an underdog or a lost cause. I'm in."

18

"You might as well go. I don't have anything to say to you."

Erin Harper sat across from me at a battered wooden table in the small visitors room at the Grantland County jail. Her arms were folded across her narrow chest, and her light brown hair was tucked behind her ears and reached below her shoulders. She wore the county jail uniform, a khaki jump suit. It was too large for her slender frame.

"You agreed to see me, Erin, I think that means you do."

"It means my lawyer insisted that I see you. I guess he thinks I'll respond to a little 'girl talk' with you. So, fine. Talk."

Her voice was flat, and her eyes showed no memory of the occasional beers and conversations we'd had at McClain's bar in the past. There was going to be no "girl talk" here.

"Okay, listen, we may not be friends, but we're not enemies. You don't have to come at me as though we are. I respect you as a police professional. You've never given me any reason to doubt your word. I hope you feel the same about me as a journalist."

After a few seconds she nodded, and I took it as a signal to continue.

"Okay. Gabe gave me the basics of your story. You lied about your alibi, you and Rob had a fight the day he died, an earring that matches a pair you have was found at the scene of the crime. You say it wasn't yours, but you can't produce the pair you own. Rob claimed you two had an affair and you wouldn't let go when he ended it. A letter that was found in Rob's office seems to support that. You acknowledge that you wrote it, but you say it wasn't to Rob, and you also say you didn't kill him. Does that sum things up?"

Again, she gave a brief nod as her response.

"Okay then. If you didn't kill Rob, who did?"

"I have no idea. It doesn't matter. The prosecutor wanted a quick investigation. Owen Fike gave it to him. Now Cliff Timmins has another talking point for his campaign for judge. He's not only a law-and-order man, but he's also impartial. He's prosecuting one of his own, a police officer."

"Hey, I'm no Timmins fangirl, and Owen and I aren't exactly tight either, but let's keep it real. From what Gabe told me, it sounds like you practically forced your own arrest."

"So why are you here?"

"Because I'm having a hard time believing that you had an affair with Rob. Also, you're way too competent to bungle a murder and lead the police straight to you. I don't want you to wind up in prison for something you didn't do. I don't know if I can help, but I'd like to try. Would you answer a few questions for me?"

I watched the conflict playing out across her face. Something was holding her back. Finally, she said, "All right, you can ask. But I may not answer the way you want."

"I can live with that."

"Is the rumor that you were preparing to file a sexual harassment complaint against Rob true?"

"Yes. Also, one for creating a hostile work environment."

"Why?"

"Because he made my work life miserable. He was after me all the time."

"Do you mean sexually harassing you, or that he was coming down hard on you for your job performance?"

"Both. It started with sexual harassment—you know, rubbing my shoulders, or brushing up against me. He'd say things like no-strings sex was his favorite tension reliever, then ask me what mine was. When I'd tell him a remark of his was inappropriate, he'd tell me to loosen up, that cops need a sense of humor."

"Did he ever make sexual remarks to you in front of other people?"

"Only his cronies and suck-ups. But they'd never say anything against Rob. They're just like him—or want to be."

"How long was the harassment going on?"

"Almost since I started."

"Why did you wait so long to decide to file a formal complaint?"

"I didn't plan on HPD being the last stop in my career. It's hard to move up if you're pegged as a troublemaker. Rob made it clear he had plenty of friends in law enforcement, and not just here. I knew it was true, so I tried to ride it out. Until I lost it at the department party out at his property a while ago. After that he was really gunning for me."

"Tell me about the party."

"All of us were at Rob's for a 'team building' afternoon—a shooting competition on his firing range and a barbecue after. Rob was a good shot, but I'm better. I wanted to beat him so bad I could taste it. I practiced for days ahead of the competition. And I did beat him. He was pissed, and I loved it. But later I took it too far."

"What did you do?"

"After the competition was over, we all lined up at the buffet table to get our food. Rob was right behind me. He saw a chance to get back at me for beating him. He reached across me for a piece of chicken, and he 'accidentally' touched my breast. Then he said, 'Sorry. I get excited when I see a nice, tender breast.'

"Somebody laughed and Rob said, 'Get your mind out of the gutter. I meant a chicken breast.' Everyone roared at that. Rob had this big grin on his face because he'd sexualized and humiliated me in front of the guys. And I couldn't do anything about it."

A wave of empathy washed over me as a quick reel of similar workplace experiences played across my mind.

"But you did something later, right?"

She nodded.

"Rob was talking to some of the guys when I was ready to leave. I walked over to say goodbye. He saw me coming and made some remark that set them all off laughing. By then, I'd had it. I thanked Rob for hosting the afternoon and said I really enjoyed it, especially winning the shooting competition. It was a small dig. If I'd left it there, it might have been all right. But then Rob said he wanted a rematch."

She paused and I saw a brief smile flit across her face.

"Don't leave me hanging. What did you say?"

"I said, 'Sure. But a word of advice. If you want to win, you need to take care of your premature release problem. You pull the trigger too fast. But I hear there's medication for that, Captain.' "

I felt a surge of surprise and admiration at the brutal assault Erin had made on Rob's ego. "Oof! That was a hard hit."

"I didn't plan to say it. I wish I hadn't. It made everything worse. The guys all laughed. Rob's face got so red he looked like he was going to explode. Then he walked away. After that everything got a lot harder at work. Rob gave me all the dullest assignments, tore into me in front of the guys, made sure I had the worst shifts. He knew it would look bad to fire the only female ranking officer in the department. In fact, the only woman at all, since Rudy Davis left. So, he tried to make me quit."

It was the same game plan Rob had used on Coop.

"Why didn't you?"

"Because I didn't want to give him the satisfaction of running me off my job. A job I really loved. I started documenting specific incidents. When I was ready, I brought things to a head on the Monday he was killed. We had a big argument in his office. I told him I had what I needed to file a formal complaint, for both sexual harassment and creating a hostile work environment. And I was ready to do it unless he stopped his behavior toward me."

"How did he react?"

"He said he'd already made sure people knew about the affair we'd had, and how I couldn't let go when he ended it. If I filed, he'd say I made a false claim to retaliate because he left me. He had witnesses who would back him up. What he meant was they'd lie for him. Then he told me if I didn't resign, he was going to ruin me."

"How did you respond?"

"I told him we both knew he was lying about an affair. There was no proof because it never happened. But the sexual harassment had, and I had plenty of documentation. He said he wasn't worried, but that I should be. That his career could withstand a phony complaint but mine wouldn't—no one was going to hire a ballbreaker like me for their department. And when he was through with me, that's the reputation I'd have.

"Then he said he knew he'd win, but he didn't want to go through the hassle. He offered me a deal. If I dropped the complaint and resigned, he'd put in a good word for me with a friend of his who's a police chief up north. I could slide into a lieutenant's position and be in line for a promotion when the captain there resigned next year. If I didn't, I'd find out what living hell was like on the job."

"Wow. He was playing hardball. What did you say to his offer?"

"It was all I could do not to jump across the desk and hit him in his smug face. I was so angry. But at the same time, a part of me knew that what he was saying was true. I was risking my career and potentially making my work life even more hellish than it had already been. He'd already undercut me with the men so much that some of them didn't respect me. Was filing a complaint really worth it? He saw that I was hesitating. He gave me 24 hours to decide. As I left, I told him he couldn't treat me like that, that he'd be sorry. He just smiled. Because he knew, and I knew, that he could."

"Where does the letter you wrote come in?"

"It doesn't. I don't know how Rob got hold of it. He didn't bring it up and I had no idea he had it. I didn't even realize it was missing until Owen shoved it under my nose and said it had been found in Rob's files. The only explanation I can think of is that Rob snooped around in my office looking for what I had on him and discovered it. I wrote it late one night at work, but I didn't send it. I shoved it in the back of my desk drawer because I couldn't decide if I should send it or not. I was shocked when Owen showed it to me."

"Well, that sort of makes sense. Except why would you keep a personal letter like that in your office?"

"You don't need to point out that it was stupid. I already know that. But

I've been pretty torn up about the end of my relationship. It was on my mind all the time. I thought if I could put my feelings in writing, it would help me. It didn't occur to me that Rob might go through my desk. It should have. He must have thought he could use it in case I didn't agree to resign."

It was definitely a bad move, but maybe the kind of thing you'd do when you weren't thinking straight during a break-up you didn't want. I moved on.

"Okay, so Monday afternoon you had an argument with Rob and left angry. What happened Monday night? Why did you go to Rob's property?"

"I hadn't planned on leaving my house that night. But I couldn't settle down. I couldn't think straight. I knew I should report Rob and let the chips fall where they may. But I didn't want to ruin my professional life—especially because my personal one was a wreck. Should I let him get away with it? Just resign and let him win? Finally, around 10, I went for a drive to clear my head. And it worked. I listened to my gut, and I knew what I had to do."

"Which was?"

"It wasn't to kill him if that's what you're thinking. I decided to go ahead with my complaint. Even if I lost and no one believed me, and I never got a job in policing again, the complaint would be on the record. The next woman—and with Rob there was always going to be a next woman—wouldn't stand alone like I had to. By the time I'd figured it out, I wasn't far from Rob's place. I knew he was out there for the night. On impulse, I drove over to tell him I wasn't afraid of him, and I was going to file my formal complaint."

"What happened when you got there?"

"His truck was there, but there weren't any lights on in the cabin. I knocked anyway, but he didn't answer. Then I noticed that his boat wasn't at the dock. I walked down to see if I could spot him on the lake, but I couldn't. It was kind of a letdown. I'd been looking forward to telling him off. Instead, I just went home. I had no idea he was dead. But I was happy when I found out. I still am."

"How do you explain the earring that was found? You said it isn't yours, but you can't produce your own pair. That's at least a little suspicious."

"Suspicions aren't facts. This is a fact: I had a pair of sapphire stud earrings. It's the birthstone for September, so probably hundreds, even thousands of women have a similar pair. I lost one of mine weeks ago. I don't know exactly when. One earring of a pair wasn't any use to me. I threw the one I still had away. That's it. End of story."

"Sadly, Erin, it isn't. The earring, whether it was yours or not, coupled with the lies you told Owen and the letter you wrote, make a pretty decent case against you. You could help yourself by saying who the letter was meant for, if it wasn't for Rob."

"I won't do that. It's got nothing to do with Rob."

19

"And that's as far as we got before Erin said she was done talking and called the guard to take her back to her cell," I said to Gabe as we sat in his office following my visit with Erin.

"You did better than I did. She didn't tell me the story about the trigger problem. I didn't expect Erin to have a sense of humor, but that's pretty funny. Too bad nothing else about this is. Do you still think she didn't do it?"

"I do. But she's sure not going to be much help to you defending her. It's like she thinks saying she didn't do it is enough. Can you imagine how she'd respond to a suspect who acted like her?"

"Just like Owen Fike did. She'd make an arrest."

"That letter is a real gift to the prosecution, isn't it?"

"Yes. Once the jury reads that, it's going to be hard to get them to doubt the prosecution's argument—that Erin was a woman scorned and she took the ultimate revenge."

"Can I get a look at it?"

"Sure. I've got a copy on my laptop."

He pulled it up and turned his laptop around so I could read the digitized copy on the screen. It was written in Erin's angular handwriting.

———————

You won't talk to me on the phone. You won't answer my emails. You ignore the texts I send you. You make sure you're never alone with me. I know it's what we agreed, but it's killing me to see you and not be able to touch you, to hold you.

I know you must feel the same way. You have to, after everything we've been to each other. I understand things are complicated. I realize there are other people involved, people who will be hurt. I'm sorry for that, truly. I'll do anything I can to lessen the pain for them. Anything except give you up. We can find a way through this. Whatever we lose, it will be worth it to be together. Don't cut me out of your life. Without you, I can't eat, I can't sleep, I can barely breathe. I've tried, and tried, but my life without you isn't worth anything.

You're the last thing I think of at night, and the first thing every morning. I'm begging you. At least see me alone one more time. If you do, and you can look me in the eyes and say you don't want to be with me, I'll walk away. If you won't see me, I really don't know what I'll do.

Erin

"Wow. I had no idea Erin was capable of that much intense emotion. Rob can't possibly be the person she feels that way about. I will never believe that."

" 'There are more things in heaven and earth, Horatio . . .' "

"Okay, don't come at me with your English major quotes. I agree, there are a lot of things to not understand in this world, especially about love. But Rob and Erin? It doesn't work for me."

"But will it for a jury? Timmins will use this letter to demolish everything Erin says about why she was at Rob's, what happened to her earrings, why she was filing a sexual harassment complaint, and anything else I can think of to use in her defense. He'll hammer on that last line. 'I really don't know what I'll do.' He'll tell the jury that what Erin did was kill Rob."

"You sound kind of like that's what you think, too. Is it?"

"No, I'm just playing devil's advocate. I don't think Erin killed Rob. But—"

"But we're going to have a hard time convincing a jury, right?"

"Right. So, let's start strategizing."

———

"Where do you want to begin? With Erin's secret lover? Maybe if we identify him, she'll be more forthcoming," Gabe said.

"Or, and remember this is Erin we're talking about, it could make her so angry she fires you. I say we leave it for now and take her at her word that his identity has no bearing on Rob's murder. We can come back to it later if we need to."

"All right. But I'm going to need something to stir up some reasonable doubt among the jury."

"Lucky for us Rob was such a terrible person. There must be lots of people who wanted him dead. But first, I think I should make sure the two most logical suspects, Harley and Rob's wife Bethany, are truly in the clear. I know you said Harley has an ironclad alibi, but he's a liar, his family are liars, and he's got a really strong reason to want Rob dead—and I don't just mean for revenge. He's got a fledgling drug distributorship to protect."

I took a brief conversational detour to bring Gabe up to speed on the night Miguel and I almost literally ran into Harley, and on Cole's follow-up visit to me.

"Harley already hated Rob for sending him to prison for 10 years. Maybe he had reason to think Rob was still keeping an eye on him. What with starting up his new illegal business, it wasn't a good time for Harley to have his nemesis looking over his shoulder. Killing Rob would get him revenge for the past and avoid future problems as well."

"How sure are you that Cole is telling the truth?"

"Semi-sure. Coop is at the beginning of an investigation into drug distribution in the area. He won't tell me anything about it, but trust me, his silence speaks volumes. That fits with Cole's story."

He shook his head doubtfully.

"Harley's alibi will be hard to break."

"That doesn't mean it's true."

"I talked to Owen myself. I think he was really thorough."

"He probably was. But still, was his full attention on Harley's story once Erin emerged as such a credible suspect? At this point, anything is possible. That's why the start of an investigation is my favorite part—before you get tangled up in dead-end leads, witness cover-ups, and false starts. I'm not ready to eliminate Harley just yet. Or Rob's wife, either. I know you said she was at a book club and then home, but do you have more detail than that?"

"Bethany drove to the meeting with her neighbor. They got home around nine. Bethany dropped the woman off at her house—she lives across the street—and then pulled her car into her own driveway, parked it, and went inside. The neighbor says Bethany's car was in the driveway all night. She noticed it when she went to bed around midnight."

"A nosy neighbor's not a bad thing if you want someone to confirm the alibi you constructed," I said.

"Do you know something that puts the wife in the running?"

"No, I hardly know her at all. I'm just wondering."

"If she's lying about it, wouldn't that mean the neighbor would have to be in on it?" Gabe asked.

"Maybe not. But to be clear, I don't have any reason to suspect Bethany beyond the statistical it's-the-spouse rule. I'm just riffing a 'what if' here. In my few encounters with her, she struck me as Rob's ideal wife—pretty, compliant, and enthralled with her lord and master. I'd like to scratch that surface a little and see what's underneath."

Just then there was a light tap on Gabe's door, and Patty Delwyn, the legal secretary for the firm, poked her head in.

"I'm sorry to interrupt, Gabe. Miller is on the line. He needs to ask you something about the Meadows file."

"Oh, right, I was supposed to call him. Leah, can you—"

"Yep, I sure can excuse you. I'll get out of your way here. It's almost five o'clock. I see a window seat, a legal pad, and a glass of Jameson in my future. I'll talk to you later."

20

"Leah, where are you going in such a hurry? Did you hear about Erin Harper? I can't believe it."

My mother was coming out of the back door of the *Times* just as I was going in.

"Hey, Mom. I did. In fact, I'm just coming back from Gabe's office. He's defending Erin. Do we have it online yet?"

"Yes, Troy just put the story up. He got a tip from a source."

I had pulled out my phone while I was talking and quickly scanned what Troy had written. It was succinct but hit the essentials. Plus, he had managed to wrestle a quote from the tightly closed lips of lead investigator Owen Fike, someone I'd rarely gotten to open up.

"This is great. All hail Troy! He's really coming along. Wait a sec, let me see what *GO News* has."

I opened the app, scanned the site, then looked up.

"There's no story on Erin yet. How can that be? Why isn't anything posted on their site yet? That's weird. Wonderful, but weird."

"That's not the only weird thing related to *GO News* today."

"Really? Do tell."

"I had coffee with Nancy Frei. She was doing the books for *GO News* until yesterday. Spencer fired her, she said."

"Why?"

"She gave him some advice he didn't want to follow. When she told him she didn't want to be part of any legal action if his creditors came after him, he told her it wasn't her worry. She disagreed, so he fired her."

"Shut the front door. Creditors? Lawsuits? *GO News* is in financial trouble? They've got more advertisers and more subscribers than we do, and we're still hanging on. How can they not be? What else did Nancy say?"

"I tried to get a little more out of her, but she wouldn't go any further. In fact, she said she shouldn't have said anything at all."

"I might try a run at her myself. We've always gotten along well."

"I wouldn't count on it. She takes her business ethics seriously."

"Don't discount my personal charm. But in case she doesn't succumb to it, I don't suppose you'd be willing to ask Paul about it and see what you can find out?"

"You suppose right. I don't say anything negative about Spencer to him, and he doesn't say anything negative about you to me."

"Even if you did, it would be a lopsided conversation. I mean because there's so very many bad things to say about Spencer, and virtually none about me, right?"

"You don't really want me to answer that, do you?"

"No, I do not. Also, I have to go. Lots of work to do."

"Your book's coming along well, then?"

"I'm fairly pleased with it."

I considered stopping there and not mentioning that I was working with Gabe to help Erin, but she'd find out anyway.

"But I'm working on something else right now. Gabe asked me to help him with Erin's case. That's why I was at his office. And I spent some time with her at the jail today."

I expected her to remind me that I wasn't a reporter anymore, that I wasn't a private investigator, and that I didn't have time for and shouldn't get mixed up in Rob's murder. Instead, she had an unexpected take on the situation.

"I'm glad. Erin is going to need help, and she won't get anyone who will fight harder for her than you. I've always felt sorry for her, you know. She keeps everyone at arm's length, even though she seems very lonely to me."

"Lonely? Erin is probably one of the most self-sufficient, independent people I know. Even now, when she's in really bad trouble, she's practically pushing help away. And she seems more angry than scared," I said.

"Anger can be a cover for fear."

"That's true, I suppose. Well, maybe I'll figure out what makes Erin tick by the time this is over. At the moment, I don't have a clue."

I balanced the legal pad on my knees, leaned back in the window seat, took a small sip of Jameson, and began plotting next steps. I started with a list of people who could tell me more about Rob. His dad, Al Porter, of course. I've loved Al since I was a kid. It had started more than 20 years ago, the night our house was destroyed in a fire. The same night my sister Annie had died. Al's the one who scooped me up in a hug and held me tight, enveloping me for a few minutes with a sense of steadiness in a world that had just shifted beneath my feet.

Now he was the one whose world had been upended. I didn't relish the thought of having what would be a very painful conversation with him. Still, he was the beginning of what I needed to know about Rob.

It wouldn't be much easier talking to Rob's wife Bethany, but at least she wasn't an old friend. I'd met her once or twice but that was it. She was a kindergarten teacher in her mid-20s, about 15 years younger than Rob. They'd only been married a couple of years. She rarely went anywhere without Rob, and always seemed to be content to let him do all the talking. Which I'm sure suited him just fine.

I tapped the edge of my legal pad with my pencil as I debated whether it was worth talking to Owen Fike. He probably wouldn't give me anything unless he had to, and I didn't have any leverage at this point. If Ross hadn't left for a trip with Allie, I would've had a conversation with him. His take on Rob would be worth hearing, but I didn't want to call him on his vacation. I considered for a minute, then decided to set up something with Owen after all, just to see how he reacted to my questions.

Then I added Jennifer Pilarski to my list.

I knew that Jen wouldn't give me any information on the investigation.

Despite our long friendship, she's frustratingly circumspect when it comes to her work in the sheriff's office. However, she's plugged into the law enforcement community. She might know something about Rob that I didn't, or about his wife. But that would have to wait until she got back from her Florida trip.

Then I came to my favorite suspect, Harley Granger. His extremely detailed alibi seemed extremely suspect to me. He could have planned it out to give himself cover while someone else did the actual killing. As far as I knew, the Grangers didn't have any hit men in the clan, but they could have imported one. Or one of Harley's prison friends might have been happy to do it. I was thinking so hard that I jumped when the door opened and Coop walked in.

"Well, that doesn't look guilty or anything. What are you up to?"

"You disturbed my concentration."

"Hmm. Why do I think it's not your book you're concentrating on?"

"You already know, don't you?"

He bridged the gap between us with a few long strides and sat down next to me.

"I heard that you're going to help Gabe with Erin's case. It looks like that's true," he said, pointing at my legal pad and the pencil in my hand. I love my laptop, but there's a weird connection between my brain and my pencil that helps me think.

"You've got good sources. Fast, too," I said.

"One of the guards at the jail told me you're working with Gabe on it."

"Does it bother you?"

"Nope. I got the girl, didn't I?"

"I don't mean that way. I meant are you mad that I'm digging into a case where you already made an arrest."

"No, I'm not. None of us are happy that it turned out to be Erin, but I'm satisfied with the case for her arrest that Owen built, and so is the prosecutor. Still, the main thing is to get to the truth. If you find something that warrants it, we'll reassess."

"But it won't make the sheriff's office look good if you arrested the wrong person."

"Come on, you know I don't want to score a win at any cost, including arresting the wrong person. Erin's a good cop. I'd be glad if it turned out she didn't do it. But based on what I know, I don't think it will. Facts are hard things and we've got a lot of them that add up to Erin's guilt."

"Maybe. But finding new facts is my specialty. Are we good, then?"

"We're good."

21

As I walked into Al Porter's office the next morning, I noted the crayon drawings from kids thanking Chief Porter for their tour of the fire station. Pictures of red fire engines, stick figures in firefighter turnout clothes, houses with flames shooting out the windows, and other artistic renditions that I couldn't quite identify festooned the wall behind him. Their colorful exuberance was a marked contrast to Al's subdued appearance.

He gave me a smile, but it was a pale imitation of his usual grin. Al is in his early 60s, and for the first time in my memory, he looked his age. He got up and walked around his desk to greet me.

When he reached out to shake my hand, I stepped forward and gave him a hug instead. I held on tight, the way he had when he had hugged me the night Annie died. When we stepped apart, I said, "Al, I'm so sorry."

"Thank you."

His eyes clouded with tears, and he blinked them away as he returned to his spot behind the desk. I took the chair in front of it.

"I wasn't sure that you'd see me, given that I'm working with Gabe Hoffman on Erin's defense."

He lifted a hand and shook his head to indicate that didn't matter to him.

"No, it's all right. I don't know if Erin killed my boy or not. If she did it, I want her punished. If she didn't, then I want whoever did kill him found. I don't have any problem with you asking questions. But I don't think I know anything about his murder that could help you."

"That's not really what I want to talk to you about. What I'm looking for from you is just a better sense of who Rob was. I know some random facts about him: he lived in Nebraska with his mother and stepfather until he was in high school, then they both died in an accident, and he moved back here with you. He went to technical college, he started out as a cop in Richland Center, and he worked a couple of years someplace else—"

"Reedsburg. Then he got hired at the sheriff's office here in Grantland County," Al said. "A couple years later, he busted Harley Granger and sent him to prison for 10 years. He'd been wanting to move over to the Himmel Police Department and that arrest sealed the deal for him. He got the job, and he did really well. Made lieutenant, then captain. He was going to try for chief, too, when Mick Riley retires."

The pride was evident in Al's voice.

"That's helpful, Al, but it's all work stuff. What can you tell me about Rob as a person?"

"He loved his job, liked people, liked to socialize. I didn't know about him and Erin, but I guess you wouldn't tell your dad that you were stepping out on your wife. I feel bad for Bethany. She said she had no idea. I'm not saying Rob didn't have his faults, he did. But he wasn't a bad person. Just human."

Actually, I did think Rob was a bad person, but there was no need to say that to his grieving father. But I must have shown something on my face, because Al said, "Rob told me once that you kind of went sour on him after he got the captain's job instead of Coop. He said you were sweet on Coop. I guess he was right, eh?"

This time the smile he gave me was genuine.

"Yeah, I guess he was. But I didn't go sour on him when he became captain. We just had a few disagreements about things."

Which was true. I was already sour on him before he took the job. Again, another thing best left unsaid.

"Well, Rob liked to have his way, I can't say he didn't. But there was more to him than that. Some real bad things happened to him when he was growing up. Things he didn't want to talk about. But I've been thinking about it and maybe it's time for them to come out. Maybe you—and some other people—might see him a little differently if they knew."

This was unexpected, but very intriguing.

"What are you talking about, Al?"

He didn't answer right away, and I wondered if he was having second thoughts. But he finally said, "It's kind of a long story."

Then he stopped again.

"I love long stories. Go ahead, tell me."

"Well, I warned you. This starts with me and Rob's mother, Jean. We got married when we were both 19—way too young. Especially me. I had a lot of growing up to do. But Jean was pregnant and it's what our families wanted, so that's what we did. I went to work in a factory, and I picked up all the overtime I could. We needed the money. I was a volunteer firefighter then, too, trying to get into the department full time. I wasn't around a lot. And when I was home, it seemed like half the time I got called out to a fire. Jean said it was like she was a single parent, and she was right. I wasn't much of a dad—or a husband. Jean got tired of it. She found somebody else, a cop from Dodgeville. We got divorced."

"I'm sorry, Al."

"To be honest, I was kinda relieved. That doesn't make me sound too good, but it's true. It was easier for me to face a fire than to walk through that door at night to Jean hollering at me and Robbie crying like he was never gonna stop. I knew what I was doing on the job. At home, I knew I was in over my head with Jean and a baby."

I was interested in this glimpse into Al's past, but I wasn't sure where it was going. His next words made me think he was reading my mind.

"I know I'm taking the long way home, but if you want to really know Rob, you gotta go back to the beginning."

"No worries, Al. Tell me the story however you need to."

"When Jean married Scott, I was fine with that. Kinda eased the guilt. He seemed like a nice enough guy. And he was good with Robbie, Jean said. But then Scott took a job in Nebraska, working in a sheriff's office out there. That's when Jean and Scott came to me with their idea."

"What idea was that?"

"They said that Scott loved Robbie, and they wanted to be a real family. I said that was good. I wanted Robbie to live in a home like the one I grew up in—two people who loved each other and loved him. I said I'd do whatever I could to support them, and that I would always be there for Rob, too."

He stopped and was obviously having trouble with what came next. I waited as he took a sip from the water bottle on his desk, rearranged some papers, and looked at the phone as though willing it to ring so he could legitimately back off from what came next. It didn't, and he finally continued.

"Jean said that was nice and all, but the thing was, Robbie was so young —he wasn't even two years old. Maybe it would be better if I let them put their family together, her and Scott and Robbie, and I sort of kept out of the way, so I didn't confuse Robbie."

"She wanted you to give up parental rights?"

"Not totally. She didn't ask me to let Scott adopt him, but she wanted full custody. She said I could write and send him things for his birthday or whatever. They'd make sure he knew that I was his biological father, but it would be a lot harder to be a family if a third person—me—had to be involved in all the decisions. With full custody, though, it would make things go smoother. Scott wanted to be a dad to Rob, she said, and I hadn't shown much interest in that."

"That was harsh!"

"Yeah. I was pretty mad, and I stormed out. But when I calmed down and thought about it, I knew she was right. I hadn't made being a father a priority. Robbie deserved a better dad than me. And Scott seemed like he really cared about Robbie . . . "

"Did you give up custody?"

"I did," he said with a heavy sigh. "I sent Robbie a card and a gift on his birthday and Christmas every year, talked to him on the phone sometimes, but it was hard. He knew I was his father, but Scott was the one he called Dad. And he didn't know me. When he was little, I'd drive down and see him, but he didn't really connect with me. Scott was the one who was there every day. I wanted him to come stay with me when he got older, but Jean always had an excuse why he couldn't. I had some friends who knew the situation, and they would always tell me I had rights and I should fight Jean."

"But you didn't?"

He shook his head.

"I figured I'd given up the right to put up a fight. Jean and Scott and Robbie were a family. They didn't need me. I hoped when Robbie was old enough, he'd choose to come and see me. I tried to stay in touch with him, but it was a one-way street. He never answered my letters, and as he got older, I didn't talk to him on the phone much either. When I'd call, most times Jean would tell me he was out with friends. I figured he just didn't have time for some guy who was supposed to be his father but he barely knew. After a while, I sort of gave up and just called on his birthday and Christmas. I still wrote to him once in a while, but I didn't know if he even read my letters. I'm not coming out too good in this story, am I?"

"Al, from what I've seen, parenting is a hard gig. You were there for Rob when he needed you after Jean and Scott died. I'm not going to judge you."

"You might as well. I judge myself for what I did to this day. I always will. See, when you said before that Jean and Scott died in an accident just before Rob came to live with me, that's what most people think. But it isn't true. They died in a murder-suicide."

22

That was a shocker.

"Al! I never heard that. What happened? How?"

"Rob didn't want anyone to know. After what he went through, I thought he had the right to decide how much information people got to have about him. It was way before Googling and all that Facebook nonsense. It would've taken a real busybody to find out the truth, and nobody did. Or, if they did, they never told."

"What is the truth?"

"That things were really bad in that 'happy family' I thought Rob was living in. Scott beat the living daylights out of Jean on a regular basis. When Rob got older, he started in on him, too."

"You had no clue that was going on?"

"None. I didn't talk to Jean that much. When I did, she always acted like things were fine. When I asked why Robbie never wanted to talk to me, why he didn't answer my letters, she said he was just busy. That all teenagers were self-centered, and he'd grow out of it. The best thing, she said, was to let him come to me in his own time. That's what I tried to do. Later Rob told me he never got anything that I sent, and Jean never told him when I called."

"Why not?"

"Rob said that she must have been afraid to. Scott was in total control of their lives. He moved them out in the country. He made Jean quit her job, then sold her car because they didn't need two if she wasn't working, he said. He wouldn't let Rob join Boy Scouts, or have kids over to play, or do any after-school activities. Jean didn't have any friends once they moved out of town, and with both her parents dead, she didn't have any family. It was like their little farmhouse was their whole world. Scott made sure they understood that what happened at home, stayed at home. Or else."

"Scott sounds like a typical abuser. Lure a partner in with surface charm that hides the inner rage. Then isolate, instill dependence, and inspire fear until the victim feels like there's no way out."

"That was the situation Rob described to me after he got here. I've never forgiven myself for what I let my son live through. To know I could have gotten him out, gotten Jean out, too, if I had pushed harder, asked more questions, driven down there to see for myself. It guts me. I thought I was some kind of a good guy because I gave up being involved in Rob's daily life so he could have a 'whole' family with Jean and Scott. Instead, I gave him to a monster! I've never felt like a more worthless human being than I did the night Rob showed up on my doorstep and told me what he'd gone through to get here."

Hearing Rob's backstory didn't make me disbelieve Erin or absolve Rob of all the bad behavior I'd seen from him. But it did slow down my roll. What kind of person would I have turned out to be if I'd gone through a childhood and early adolescence like that?

"Are you saying that Rob literally showed up on your doorstep, on his own? You didn't go to Nebraska to bring him back, after you were notified that Jean and Scott were dead?"

"That's not how it happened. I wish it was."

"Tell me."

"Three days before Rob showed up at my place, he got off the school bus at home. He went inside the house, found Scott half-drunk at the kitchen table and Jean huddled in a corner. She was beaten up so bad she could hardly move. Scott told him to go to his room. Up until then, Rob had just kept his head down and did what Scott told him. That day, he said no, and tried to help his mother up.

"Scott came over, yanked him away from Jean, and smacked Rob across the face. Something snapped in Rob. He was a big guy, even at 14, and strong. He hit Scott back, knocked him off-balance. And then he did it again. Scott fell and hit his head so hard on the floor it knocked him out cold. Rob told Jean they had to leave and not come back. Jean said no. Scott had told her a hundred times that if she ever left him, he'd find her and kill her. She believed him.

"But she told Rob he had to go. She couldn't protect him, and the cops wouldn't. They were Scott's buddies. She'd called for help once, and things were worse for her after they left. She told Rob to take the money out of Scott's wallet, get to the bus stop in town, and buy a ticket to Himmel. She wrote my address down for him."

"You must have been surprised when Rob showed up."

"You could've knocked me over with a feather. When I opened the door, he just stared at me. I opened my arms to him, and he fell right into them. Hugging my boy was one of the greatest feelings I've ever had. But when we went inside and he told me why he was there, that was one of the worst feelings. I was so ashamed of myself for letting him go through that. He started crying when I said I had to call Jean and let her know he was all right. He was afraid I was going to send him back. I've never felt lower than that. I realized he didn't have any idea that he could trust me to take care of him. Why would he?"

"What did Jean say when you reached her?"

"I didn't. A cop answered the phone, a deputy Scott worked with. He was at the house because Scott hadn't shown up for his shift and wasn't answering his phone or his radio. He found Jean and Scott, both dead. Shot. They were just trying to locate Rob when I called."

"Al, that's awful. I suppose that Scott killed Jean and then himself when he realized that Rob was gone. Everything would come out, Jean would leave him, and he'd go to prison."

"No, that's not what happened. Scott didn't shoot Jean, she shot him and then killed herself."

"That's a nightmare scenario, Al. But I hope you don't think you own the blame for it. That's on Scott."

"I'm the one who put my son in his hands. A father should protect his child. I didn't. After he came to me, I did my darndest to make it up to him. But how do you make up for something like that?"

That was a question I couldn't answer.

"I wanted Rob to go to counseling, so he could figure things out, get to a better place in his head. But he wouldn't do it. He begged me to just let him be 'normal.' That's what he kept saying. 'I just want to be normal. Not a loser freak.' He wanted to play sports, have a girlfriend, hang out with friends—all the things Scott never let him do. He didn't want anyone to know. It's like he was ashamed, even though he hadn't done anything wrong."

"I've done a lot of stories on domestic violence situations and talked to a lot of social workers and psychologists about it. Kids are under tremendous pressure to keep what's happening at home secret. They internalize the idea that it's their fault somehow, that something in them brought on the abuse. That's where the shame comes from. And it can affect them for a very long time," I said.

"I know I should've pushed Rob harder to see someone. Maybe things would have been better between us if I had. Maybe if we'd both gone."

Based on my own recent experience with therapy, I thought that was quite possibly true. I also thought Al was heaping enough guilt on himself. He didn't need me to give him any more.

"Better how, Al? Didn't you and Rob get along?"

"We did okay. But we were never close like I wanted us to be. When he wouldn't talk with a counselor, I tried to get him to talk to me. Told him it was okay if he was angry at me, I understood. He always just said, 'We're good, Al. Don't worry about it.' "

He rubbed his face with his hands and then looked down at them for a minute before he began again.

"I wanted Rob to call me dad, but he said he'd rather not. It stung a little every time he called me Al. He knew it hurt me, but I think he wanted that small piece of payback for me not being a father to him when he really needed it."

Now that sounded a lot more like the Rob that I knew. But Al was obviously feeling so low that I tried to channel Father Lindstrom, my spiritual north star, and find something wise and comforting to say.

"When people are hurting, they sometimes do things that hurt other people. Rob had to know you loved him, and I'm sure he loved you."

"I'd like to think so. But regardless, the only thing I can do now is try to be there for Bethany, Rob's wife. She's awful young to go through something like this on her own. Do you know her?"

"Not really. What's she like?"

"Real nice. Pretty, too. She's kind of a homebody, I'd say. Rob liked to go out, have fun. Bethany, she's a little on the shy side. I was kinda surprised when he married her, to tell the truth. After what his first wife did, he said he was through with marriage."

"Rob's first wife? He was married before?"

How had I missed that?

"Yeah, for a couple of years. Jody was her name. Bethany reminds me a little of her. Jody was a real pretty girl. Shy, too, like Bethany. One day, she just up and left him."

"When was that? What happened?"

"It's been maybe eight years ago now. Things seemed to be going well enough for them, from what I could see. Rob was real busy with his job and things, so I didn't get to see them that much. But then Jody lost a baby. Couldn't seem to get over it. Rob tried to help her, but he couldn't get through to her. Then one morning, he got home—he was working night shift then—and she was gone. Left him a note, said she was sorry, but she just couldn't cope. She wasn't any good to him or herself and she needed to leave."

"Where did she go?"

"Don't know. Rob tried to find her, but I guess she didn't want to be found. After a year or so he filed for divorce. Said he was through with marriage. But then he met Bethany a couple of years ago. I was really hoping I might have a grandkid or two one of these days to kind of give me a second chance but . . ."

His voice trailed off and his face clouded with pain again.

I put my notebook away and stood up to leave.

"I'm sorry, Al. I appreciate you trusting me enough to share all that."

"I hope it helps, Leah. Like I said, I wasn't the best father in the world, but I loved Rob and I tried to make up for letting him down as best I could. But some things, you just can't fix, I guess."

23

I sat in the parking lot of the fire station for a few minutes after I left Al, thinking about what he'd said. I felt bad that he was both grieving for his son and tormenting himself for his mistakes as a father. He'd tried to do the right thing—even though it had all gone so wrong. And he'd certainly stepped up when Rob came back into his life.

I didn't believe it was Al's fault that Rob had grown up to be the man I knew. His early experiences were horrific, but after he came to live with Al, he had the opportunity to make choices about how he wanted to live his life. Although to be fair to Rob, which it pained me to be, the damage done to him as a kid might have run so deep that he wasn't capable of seeing the different path Al offered. He'd buried his pain under a frantic hunt for normalcy that had left him no room for self-reflection and growth. He'd become the Rob that I knew, a self-serving manipulator who had gone through life hurting others.

Al's story had reminded me again how hard it is to raise a kid and reaffirmed my feeling that maybe it wasn't for me. I hadn't learned much that was helpful from Al, and I was sorry that talking to me had pulled up such painful memories for him.

I glanced at my watch, and when I saw the time, I hurried over to the Elite to pick up some coffee and cookies before I went to see Bethany

Porter. If I showed up bearing gifts, it might increase my chances of her inviting me in.

When I got back into the car with my purchases, I remembered to check the *GO News* site to see what they were up to. Their coverage of Erin's arrest had been oddly low-key to date. The story was the stuff their yellow journalism dreams are made of—beloved community leader cut down in his prime, illicit romance, woman scorned, blah, blah, blah. But yesterday, they'd steered away from it. I opened my phone and saw what a difference a day makes.

It's Coming from Inside the House! blared the headline on the lead story. It breathlessly detailed the unverified romance between Erin and Rob, tossing in an "allegedly" here and there for cover. It painted Rob as a heroic figure brought down by a woman who couldn't let go. The article was accompanied by a dashing photo of Rob in his dress uniform, and a terrible mug shot of Erin, looking sullen and very capable of killing an ex-lover.

After a round of speculation by anonymous sources, the story went on to trash the sheriff's office, implying that there had been an attempt to cover up for a fellow cop by shifting the blame to, and I quote, "a remorseful man who paid his dues for a youthful mistake, struggling to rebuild his life after prison." Yes, that would be Harley Granger.

The rest of the story rehashed the "incompetent and ethically compromised investigation" the sheriff's office had conducted into the murder of local businessman Bryan Crawford a few months earlier. Of course, it had been neither incompetent nor unethical—though Charlie Ross had skated pretty close to the line. But he'd been sidelined, disciplined, and paid a price for leading with his heart instead of his head.

I hated that Spencer and his crew were regurgitating all that bile. But I hated even more that once again, Spencer was trying to make Coop out to be the kind of cop who tried to cover up and divert blame when another cop was involved.

If I didn't have two hot coffees cooling fast, I'd have run over to the *GO News* office right then. Instead, I put a conversation with Spencer on my list of to-dos. I hadn't forgotten the fascinating tidbit my mother had picked up from Nancy Frei about possible financial troubles for good old Spence. I had a lunch lined up with her after I saw Bethany. Our conversation might give me some insights I could use to needle Spencer—one of my favorite pastimes.

The Porter house was a two-story brick home on a tree-lined street in a pleasant neighborhood on the north end of town. The lawn was well-tended, with a pretty border of flowers along both sides of the wide drive-way. As I got out of the car, an across-the-street neighbor mowing her lawn gave me a friendly wave, a kid rode by on a bicycle, and I heard a dog barking up the block. All that was missing from this Norman Rockwell picture of small-town life was a line of residents waving small American flags as a high school band marched by playing "The Stars and Stripes Forever."

It's what a lot of people think small towns are like, if they don't live in one. On one level, they're not wrong. Those things can all be part of it. But I never make the mistake of thinking that's the sum total of life in small communities. Beneath the pleasant surface, despair, sadness, guilt, fear, and loneliness live—as they do in any place that humans inhabit. I knew that I was about to confront one or all of those things as I waited for Bethany Porter to open the door of her lovely home.

"Hi, Bethany. I'm not sure if you remember me. I'm Leah Nash."

She was two or three inches shorter than me, and unlike me, she was fine-boned, with small features and delicately formed hands and feet—the kind of petite woman who makes me feel like a lumberjack. Short blonde hair with curls that seemed almost too assertively sassy for her subdued demeanor framed her heart-shaped face. Her soft brown eyes looked at me warily.

"Yes, I remember you, Leah," she said in a whispery voice that I had to lean into a little to hear. I lifted up the cardboard tray that held the coffee and cookies I'd brought to help me gain entry.

"I hope this isn't a bad time to stop by. I'd just like to talk with you for a few minutes. I brought some coffee and cookies to share if you have time."

"Well, I—"

"I'll keep it short. I promise. I really appreciate it," I said, rolling past her hesitancy with my best smile and a subtle insertion of myself into the opening between the edge of the door frame and wee Bethany.

She didn't shut the door on my foot, so I said, "Kitchen? That's always a nice place to talk."

She nodded and I followed her down the hallway into a surprisingly vivid red and white kitchen. I had expected Bethany to go with more of a pastel palette, like the pale-yellow top she wore with her light gray shorts.

"I like your red kitchen."

"I can't take credit for it," she said. She got a plate for the cookies out of the cupboard and set it down on the kitchen table, and then took a seat herself and pointed to indicate I should do the same.

"Rob had this house before we were married. I would've chosen lighter colors, but he likes—liked—the bold ones. And he didn't like to change things."

"Bethany, I'm sorry about Rob, and for what you must be going through. I wouldn't have intruded on what I know is a very tough time for you, but—"

"But you're working with the lawyer who's defending Erin Harper. Yes, I know. One of Rob's officers told me. They've all been so good to me, calling or stopping by every day to see if I need anything. He said I should expect you to come by, and that I shouldn't talk to you."

"Really? Why?"

"Why did he say that, or why am I talking to you?"

"Both."

"He said it, I suppose, to protect me from being upset. But when your husband is murdered, it's impossible not to be upset. I didn't send you away because I guess I'd like to know why you're helping the woman who killed Rob."

"Because Erin says she didn't do it, and she needs help to prove that."

"Do you think you're smarter than the detectives who arrested her?" Her voice was still soft, but her words were a bit harsh.

"Not smarter, no. But not dumber, either. Sometimes a different approach or perspective can help. Erin is going to go to prison for a very long time if she's found guilty. She says that she didn't kill Rob. I know Erin.

I'm inclined to believe her. I'm doing some checking to see if there's any evidence to support that belief."

"If she killed him, she deserves to go to prison."

"I agree. If she's guilty, she should suffer the consequences. But what if she isn't?"

"Isn't that for a jury to decide?"

"Yes, it is. I'm just trying to make sure that Erin's attorney has as much information as possible to present to the jury before they make that decision. I talked to Rob's dad earlier this morning. He wants justice for his son, too. But he doesn't want the wrong person sent to prison. I don't think you do either."

"Of course I don't. But this whole thing is so confusing, so unreal. I don't know how I'm supposed to feel. My husband was murdered. My husband was cheating on me? I had no idea. It's all just so much. Sometimes I don't think I can get through this. I really don't. I just . . ." Her lips began to tremble and suddenly she burst into tears. She put her face in her hands then and gave in to uncontrollable sobs.

Okay, that made me feel pretty bad. I reached across the table and patted her awkwardly on the shoulder. I could see that wasn't helping, so I pushed a napkin over toward her and sat back, waiting for her to cry herself out.

After a few minutes her sobs slowed down, and her hand reached out to grab the napkin. She blew her nose and looked up at me.

I opened up one of the coffee containers and slid it over to her. But when the rich, earthy smell of the brew wafted outward, Bethany abruptly pushed away from the table and ran down the hall.

24

Bethany's surprising departure was quickly followed by the sound of retching and the apparent disgorgement of everything she'd eaten that morning. I don't know a lot about pregnancy, but when Jennifer Pilarski was pregnant with her twins, I'd witnessed a number of similar quick exits.

When Bethany returned, her skin was very pale, and she was dabbing at her face with a washcloth.

"I'm pregnant," she said in a flat rather than joyful tone. "I've been having some morning sickness."

"Oh, Bethany! How far along are you?"

"I'm not sure. I did a home pregnancy test. Three times. It was positive every time. But I haven't seen the doctor yet. I can't seem to get myself together to do anything about anything. I'm 25 years old. My husband was sleeping with another woman. Now he's dead. Murdered. And I'm going to have a baby, and I'm all alone. It wasn't supposed to be like this."

"Were you and Rob planning to start a family?"

She shook her head.

"No. Rob said the timing wasn't right now. He was going to be named police chief when Mick Riley retires in the fall, and he wanted to be able to focus on the job for a while. Now he's dead, he'll never be chief, and I'm having a baby without him. Without anybody."

Her eyes filled with tears, but she didn't cry this time.

"What about your family? They'll step up, I'm sure."

"I don't have a family, not really. My parents weren't married, and I never knew my dad. I don't have any brothers or sisters. My mother had a stroke four years ago. She's in a nursing home in Marinette."

"I'm sorry. But you must have friends. If you reach out, I'm sure people will be there for you."

"You're wrong. I don't have any friends. Oh, I know people at work, but they're more acquaintances than friends. I've never socialized with them. Rob liked me to be home and I liked to be here for him. Besides, I've always been really shy. That's one of the things that attracted me to Rob. He was just so confident, so at ease everywhere."

"How did you and Rob meet?"

I felt a tiny twinge of guilt for riding the wave of her emotional storm all the way into the place I wanted to land—her relationship with Rob. But not guilty enough to ignore the lead she'd handed me.

"I had a job interview in Omico, and I got lost. My sense of direction is pretty bad. Even with a GPS I still manage to turn too early or too late, and it's always rerouting me. Somehow, I wound up in Himmel, and as I was getting back on track, I was really worried I was going to be late for the interview. I started speeding pretty fast.

"Rob pulled me over. I was so nervous about the interview and then getting stopped by a cop—which I knew would make me even later—that I burst into tears. Rob told me not to cry. He said he didn't want to give me a ticket, he wanted to ask me out. I was so relieved I said yes."

"I see. How long after that did you get married?"

I kept the judgy tone out of my voice as best I could. Bethany seemed to think it was a "meet cute" story. Given what I knew about Rob, it seemed more like a predatory move than a romantic one to me. Especially because three years ago, he was 37 and she was 22.

"From there it was a whirlwind romance. We got married in Las Vegas a month later. It was just the two of us, because the thought of a big wedding just overwhelmed me."

"Rob didn't mind? He was pretty extroverted. It seems like he would've been all in on a big party."

"He said he and his first wife had a big wedding and then a bad marriage. So, he was willing to try a small wedding and a good marriage."

"Yes. Rob's dad told me that his first marriage didn't end well."

"It didn't. His wife walked out on him. He just came home one day, and she was gone. Left a note and that was it."

"He never heard from her again?"

"No. He tried to find her, but there was no trace. It was like she just disappeared. He filed for divorce on abandonment grounds. After that he didn't trust another woman, he said, until he met me. That's really all I know about Jody. Rob didn't like to talk about her, and I wasn't really that anxious to talk about his first wife either."

There was something about that story that bothered me. Rob wasn't just a cop. He was a detective. He had training, experience, and access to resources a civilian wouldn't have. That he'd turned up nothing on his ex-wife was hard to believe.

"Sure, I can understand that. Did Rob ever talk to you about growing up in Nebraska, before he moved in with his dad?"

"Not a lot. He said that his stepfather was an alcoholic and really strict. His mother was okay. He used to tell her they should leave, but she was too weak to do it, Rob said. Then one day it must have finally got to be too much for her. Rob wasn't there, thank goodness, but she shot her husband and then herself. Rob came to Himmel to live with his dad then. I didn't ask him any more about it because I could see how upset it made him."

"Yeah, I can imagine."

I noticed her glancing at the clock.

"I just have a couple more things to ask, and then I'll be on my way," I said to reassure her. "Were you worried when Rob didn't come home the morning after he went fishing?"

"No. When he stays—stayed—all night, sometimes he showered at the cabin and went to work from there. He told me he wouldn't be home— that's why I went to the book club with my neighbor. Rob liked me to be here when he got home from work, so I don't usually do things in the evenings. I didn't expect to see him the next morning, so I didn't worry. I didn't even think about it until his dad called looking for him. Now I can't stop thinking that I was at a book club meeting, talking and laughing, while he was on the lake, dying. I feel like I should have known something terrible was happening to the man I was married to. But then, I didn't know he was having an affair either. I guess I'm just not very smart."

"Hey, if Rob was having an affair, he would have done everything he could to cover it up and make sure you didn't find out. That doesn't make you stupid, it makes him dishonest."

Having been in that situation myself—minus the murder part, though it did cross my mind when I found out—I felt a degree of solidarity with Bethany.

"Bethany, did Rob talk to you much about his work? Did he mention Harley Granger, or any problems he was having with Erin Harper?"

"He thought the story *GO News* did about Harley Granger being reformed and wanting a chance to start over was a joke. He said he'd have the last laugh though, because Harley would never change, and he'd wind up back in prison. He never mentioned Erin Harper to me at all. Do you think it was Harley Granger, not Erin, who killed Rob?"

"At this point, I really don't know. That's why I'm asking questions. Thank you for talking to me, Bethany. I'm very sorry that you're going through so much right now."

She teared up again, like you do when you're barely holding it together and someone is nice to you.

"Thank you."

25

As I walked down the driveway, a car pulled in and parked next to mine. The man who got out was Shane Jennings, the cop source that Troy was cultivating. Shane is about 30. He's always seemed like a pleasant enough guy, though there's nothing particularly memorable about him, except for his red hair. It's not strawberry blond, like Owen Fike's. It's full-on Ron Weasley red.

"Shane, hi. How are you?"

"Hi, Leah. I'm good. What are you doing here?"

He sounded a touch wary.

"I just had coffee with Bethany."

The answer was truthful, though not very complete.

"How about you? What are you up to today?" I asked.

"It's my day off. I came to do some yard work for her. Me and some of the other guys are kind of keeping an eye out for her. You know, making sure she's not alone with everything going on about Rob and stuff."

"That's nice. She's got a lot to cope with."

"Yeah, she does. Are you a friend of hers?"

"No, more of an acquaintance."

"You're not writing a story for the paper, are you? You know, Beth really needs some space and some privacy. Her husband was murdered, and she just found out Rob was having an affair. She's hurting. She's not just another news story," he said.

His protectiveness toward Bethany didn't surprise me. Lots of men are attracted to the kind of fragility she projected. But his use of "Beth" instead of Bethany was unexpected. I hadn't heard anyone else refer to her as anything but the more formal Bethany.

"I know that, Shane. I suppose by affair you mean Rob's alleged romance with Erin. It sounds like you believe that story is true. Do you?"

"Is that what you were talking to Beth about? Because if it was, you need to cut her some slack. She's too stressed to deal with those kinds of questions."

"I'm working with Gabe Hoffman, Erin's attorney. I'm just trying to find as much information about Erin and Rob as I can. You worked with Erin. You didn't answer my question just now. Does it seem likely to you that she had an affair with Rob, and that she killed him because he broke it off?"

"That's what the sheriff's team came up with. I wasn't part of it. I don't have any insider knowledge," he said.

That wasn't exactly true, according to Troy. Shane had witnessed the argument between Rob and Erin that had been one of the factors in her arrest. He'd also told Troy about the rumors circulating about Rob and Erin.

"But you saw them together on a daily basis, right? And you had to have heard the rumors that were going around. Does the motive—Erin as a woman scorned out for revenge—seem plausible to you?"

"Erin was my supervisor. She didn't confide in me. And Rob was her boss. I don't speculate about my superiors."

"Really? Because if that's true, you must be the only employee in America who doesn't. Shane, I'm not asking you to testify under oath here. We're just having a conversation."

He held his ground. "Like I said, I don't know anything about the captain's murder."

I changed the subject abruptly to see if I could shake him up.

"What do you think about Bethany as a suspect?"

His voice was incredulous as he answered.

"Bethany? No way. She'd never do anything like that. I can't imagine her shooting anyone, especially not her own husband."

"Hey, I'm not saying I suspect Bethany. She seems like someone who's dealing as well as she can with some very hard things right now. But you know the rule is look to the spouse first. I just wondered if you had any thoughts about that."

"I don't know anything about their relationship. It's not like I hung out with them. And the captain sure never talked to me about anything personal like that. But if you're thinking Bethany had anything to do with killing the captain, I'm sure that you're flat out wrong."

"Shane, I told you, I'm not thinking that. Not yet anyway. I'm just asking questions, and there aren't many answers so far."

"Okay, well, look, I've gotta go. Nice seeing you."

I knew that was not true. He'd been very uptight during our brief conversation, especially when I offered Bethany as a potential suspect. I might be circling back later. For the moment, I let it go.

"Nice seeing you, too."

As I turned out of the Porter driveway onto the street, I heard someone shout my name.

"Leah! Leah!"

I turned my head to the left and then smiled. Tracy Roach, who lives on the other side of the Porter house, was gesturing wildly to indicate she wanted me to pull into her drive. I happily obeyed, because I love Tracy, who happens to be my godmother.

"Come have a cup of coffee with me," she said, leaning into my open window.

"I'd love to, Tracy, but I really can't. I—"

"Oh, I know, I know. You're very busy. My goddaughter the newspaper-baron-slash-true-crime-writer. And now I hear you're going to be the next Sue Grafton. At least that's what your mother told me. I'm sorry I missed the big announcement about you and Coop—it's about time, by the way. If you think I'm going to let you get away without at least a quick catch-up chat, you are badly mistaken."

She attempted a stern look to accompany her faux outrage, but it was overpowered by her wide smile. She moved back and opened her arms for a hug. I got out of the car, bent down—Tracy is mighty, but she's small—and hugged her hard.

"Hey, don't give me grief. I called last week. But then all this other stuff came up and I didn't try again. I'm sorry I didn't make more of an effort, but this fiction writing along with everything else is kicking my butt."

"I know it is, hon. Your mom said. We had drinks last night. I understand. I've been caught up in some creative frustrations myself. A painting I'm working on just wasn't coming together the way I wanted it to. But I think I've finally got it now. Come and have a coffee with me to celebrate. It's the kind you like so much that my friend Enriqué hand roasts."

"Well . . . " I said, looking at my watch and weighing how much I like that coffee against how much time I had until I was due at Nancy Frei's.

"Oh, come on, you can take a few minutes," Tracy said.

"All right. I'd love to hear what you've been up to. I can't stay long, though."

"Well then, let's get going. But I want to hear about you. We can do me another day."

A few minutes later we were seated on Tracy's patio, coffees in hand. It made me smile to look over and see her feet barely touching the ground.

"You know, I really miss you when you're in Mexico for the winter," I said.

A few years ago, to the dismay of her many friends in Himmel, Tracy made the decision to move to Mexico, though she still returns to Wisconsin for extended stays several times a year. In Oaxaca she found a place and a people that she really loves, and the time to pursue her painting. She's had multiple fulfilling careers in her adventurous life—FM radio host, attorney, yoga teacher, travel agent, entrepreneur—but she seems the happiest to me now.

"I miss you, too. I'll always love Himmel—it's why I still have my house here. But there's something about Oaxaca that is so special to me."

"Well, it's obvious that it's good for you. You look wonderful."

Tracy's hair was once a soft and shiny blondish brown. Now, it's still shiny, but it's trending toward white, and she wears it in a long braid. Her eyes, a lovely blue-green color, crinkled with a smile at my comment.

"Flattery will get you everywhere. Thank you. You're looking good yourself. Now, I want to hear the inside scoop on Rob Porter's murder. Your mother told me Gabe Hoffman is defending the woman who's in jail for killing him, and you're helping him. By the way, I'm glad you threw Gabe back into the water for someone else to catch. He's a good person, I think, but he wasn't right for you."

"Oh, really? Why is that?"

"He's a little too nice to contend with someone like you. He'd let you boss him around too much. Not that a little bossiness is a bad thing. Sometimes it's necessary. But you need someone who occasionally pushes back. I think Coop is up to the job."

I started to object to her characterization of me, but she rolled right over me.

"You're on a tight timeline. We can discuss your need for control later. Tell me why you were at Bethany's this morning. Is she a suspect?"

"Tracy, slow down. Nobody's a suspect and everybody is at this point. I don't know enough about anything yet. I just wanted to hear what Bethany had to say about Rob and their life together. They're your next-door neighbors. What do you know about them?"

"Rob lived there for 10 years. He was an ass. Bethany's been married to him about two or three years. I don't know her, really. But she reminds me of Rob's first wife, Jody. She's quiet, seems compliant, the way I think Rob liked women to be."

"I didn't even know Rob had been married before until Al told me this morning. Were you friends with his first wife?"

"Friendly more than friends. Most of our conversations were just hello, and a little casual chatting out in the driveway, that kind of thing. Except for two occasions, both of which I remember quite well."

I sensed something interesting coming.

"Don't stop there. What were they?"

"The first was when Jody found out she was pregnant. I don't think she had many people to share the news with. She told me once that her only family was a grandmother in Omico. I never saw friends dropping in on her either. I guess that's why she came running over to tell me. It was fun to hear the news because she was so excited. She told me that she and Rob hadn't planned to start a family yet, and she hoped he'd be as happy about it as she was."

"And was he?"

"When I congratulated him later, he seemed sort of blah about it. Not excited, but not upset either. When she lost the baby, I thought he seemed more relieved than grieved."

"Al told me that Jody went into a major depression after she had the miscarriage. He said Rob tried to help her, but she didn't get any better, and that's why she left."

"There's more to that story than Rob told his dad. I don't know how a nice person like Al could have had a son like Rob. Of course, Al didn't really raise him, so there's that."

"What more to the story is there?"

"Normally, I wouldn't be telling you this. I haven't told anyone else. But with Jody long gone and Rob dead, I don't see how it could hurt either of them now. Rob had a vasectomy right after Jody miscarried, without telling her. I'm not saying she wasn't depressed about losing the baby. Of course she was. But she was also really devastated and overwhelmed when she found out what Rob had done. Jody wanted children and Rob unilaterally made sure that wasn't going to happen."

Tracy continued talking, but I wasn't processing anything she was saying. My brain was working too hard to hold two contradictory thoughts at the same time. Bethany was pregnant, now. But Rob had had a vasectomy 10 years ago.

26

"Tracy, are you sure Rob had a vasectomy? How do you know? It doesn't seem like the kind of thing a man as hung up on his masculinity as Rob was would do."

"I know because Jody told me herself. That was the only other time we had a truly personal conversation."

"If Rob didn't tell her, how did Jody find out?"

"She was listening to the messages on their answering machine. They still had a landline then. Rob—or someone from his doctor's office—must have mixed up his cell phone number and their home number. The call went to their landline, and the message was to reschedule his post-vasectomy follow-up. That's how Jody discovered it."

"Wow. Right after losing a pregnancy, to learn there wasn't ever going to be another one, and that Rob had made the choice for her . . ."

"She was devastated. I doubt she would have said as much to me as she did if she hadn't been so distraught."

"What all did she say?"

"That she'd confronted Rob. That he told her he didn't want kids, that was final, and he wasn't going to discuss it anymore. When she said he had no right to make that decision without talking to her first, he grabbed her and shook her so hard her head hit the wall. Then he stormed off."

"Rob was physically abusive to her?" I asked, thinking about the example Rob's stepfather had given him growing up.

"She backtracked when I pressed her on that. Tried to downplay it, said it was an accident, she'd slipped, he didn't do it on purpose. But I saw the bruise. There were fingermarks on her arm."

"What did you do?"

"I didn't hold back. I told her that no one, no matter how angry they were, no matter who they were, had the right to hit her. But she kept saying it wasn't like that. She also said she shouldn't have told me about the vasectomy. She begged me never to say anything to Rob. Or to anyone else. She was almost hysterical. I promised her that the conversation was just between her and me. Don't look at me like that," Tracy added.

"Like what?"

"Like I should've bundled her off to the nearest women's shelter."

"I wasn't," I said—though maybe a little I had been.

"You can't force people to save themselves, Leah. I keep a handful of cards from the local women's shelter around because you never know. I gave her one, and I wrote my number on the back. I told her to call the shelter if things got bad, or if she couldn't bring herself to do that, to call me, any time. But later that evening, when I was cleaning up, I found the card. She'd tucked it under a placemat and left it behind."

"What happened after that? Did you check on her?"

"I was leaving for Mexico the next day. She was at work. I didn't dare leave a note in case Rob found it. I called her cell phone when I got to Oaxaca, but it was out of service. I called your mom and casually mentioned Jody. I couldn't be direct because I'd promised not to say anything. Carol told me that Jody had left Rob, taken off with just a note left behind, and it was causing quite a stir in town. I was surprised she'd found the courage, but glad for her. I was gladder still that he never found her. I hope she's living a brand-new happy life somewhere else now."

"Tracy, this is pretty explosive information. How sure are you of it?"

"As sure as I can be without actually witnessing him hitting her myself. I used to volunteer at a shelter, Leah. Jody presented with a lot of the characteristics of a domestic violence victim—low self-esteem, socially isolated, taking on blame, making excuses for Rob. Plus, there was that ugly finger-mark bruise on her arm. So, I'm pretty sure."

A ghost of an idea flitted across my mind as Tracy spoke, but it disappeared before I could grab hold of it. I knew it would come back later, probably when I least expected it. The unconscious, mine anyway, works on its own time. I haven't found a way to rush it, so I moved on.

"What about his current wife Bethany? Do you think Rob beat her up, too?"

"I've worried about that, but I haven't seen any sign of it. Although I almost never see Bethany at all. She keeps to herself. You spent some time with her just now. How did she strike you?"

"Shy, passive, not very confident. She didn't have anything bad to say about Rob. She didn't even seem very angry about the rumor he and Erin had an affair. More bewildered than anything else."

"Is the affair just a rumor, or did they actually have one?"

"Erin says no, and I'm inclined to believe her. I definitely can't wrap my head around her having a fling with someone like him. But it's early days."

It wasn't quite as early as I was indicating, however. But I couldn't share that with Tracy.

"Tracy, when I was leaving Bethany's, I ran into Shane Jennings. He's a cop with the Himmel Police Department. Have you seen him there before?"

"There are always cops from the department coming and going over there. I think Rob used the younger guys under his command like indentured servants. He had a couple of them re-roof his garage last summer, and the year before they helped him do the driveway. But I don't know any names. What's Shane look like?"

"He's pretty average looking. But he does have one very distinguishing feature."

"Is he the redhead?"

"Yep, that would be him. Have you seen him at Rob's since you've been back?"

"He was here a lot last summer. I haven't really noticed him much since I've been back. Hey, if you're looking for the nosy neighbor from *Bewitched,* you should be talking to Ada Dillon across the street, not me. She literally keeps a pair of binoculars on her windowsill—front and back. She says she's an avid bird watcher. Maybe so. But she can also tell you everyone's comings and goings on the block."

"Which house is hers?"

"The stucco one with the green door."

"Thanks, maybe I'll get in touch with her later. Right now, I really better get going. I'll call you soon for lunch."

"I'll hold you to that."

I made a phone call to the county medical examiner as soon as I left Tracy's.

"Connie? Hi, this is Leah. I have a question."

"You always do, Leah. I heard you were working with Gabe on Erin Harper's defense. Sorry, but I'm not authorized to speak on the case, per Cliff Timmins. You need to check with him."

"As if our not-esteemed prosecutor would ever give me anything. Come on, Connie. I just have one thing to ask."

"You can file an Open Records Act request and get a copy of the autopsy."

"I know, but that will take too long. This is really easy, and your answer will be the deepest of deep background, I promise. I just need you to answer this one little question. Please? I'll owe you one."

"By my count, that'll bring your total up to an even one hundred that you owe me," she said, but I could tell by her tone that she was going to answer me.

"Did Rob Porter's autopsy show evidence of a vasectomy?"

"Yes, it did. The vas deferens were severed."

"He was infertile, then. No sperm, right?"

"That's the hoped-for outcome of a vasectomy, and the usual one. But there's still a reserve amount, let's call it, of sperm for a period of time after the procedure. Birth control is advised for the three months following."

"But after all this time, there was no way he could impregnate someone."

"That's right."

"Okay. Thanks. Bye."

I hung up before she could turn the tables and ask me any questions. I needed time to process what she'd just said. But I didn't have any right then. I'd just pulled up in front of Nancy Frei's office, and I had to switch gears.

Talking to Nancy didn't have anything to do with tracking down information on Rob. But I hadn't given up on my quest to find what Spencer was up to. After the call I got from Harley, and then Cole's oblique hints and what my mother had told me about Spencer firing Nancy, I knew something was going on.

And I can do more than one thing at a time. As I pulled up in front of Nancy's office, I switched my focus off Rob's murder and on to Spencer's secret life.

27

Nancy's bookkeeping service is a one-woman shop. She runs it out of her home, which is about a mile outside of the Himmel city limits. When I'd called her to set up a time to talk, she'd invited me to lunch.

"Leah! Hi! It's been a long time since I've seen you. How are you doing? I thought we'd eat out in the backyard, it's such a nice day," she said when she opened the door to my knock. One of her three cats had appeared at her feet and meowed at me in greeting until she shooed him back in.

"Yeah, it's been a minute," I said as we walked around to her backyard. "I think maybe since you did my taxes last March."

Nancy is somewhere in her early 50s, but you wouldn't know it. Her skin is clear and smooth with just a few laugh lines around her hazel eyes. As we reached her backyard, the wind caught a few strands of hair that had fallen from the loose bun on top of her head. They floated in the air like spun gold.

"You have the hair of my five-year-old dreams, Nancy. Like my Holiday Barbie before the neighbor's dog ate part of her head."

"Thanks. I think."

She said it as though she thought I might be teasing her. I wasn't. I don't envy other people much. I'm okay with the way I look—average to maybe high average on good days. And I'm a little vain about my eyelashes. But my hair has always been the bane of my existence.

"No, I mean it. If you took it down and shook your head, it would cascade onto your shoulders in gorgeous waves. If I pull the clip out of my hair, it will just hang there like a curtain. A sort of rusty brown, fuzzy curtain."

"Oh, stop it. Get some food and you can tell me what it is you didn't want to get into on the phone when you called."

As we fixed our plates, she said, "I'm sorry but I only have about half an hour, Leah. I forgot that I have a conference call at 12:45 with a client who can be a little high maintenance."

"No need to apologize. I'm the one intruding on your business day. But speaking of clients, I wanted to talk with you about one of them," I said.

"Okay. This is about Spencer Karr, isn't it? I thought it might be when you called. I shouldn't have said what I did to your mother. I was feeling frustrated and a little angry. I'm not going to make that mistake worse by talking to you about *GO News* and Spencer."

I'd been afraid she might say something along those lines. She looked pretty firm in her resolve. I tried to soften her up a little.

"I understand completely. That's why I'm not asking you to talk about anything specific. I just want to confirm that you told my mother you gave Spencer some advice he didn't want to take, and that when you told him you didn't want to be involved in any legal action, he fired you."

"You're confirming what your own mother told you? You don't believe Carol?"

"Like they taught us in J-school, 'If your mother says she loves you, check it out.' So, is it true, did you tell Mom that Spencer fired you? I'm just fact-checking my mother. Not doubting her. Or you."

"Yes, I did say that to Carol."

"Is *GO News* in financial trouble?"

"I can't answer that."

"Did Spencer ask you to do something unethical?"

"Again, no comment."

Nancy's business and personal ethics might keep her from talking, but I heard the answer in what she didn't say.

Almost every day I have a reason to be glad that I had worked my way up from a small-town weekly paper to a regional daily, because in doing so I had written hundreds of stories that taught me things I never would have known otherwise. One of those things was how an LLC, which *GO News* is, operates.

A limited liability company is set up to provide protection for the owner's personal assets. Which means that if your LLC business goes under, creditors can't come after you personally. However, you can lose that protection if you mix your personal and business funds. For instance, if you pay your car payment from your business account, or if you deposit a check made out to your business account into your personal account.

If that kind of thing is happening, and your business gets into a bad place financially, your creditors can come after you personally, by making the case that you didn't stick to the rules for an LLC. In which case a judge is very likely to "pierce the corporate veil" for creditors—meaning all bets are off, and you're on the hook for your company's debts.

Spencer was smart enough to know better, but arrogant enough to think the rules didn't apply to him. He'd have no second thoughts about firing someone like Nancy who stood up to him, I was sure.

"Nancy, this is what I think. Spencer is doing things he shouldn't with his business, and as a result his personal and business accounts aren't really separate. Which means if *GO News* is in financial trouble, his LLC won't protect him from personal liability. I think you told him that, and he refused to take your advice and fired you. I wonder, do you think I'd be wasting my time if I did some digging into where Spencer's money is going?"

"My mother always said that it's never a waste to learn something new."

"And mothers know best, don't they? Wait, don't tell my mother I said that. Thanks, Nancy, I appreciate it."

"For what, Leah, passing on my mother's wisdom?"

"Exactly for that, Nancy."

28

As I left Nancy's and drove back toward town and the meeting I'd arranged with Owen Fike, I felt cautiously happy. Nancy's carefully worded responses to my questions about Spencer had put a little song of hope in my heart. Maybe *GO News* was on the edge of collapse and would take Spencer down with it.

Sternly, I pulled myself back from the brink of dancing on Spencer's metaphorical grave as I drove into the parking lot at the EAT diner. The EAT is a local restaurant known for its great coffee, so-so to truly bad food, and extremely cheap prices.

Owen was seated in the last booth. He looked up from the burger he was finishing as I slid in across from him. A waiter approached, but I waved him off.

"Owen, thanks for meeting me."

"When the sheriff's girlfriend asks to see me, what else can I say?"

He smiled but it didn't reach his eyes. He wasn't happy.

"You can say no. I'm not 'the sheriff's girlfriend.' I'm a journalist looking for some answers. If I gave you the impression that I was using my connection to Coop to force you to see me, I'm sorry. That's not the case. Do you want to cancel this meeting?"

I hadn't really thought through how my new romantic relationship with

Coop might have an impact on things I needed to do. I didn't really care why Owen had agreed to see me, but I didn't want Coop to get labeled as someone who threw his weight around to give special favors to his lady friend. Which he most definitely did not do—though I'm not saying I wouldn't have enjoyed the perk.

He shrugged.

"No, ask me whatever you want. I'm a little curious myself."

"About what?"

"About what you find worth your time in an open and shut case like this. Look, I'm not happy that Rob's killer turned out to be another cop. We get enough bad PR as it is. But the truth is the truth. Erin's a cop, but she's a killer, too. The evidence doesn't leave room for any other conclusion."

"Erin's case wouldn't be the first one where the evidence pointed to the wrong person. Even if she and Rob had a thing, which if you knew Erin better, you'd find it very hard to imagine, she's not someone who goes off the deep end because she got dumped. She's got ambition, drive. Her career means a lot to her. I don't believe she'd throw it away because someone like Rob broke up with her."

"It's true. I don't know Erin as well as you do. But I do know when a suspect is lying to me. Her phone records show that, and her letter to Rob proves it. That whole 'I wrote it to someone else' defense she's trying on is a pretty stupid attempt to lie her way out of what she did. In fact, everything she said in her interviews turned out to be a lie—she did have an affair with Rob—the letter proves it. She did go to Rob's that night. Her phone records show it. We've got a witness who heard her arguing with Rob and threatening him the day he died. She lost one of her damn earrings at the scene. What more do you want?"

"You can't prove that it's her earring. You've got no DNA, nothing else to identify it."

He shook his head.

"You and her lawyer must really be desperate. We didn't build our case on the strength—or weakness—of the earring at the scene. It doesn't matter if we can prove it's hers or not. We've got motive, means, and opportunity—all of which she lied about. The DA is pretty happy with the case. I am, too. If you signed on so you could win the game and show me up again, like you did with Jancee Reynolds, it's not going to happen."

"Owen, I'm not playing a game and I don't want to show you up. I want to be straight with you, and I hope you'll be straight with me. We might even be able to help each other."

"Look, I told you before. It's not personal. I just don't believe in making nice with the press so I can get some good publicity. Journalists get in the way a lot more often than they help. And I don't have any interest in being your pet policeman like Charlie Ross."

"Well, since you brought it up, you made a mistake with Jancee Reynolds. A big one. This time, maybe you're right and I'm the one who's wrong about Erin. But this is about Erin's life, not about some contest between you and me. Coop says you're a good cop. If you are, then don't you want to be sure you got it right this time?"

"I did. And I don't need your 'help' to know that. I did some research on you. You used to be some up-and-coming journalist. But you flamed out, didn't you? You came back here because you couldn't make it in the big city. I think you stayed because you decided it was more fun to be a big fish in a small pond. Now, you write your books, and run your little newspaper, and as a sideline, you second-guess every investigation that doesn't come out the way you like."

He didn't say it with anger in his voice. He spoke as though it was simply a matter of fact. I tried to respond as calmly, but I was furious at his condescending assessment of my motives.

"That's not true."

"You didn't get fired? You didn't come back because no one would hire you?"

"I did get fired. But I didn't stay in Himmel because my ego is so big, I only felt safe in a small town. I don't need to stay here. I can be a writer anywhere. I choose to live in Himmel because I like it here, and because I think my newspaper can help what Miller Caldwell is trying to do bring some life back to this town."

"Whatever you say. Just know that I take policing seriously. It's not a hobby for me. And because I'm serious, and careful, and thorough about what I do, I don't see that I need any help from you. My boss—your boyfriend—agrees with the case I put together. The district attorney is pleased. And I'm satisfied with what I did. If you have any new, substantive evidence, let's hear it. Otherwise, I don't see the point to this or any future conversations about this case."

Owen's mind was obviously made up. I hadn't been sure whether or not to tell him what I'd learned about Bethany's pregnancy and Rob's vasectomy. I saw now there was no point unless and until I had the details firmly nailed down. Ross wasn't my "pet policeman" by any means, but at least he listened to me. Owen wasn't interested in any kind of dialogue. I stood up.

"I've turned up a few things, and made a couple of connections, but no, I don't have anything that would pass your rigorous scrutiny as evidence, I'm sure. Thanks for your time."

He nodded. "You're welcome. Will I be hearing about this meeting from my boss?"

"Not by way of me," I said.

"Good to know."

29

When I left Owen, I felt the urgent need for a fountain Diet Coke with extra ice. I picked up a large one before heading to Riverview Park to think. Jameson is for relaxation, consolation, and gently stimulating the creative flow. But when I have hard thinking to do, nothing beats the fizzy, bubbling, caffeine-laden rightness of my favorite soda.

I left my car at the edge of the grounds and walked all the way to the back of the park, to an old maple with a tangle of above-ground roots. Over the years they've managed to weave themselves into a perfect sitting spot. When you sink down onto it, your back is supported, your sides are comfortably snug, and your arms have a place to rest. I settled in and pulled out my reporter's notebook to review what I'd found so far. I put aside thoughts of Spencer, because my first duty was to the work I'd promised Gabe I'd do.

I read the notes I had taken while talking to Al. I couldn't help feeling sorry for the kid that Rob had been. His home, the place where most children feel safe, was instead the place where Rob must have felt the most fear. Children of domestic violence have a lot of rage to discharge. Sometimes they turn it inward and become victims as adults. But they can also turn it outward and become abusers themselves. From what Tracy had said, it looked like that was the path Rob had taken.

Although Al had said that Rob tried hard to find his first wife when she took off, I doubted it. He wouldn't have wanted to run the risk of having it come out that she left not because she was in despair over her lost pregnancy, but because she was terrified of her abusive husband. And once she had found the courage to escape him, she would have worked very hard to keep him from finding her. It was better for Rob to assume the role of a husband devastated by his unstable wife's abandonment.

A few years later, Rob had married a woman who was very like Jody. It was likely that Bethany, too, had been a victim of Rob's rage. Abusers don't stop without some serious intervention and rehabilitation. But maybe, unlike Jody, Bethany hadn't had to run away, because she found someone to help her.

Shane had been very protective of Bethany when I talked to him. And he'd called her Beth, a nickname I hadn't heard anyone else use when speaking of her. Shane had been at the Porters' frequently the previous summer, and although Tracy didn't recall seeing him specifically of late, that didn't mean he hadn't kept coming back. I jotted down a note to talk to the across-the-street neighbor with the binoculars, Ada Dillon.

I went back to thinking about Shane and Bethany then. Shane was young, much closer to Bethany's age than Rob. He was different from Rob —not as sure of himself, kinder, perhaps more gentle, too. Someone like Shane might have been very attractive to Bethany. And Shane hadn't been able to hide his admiration for her when he and I talked. It was possible that they'd begun an affair—though it would have been fraught with peril for both of them.

In Bethany's case, Rob's anger would have been fierce. She had violated his ownership rights by choosing to be with Shane. If he found out, the terrible affront to his ego and the defiance of his control could easily set off a titanic eruption from his bottomless pit of rage. There was no way to ensure that Shane could keep her safe.

As I took another drink of my soda, I thought how lucky it was that Bethany hadn't realized she was pregnant while Rob was still alive. He would have known immediately that she'd been unfaithful, and then not just she, but her baby, too, would have been in serious danger. She—

I stopped. An idea had just popped into my brain, perhaps courtesy of my carbonated elixir. What if Bethany had found out she was pregnant not just a few days ago, but a few weeks ago? She might have known about Rob's vasectomy, too. If so, she and Shane would have had to make a decision. It wasn't just about them. There was a baby to protect.

Their options weren't great. Give up their jobs, leave town, and hope Rob left them in peace. Stay, file for divorce, and hope a restraining order—if Bethany could even get one—would be enough to keep Rob from doing anything. There was one other choice, though. Take Rob out of the picture for good.

It really wouldn't be that hard to do. Bethany would get close scrutiny if Rob were murdered, so she'd need a good alibi. But Shane could do the actual killing. No one would ask him where he was that night, because no one knew about the secret romance. Suspicion would fall on someone like Harley Granger, or some other low-life Rob had dealings with. Or on Erin Harper.

And it was Shane who had pointed a finger at Erin by telling Troy, and presumably Owen, about the rumors and the argument Erin had with Rob. Now that an arrest had been made, Bethany could announce her pregnancy. Who wouldn't think it was nice that Shane was stepping up to be her rock? And later, how natural it would be that they had fallen in love. No one would blame her for turning to Shane after Rob's betrayal. Was Bethany quick-witted enough to see that my visit was an opportune time to start rolling out the story? Could she have deliberately told me that she was pregnant, while she claimed to be both grieved at the loss of Rob and bewildered by his affair?

It wasn't an airtight scenario, but it was within the realm of possibility. And that's what Gabe needed—possibilities that didn't point to Erin. I wasn't ready to stop the hunt for alternate suspects just yet. I'd still relish the chance to find a flaw in Harley Granger's seemingly ironclad alibi. I'd love to see Gabe give Harley some bad moments in court. But I was pleased with where things stood at the moment.

Except for my run-in with Owen. I felt like I hadn't handled it very well. From Owen's perspective, he'd taken the case, turned up the evidence, and shown himself to be a detective who got results. Then I popped up. He didn't see my involvement as an honest attempt to get to the truth. He saw it as me wanting to win the second round in a fight I hadn't realized we were having.

Plus, he was concerned that I had undue influence over Coop, and thus unwarranted access to sheriff's office business. That, of course, would be my dream. It was too bad Owen didn't know how unbendable Coop was about maintaining the integrity of his office and supporting his team. Our romantic relationship made it harder, not easier, for me to get information.

If Ross weren't on his trip with Allie, maybe he could have eased Owen's mind about me. Although on second thought, given the derisive way Owen had referred to Ross as my "pet policeman," he probably wouldn't listen to him.

30

On my way back home, I called Gabe to share the good news that there was a hairline crack in the case against Erin, and maybe we could widen it enough to let the light in.

"Hey, Gabe, can you talk?"

"Not for long. I'm in line at the bank drive-through."

"I'll just hit the high points."

I gave him a condensed version of my morning's interviews.

"You did good, Leah."

"Thanks, I'm kind of pleased myself. This gives you something to work with, right?"

"You bet. My fallback in a case like this is to show jurors that someone besides the defendant had means and motive to kill the victim. But it's tough when all you can point to is some unnamed person. To make that work, you have to convince the jury that the police were either incompetent or negligent. They don't buy that argument very often. It's much better to have actual alternate suspects."

"We're not quite there. I need to talk to Shane, find out where he says he was the night Rob died. I want to talk to the neighbor, Bethany's book club friend, to see what she knows or might have seen, too. But at least you can tell Erin that we're moving forward. When do you see her next?"

"Tomorrow afternoon at three."

"Good. I might have more by then. I'm still going to work the Harley Granger angle, too. I'll talk to you later."

"Oh, Leah?"

"Yeah?"

"Thanks. I knew you'd come through, but I didn't expect it this fast."

"Well, you know me, I like to check things off my list."

I called Coop next to see how his day was going and let him know that I was having a pretty decent one.

"Hey, you. I was just thinking about you," he said.

"That's what I like to hear. Where are you?"

"On my way to a meeting."

"Would that be about the undercover drug investigation you're working on?"

"Are we doing this again? Because I feel like we've had this conversation before. I told you—"

"I know, I know. You can neither confirm nor deny, there are no girl-friend perks about confidential matters, and you don't trust me. That's okay, I get it, I'm just checking in case anything has changed."

"It's not a matter of trust, it's a matter of ethics, Leah. If I could tell you anything, I would."

"I told you, it's fine. I was just teasing. I'm not mad. No worries."

"You must have had a really good day."

"Oh, I did. If things get any better, you may have to reopen your investigation and look for a new suspect, because Erin will be released."

All right, so that was exaggerating a bit—a lot—but I was feeling pretty pleased with myself.

"That good, eh? I know you want Erin to be innocent. I'd like that, too. But you and Gabe have a lot of facts to overcome. Don't get out too far over your skis."

"I won't."

"What does Gabe say?"

"That I'm the world's best investigator, he couldn't carry on his work without me, and he is deeply appreciative of my wise counsel."

"That doesn't sound like something Gabe would actually say."

"Those weren't his exact words, I'm paraphrasing. But that was the subtext. He said he was happy, things were looking up, and what I found will help him build a better case."

"What exactly did you find out?"

"I'd give you the details, but I just can't. I love you, but my higher duty is to confidentiality and ethics. You understand."

"I understand payback, that's for sure. All right, fine. I can wait."

"Are you coming over after work?"

"No. Work doesn't end until pretty late for me. I've got a budget committee meeting I have to be at. Augie Marshall is doing a presentation. If he runs true to form, and I don't know why he wouldn't, we're in for at least an hour of PowerPoint slides and a lot of handouts. It'll be after 10 before we're done."

"Oh, that makes me sad."

"Because you thought I'd feed you, right?"

"No. Because every moment away from you is an eternity. But also yes, because I thought you might make me a hamburger on the grill. I'm dying for one of your burgers."

"I can do that tomorrow. How about it?"

"Works for me. My place or yours?"

"Mine. I want to show you something."

"What?"

"You'll have to live in suspense."

⸺

My phone rang as I was walking through my apartment door.

"*Chica!* Where have you been? I haven't seen you in forever."

"Oh, come on, Miguel. We had coffee at the Woke on Sunday." The Wide Awake and Woke coffee shop is across the street from the *Times*.

"That was days and days ago. And just for like two minutes! It's

Wednesday now and I had to hear from Carol this morning that you are working with Gabe to help Erin."

"Sorry, it came together kind of fast. You want to come up now? I'm home."

"I can't. I'm shooting some pics in Hailwell. I was just checking to see if you still love me."

I laughed.

"Yes, I still love you. So much so, that I'll spring for pizza if you want to come over for dinner. Unless you're too busy."

"For you? Never. You call it in, and I'll pick it up around six at Bonucci's on my way to you."

"Sounds good, see you then."

31

You can keep your deep-dish pizzas. Give me a Bonnuci's with a crust so thin and crisp sometimes it makes an audible cracking sound when you bite into it. As soon as he got to my place just after six, Miguel and I set to work demolishing a large pizza. It was well done, just this side of burned, with big, airy crust bubbles that were slightly blackened on the edges. My perfect pizza.

Both of us were too busy chewing and wiping our chins with napkins to do much talking as we sat at the island in my kitchen. When I reached the point where I knew one bite more would send me over the edge from satisfaction to discomfort, I shoved the box toward him.

"Here, you take the rest while I'm still on the right side of regret."

I stood up as I spoke and began cleaning up the remnants of our feast, which didn't take much, because they consisted of paper plates, napkins, and the delivery box. As Miguel finished his last bite, I said, "Let's go into the living room. We did more chewing than chatting and I want to catch up with you, too."

Once seated on the couch, both of us facing each other, Miguel said, "You go first."

"Okay, but this is off the record for your ears only at this point."

I ran through the day's work on Erin's behalf and shared my growing certainty that Bethany and Shane had a much stronger motive for killing Rob than Erin, despite the evidence against her.

He was nodding his head before I even finished, which was much more satisfying than Coop's advice not to get too far ahead of myself.

"You think I might be onto something, then?"

"I do, yes! I can see it in my mind."

He jumped up off the couch then, and I knew an animated re-enactment was coming. Miguel did not disappoint.

"Shane, he is young, much younger than Rob. He is nice, he likes to help people. That's why he's working on Rob's roof on his time off. Bethany, she brings him water on a hot day, he talks to her about her teaching job, he listens, he's interested. He's not flashy like Rob, not so *macho*, maybe not so very handsome."

He shrugged.

"Maybe Shane is even—no judging—a little bit dull. But he is kind. And that is very attractive to Bethany, who has no one to be kind to her. Rob has made sure of that. And Shane, his love for Bethany starts slowly, but it burns very hot. Rob pays no attention. Why would he worry about boring, plain Shane?

"When the roof is done, Shane keeps coming back to help with this or that. Rob, he has a big ego. He thinks Shane is trying to impress him, trying to get ahead. He never thinks that it's Bethany Shane wants to be near. One day, Shane can contain himself no longer. He confesses his love to Bethany, and he finds that she loves him too. They are carried away by their passion, and the affair begins."

He paused for effect before rolling on to the big finish.

"Soon, Bethany tells Shane that Rob has been violent toward her. It is a shameful secret she has never shared with anyone because she believes it is her fault. That's what Rob tells her. Shane is outraged. He wants to take her away immediately! But Bethany, she knows how dangerous Rob is. They must plan carefully.

"But then, they are not so very careful. Bethany becomes pregnant. Now there is no more time to think, they must act. They make an alibi for Bethany, and then Shane kills Rob. It goes perfectly—especially when Erin is arrested. They are safe. But they did not count on you."

He pointed at me with a flourish as he finished, and then flopped down next to me on the sofa, his energy spent.

"You made a case Jack McCoy would be proud of. I take it you don't have any problem believing that Rob was an abuser?"

He shook his head.

"No, because I knew Rob's first wife, Jody."

"You did?"

My first reaction was surprise, but then I reconnected with reality. Miguel's life is like an amped up version of Six Degrees of Separation. I'm convinced that while the rest of us may be no more than six connections away from everyone else on the planet, in his case it's easily three degrees or less.

"Yes. In high school when I worked weekends for my Aunt Lydia at Making Waves, Jody was a stylist."

"She told you Rob beat her up?"

"No, but one time, she was off work for a week. That's a long time for a stylist because they don't have any backup—no one to do their job if they aren't there. And the clients, they don't like substitutes. When she came back . . . " He shook his head.

"When she came back, what?"

"I was joking with her about making sure she was healthy. I leaned in to put my hand on her forehead, like I was checking for a fever. She jerked back as though I was going to hit her. That's when I saw she had a big bruise on her cheek. She covered it up with concealer, but already in high school I had the eye of a makeup artist. I could tell right away. She said she tripped and fell, but I didn't believe her."

"Why not?"

"Her eyes—she had big, brown eyes, like a deer—they were so scared. And she looked away when she told me the lie. My best friend's mother when I lived in Milwaukee, she would always have the same look after her boyfriend hit her."

"Did you tell Jody you didn't believe her?"

"Yes. I told her about my friend's mother. She told me I was wrong. It wasn't like that. And she begged me not to say anything like that again to her, or to anyone. Then her client came in, and the salon was getting busy, so there wasn't any time for more talking that day. The next time I worked, my aunt told me that Jody had left her husband and moved away."

"That's what Al told me, without the Rob-hitting-her part. Miguel, I'd really like to talk to Jody. Do you know if any of her friends at the salon heard from her after she left?"

"She didn't have any friends, or family either. She told me one time that her grandmother lived in Omico, but that was her only family besides Rob. Sometimes people at the salon would invite her to go out after work, but I don't think she ever did. She said Rob liked her to be there when he was home."

"Your Aunt Lydia? She never heard from her either?"

"No, she asked Rob where to send Jody's tax information, but he told her he didn't know. He sounded very depressed, Aunt Lydia said. But I knew he wasn't, because of how Jody had been that last time I saw her."

"Did you say anything to Lydia?"

"No. I promised Jody I wouldn't. I only told you because, well, it's you. And because Jody's life then seems like Bethany's life now. You know, if Bethany did kill Rob, I am not that sorry. I feel bad for her."

"I'm not happy either that the way to help Erin is for Bethany and Shane to become legit suspects. But it's not right for Erin to go to prison for a crime she didn't commit, either."

"*Chica*, I don't even want to say this but . . ."

"But what?"

"What if Jody didn't run away? What if Rob didn't find her because he didn't really look? Because—"

"Because he killed her?" I asked.

As soon as Miguel had begun speaking, the half-formed thought I'd had when Tracy told me about Jody popped up, held out its hands, and caught the idea he was tossing toward me.

"Yes! Do you think that could be? Or is it too crazy?"

"No, it isn't too crazy, given what we know about Rob. I'll even go you one better. What if the convenient death of Rob's parents by murder/suicide was really murder/murder—by Rob?"

Miguel's eyes widened at the suggestion.

"I'm just thinking out loud. But things definitely started breaking Rob's way after they died. He moved in with a father who couldn't do enough for him to make up for all that Rob had suffered."

"But to kill his own mother!" Miguel shook his head.

"I know. I'm not saying it's likely, but we don't know exactly how bad things were for Rob. And he was a kid, not fully in charge of his impulses. If his stepfather started punching him, and Rob's anger had reached the explosive point, maybe he did more than punch back, like he told Al. Maybe he killed him."

"But his *mamá*! He wouldn't do that."

"You wouldn't. I wouldn't. But our mothers didn't stand by and let someone beat the hell out of us. Maybe she tried to intervene when he shot his stepfather. By then he was in a blind rage, incapable of rational thought, and he turned around and shot her. It could've happened."

"But it won't make any difference to Erin or to Bethany, will it?"

"I don't know. Part of the prosecution's story is that Rob was a super citizen, dedicated himself to public service, put his life on the line every day, a good man cut down in his prime. If instead he was a man with a history of violence, maybe Gabe could do something with that."

"Even if it didn't help Gabe make a case, it would be a very big story if it's true," Miguel said.

"Don't get too excited. We're pretty much building this idea on the fly without anything solid to rest it on."

"Are we taking a road trip to Nebraska?"

"Not yet. Let's find out if there's a reason to dig deeper first. I'm going to ask Coop for a little help. If he's willing to make a call to the cops who investigated the murder/suicide of Rob's stepfather and his mother, he'll get answers quicker than we would."

"Do you think he'll do it? He doesn't always like when you're mixing in his investigations."

"Correction. He never likes it. But his office isn't investigating Rob's life in Nebraska, and he's satisfied with Owen's investigation. So, he might. Especially because if I'm wrong, he'd be entitled to a victory lap and another chance to warn me not to get too far over my skis. That might motivate him."

Miguel gave me a look.

"You're right. That would motivate me, but Coop's not as small-minded as I am. Maybe I'll have to try persuading him with my sexy, sexy ways," I said, reaching up to pull the clip out of my hair. I intended to shake my head to make my tresses cascade on my shoulders while I batted my eyes flirtatiously. But the clip got caught, I pulled out a significant number of strands by the roots trying to untangle it, and Miguel had to reach over and release it.

"Maybe you should just try saying please," he said.

"Noted. But anyway, while I'm getting more information about the murder night from Bethany's gossipy neighbor and Shane, would you see if you can find anything on Rob's first wife? Talk to her grandmother in Omico. If she's Jody's only relative, it's hard to believe Jody hasn't contacted her in all these years. Also, I need your help on something else, but it doesn't have anything to do with Rob's murder."

"What?"

"I think this will go down easier with an after-dinner Jameson."

32

Miguel had declined my offer of alcoholic refreshment and stayed with his water. I fixed myself a short Jameson and took a sip before I sat back down with him.

"The man of the hour, and the object of your mission should you choose to accept it, is Spencer Karr."

"Spencer? Is that because of what's happening at *GO News*?"

"Wait, what do you know about it?"

"Courtnee told me that her friend Destiny, the receptionist at *GO News*, quit today. Also, Andrea Novak is looking for a new job, and everyone else who works there is ready to do the same thing."

"Really? Why?"

"Courtnee said that people aren't getting paid on time. Spencer is hardly ever there, and if anyone complains, he fires them, or tells them to quit if they don't like it. It started a couple of months ago, and he's getting worse."

"That's interesting. I doubt Spencer was ever anyone's dream boss, but I'm pretty sure he used to make payroll. Does this Destiny know what's up?"

"She told Courtnee that Spencer is acting like he's high most of the time."

I was silent as I combined Courtnee's intel, what Cole had told me, what Nancy Frei had said—and not said—and what I'd observed myself.

"Hey, hello in there? Are you still here?"

"Sorry, yeah, I am. I was just putting some pieces together. Courtnee's not good at a lot of things, but she does pretty well with gossip. What she told you fits with something I got from another source. Spencer has been mixing his business and personal finances, which is a no-no for an LLC, which is the legal structure *GO News* operates under.

"Also, when I saw him at the fundraiser, he looked really rough. His eyes were bloodshot, and he kept sniffling. He said it was allergies, but he seemed a little twitchy, too. In hindsight, I'm wondering now if he was using coke that night."

"A cocaine habit can be very expensive. Do you think Spencer was buying from Harley the night we saw him?"

"Yes, but I don't think that's all that was going on between them."

"Why?"

"Because of something Cole said to me."

"When did you see Cole?"

"Didn't I tell you?"

"No, you did not. When was this?"

"Last Monday. He delivered a warning from Harley to stay away from him, his property, and all things Granger. Although Harley had already called me with a similar warning."

"You said Harley wouldn't recognize us because it was too dark."

"Harley didn't recognize us. Spencer told him it was us."

"How could he know? He was already gone before Harley came running after us."

"Yeah, well, the thing is, I screwed up. I was talking to Spencer at the Players fundraiser, and he kept needling me. I poked back. I asked him why he was meeting Harley in the woods in the dark of night. That shook him up, which was very satisfying in the moment. But then Spencer didn't waste any time going to Harley with the information. Apparently, Harley was more than a little peeved that we had invaded his space, and he was ready to teach us a lesson about private property."

"Harley was going to beat us up?"

Miguel's alarm caused his normally pleasant tenor voice to move up the register and end on an almost squealing note.

"Well, that's how Cole made it sound. That was probably just to make himself look like some kind of a hero who intervened and calmed Harley down. I'm sure he was just exaggerating."

Miguel did not look reassured.

"What else did Cole say?"

"He tried to enlist me in a coup attempt against Harley."

I explained about Harley deposing Cole as king of the Grangers, and Cole's worry that his brother's new drug business was going to drag the whole family down.

"Why would he tell you so much bad about his family?"

"He was offering a quid pro quo. He wanted Coop to know about Harley's plans but didn't want to risk being ID'd as the one who ratted out his brother. I guess the Grangers are fussy about that. In return, he offered me information about Spencer that he said I could use to bring him down."

"What was it?"

"I don't know. I said I wasn't interested in partnering with him on anything because I don't trust him. But with everything else that's starting to surface about Spencer, I'm thinking Cole was on the level for once. Maybe he does have some seriously damaging information about Spencer."

"More than a cocaine habit?"

"I think it has to be more. Lots of people have alcohol or drug problems. It's no one's proudest moment, but I don't see how revealing that would destroy *GO News*."

"What is it, then?"

"That's what I need you to help me find out. First, I want the real story about Spencer's years in Chicago, and why he returned to home sweet Himmel. To hear his mother tell it, Spencer was the Alexander the Great of the marketing world. With no more worlds to conquer, he left his amazing partnership at the greatest agency in the history of marketing and came back to help revitalize his old hometown and spend more time with his family. That story never matched the Spencer we know and loathe. I'd like to know why, if he was such a winner, he came back to town."

"Well, to be fair, it is sort of what you did."

"Ah, but I did not return as a conquering hero. I had to come back because I screwed up, lost my job, couldn't find another one, couldn't pay my bills, and it was my only option. And everybody knew it. But what if Spencer and I actually share a similar backstory? Maybe he didn't do as well in Chicago as his mother and he claim. How about it, can you do some checking?"

"I can, but does it matter? If Spencer has a coke problem, then maybe he'll go away again, and *GO News* will go out of business, and we won't have to worry about it anymore."

"And that will be the day you see me do my happy dance to 'Heat Wave.' But there's something going on with Harley and Spencer and I want to know what it is. You saw and heard the same thing I did that night at the sugar shack. What was your impression?"

"That Spencer was very scared of Harley. But *I'm* very scared of Harley, too."

"But you're scared because we were caught on Harley's property where we weren't supposed to be. Why would his old high school friend Spencer be scared of him, if they just have a regular, transactional, Harley sells coke, Spencer buys it relationship?"

"Maybe Spencer got drugs on credit from Harley, and then he didn't have the money to pay him?"

"It's possible but Harley's never been a very trusting sort. I don't think he'd give coke on credit."

"But that night we saw them together, when Spencer was leaving, he told Harley that he should trust him because he came through, or something like that. Couldn't Spencer have meant that he paid Harley back for the drugs, so now Harley could trust him?" Miguel asked.

"Yes, except remember, then Harley told Spencer he'd only made a down payment on trust. That sounds like Spencer owes Harley big—or that Harley is holding something big over him. I'd really like to know what it is. And I'd like you to start with Spencer's recent past, just before he erupted into our lives like a cold sore. Are you in?"

"Ugh, I don't like that mind picture you just gave me. But yes. I'm in to find Spencer's life before *GO News*. And I won't forget to talk to Jody's grandmother."

I had texted Coop to call me when he got out of his meeting with the budget committee, but I was surprised that it was after II when he did.

"Wow, that must have been some PowerPoint that Augie presented."

"It wasn't the presentation so much as the discussion after. Everyone on the committee felt the need to comment, ask questions that were already answered, and then circle back and do it again. I had to sit through it all, and in the end, they tabled the proposal. By then, everyone was ready to go home, so I had about five minutes to go over my funding request before everyone fell asleep, or mutinied."

"Did you get the money?"

"They tabled my request, too. How was your night?"

"Quite a bit better than yours. I'll tell you more tomorrow, but I have a favor to ask."

"What is it?"

"Could you call the county sheriff's office in Nebraska where Rob used to live, and see if you can get some information on the investigation that was done when Rob's mother and stepfather were killed? I think you could get the answers easier than I could."

He was quiet for so long that I said, "Coop? Are you still there?"

"Yes. I'm just trying to work out why you want to know about that."

"I want to get confirmation that the death of Rob's stepfather and his mother was murder/suicide. That there wasn't anything odd or unanswered about it."

"No need for a call. Al told Owen the same thing he apparently told you. And Owen checked on it."

"Can you tell me what Owen found out?"

"The evidence was clear, nothing 'odd or unanswered' in the investigation. Tests showed a high level of alcohol in the stepfather's blood. He was shot three times. The angle of the bullets and the blood spatter pattern corresponded to the fact that Jean was significantly shorter than her husband, and that she was left-handed. Jean was shot once in the head. Her fingerprints were on the gun, which had fallen at her side, and there was gun residue on her left hand."

"That sounds pretty definitive."

"And you sound pretty disappointed."

"I am, a little. I was hoping Rob was a serial killer, but it doesn't look like that's going to pan out."

"Why would you—never mind. I'm not even going to ask. I'll see you tomorrow for burgers at my place, right?"

"Absolutely. Good night."

A few seconds later my phone pinged with a text. It was a heart emoji. Some, including me at one time, might have considered that a little sappy. But it made me smile, not scoff. I sent one right back and went to bed happy.

This despite the fact that Coop's information had caused the premise that Miguel and I were developing to die aborning. Rob had not killed his parents. But he wasn't absolved for the murder of his first wife. And tomorrow was another day.

33

No one answered the door when I knocked the next morning at Ada Dillon's house, but there was a car in the driveway, so I followed the pavers around the side of the house to the back.

A woman stood there with a pair of binoculars trained on the backyard of a house at the far end of the street.

"Mrs. Dillon?"

She jumped slightly when I spoke. As she turned, she lowered the binoculars in her hands.

"Oh! You surprised me! I was just watching a Northern Flicker in the Stockmans' yard. I'm an avid birdwatcher," she said.

"Oh, I see. I don't know much about birds."

Unless her binoculars had the magnification power of the Hubble telescope, she wouldn't be able to see a Northern Flicker that far away. She would, however, have quite a good view of the man and woman arguing on the deck of the house she was staking out.

"Oh, it's a wonderful hobby. There are so many different varieties right in our own neighborhood. It's so interesting!"

Ada Dillon's eyes were round and bright as she tilted her head and looked at me with undisguised curiosity. She had a sharp, almost pointed nose and wispy gray hair that feathered out around her narrow face. Her voice was light and chirpy and altogether she reminded me of a little bird herself.

"I'm sorry I startled you, Mrs. Dillon. I'm Leah Nash, the one who phoned you this morning. Thank you for seeing me."

"Please, call me Ada. Everyone does. You signed a book for me at the library last year. I think it's absolutely thrilling that you're investigating Rob Porter's murder. I love true crime. I'm a huge *Dateline* fan."

Clearly, I wasn't going to have to coax information out of her, so I didn't bother with a lead-in.

"I understand that Bethany Porter attended a book club with you the night Rob was killed. Was that something you two did together regularly?"

"No, never. I'd asked before but she always said no. She's very shy. And Rob was very old-fashioned, I think. He liked to have her home, even when he wasn't."

"How did you convince her to go?"

"Oh, I didn't. This time, she asked me. She said she'd read the book we were discussing—it was *Where the Crawdads Sing*. Have you read it? It's very good."

"Yes, I loved it, too. But getting back to Bethany . . . "

"Oh, yes. Well, I was glad she wanted to come. I don't think it's good for a marriage when one partner—man or woman, and I've seen it both ways —calls all the shots. My husband Stan and I were always 50/50."

"But it wasn't that way for Rob and Bethany?"

"Well, I couldn't say for sure. No one knows what goes on behind a neighbor's closed doors, do they?"

I nodded agreement, although I'd be willing to bet that Ada spent a good portion of her time trying to find out.

"But it looked to me as though Rob was in charge. She didn't seem to have any friends of her own. She was always with Rob, or home alone, except when she was at work. But I'm not one to interfere. It was her life. And she seemed happy enough, usually."

"There were times when she wasn't?"

"Well, nobody's happy all the time, are they? It was just the one time, really. I was in front, watching a red-tailed hawk that was sitting up in the big oak in the Porters' side yard. Bethany was out there, trying to get her puppy to come back in, but the little rascal kept running away from her. Rob came out, I thought to help her. Instead, he grabbed her by the arm and said something. She started to cry, not out loud, but with tears streaming down her cheeks."

"You could see tears on her face from across the street?"

"I had my binoculars—because I'd been looking at the hawk. I just swung them around when the commotion started."

"Of course."

"He dropped her arm then, kind of flung it away. And he went stomping over to his pickup truck, got in, and drove off. I went over to see if she was okay. She said it was nothing. The puppy had chewed one of his toys up and the inside stuffing was scattered all over the living room. Rob liked things to be tidy, Bethany told me."

"It seems a bit of an overreaction, though," I said, encouraging her speculation.

"It did to me, too. He was a puppy. He was going to chew. I said as much to Bethany. She told me that Rob just had a lot on his mind. I could tell she didn't want to talk about it. Ah well, the honeymoon doesn't last forever."

"I suppose not. So, about the night Rob died. What time did you and Bethany go to your book club?"

"We left around seven. The meeting was at Ginny Daley's house, and she is such a good hostess. We had all kinds of fancy little hors d'oeuvres, and a really lovely cake."

"That sounds like my kind of book club. What about after, did you and Bethany carry on with your girls' night, or did you just go home?"

"It was after nine o'clock when we left, so we came straight home. Bethany dropped me off and we chatted for just a minute in my driveway, and then she drove into hers and went inside the house, and I went into mine."

"Did you go right to bed after you got home?"

"No. I read for a while. I just started the new John Grisham and it's very exciting."

"Ada, are you certain that Bethany didn't leave her house after you both got home?"

"Oh, yes. I noticed when she drove us to book club that her muffler was a little loud. It was even louder on the way back. I'm sure if she'd left, I would have heard her car."

"I see. Do you know if anyone came to see Bethany later in the evening?"

"Yes and no. I mean she saw someone later, but it wasn't a friend or anything like that. She got a delivery from Bonnucci's pizza around 10 o'clock or so. I heard a car across the street, and I just happened to glance out the window as the delivery boy was ringing her doorbell. I was surprised Bethany was hungry after all the food at Ginny's. But I have a sister like that. She's a tiny little thing, but our mother always said Eileen had a hollow leg!"

"But that was it, no other coming or going at Bethany's that night?"

"No, nothing else. I went to bed a little later than usual—just after midnight. I wanted to finish the chapter I was reading. Bethany's car was still in her driveway, and the lights were off in her house. I know for sure, because I always stop at the stairway window and look out at the neighborhood when I go to bed. That's when I wish everyone pleasant dreams. Stan and I always said that to each other before we fell asleep. After he died, I didn't have anyone to say it to. So, I started saying it to everyone on our street on my way to bed. I know it sounds foolish, but it makes me feel less alone, somehow," she said with an apologetic smile and a shrug.

"I don't think it's foolish, Ada. I think it's very nice."

What I didn't think was very nice was me. I suddenly felt ashamed that I had dismissed Ada offhand as a neighborhood busybody. She was flighty, and maybe a little too interested in other people's lives, but that was probably because she was lonely.

Father Lindstrom has a favorite quote that he's shared with me more than once. "Remember that everyone you meet is afraid of something, loves something, and has lost something." It always resonates with me when he says it, but when it comes to living my regular life, I usually forget it until an encounter with someone like Ada reminds me.

"I know you're asking all these questions about Bethany because it's usually the wife when there's a dead husband. I see it all the time on *Dateline*. But if you had seen Bethany the next day, when she found out Rob was dead, you wouldn't believe for a minute that she had anything to do with it.

I thought she would make herself sick with crying. She was that grief-stricken."

Or possibly that relieved that her abuser was dead.

"I'm just gathering as many details as I can, that's all. But I've taken up enough of your time. Thank you, Ada. I appreciate it."

34

If Bethany and Shane actually had conspired to kill Rob, they'd done a decent job on setting up Bethany's alibi. It was tight, but not too tight. Her neighbor Ada was with Bethany through about 9:30, then Bethany was alone. It was, according to Tracy, well known that Ada kept an unofficial one-woman neighborhood watch. Also, ordering a pizza meant there was a second witness to confirm Bethany had stayed put after she got home from the book club. Ada's final look before bed served to strengthen Bethany's alibi.

The question now was, what about Shane's alibi? And there was no time like the present to ask him about it. I'd already checked at HPD, and he was on afternoon shift for two weeks. I knew he'd be home when I got there. Except he wasn't.

Shane lived in a nondescript white duplex without a garage. His car was in the driveway. But when I knocked, there was no answer. I tried again, this time pounding hard on the door in case he was a heavy sleeper.

"Hey, you lookin' for Shane? He's not here."

The man who asked was young, early twenties maybe. He had come out the front door of the other unit in the duplex. He had a round, open face and the smile he gave me was wide and welcoming.

"I am. Do you know when he'll be back?"

"Pretty soon, I'd say. He said he was just doing a short ride when he left, and that was about an hour ago. Was he expecting you?"

"No, I was just hoping to catch him. I need to ask him some questions about his former boss, Rob Porter."

"Oh, wow. The guy who got murdered. Yeah, that's pretty wild. Are you like a private eye? I'm Mac, by the way," he said, and held out his hand.

"Hi, Mac. I'm Leah. Yeah, I guess I'm sort of like a private eye. I'm actually a journalist. I'm doing some background research for an attorney."

"Yeah? Good thing Shane's a cop, not a suspect," he said with a grin.

"Why's that?" I asked, keeping my voice as casual as I could.

"Shane's got no alibi. Come to think of it though, I don't either."

He laughed then at his own joke.

Could anyone really be as utterly guileless as Mac? I felt a slight twinge of guilt at taking advantage of his general cluelessness, but not enough to stop doing it.

"How's that, Mac?"

"Shane said he was gonna stay in and watch the Brewers game that night. I was going to go over to his place and watch it with him. But he called and said he had a stomach bug or something and he wasn't feeling real good."

"I see. You mean because you didn't get together, you were each home alone. You can't alibi each other."

"Well, one of us was home alone. I can't speak for Shane," he said, laughing again.

I kept my voice noncommittal, even though my pulse had picked up the pace.

"How's that?"

" 'Cause I went over there when my TV crapped out in the 10th inning. The bases were loaded, and the Brewers only had one more out. I figured I could deal with catchin' whatever Shane had better than I could missing the end of that game. Shane's car was in the driveway, but his place was dark, and he didn't answer. So, I used my key. I made it just in time. The bottom of the 10th was a beautiful thing. Best game in years."

"Where was Shane? Sick in bed?"

"Nah, I checked his room. He wasn't in bed. I think he made up the story about being sick, and he dumped me for a girl," he said.

"What did he say when you asked him about it?"

"I didn't. See, this one night, I got home from the bar kinda late and this car was just pulling out of Shane's driveway—it wasn't his. I looked and a woman was driving, but it was too dark to see much of her. I asked Shane who his girlfriend was, and he cut that conversation right off. Got a little pissy, in fact, and that's not like him. So, I figure he's got something going but he wants to keep it low key, like maybe she's married. But that's his business. Like the French say, *C'est la vie*."

He mispronounced the French phrase for "that's life," as "Sest la veye," but it did not diminish my growing affection for the oblivious Mac and his outpouring of incriminating information.

Mac's phone rang.

"Man, I gotta take this. Sorry. Like I said, Shane should be back any minute."

"Thanks, Mac. Nice meeting you."

He smiled and waved as he began his phone conversation and walked away. Shane rode up on his bicycle just as Mac entered his side of the duplex.

He looked both surprised and unhappy to see me.

"What are you doing here?"

"Hi, Shane. I just have a quick question for you."

"Yeah? Well, here's my answer. I don't have anything to say to you."

His eyes had narrowed, and a bright red flush of anger rose on his cheeks that rivaled his fiery red hair.

"Why so hostile, Shane?"

"You know why. You really upset Beth yesterday. She could hardly stop crying. You had no right to harass her like that. And you'd better not do it again."

His voice was harsh, and his eyebrows were drawn together in a fierce frown.

"I'm sorry that Bethany was upset. That wasn't my intention. I just needed a little information. Erin Harper's life is on the line, you know."

"Erin isn't my problem."

"But Bethany is?"

"She's all alone. I'm just trying to look out for her."

"Erin's all alone, too, Shane. And I'm trying to look out for her. I just have one question to ask you. Think carefully about the answer. Where were you the night Rob was killed?"

"That's none of your business."

"It is, though. I need as much information about that night as I can get. Why is that a big deal?"

"It's not. It's just none of your business. I was home, all right? Watching the Brewers game."

"That's strange. Your neighbor Mac, he says he wanted to watch the game with you, but you told him not to come over because you had a stomach bug."

"Yeah, so what? I didn't want my friend to get sick."

"Nice of you. But according to Mac, that wouldn't have been a problem. Because when his TV went out, he came over to catch the end of the game. You didn't answer when he knocked so he let himself in. He thought you were asleep in your room, but when he poked his head in to see, you weren't there. Where were you, Shane?"

"What I do and where I go is none of your business. Or Mac's either. And you've got no business on my driveway. You'd better leave, now!"

"Or what? You'll arrest me for asking a question that you don't want to answer? That wouldn't look so good, Shane. I'd advise against it. But no problem, I'm leaving. Thanks for your help."

35

I drove away from Shane's pretty confident my hypothesis that he and Bethany had conspired to kill Rob was correct. But I didn't feel great about that. I wasn't a hundred percent sure that I would've done things differently, given the loathsome creature that Rob was. Though I was glad that my faith in Erin was justified. I believed without reservation her accusation that he'd sexually harassed her and created a hostile work environment. I've been in similar situations a time or two—most women have. But as a general rule, we don't kill our bosses because of it. You either suck it up until you're in a position to leave—which I don't recommend, the stress is almost unbear-able—or you report it and face the fallout. Unfortunately, there's almost always fallout.

It was only 11 a.m. And already I had the case solved. I love the smell of vindication in the morning. I couldn't wait to tell Coop. Who's getting too far out over her skis now?

Then I reined myself in a little. I wouldn't be able to say anything to Coop just yet. Gabe was trying to build a defense strategy, and Coop was not on our team on this one. I'd have to be satisfied with keeping the thrill of victory between Gabe and me for a while.

I called Gabe to update him. It went to voicemail, so I just hit the highlights and told him to call me for more details on the amazingly good news I had for him.

When my phone rang a couple of hours later, I was at my desk, virtuously typing away, trying to push through an unexpected road block my plot had hit. I was back to wondering why I ever thought I could write a fictional mystery. Even though, as my morning's work showed, I was pretty good at solving real-life ones.

"Gabe, hi. Great news, right? I—"

"Leah, it's me."

"Oh, sorry, Tracy. I'm expecting a call from Gabe. What's up?"

"Can you come over?"

"Right now? It's just I'm kind of in the middle of something and—"

"Yes. I need to see you right now."

Her voice was so serious that I didn't protest anymore.

"All right. I'll be right over."

"I lied to you yesterday, Leah. I'm sorry."

Tracy spoke without preamble as soon as we were seated at her kitchen table.

I was taken aback. Tracy isn't a liar. If anything, she can be painfully and sometimes inconveniently honest.

"About what?"

"About Bethany Porter and Shane Jennings. I acted like I didn't know who Shane was when you asked me about him. And then I fobbed you off on Ada Dillon. But in this case, I'm the real Mrs. Kravitz of Collingwood Drive. I knew who Shane was. And I know he and Bethany have been having an affair."

"I don't get it. Why didn't you say that yesterday?"

I was puzzled, but not angry. It didn't matter because I already had the answers I needed about Shane and Bethany.

"I told myself it wasn't any of my business. I still think that. Frankly I don't blame Bethany for finding someone who would treat her better than Rob did. But their personal lives are tangled up with a murder investigation. I shouldn't have filtered the truth because I didn't want to violate Bethany's privacy."

"Tracy, don't sound so conscience-stricken. Sure, you might have saved me a step or two if you'd confirmed what I suspected, but I found out through other means. Besides, you helped me more than you knew."

Now it was her turn to look puzzled.

"You said Rob had a vasectomy years ago. I confirmed it with the medical examiner to make sure he hadn't had it reversed. Bethany is pregnant. Obviously, it's not Rob's baby."

"Pregnant? That poor kid. What she must be going through. Especially if Rob didn't tell her about his vasectomy—like he didn't tell his first wife. Bethany must be wondering if it's Rob's baby, or Shane's."

"I feel sorry for her, too. But their affair gives both Bethany and Shane a good motive for murder."

"You think one of them killed Rob? But they couldn't have."

"Look, I know they're both nice people, Tracy. But nice people when cornered can do some really bad things, including murder."

"No, no. I don't mean they're too nice to kill someone. I mean they actually, physically couldn't have done it."

"I'm afraid they could have. Shane's story is that he was home watching the game all night. I found a witness who can prove that he wasn't. I'll concede that it's possible that Bethany didn't know about it, and Shane killed Rob on his own to protect her, but I don't think so. See—"

"Stop. Listen to me. Shane has an alibi, too. He was at Bethany's from 8:30 on. He didn't leave until five in the morning. I saw him."

"Wait—what are you saying to me?"

"I'm saying that Shane spent the night at Bethany's. He's done it before when Rob is away. Shane rides his bike down the alley between my house and the Porters'. He parks it behind their shed, and he goes in through the back door of the house, I assume. The alley doesn't get much use—no cars, ever. A few kids use it as a shortcut, but that's always in the daytime. Shane is pretty free to come and go on his bicycle with no one the wiser. Except for me because I'm an insomniac who is up at all hours. According to the paper, Rob was killed between 8:30 and midnight. It couldn't have been Shane who did it."

I shook my head to clear it of the sound of my theory of the crime collapsing.

I cast about for a way to shore it up. I knew from Ada's surveillance report that Bethany's car hadn't left the driveway, but there was still Shane's bike.

"You didn't watch the house all night, did you? Shane could have ridden his bicycle to Rob's hunting land, killed him, and then ridden back to tell Bethany it was done."

"Leah, seriously? I know math isn't your strong suit, but it's almost 15 miles to Rob's property. Shane may be a decent cyclist, but he's not a qualifier for the Tour de France. It would take him close to an hour to bike there, and another hour to bike back, and some significant amount of time in the middle to kill Rob."

"You saw him arrive around 8:30. Maybe he left again."

Tracy shook her head.

"I was keeping a friend's dog for her while she was out of town. I took her for a short walk down the alley to do her business around 9:30. Shane's bike was parked behind the garage. It was still there at 11:30 when the dog, who has a bladder the size of a pea, wanted to go out again. The time frame doesn't fit."

I sighed heavily as I accepted the death of my thesis.

"I thought—no, I was sure—I had it figured out. I guess I owe Shane an apology. I didn't accuse him of killing Rob, but I came pretty darn close."

"I'm sorry," Tracy repeated. "I should have said."

"It's okay. I understand why you didn't tell me. And, sadly, this isn't the first time a faulty premise has blown up in my face. But listen, I better get going. I want to try to catch Gabe at his office. I need to let him know we're back to square one before he gets Erin's hopes up when he sees her later this afternoon."

36

When I walked out of Tracy's house, I noticed a car in Bethany's driveway. Shane was just getting out of it, and Bethany was walking down the drive to greet him. I might as well get it over with.

"Shane! Bethany!" I called as I hurried across the lawn. Shane was standing next to Bethany by then, and they both looked over as I shouted. Their expressions were not welcoming. In fact, they both turned without a word and moved toward the front door.

"Wait, please. I need to talk to you both," I said.

"Well, we don't need to talk to you," Shane said. "Beth, go on inside. I'll handle this."

"No, please," I said as I approached. "There's nothing to handle except an apology. Mine. I'm sorry, I was wrong."

They looked at each other and then at me.

"All right. Say what you have to say. You've got two minutes," Shane said.

"I know neither of you had anything to do with Rob's death. I got it all wrong, and I'm sorry."

Bethany's face looked slightly more forgiving than Shane's, so I focused on her.

"I know you two have been having an affair—that's your business," I added quickly. "I have reason to believe that Rob was an abuser, and I think that's why his first wife left him. I think he was doing the same thing to you, Bethany. When you told me you were pregnant, I realized that gave you both a motive to kill Rob. You were afraid he'd find out about you two, and with his temper that would be very dangerous to you, and to the baby you're carrying. I don't blame you for being scared. But I did some digging into your alibi, Bethany, and found out that it's solid. What I didn't know until just a few minutes ago is that Shane's is, too. There's a witness who can prove it."

"Who?" Shane blurted out, surprise in his voice and relief on his face.

"Tracy Roach. She's seen you here before, Shane, when Rob was away. And she saw you park your bike behind the garage around 8:30 the night Rob was killed. She was dog sitting for a friend, and at 9:30 she took the dog for a walk. Your bike was still behind the garage then, and it was there later, when the dog wanted to go out again at 11:30. Neither of you could have killed Rob. The timing doesn't work."

"Oh, thank God," Bethany said, clutching Shane's arm. "I've been so scared ever since Rob was killed. I thought if anyone knew about the way Rob used to hit me—then it would look like I killed him. And if it came out about Shane and me, we'd both be arrested for sure. Everything's been so terrible. And then I found out I'm pregnant, and I don't even know yet if it's Rob's baby or Shane's, and . . ." By then she was crying too hard to finish.

Shane put his arm around Bethany.

"It's okay. I told you everything will be all right. A baby is happy news, Beth. Don't cry. It doesn't matter to me who the biological father is because you're the mother. I love you, Beth, and I love that baby, and I'm going to be the best dad I can be, okay?"

She continued weeping, though more quietly. I must have gotten something in my eye because I teared up a little, myself. It was time for me to go. But not before I passed along an important bit of news. I made a discreet swipe at my eye, then gave a little cough to regain Shane and Bethany's attention.

"I'm leaving, but I just want to say again that I'm sorry, Beth, and I want to tell you something I don't think you know yet. Rob had a vasectomy more than 10 years ago."

They both looked at me with blank expressions, like what I'd said didn't compute.

"Let me put it this way," I said, turning to Shane. "Congratulations, Dad."

⸻

I was almost to Gabe's office when my phone rang, and his caller ID popped up.

"Gabe, hi. Listen, I need to talk to you. I'd rather do it in person, I—"

"Erin wants to change her plea. She says she's guilty and she just wants to be done with things," he said, talking over me.

"What? No. When did that happen?"

"A few minutes ago. I just left her."

"I thought your meeting was at three."

"It was, but I had to see another client at the jail. I finished early, so I stopped to see Erin. I was excited to tell her we might have a path forward with two possible alternate suspects."

"And that made her decide to change her plea? That doesn't make sense."

"She wanted to know who the suspects were. I told her, and she didn't say anything for a minute. I thought she was overwhelmed with emotion—so relieved she couldn't talk, or that she was holding back tears."

"Clearly you don't know Erin."

"When she did speak, she said she was changing her plea to guilty. I was shocked. I told her we were closing in on a defense that might actually work. I begged her to think it over, but I couldn't get through to her."

"I don't get it."

"She said she killed Rob and that she didn't regret it. She lied because she didn't want to go to prison. But she doesn't want to lie anymore. She wants me to enter a guilty plea for her."

"If worrying about Shane and Bethany is driving her decision, she can stop right know. They're out of the picture. I just found out. That's why I was trying to reach you."

"Shane and Bethany are in the clear? What happened?"

"It turns out that I'm not as smart as I think I am."

I explained the discovery that Shane had an alibi and an eyewitness to prove it.

"That caps it, then," Gabe said.

"Not necessarily."

"Leah, remember when you said you believed Erin was innocent, because if she was guilty, she'd own it? Well, she's owning it now. She confessed. We can talk more later, but I've got a court appearance, in about . . ."

There was a slight pause as Gabe must have looked at his watch.

"Oh-oh. I've got about five minutes to get there. I know you hate to give up. But you don't have a choice. Thanks for your service on the Erin Harper defense team, but there really isn't one anymore."

37

"Thanks for seeing me, Erin. I wasn't sure you would."

She sat across from me at the small table in the room set aside for inmates to meet with their attorneys. I hadn't told Gabe I was going to try and see Erin. This was just between her and me.

"I'm done, Leah. I told Gabe, and I'll tell you. I killed Rob. I want to change my plea. I'm at peace with my decision."

The slight quaver in her voice at the end and the tension that radiated from her gave the lie to her last words. Her lips compressed in a straight line when she finished talking. Her hair was scraped back in a ponytail so tight, I doubted she'd be able to raise an eyebrow if she tried. She had folded her hands together and they were clasped tightly enough to make her knuckles show white.

"Erin, when I talked to you just days ago, you swore you didn't kill Rob. Yet when Gabe told you the first good news we had—that Bethany and Shane had a strong motive to kill him—instead of giving you hope, it made you change your plea. Why?"

"Isn't it obvious? Because I lied, and I'm tired of lying. I killed Rob. We had an affair, he rejected me, I couldn't handle it. Owen got it right."

"If you're worried about Bethany and Shane, don't be. They're both out of the picture now."

"Good. I'm glad."

"But don't you see, Erin? You don't have to plead guilty to save them."

"That's not why I confessed. I'm changing my plea because I killed Rob. How many times do I have to say it? I have to own what I did, and I'm ready to do the right thing. I'm not sorry Rob is dead. But I can't risk someone else getting blamed for a murder that I committed."

"That sounds super noble and all, Erin. But I don't think you're telling the truth. At least not all of it. The more I learn about Rob, the less I can believe that you and he were lovers. I can't accept that he was the man who inspired that letter from you, or that you were so carried away by your passion for him that you killed him because he rejected you. The Erin I know would never be attracted to a misogynist like Rob."

"Maybe I'm not the Erin you think I am. It doesn't matter if you 'can't accept' that I was in love with Rob. You'll never understand it."

"Try me."

She sighed and unclasped her hands, then rested them on the table as she leaned forward a little and looked me directly in the eyes.

"It wasn't really love. I was obsessed with Rob. I knew what he was like, but I couldn't help myself. When he broke up with me, I was devastated. At first, I tried to hurt him as much as he had hurt me. I enjoyed humiliating him at the shooting competition. I accused him of sexual harassment to pay him back for leaving me. But I couldn't get him out of my mind. God help me, I still wanted to be with him. And I wanted to believe he felt the same. I was desperate to have him back in my life. That's why I wrote the letter to him. Only he didn't respond."

"And that made you angry enough to kill him?"

"Not at first. I convinced myself that he didn't receive it—that it got lost in the mail. You read about it once in a while—a letter that gets delivered years after it was sent. Don't look at me like that. I know it sounds pathetic. It *was* pathetic. But at the time it was the only explanation I could live with. I bared my soul to him—I couldn't let myself believe that he had read it, and just ignored it. When he called me into his office that day, I was happy. I thought it meant he wanted to reassure me, to apologize, to explain that he'd just received the letter."

"But that didn't happen."

"No. The part I told you about him offering to get me a job in a police department up north was true. He didn't even mention the letter. He said my career in Himmel wasn't going anywhere and I should consider a move. He told me if I dropped my threat of a sexual harassment complaint, which we both knew wouldn't go anywhere, he'd put in a good word for me with a police chief he knew up north. He acted like we'd never been anything to each other but boss and employee."

"You didn't bring up your letter? You didn't tell him all the things you were feeling?"

"No. I was gut-punched. I couldn't think straight. And I was afraid that I might start crying, right there in the office. Rob hated tears. I just walked out. I think I might have said something like 'You can't treat me like this.' Meaning don't gaslight me and pretend you never loved me. But I couldn't get into anything with him there in the office."

"Why did you drive to Rob's property that night?"

"Because I had to see him. You see, when he broke it off, we both agreed it would only be bearable to be around each other if we kept everything very professional, very distant at work. I decided I'd played my part too well, and he thought that I was over him. Then I was sure he hadn't read my letter. If he had, he'd know I loved him as much as ever. I had to see him to say to him face-to-face what I'd written in the letter. I was desperate to hear him tell me the same."

"And that didn't work out the way you expected?"

"No. Instead, that night on his dock, he couldn't have been any colder. He dismissed me like I was nothing. When I looked at his face, there wasn't even pity in his expression—just contempt. He was so obviously done with me. It shattered me, and it humiliated me, but it opened my eyes. Finally, I saw what had always been true. He didn't love me. He never had. He loved the control he had over me. I was strong, but he made me weak. It was just a game to him. Everything he'd said, everything I'd believed was a lie. I felt a wave of hatred inside me that was as strong as the obsession I'd felt for him. Stronger, even."

"Is that when you decided to kill him?"

"I didn't decide anything. I just reacted. His gun was lying on the dock. I picked it up and I pointed it at him. I was shaking with fury, and I shot it. The bullet went wild, but I had his full attention then. I shot again. That time he went down. As I stood looking at him bleeding out, it was like my fever broke. The love was gone. The hate was gone. The only thing I felt was satisfaction that Rob was gone, too. I wiped the gun off. Then I undid the rope and pushed the boat away. I watched Rob float out of my life forever. I wasn't sorry then. I'm not sorry now."

"So that stuff you told me when we first talked about the meeting you had with Rob the day he died—that you went to tell him you were filing formal sexual harassment charges against him, that he threatened to ruin your career if you didn't drop it and resign, that was a lie?"

"Yes. I didn't threaten him with my sexual harassment complaint. I'd dropped the idea weeks earlier, once I realized I had to have him back in my life. I just wanted him to love me again. I didn't go to his place to tell him I wasn't giving up my complaint. I went to beg him to come back to me. Are you satisfied now? Did I humiliate myself enough for you?"

I ignored her question and followed up with another of my own.

"What about the earring, Erin? The one they found at Rob's. Is it yours after all?"

"Yes. I didn't know it was missing until the next morning. I realized I had lost it at Rob's the night before. But I wasn't too worried. It was a small earring. I thought there wasn't much chance it would be found."

"Why didn't you eliminate the possibility of connecting the earring to you by buying another pair to replace the one you lost?"

"I was going to, but I just ran out of time. They were nice earrings, from a jewelry store, not a mall kiosk. I knew I wouldn't be able to find a pair here, and anyway, I couldn't take the chance that someone would see me buying them and remember. But it was chaotic the first couple of days after Rob's body was found. I was acting captain and there were constant media calls, and meetings with the chief, and with my officers. Everyone wanted me to be on top of everything. Before I could get to Madison to look for a similar pair, Owen had made me his chief suspect and it was too late."

"Something else bothers me."

"What's that?"

"The letter. All right, so you believed Rob hadn't received it, but you knew you'd sent it. There was always a possibility that it would show up. You're a meticulous, smart, logical person. That's a big loose thread to leave hanging without having an explanation for it ready, in case you needed it."

"I know that now, but at the time I wasn't thinking in a 'meticulous, smart' way. I wasn't thinking at all. I guess I'm just better at being a cop than being a killer."

"Erin, at first you claimed you didn't kill Rob and I believed you. Now you say you did, and you expect me to believe you. I'm kind of at a loss here. Were you lying then, or are you lying now? I really don't know."

"I lied at first because I didn't want to spend my life in prison. But I've had a lot of time to think. I told you, I'm not sorry I killed Rob, but I can't live with the lie, and I can't let someone else pay for what I did. Why is that so hard for you to understand?"

"I guess because I can't believe that you were ever involved with Rob—certainly not to the point of obsession. He was a liar, a cheat, a hypocrite, and quite likely an abuser who beat up women as well. I don't believe he's the man who inspired that level of passion in you. I don't believe the letter you wrote was to him. But I have no problem believing that you would do anything to protect someone you truly loved. I think you're sacrificing yourself for whoever that man is."

"Don't be ridiculous," she snapped. "There was only Rob. There isn't any other man in my life."

"It's not ridiculous. You're afraid that if I keep going with this, I'll turn up who that man is. Look, Erin, if he's got nothing to do with the crime, I'm not going to drag him into it. But maybe you should reconsider whether he's worth the sacrifice that you're ready to make for him. You're in serious trouble, and he's abandoned you. What kind of love is that?"

She pushed back from the table and sat perfectly straight in her chair. Her eyes had narrowed to slits. When she spoke, her voice was tight and clipped.

"I don't need your questions or your advice. I'm done."

She began shouting for the guard. He appeared in seconds and addressed me.

"Is there a problem here?"

Erin answered instead.

"No. No problem. I'm done talking and I want to go back to my cell."

He hesitated a second, looking at me.

"I guess we're done," I said.

38

"What is going on here?"

I'd shouted for Miguel to come in when he'd knocked on my office door. He found me sitting on the window seat surrounded by wadded-up sheets of paper from the yellow legal pad on my lap. He sat down next to me.

"It's the death throes of my theory," I said.

I explained about Bethany and Shane, and Erin's sudden reversal to a guilty plea and her insistence that I drop the investigation.

"I'm having trouble deciding where to go next."

"But there is no next, right? Gabe said he's done, that he doesn't need you. Erin, she doesn't want you."

"Gabe's her lawyer, he doesn't have a choice. But I still do. I don't believe Erin killed Rob."

"But why would she confess?"

"The same reason she wouldn't say who she wrote that letter to. She's protecting the man she loves."

"You mean Erin's lover killed Rob?"

"No, I mean she's afraid of the collateral damage he'll suffer if the affair comes out. And she's afraid that if I keep digging, I could find out who he is. In her letter, she tells him that her life is worth nothing without him. So, maybe if she believes her life isn't worth anything, she's willing to give it up to make sure his is—with an intact family, career, whatever, untouched by any consequences the discovery of an affair with her could set off."

"That's a lot of love, *chica*."

"Agreed. But I think Erin's someone who is all in once she commits. She wants to protect him. Maybe he has a wife who would keep him from his kids if the affair came out. Or he's a judge, or a politician, or a priest even. Someone whose career would be ruined by a scandal."

"Or maybe his wealthy family will cut him off because he brought disgrace on them, and he'll have to live in exile for the rest of his life!"

"Okay, you've been bingeing *The Crown* again, haven't you?"

He shrugged. "It's very good. And it really happened."

"I'm aware. I don't think we've got another King Edward VIII situation here. But whatever the reason, Erin is willing to give up everything for him."

"So, you're going to keep investigating?"

I shrugged, and then nodded.

"I have to, Miguel. Once I start, I can't stop. Sometimes I'd like to, but I just can't. When I figure things out, it's not because I'm so brilliant or so intuitive. It's because something in me just won't let me quit."

"No. I will not allow that kind of talk. You find the answers because you are *very* smart, and very brave, and very strong."

I leaned over to give him a hug.

"Thank you. Everybody needs a Miguel in their life. But I think it comes down more to stubbornness. Anyway, I'm going ahead without Erin, and I'm going back to square one. The person with the best motive and the means to kill Rob is Harley Granger."

"But Harley has the perfect alibi."

"Does he, though? Harley's story is he took his mother and his aunt to a Brewers night game in Milwaukee. He's got the receipts to prove it—literally. Time-stamped and dated receipts from here to Milwaukee and back. What does that sound like to you?"

"An unbreakable alibi?"

"No. It sounds too good to be true. What innocent person would have that much evidence at the ready when the cops came to call?"

"But then Harley would have to have someone else do the shooting for him."

"Exactly! And he'd be as guilty of murder as the person who actually pulled the trigger. But if the triggerman didn't appear to have a motive for the killing, he wouldn't be a suspect, so he'd get away with it. And Harley, having set up the perfect alibi, walks away, too. See, even though I was wrong about Shane and Bethany being the killers, I might not be wrong about the structure of the murder—that it took two people, I mean."

"Who is the other person? Cole?"

"I think Cole would draw the line at murder—though I'm not sure. But I don't see him doing anything that would help his brother out. He basically hates him. But the Grangers are a big family. Harley has a lot of loyalists he could choose from. Or it's possible that his business friends from Milwaukee did him a favor. It's—"

Miguel's phone rang. He glanced at the ID and answered it.

"I'm with Leah, but I can . . .Yes, Courtnee, I know you do, but . . . Okay, I'm on my way down."

Before he could explain the call, I said, "What? You're going to leave me hanging mid-brainstorming here? For Courtnee?"

"No, there's someone waiting to see me, but it's almost five o'clock and Courtnee couldn't stay. She's at her boyfriend's. She forgot to tell me before she left that someone's waiting."

"She just left a random stranger sitting in the reception area and walked away?"

"But she called to tell me. That's progress, right?"

"I guess. Don't be too long, please. You're disturbing my creative thinking flow here."

"I know, I'm sorry. Just hold your thoughts. I'll be right back."

While Miguel met with his surprise visitor, I started thinking about who could help me flesh out my Harley conspiracy conjecture. Cole, for sure. Maybe, but not likely, Coop. Still, I'd ask.

When my door opened, I realized Miguel was talking to someone. I looked up. He was with a woman maybe late 20s, early 30s. She was petite, pretty, with short brown hair and glasses. I'd never seen her before.

Miguel saw the puzzled look on my face and said, "Leah, this is someone I know you'll want to meet. My friend, Jody. Jody, this is Leah."

I walked toward her, my hand held out to shake hers, when my brain kicked in. The involuntary double-take I did, complete with dropping jaw and eyes popping, would have done a sitcom actor proud.

"You're not dead! You're Jody, Rob's wife, aren't you?"

She smiled at my reaction and said, "Ex-wife, yes. And also yes, I'm not dead. But I'm not Jody anymore, either. I haven't been for almost eight years. My name is Hannah Johnson now."

39

Once we were all seated at the kitchen island with a glass of water each, I started in.

"Miguel, why didn't you tell me you'd found Jody? Sorry, I mean Hannah. Also, Hannah, I get the last name change—you're remarried, right? But what about the first name?"

"I didn't find Hannah," Miguel said. "I didn't even start looking yet. She found me. Hannah, you tell her."

"Somebody tell me, please. And start at the beginning."

"All right. It's a long story, but you asked," Hannah said.

Her voice was soft and pleasant, like Bethany's.

"I'm from Omico. I met Rob the night I finished cosmetology school. I'd been out celebrating with some friends. Rob stopped me for speeding. He was very nice, very understanding. He told me I should get a ticket because he could smell the alcohol on my breath. But he said he'd follow me home and let me off with a warning if I agreed to go out to dinner with him."

"Oh, that's not creepy at all," I said.

"It is, but I didn't see it that way then. He was cute, and funny, and I thought he was really sweet to let me off without a ticket. We only dated for a month before we decided to get married."

"You were so young!" Miguel said.

"I know. That's what my grandmother said. I was living with her then. She raised me after my dad died when I was nine, and my mother married a man who didn't like kids. I didn't listen to Gran. I was sure Rob and I were forever. And for the first year or so, I was really happy. Rob knew so much more than I did about everything. I didn't mind that he made all the decisions. It felt good to be taken care of. But then things started to change."

"How?" I asked.

"The salon I was working at closed. Rob wanted me to stay home and take care of the house. But I loved doing hair and makeup. I was good at it, and I didn't want to quit my career. When I told him that, he said I was just a stupid hairdresser, not a brain surgeon. I didn't have a career. I had a job. Besides that, I didn't make enough money to make any difference anyway."

"Hannah! That is so terrible," Miguel said.

"He'd never spoken to me like that. I felt stupid, and useless, and angry all at the same time. I started to cry, and he shook me hard, then flung me away and left. I couldn't believe it. He'd always been so sweet to me. I was still crying when he came back a few hours later. He was carrying a big bunch of flowers. He apologized. He said that he was under a lot of pressure at work. That me saying I wanted to get another job made him feel like I was saying I didn't trust him to take care of me. That hurt him, so he lashed out, but he didn't mean it."

"What did you say to him?"

"If you can believe it, I wound up apologizing to him for making him get angry with me."

"Oh, I can believe it, Hannah. It's textbook abuser behavior. Make the victim believe it's her fault," I said.

"It took me a long time to learn that. Anyway, after that night things were really good again. I started at Making Waves, and I built up a clientele. I really enjoyed the work. And I was happy with Rob. But then one night—I can't remember now what I did to 'make' him get mad at me—it happened again. Only that time, he didn't just shove me, he slapped me so hard, I fell into the wall. I ran upstairs and Rob left. When I heard him come back, I locked the bedroom door. I was afraid of him."

"Oh, Jod—I mean Hannah—I'm so sorry! What a terrible man!" Miguel said.

"He begged me to forgive him. I kept telling him to just go. But then he started crying, these huge sobs, like his heart was breaking. If you knew Rob, you know what a big man he was, how strong and confident he was. To hear him sobbing like a child, well, I couldn't stand it. I opened the door, and I hugged him while he cried, and then he begged me not to leave him.

"After that he was so sweet. He couldn't do enough for me. Then slowly, the tension started growing in him again. I tried not to upset him, I tried to keep the house the way he liked, to cook the things he liked, to be home when he was home, but it didn't make any difference. It always came back —the violence, I mean—and it got worse every time."

"You should have told me, I would have helped you," Miguel said.

"Miguel, you were just a kid! I wasn't about to get you involved in my problems. I didn't tell anyone. Not even my grandmother. I was ashamed. I felt like I was failing, that if I was better at being a wife, it wouldn't be happening. Besides, Rob was a policeman. He was a good neighbor. He was always joking around. People liked him. They respected him. No one would believe what I said. I could barely believe it. And by then I'd started to think that it really was my fault, that I didn't deserve to be loved, and that if Rob didn't love me, nobody would."

"Oh, Hannah, I'm so sorry," I said.

"We fell into this pattern where Rob would get violent and assault me, and then he'd beg me to forgive him, and he'd be super nice and loving, and then he'd get violent again. It seemed like the hitting was the price I had to pay to be loved. But then the beatings began to escalate. They happened more often, and they kept getting worse. But he was careful to hit me where it wouldn't show—my back, my stomach, my upper arms."

"What finally made you decide to leave?" I asked.

"I got pregnant. It wasn't planned. I had wanted to start a family. Rob had said he wasn't ready. He was focused on his career. He said he was finally getting the recognition he deserved."

"What did he mean by that?" I asked, though I thought I knew.

"Right after we got married, he was part of a big bust that shut down a meth lab and put a local drug dealer in prison. That's what helped him get into the Himmel Police Department. He had big plans. He'd already made sergeant and he was trying to get a promotion to lieutenant. I knew how important his career was to him, so I was all right with waiting. But when I got pregnant by accident, I was thrilled. I thought having a baby would make us a family, and maybe Rob wouldn't hit me anymore."

"What did he say when you told him?" Miguel asked.

"He said I tricked him. I'd gotten pregnant on purpose to get my way. That I had defied him. Then he just left the house and didn't come back for hours."

"Did he do anything to you when he came back home?"

"No. It made me nervous, but I waited for him to bring it up. He didn't, though, and that worried me. I didn't tell anyone I was pregnant—well, I did tell our neighbor the day I found out. I was so excited I couldn't help it. But I told her I didn't want to share the news with everyone until I was through the first trimester. It was really that I was waiting until Rob came to terms with it and was as happy as I was."

"And did he come to terms with it?"

"No. One night at dinner, he got upset because I burned the roast. He started yelling and getting worked up. That was usually the start of a beating. I was worried about the baby, so I tried to run upstairs and lock myself in the bathroom until he calmed down. I didn't make it. He caught me at the top of the stairs. He was furious. He punched me in the stomach and then he hit me in the face. I fell down the stairs and lost consciousness.

"When I woke up, I was in the hospital. Rob was sitting beside my bed, talking to a doctor. I recognized him. He played on Rob's softball team. Rob was telling him that he wasn't home when it happened. He'd found me at the bottom of the stairs.

"I tried to talk then, to say that wasn't true, but Rob grabbed my hand and squeezed it, hard. Then the doctor told me that I'd had a miscarriage, but that I'd be fine. Then he patted Rob on the shoulder and told him he was sorry for his loss. I knew then it wouldn't do any good to try and tell anyone what really happened."

"That was the time you were gone from work, and you covered up the bruise on your cheek with the makeup," Miguel said.

She nodded.

"But I didn't have the guts to leave Rob, even then. It wasn't until I found out that he had a vasectomy without telling me. I wanted a baby so bad, and he knew that. And I put it off because he wasn't ready. But then he not only made me lose my baby, he made sure that we would never have one. I finally understood that he didn't love me, he didn't care about me, he didn't want me to be happy. He wanted to control me, and he would keep trying to control me· until he killed me. That's when I told my grandmother the truth. She's the one who really loved me. She helped me get away."

40

"Okay, short pause," I said. "I need something a little stronger to drink. How about you guys?"

"No, I'm fine with water," Hannah said.

"I'll take a White Claw if you have one," Miguel said.

"If I have one? Miguel, it's your summertime favorite. Yes, I have one."

I refilled Hannah's glass, handed Miguel his White Claw, and replaced my Diet Coke with a short Jameson over ice.

"Hannah, carry on, please. You had just asked your grandmother for help."

"Yes. I hadn't told her anything before then because I didn't want to worry her. She has a heart condition. Also, she's pretty feisty. I was afraid she might confront Rob and I wasn't sure what he'd do. But when I finally told her, she didn't remind me that she hadn't wanted me to marry Rob, that she'd never liked him. She hugged me and said it would be all right, because she knew how to fix things. I felt like maybe it was going to be all right, after all."

"What did she do?" Miguel asked.

"She has a friend who used to run a shelter for domestic violence victims. I didn't know about Blanche—that's her name, Blanche—before that. But when I told Gran, she went into her take-charge mode. She called Blanche, they made a plan, and they set everything up."

"What was everything?" I asked.

"Blanche told me I was going to stay with her for a while. She said to take photos of any bruising I still had for evidence. Then text them to her, and after that delete them from my phone so there was no chance Rob would find them. She explained the California Safe at Home law. Domestic violence victims can change their names, their social security numbers, and keep motor vehicle records, voter registration records—almost anything that an abuser could use to track you down—confidential. She said she'd help me work through it once I got there.

"But I couldn't even buy my own bus ticket to leave. I didn't have enough cash. My paycheck was direct deposited. Rob controlled that account and gave me an allowance. He had an alert set up for our credit cards, so he knew anytime I charged anything. But I couldn't use those anyway because he'd be able to find me that way. Gran bought me the bus ticket to Blanche's."

"Without any money, you were like Rob's prisoner," I said.

She nodded.

"I didn't realize it until I tried to leave him."

"Why did you choose the name Hannah?" Miguel asked.

"Because that was my favorite teacher's name. I'm not married, Leah," she added, turning to me. "Gran came up with the last name Johnson. She said there are almost two million Johnsons in the United States. If Rob tried to find me, he darn well was going to have to work for it."

"I like the way your grandmother thinks," I said.

"But weren't you afraid that Rob would find out what you were planning?" Miguel asked.

"I was, but I was more scared of staying. Blanche talked me through what to do. She said it was important to leave a note. If I just walked away, there'd be an investigation, and a lot of people would be looking for me."

"What did your note say?" I asked.

"What Blanche told me to say. That I had been depressed since the miscarriage. That Rob had been great, but it wasn't fair to him. I had to work through the pain on my own. I told him I'd be in touch when I was ready."

"That was good. Your note took it out of the criminal realm and put it into a personal matter between husband and wife. Plus, it let Rob save face and come off as the unappreciated, caring husband who tried."

"Yes, Blanche told me Rob would be angry that I left. But he might let it go if I didn't say anything about his violence. She also told me to get my birth certificate, passport, and social security card—that I'd need them to go through the name changing and everything. I had to wait until Rob was on the night shift. After he went to work, I broke into his desk drawer to get the documents. He always insisted he needed to keep them because I was too careless. I found something else there to take, too. Ten thousand dollars in cash."

"How did Rob have that much cash lying around on a cop's salary? And why was it at home, not in the bank?"

"I don't know. It was a surprise to me. He never said anything to me about it, and he knew I'd never dare get into his locked desk drawer. But when I found it, I figured he owed me at least that much."

"He must have been very, very mad when he found it gone," Miguel said.

"I'm sure he was furious. But by the time he got home, I was hours away. Gran drove me all the way down to a bus station in Chicago so there wasn't a chance anyone would see me leaving from a local bus stop. Then I was on my way to California."

"That took courage after what you'd been through," I said.

"I wasn't brave at all. I was shaking the whole time I was traveling. When I got to California, Blanche picked me up and took me to her house, and I stayed there for almost nine months. She helped me get everything sorted out. She's the one who convinced me to buy a gun and learn how to use it."

That surprised me a little, though it probably shouldn't have, given the fear that Hannah must have lived with.

"I didn't want the gun at first, even though I was so scared Rob would find me. But I found that having it, and knowing how to use it, helped me get over feeling terrified all the time. I knew I'd at least be able to fight back if Rob ever found me. The longer I was away, and Rob didn't show up, the more confident I felt that I had gotten away with leaving him. Still, there's nothing like carrying a gun in your purse to remind you that someone out there wants to kill you."

"Hannah, what about your grandmother? It must have been awful to leave your only family behind. I assume you've never come back to the area until now, have you?" I asked.

"No, I didn't dare. But Gran came out to visit me a couple of times a year. The only reason I'm here now is that she had a bad heart attack a few weeks ago. I couldn't not come, no matter how scared I was of Rob. I cut my hair short—I've always worn it down to my shoulders. I did a quick color job—I'm really still a blonde. And I bought these fake glasses," she said, pointing at the black-framed pair that kept sliding down her small nose.

"I didn't think anyone would recognize me unless they got really close. But Miguel did as soon as he saw me. And it's been 10 years!"

"Not as soon as I saw you, but as soon as you said hello. It was your voice, and then your smile, that's how I knew. But how is your grandmother? Is she okay?"

"Yes. It was really scary for a while, but she's much better now. Her doctor is surprised how fast she's coming along. Gran says it's because I'm here. I'd like to think so. She's getting moved to cardiac rehab tomorrow. I plan to stay on a while longer. With Rob dead, I don't have to be worried anymore."

"That must be such a relief—both that your grandmother is doing well, and that Rob isn't a threat to you now," I said.

"You have no idea. From the moment I got here, I've been looking over my shoulder, afraid that Rob would be following me. Whenever I turned a corner, I worried that he'd be there," she said with a slight shudder.

"You were here before Rob was killed, then?" I asked.

She nodded.

"I got to town the week before. It was touch and go with Gran and I never left the hospital. But she started to do better over the weekend. On the Monday night Rob was killed, Gran was doing so well that I slept at my motel for the first time since I got here. And I mean slept! I didn't wake up until almost noon. When I got to Gran's room, she was watching the local news. The report about Rob's murder came on. Both of our mouths dropped open, and Gran—who never swears—said, 'Ding-dong, the bastard's dead!' Then she high-fived me."

"I don't blame her—or you."

"I don't feel guilty about it. It means Gran doesn't have to worry about me anymore. It means that I don't have to wonder when an unknown number calls if it's really Rob trying to find me. It means I don't have to carry a gun anymore. You have no idea what a weight has lifted from my shoulders. Literally," she added with a smile.

"I'll bet," I said.

"And now I'm free to see some of the people who were important to me when I lived here. I didn't have any friends really—Rob made sure of that. But the people at work meant a lot to me. Like Miguel and his Aunt Lydia. I already stopped at Making Waves to see her. That's how I knew where to find you. I've always felt bad that I left without a word to you," she said, looking at Miguel.

"No, no. You had to leave. I understand."

"Well, I want you to know that you made a real difference in my life back then. I had some really dark days, but you could always make me smile. Thank you."

"You are very welcome. I'm so happy you are here, and your grand-mother is fine, and you're fine, now," he said with a big smile.

Hannah smiled back.

"Well, listen, I've taken up enough of your time. Miguel, maybe we can have dinner before I go back, and really catch up. I want to hear all about you, not just talk on and on about myself."

"Yes. I would love to have dinner with you. Just let me know when," he said.

"Okay, I will."

She stood to go. "I want to see Gran before she gets too tired. She'll be excited to hear how my day went."

"Hannah, I just have one more question. Where do you think Rob got the $10,000 in cash that you found in his drawer?"

"I have no idea. I wasn't allowed to know anything about the money. But I'm sure he was pretty mad when he found out it was gone. Thinking about that is what kept my spirits up on that long cross-country bus trip."

41

I sat thinking hard while Miguel walked Hannah downstairs. When he came back, he said, "Why don't you look happy? We found Hannah—well, she found us. Rob didn't kill her, but we know now for sure that he abused her, like he did Bethany. Are you sad because Rob wasn't a murderer?"

"I'm not *that* much of a true crime junkie, Miguel. No, I'm not unhappy that both of Rob's wives survived his abuse. That was just an idea that didn't pan out, and I'm glad for Hannah's sake that it didn't. This is my thinking face, not my sad face."

"What are you thinking about?"

"Where Rob got $10,000 in cash to leave in a drawer. How did he have that much money? He wasn't even a lieutenant yet and I know for a fact HPD doesn't pay its sergeants enough to have that kind of money lying around. Besides, if he'd somehow managed to get it legitimately, why didn't he put it in the bank? Or in a money market, or invest it, so he'd get some kind of return?"

"Are you asking me because you want to know, or because you want to tell me?"

"I'm asking because I want to get your reaction to my idea about it."

"Which is?"

"That a cop with that much cash was on the take. And who around here might he have been taking from? Perhaps a drug dealer like Harley Granger?"

My phone signaled a text just then. As soon as I looked at it, I jumped up.

"Oh-oh. I was supposed to be at Coop's half an hour ago. I have to go, Miguel."

"But you didn't finish telling me. And I didn't even start telling you what I found out about Spencer today."

"I'm sorry, I really want to know, but I can't leave Coop hanging. I'll call you later."

"You can't. I mean you can, but I won't be able to talk. I'm recording my podcast tonight."

"Tomorrow then, first thing."

"In summary, Bethany and Shane didn't kill Rob, Hannah isn't dead, Erin is changing her plea, and Gabe basically fired me," I said as I helped Coop clear away the dishes from our hamburger feast. "But on a positive note, dinner was all that I dreamed of—perfect burgers, baked beans, and chips. Thank you."

"You're welcome. You don't seem very down about your investigation ending without the resolution you wanted. Your idea about Bethany and Shane didn't pan out, Rob wasn't a serial killer, and Erin confessed."

"I'm aware of that. But I like Shane and Bethany, so there's an upside to them not being killers. And for Al's sake, I'm glad his son wasn't a murderer as well as an abuser—and my investigation isn't over, because Erin didn't do it."

"Leah, come on. She confessed."

"You've never heard of a false confession?"

"Yes, I have, but that's not the case here. False confessions happen when a suspect is intimidated, or sleep deprived, or set up, or has some mental health issue. That isn't the case here. Erin is no intimidated suspect. She confessed for the exact reason she gave. She didn't want someone else to go on trial for something she did."

"You left out another reason for a false confession."

"What's that?"

"Protecting someone else."

"Who would that be in Erin's case?"

"The person she really wrote her letter to. The mystery lover that she refuses to identify."

"It's only a mystery to you because you don't want to be wrong about Erin. She wrote the letter to Rob."

"That's what she says now, but I think her original story—that she wrote a letter to the man she was seeing, but she didn't have the courage to send it—is the real truth. She's changing her story now, because she's afraid if the investigation goes on, his identity will come out."

"I don't think we're going to see eye to eye on this."

"Then let's look at it from a different angle. Take Erin out of the picture for a minute. Pretend the investigation is just beginning, and you're looking at plausible suspects who have a motive. Where does that take you?"

"Erin Harper?"

"No! Come on, Coop. I said take her out of the picture. Who comes out on top? Harley Granger. Rob sent him to prison for 10 years, and he's had a long time to plot his revenge. And what about the $10,000 Hannah found in Rob's desk drawer the night she left? It looks to me like Rob was on the take. That implies a Harley-Rob connection, don't you think?"

"There's no proof of Hannah's story about the money. Even if it's true, there's no link between the money and Harley, except the one you created in your imagination. Also, if Rob was on the take and then set Harley up, why wouldn't Harley shout that to the rooftops and bring down Rob at the same time *he* was going down?"

"Because he knew Rob held all the cards. Like you said, there's no evidence that Rob was getting cash from Harley, even Hannah didn't know. And it's not something Harley would've been keeping records of. Rob could just deny it and say Harley was lying because he got caught. Be honest, who would take Harley's word over Rob's?"

"You're speculating about a past where Rob *might* have been extorting money from Harley to stay quiet. But we're in the present now, and it doesn't matter whether or not Rob was a dirty cop, or if Harley had a reason to kill him. We know Harley didn't kill Rob because his alibi is solid. And because Erin confessed that she did it. Give it up, Leah."

"You know those are fighting words, Coop. I'm not going to give up until I find the truth."

"The truth, or the answer you want?"

"Same thing. The answer I *want* is the truth. If it turns out to be Erin, well, you can have gloating rights."

"I don't want to gloat. I want the right person to face the consequences. Everything points to Erin. I wish it didn't, but it does."

We finished loading the dishwasher in silence, but I was thinking all the while. And I came up with a reason for Coop's refusal to engage with the idea that Harley could be responsible.

"Wait a second. Are you ignoring Harley because he's not the target of your drug investigation, he's the informant? Is that really why he got out of prison early, not for being a model prisoner but because he had useful information? Does he get a pass because he's like a low-rent Whitey Bulger and his law enforcement handlers want him to keep informing?"

He shook his head.

"We're not getting anywhere here, and I don't want to fight with you. But if you're determined to dig around in Harley's life, remember he's not the same guy we knew in high school. He was a mean kid then. Now, he's a dangerous man."

"I know that. And I don't want to fight, either. Let's drop it for now, all right?"

"Fine by me."

"Okay then. Listen, you said you had something to show me. What is it?"

He smiled then. It's one of Coop's better qualities. He doesn't get mad that often, and when he does, it's usually not for long.

"Let's go into my office. You can see it better on the computer than on my phone."

Coop's home office was, like the rest of his house, neat and well organized. No piles of paper, no empty cups, no random sticky notes on the wall above his desk. In other words, it didn't look anything like mine. I leaned over his shoulder as he brought up the photos he wanted me to see.

"What am I looking at here?"

"It's property I'm thinking about buying. A few acres, some woods, a stream. First impression, what do you think?"

"You're moving?" I asked in surprise. "Where is it?"

"Not that far out of town. It's only about a mile from the old Cepak farm. And I'm not sure I'm moving. I'm just looking right now. The house needs a lot of work, but Dad could help me with that. It's a really pretty spot out there."

"I know the general area. Claire and William Montgomery bought the Cepak place, did you know that? But why do you want to move? You've got a nice house here, a workshop in the garage, you're close to work—close to me, too. Why is this the first I've heard about you moving?"

"Because I just started thinking about it. I'm feeling like I need a little more room."

"For what? What's wrong with this house? You've got two bedrooms, an office, a living room—your kitchen's a little small, but you could expand that. It'd be cheaper than buying something bigger. Also, that house in the photo needs more than 'a little work.' A complete tear-down is more like it."

"It isn't really this house that's a problem. It's more that the location is. I said when I ran that I'd be a sheriff who was accountable. That I would answer to the people in the county. I didn't realize so many of them would feel free to drop by the house instead of come to my office to share their views."

"People are coming to your house?"

"At first it was just once in a while. Somebody would see me working in the yard or taking out the trash and they'd stop to talk to me. But word must have spread that it's open house at the sheriff's, because the last few weeks five different people have dropped in with a question, a complaint, or an idea for how to run a better office. I'm feeling like maybe I'm a little too accessible. You don't like the property?"

"No, it's not that. I'm just thinking you won't be as accessible to me, either. I like knowing you're just across town. Especially when I find a giant, hairy spider in the bathtub."

"Hey, no matter where I am, I'll always answer a spider call from you. And I haven't decided anything yet. Maybe you and I can take a drive out there sometime this weekend and look it over."

"Maybe. Let me see what tomorrow brings and I can let you know for sure."

42

When I got home the next morning around eight, Miguel's car was in the parking lot, so I went straight to the newsroom. He was talking to Maggie, and when she noticed me, she waved me into her office.

"I understand there might be more to the Rob Porter story than meets the eye. A first wife who shows up and says she ran away because he beat her, and a second wife who has a similar story? Plus, the possibility that he was on the take? Looks like I'd better put our top reporters on it."

"Maggie, Troy and I are your only reporters—full-time, anyway," Miguel said.

"You're tops with me, no matter how many I have, kiddo. Hey, that reminds me, is there anything to Courtnee's story that there's trouble at *GO News*? Some kind of staff exodus? I hope so, we could use a break," she said, knocking on her wooden desktop.

"We sure could. Knock on wood again and see if you can conjure up a bankruptcy for them," I said.

"Sorry, my powers are limited to one evil wish per day."

"In my mind, *GO News* folding would be a wish for the good, ours and the whole county's."

I caught Miguel's eye and signaled him not to say anything about Spencer. I didn't want Maggie in on that just yet. I wondered briefly if that was how Coop felt when an investigation of mine had the possibility of colliding with one of his.

"Oh, Miguel, if you've got time," I said as I turned to leave, "could you come up to my place for a minute?"

"Sure, unless Maggie needs me."

"Get out of here, you two. I may be old, but I'm not stupid. I saw Leah give you the nod. Obviously, she's got a secret assignment for you—or you just completed one for her. Go ahead. Troy won't be in for another half hour. When he gets here, I want to talk to the two of you together."

———

"Do you want coffee or anything?" I asked Miguel when we got upstairs.

"No, I stopped at JT's on the way in. I saw your boyfriend Cole there, by the way."

I made a face.

"Don't even use the words Cole and boyfriend in the same sentence. Did you see him to talk to, or just notice him in passing?"

"I talked to him. He was working behind the counter."

"That's odd. I thought he was high enough on the family food chain not to have to work at his uncle's store anymore."

"I asked him that. But nicer. He said that his uncle broke his wrist, so everyone was helping out. Also, he told me to give you his best. If you ever want to make Coop jealous, I think Cole's your man. He's got a thing for you."

Miguel wiggled his eyebrows up and down.

"Please, don't go there. It's too early in the day for me to express the extreme disgust that suggestion makes me feel."

"Okay, I'm just sayin' he's got it for you, girl."

He grinned and I reached over and gave his head a thorough rubbing that left his beautiful hair in wild disarray.

"Not the hair! I had to wash it twice to make it go right this morning," he grumbled. He got up from the stool he was sitting on and headed for the mirror on the wall to repair the damage.

"Sorry, but you deserved that for coupling me with a Granger, even in jest. Now, please give me what you got on Spencer before Maggie calls to tell you recess is over, and you have to get to work on your real job."

"It isn't very much, but it's very good. I called McEachin and Miles, Spencer's old agency. All I could get was when he worked there and when he left. Then I tried his LinkedIn profile and I found two connections that we both had. One I couldn't reach, but the other one was very helpful, probably because she doesn't work there anymore."

"How on earth do you and Spencer have two of the same connections? No, you know what, never mind. Just tell me what you found out."

"Spencer did very well at the agency, just like his proud *mamá* said. He was on track to become a partner."

"On track to become? Marilyn told everyone he made partner."

"His mother, she exaggerated a little, that's how mothers are. But then things started to go bad his last year there. He was late most days, he was moody—way up or way down. He missed meetings. He was rude to staff and to clients."

"That doesn't sound a whole lot different than the Spencer I've known almost all my life."

"Maybe, but Spencer's fashion sense is fire. My friend who worked there said also that he was wearing just anything, like he didn't even care toward the end."

Disinterest in fashion signaled a troubled soul to Miguel. Except in me, where he considers it as evidence of a genetic mutation—because he has always admired my mother's sense of style.

"Rumors started that he was too much into the party life, that his girlfriend ghosted him, that he was losing clients for the firm, that he had a problem with cocaine. Then he got arrested."

"Spencer was arrested?"

"He got swept up in a drug bust at a club. At first the charge was trafficking."

"Holy cow, that's a felony! But I'm guessing since it's Spencer, and he's walking around free and easy, he got out of it somehow."

"He did. His parents got him a good attorney. But his agency fired him. Then he went to rehab. But my friend Mia didn't know what happened after that."

"Well, we do. He got his drug problem under control, but not his jackass problem. His parents set him up with *GO News*. He came back home after destroying his career and now he works at destroying ours with his alleged online 'news' site. But it looks like making stuff up and ruining other people's reputations didn't make him feel whole again. Given what we've heard about his business troubles, and the way he's been behaving, and who he's hanging out with, I'd say it's a for sure that he turned back to his cocaine ways. Good work, Miguel."

"What is next?"

"For you, getting back downstairs to your real job. For me, I think I'm going to take a run over to JT's for a little chat with Cole. No—don't say it. I know you want to, but you'll force me to retaliate if you do."

"No, no. I won't bring up unrequited love," he said, moving quickly to the door and out of my reach. Then, with his hand on the doorknob, he looked back over his shoulder.

"Let me know what you find out. But if you really want Cole to help you, work it a little. I know you can."

43

JT's party store is a Himmel institution. The original JT is long gone, but the name has lived on even though it's been owned for years by Cole Granger's aunt and uncle. They're *in* the family, but not really *of* the family —that is, they've maintained family ties, but managed to actually go legit, for the most part.

A light rain was falling, and as per usual, it ran down the faded and badly positioned awning over the entrance to the store and from there straight down the necks of incoming customers, of which at the moment I was one. As I pushed through the door, a little bell jingled to announce my arrival. I was greeted by the smell of strong coffee and overcooked hot dogs roasting in a roller grill on the counter. Cole was standing next to it, behind the cash register.

"Well now, good mornin', Leah. I seen your little Mexico friend already. He told you I was workin' today, and you just couldn't stay away, am I right?"

"Miguel is from Milwaukee, not Mexico. I need to talk to you."

"I'm kinda busy right now. Maybe I should drop over to your place tonight after work. We could have a real nice talk then," he said with a smirk.

"You're not busy. There's no one here. Let's go in the back. I don't want anyone walking in on our conversation."

"I appreciate your direct approach in gettin' your needs met, but I really can't help you out during business hours. Like I said, I can come by after—"

"Cole, come on, please. I really need to talk to you, and I don't have time for your faux flirting," I said, and marched toward the office at the back of the store.

The room designated as the office wasn't much larger than a closet. Cameras were mounted on one wall to oversee the main part of the store, and the front and back parking lots. Cole took the chair behind the desk, facing the cameras. I sat on a folding chair in front of him.

He leaned back, hands clasped behind his head in a classic power position pose. It irritated me, but he did have the power at the moment, because he had something I wanted: information.

"You said before that you and I could help each other out. I helped you. I told Coop about Harley and what was going on. Now I want you to come through for me."

"Oh, you do? That's kinda funny 'cause as I recall you said you wouldn't partner with me under any circumstances—or some other hurtful words to that effect."

"I know what I said. I changed my mind. I want to know what you know about Spencer that could bring him down."

"Sorry, that offer was good for a limited time only."

"All right, how about this? You tell me what you know about Spencer, or I'll tell Harley that you ratted him out to the cops."

His chair crashed down abruptly, and he leaned forward with his hands on the desk.

"Ah, I see I have your attention now," I said.

"You wouldn't do that. Do you know what would happen if Harley thought I give him up to the cops?"

"Tell me what you know about Spencer and Harley, and you won't have to worry. Come on, you're already partway there. You told me he and Harley are in business together."

"No. No, ma'am, I did not say that. I said Spencer was providin' some assistance to Harley. They was old high school buddies, you know that. It's just a natural thing to do."

"Stop it. We both know there's nothing natural about Spencer Karr helping someone out. If he's helping your brother, it's either because he's getting something out of it, or he's being forced to do it. Spencer's got a cocaine problem and it's getting worse. Harley is his supplier. I'm sure of that. But what else is going on between them?"

"I never told you that," he said, his eyes darting nervously toward the door as if he expected Harley, like the devil, to appear at the mention of his name.

"But Harley doesn't know that, does he? If I were to tell him that when you were supposed to be scaring me and warning me away from Granger property, you were actually enlisting me to bring him down, and when I said I wasn't interested, you went directly to Coop yourself, that wouldn't be so good for you, would it?"

He stared at me with his close-set, hard little eyes, trying to determine how far I would go. I stared back, hoping he wouldn't be able to tell that even though he was a conman, a petty thief, and a liar who had caused my family a lot of pain in the past, I still couldn't put him in Harley's crosshairs.

Finally, he sighed.

"I don't know if you'd really turn the wrath of Harley loose on me or not. But I never seen you break a promise. So, if I tell you, I want you to promise you ain't goin' direct to Harley, usin' me as your source. You hear?"

"I hear."

"You need to promise."

"Yes, fine, I promise. But I can't do anything about it if Harley makes the connection on his own."

"There's a few others in the family who know the story, and a few more who know some of it. As long as Harley don't know it's me for sure, I can get him lookin' in another direction."

"Nice," I said, shaking my head at the Granger family's *Lord of the Flies* lifestyle. "Whatever machinations keep the Granger family gears grinding, I guess. Now, tell me everything you know about Spencer and Harley's relationship."

44

Cole's eyes had brightened at the possibility of his brother's imminent downfall, and there was an undertone of glee in his next words.

"The cops are workin' on it, are they? Ol' Coop's keepin' it mighty quiet. I haven't heard nothin' about nothin'. I just hope they're plannin' some kind of big bust-up soon. I'm tired of Harley lordin' it over me."

"Tell it to Dr. Phil. You're not going to get me off topic here. What's the deal with Spencer and Harley?"

"I hear Spencer is havin' some financial troubles. That's probably because all his money is goin' up his nose. Cocaine ain't Harley's regular line. He's mainly meth and oxy. But he does special orders for certain customers. Spencer's been gettin' his coke from Harley ever since he got outta prison. But things took a turn a while ago."

"What kind of turn?"

"Your average cocaine addict don't have a lot of impulse control. This one night, Spencer had a powerful need. He picked up a big bunch of baggies from Harley at his business office—that would be the old sugar shack to you. Spence, he took his first snort before he even left the building and he drove away like he was flyin' . Right in the direction of Rob Porter's property. You know it's only a couple miles north of us, right?"

I nodded.

"Well, Spencer, he had some real bad luck that night. Happens Rob was just comin' out of his place when Spence goes zoomin' by and almost hits him. Rob put his cop light on his truck and took off after him. They had a little chase before he forced Spencer off to the side of the road and stopped him. Spencer was high as a kite. He had a pile of little baggies he was tryin' to stuff under the seat when Rob leaned in the window."

"You weren't there. How do you know all this?"

"I was there for the tellin' when that dumbass Spencer fessed up to Harley. I'm just addin' a little color commentary to the story."

"Just stick to the facts, please. If that's all true, why didn't Rob arrest him?"

"Because Spence, he offered Rob 500 bucks to forget all about it."

"Rob took a bribe?"

"He was always up for a share of the action. That's how he and Harley fell out and Harley wound up in prison. He knew what Harley was gettin' up to with his meth lab, and Rob wanted a piece of it. But then he wanted more. When Harley said no, that's when Rob set him up. He got to be a big hero for bustin' a drug operation, and Harley got himself 10 years in prison."

I wished that Coop was there to hear that my idea about Rob was more or less right.

"Why didn't Harley turn on Rob, tell the prosecutor what he was doing?"

I knew the answer, or thought I did, but I wanted confirmation.

"Harley's not the sharpest knife in the drawer, but even he knows his word against Rob's wouldn't get him anywhere. Who'd believe a Granger against one of Grantland County's finest? Besides, Mama didn't want no one lookin' into things too deep and findin' somethin' else to come down on us for. She leaned on Harley pretty hard."

"Harley took one for the team and went to prison without a whimper?"

"I wouldn't say that. He did get some promises from Mama, and she kept 'em. That's why he's back sittin' in the boss seat now."

"Interesting. But we're getting off-track here. You still haven't told me what 'assistance' Spencer is giving your brother and why."

"I'm tryin' to. After Spencer paid Rob off, the dumbass went and told Harley what happened. He was shook up, I guess, because he spilled it right out while I was sittin' there with Harley."

"What happened then?"

"I thought Harley was gonna take him out right there. Harley smacked him a good one. Then he started screamin' about Spencer bringin' Rob down on him again, and he wasn't goin' back to prison, and Spencer was the one who was gonna pay.

"I thought Spencer was gonna start cryin'. He sure was babblin' fast and breathin' hard, sayin' he didn't tell Rob anything, he had it under control, he paid Rob off, blah, blah, blah. Harley was havin' none of it. I could see there wasn't any need for me to be there, so I just kinda sidled over to the door and left. Harley was spittin' fire and he didn't even notice. I wasn't sure ol Spence was gonna get out of there alive."

"Thank goodness for your heroism, or he might not have," I said.

"Hey, don't try to shame me. It wasn't my fight, and I wasn't about to put myself in the middle of it. When Harley gets that mad, nobody's safe."

"Harley obviously didn't kill Spencer. So, what happened?"

"I told you, I don't know exactly, but I got my suspicions."

He stopped then as though he was having second thoughts about coming clean.

"I can go right from here to your brother and tell him—"

"No, don't do that. I just want you to understand I don't know this for a fact. I'm just tellin' you what I think."

"You're not usually that careful with the truth."

"There you go again, tryin' to make me feel bad about myself. When I'm just tryin' to make sure I don't give you the wrong idea. This isn't what I *know*, it's what I suspect."

"Consider me cautioned. Get to the point, please."

"Harley told me one time that instead of givin' Rob a cut back in the day to keep him quiet, he shoulda just killed him. Now, as a rule, Grangers don't go in for killing. Too much risk. But I told you, Harley picked up some bad ideas in prison. Ideas I don't personally support."

"Okay, well, Harley didn't kill Spencer, so where is this story going?"

"I'm just givin' you some context here. Harley was about as mad at

Spencer as I ever seen him. I can't say as I blame him, because there is negative zero chance that Rob didn't connect Spencer barrelin' down a dark country road in the middle of the night, with baggies of cocaine, comin' from the direction of Granger property, with Harley's past drug enterprises. Even if he didn't do it that night, sooner or later, Rob woulda pressed Spencer until he spilled his guts about Harley."

"And that would put Harley under Rob's thumb again."

"Exactly. And them boys from Milwaukee that Harley's in business with, they wouldn't think twice about cuttin' ties with Harley—and by that I mean killin' him—to protect their bigger operation."

"Harley, he already had a revenge need from the past for *Rob* to be dead. After Spencer told him what he did, Harley had a survival need from the present for *Spencer* to be dead."

"But Spencer isn't dead."

"Do you want to hear this, or do you wanta keep cuttin' into my story flow?"

"All right, then. I believe to save his sorry ass, Spencer made Harley an offer that he couldn't refuse."

"I think Spencer killed Rob for Harley, in exchange for Harley not killin' Spencer."

For once, I had no words.

Cole's story made sense. So did Harley's rage. But my willing suspension of disbelief stopped there. Spencer was a lot of things, but I couldn't believe that a hitman was one of them.

"I can't remember that I've ever had the pleasure of baskin' in your silence before," Cole said.

"Listen, I've had some wild ideas about Spencer's relationship to Harley, but I never thought it was hitman to client. Do you have any proof there was a conspiracy to commit murder between the two of them?"

"Not as such. But I am a student of human emotions. Harley was mad enough to kill when I left. Spencer was whimperin' like a baby, sayin' he's a loyal friend, begging Harley not to hurt him. When I ask a few days later how things went down with Spencer, Harley tells me he passed his first loyalty test. I ask him how. He says Spencer got rid of a big problem for him. I don't ask more because I don't wanta know more. But I can tell what he means."

"No. Spencer's a pretty bad guy, but I don't see him as a killer."

"You know Spencer better'n I do, but if you saw the way he was cryin' and beggin' when I left, I'd say he was ready to do about anything to get himself out from under."

"Why would Harley trust Spencer to do it and not rat him out?"

"Because Spencer is more scared of Harley than of the law—with good reason. And with Spencer doin' the dirty work, Harley could set himself up a nice alibi. Which, as you know, he's got."

I weighed the idea. Spencer doesn't have much of a moral code to rely on. Self-preservation would be his guiding principle.

"So, Harley gets rid of Rob, Spencer escapes Harley's wrath, and Erin gets the blame. All's well that ends well—for those two, anyway, not for Erin."

"*Maybe* it ends well for Spencer. Jury's still out on that. I don't think Harley's all the way comfortable with the idea of Spence walkin' around knowin' all he does. A man with a bad coke habit like Spencer has, he's not a very reliable person. If I was him, I wouldn't be restin' too easy right now."

Cole had been keeping an eye on the security cameras to watch for customers while we talked. Suddenly he said, "Shit! You got to get outta here. My sister Tabitha just pulled into the parkin' lot. Go on out the back door."

"Why are you rushing me out of here? I'm not scared of seeing Tabitha."

"You should be. She hates you."

"Why? I barely know her."

"Because you're the person she blames for her husband Monroe bein' in jail."

"I didn't have anything to do with that."

"Tabitha don't agree. You was the one who stirred up everything at that strip club where Monroe was workin'. She's not enjoyin' life as a single mom. Go on now, get out of here!"

45

I felt cautiously optimistic as I drove away from JT's. The more I thought about it, the more plausible it seemed that Spencer had killed Rob to save himself. And what Cole had told me explained what Miguel and I had witnessed between Spencer and Harley at the sugar shack. I took several deep breaths to tamp down a sudden feeling of malicious glee. Not because it was wrong to take joy in the troubles of others, but to calm myself in case it wasn't true.

My first instinct was to call Coop. My second was to wait. I'd already fallen on my face by homing in on Bethany and Shane. I hadn't exactly covered myself with glory with my Rob-killed-his-parents-and-his-first-wife conjecture either. This time, I wanted to do some additional checking before talking to Coop.

But I couldn't completely erase the feeling of renewed hope. If Erin knew, it might change her mind about changing her plea. If Spencer and Harley had colluded to kill Rob, Erin wouldn't be in the picture anymore, and that meant her lover wouldn't be either. I called the jail to set up a visit with her.

"I can't schedule you. Erin took you off her list of visitors," the jail visitation clerk said when I called.

"Are you sure, Deenie?"

"Yes."

"Could you ask her to put me back on it? I have something to tell her she really should hear."

"It's up to the inmates to put people on their lists. I don't have time to run around asking every one of them if they have any additions to make. I don't make the rules," Deenie said. Although it was clear that she delighted in them.

"How do I get hold of her to ask her to put me on her list?"

"You can email her. But she still has to agree to receive email from you before it will get delivered to her."

"Wait a second. First you say that I can't see her because I'm not on the list. Then you tell me the only way I can get on her list is to ask her to put me there. Only she won't get my email asking to be put on her list, because I'm not already on her list. That's a pretty strong Catch-22 vibe you've got going there, Deenie."

"I don't make the rules," she repeated. "There's a form you can fill out on the jail's website to make a request to send her email. She'll be informed of your request, and can say yes or no."

"All right. Thanks."

I called Gabe to update him and see if he could run interference for me.

"Hey, Gabe, I just tried to set a visitation time with Erin. I made Deenie's day because she got to tell me about rules. Can you get Erin to put me back on her visitors list?"

"I can't. Erin doesn't want to see you, Leah. Don't take it personally, she doesn't want to see anyone."

"But I talked to Cole Granger this morning. If what he told me holds up, Erin won't have to change her plea, and she won't have to go to trial, either."

"I feel like we've had this conversation before. Erin confessed. You don't need to keep investigating. Unless you've got a signed confession from another suspect, it's no good. Do you have that?"

"No, but what Cole said could lead there."

"That won't be enough for Erin, and it's not enough for me to go against a client's wishes. It's over, Leah. There's no point in you continuing. This conversation needs to be over, too. I can't talk to you about a client when you're not part of the case."

"But Gabe—"

"I'm sorry. This is Erin's decision. It's not appropriate for me to discuss it with you."

"Why are you acting so formal, like we're not even friends? Do you not trust me because I got Shane and Bethany wrong? Because I think the concept was right, I just had the people wrong. See, Cole—"

"I'm not acting like we're not friends. I'm acting like I'm Erin's lawyer."

"Wait, just listen, for just a minute. Please?"

I didn't wait for him to agree, I just plunged ahead. I ran quickly through what Cole had told me and reiterated my belief that Erin had only confessed to protect the identity of her lover.

"I'm going to find out where Spencer was the night Rob was killed, and if his alibi doesn't hold, we're in business," I said.

I couldn't see him, but I could almost feel Gabe shaking his head as he answered.

"Why are you so sure this is the lead that will pan out?"

"Why are you so sure it isn't? Don't you believe what I just told you about Spencer and Harley?"

"I believe you. I don't trust your source. Leah, you're great at finding the links, but you're not great at letting them go when they don't connect to anything that matters. I know it's hard for you to give up. But it's time. Don't let your need to be right get in the way of accepting the facts."

I felt a wave of both hurt and anger at his words.

"I don't 'need' to be right. But I'm not so scared of being wrong that I stop trying to find the truth. I'm sorry you think that it's my big ego that pushes me on."

"I didn't say that. But bottom line, Erin confessed. I believe her. I think you should, too."

"Thanks for the advice."

"Leah—"

I hung up without giving him a chance to finish. Although I'd punched back hard, underneath I felt disoriented, angry, and a little abandoned, too.

Gabe had always backed me before, even when I was on shaky ground. His resistance this time had stirred up doubt—even though I hadn't admitted it. Was he right? Was pursuing the investigation more about my need to be right than it was about helping Erin?

Normally in such circumstances I would visit Father Lindstrom to check the readings on my moral compass and do a reset if necessary. But he wasn't back yet.

However, there was Claire. At my final session with her, she'd encouraged me to call if I ever felt the need. Right then, I definitely did.

46

"No, I'm sorry, Leah, Claire isn't in. She's working from home today, " her secretary said when I called.

"Oh, okay. I'll catch her later. I just wanted to ask her something," I said, trying to conceal the disappointment I felt.

"Do you want to leave a message?"

"No, that's okay, Barb. Thanks."

But after I hung up, I decided it wasn't okay. I found Claire's personal cell phone number in my contacts and called her direct.

"Leah, don't apologize," Claire said when I reached her. "It's fine that you used my cell phone number. It's why I gave it to you. And no, I'm not too busy to see you. In fact, I'd welcome a break from what I'm doing. But would you mind coming out to my home office?"

"No, of course not. What time?"

"Let's say 3:30. Oh, in case you didn't know, we're not in town anymore. We finally finished the renovations on the house, and we moved in last week. You know where we are, don't you?"

"It's the Cepaks' house on Washington Road," I said.

She laughed.

"We like to think of it as the Montgomery house. I wonder how long it will be until people stop calling it the Cepak house?"

"After you sell the house. Then no matter who buys it, locals will call it the Montgomery house until those people sell it. It's Himmel's way of keeping history alive."

"I don't mind. I like being part of an ongoing line of Himmelites. I'll see you at 3:30 then."

"Yes, thanks, Claire."

When I got out of the car in Claire's driveway, I paused to admire the renovations she and William had done to the house. Ken and Miriam Cepak, the previous owners, had passed away in their 90s, within days of each other—without leaving a will. Consequently, the family farm had been tied up in litigation for more than 20 years while their children and later their grandchildren fought over the small estate. By the time things were settled, the house was in as much disrepair as the family relationships. The last time I'd driven by it, the windows had been boarded, the front porch steps were missing, and the roof sagged.

Now I saw that the exterior of the two-story brick house had been cleaned and restored to its original cream color. The tall, narrow windows, flanked by black shutters, sparkled in the afternoon sunlight. Two rebuilt chimneys poked up on either side of the square-windowed cupola on the roof.

"What do you think of the renovation?"

I didn't need to turn around to know who was speaking. William's distinctive voice sounds the way a warm hug feels.

"Hi, William. It's really amazing. You guys did a wonderful job," I said.

"Thank you. It took much longer than we expected. We hired a contractor, of course, but we did a lot of the work ourselves. It was hard work, but it's been a labor of love. I think you're here to see Claire?"

"Yes, is she in her office?"

"No, she ran into town to pick up the children. But she should be back in a few minutes."

He didn't indicate that I should go to Claire's home office and wait. I didn't want our encounter to slide into another discussion of my lost sheep status, as it had at the Players fundraiser. So, I took charge of the conversation and kept it on firm secular ground.

"How much acreage do you and Claire own? Are the woods part of your property, or just the house?"

"Both. Claire fell in love with the house, but the woods are what attracted me. I'm quite anxious for hunting season to begin this fall."

"I didn't figure you for a hunter, William."

"Is there a Wisconsin native son who isn't?"

He smiled. It was quite a sweet smile, really, and I liked his unexpected flash of humor.

"I know one or two, but they're rare creatures," I said.

"My father took my brother and me hunting every year until he died. Keith—my brother—and I have kept up the tradition. We get together every fall to hunt. For us, it's not as much about the hunting as it is about the memories we have of being with our father. I'm looking forward to this fall."

"Well, now that your house is finished, I hope you'll have plenty of time for hunting."

"Yes. We still have a little painting to do, some other odds and ends, but essentially we're done. My next project is centered on the church. We're starting a major fund drive to replace the roof."

"That sounds like a big undertaking. I'll mention it to Maggie at the paper. It would make a nice feature for the religion page."

"Thank you, I'd appreciate that."

"No problem. But I shouldn't keep you standing here in the driveway," I said to forestall any more invitations to Sunday services. "If it's all right, I'm happy to wait in Claire's office."

"Oh, of course. Yes. Follow me."

William set off at a brisk pace over a walkway leading to the backyard. I hurried behind him to a stand-alone structure the size of an extra-large garden shed that sat about 20 feet from the back of the house. A bright red door and a red flower box under the window provided a pop of color against the plain gray siding.

Inside, Claire's stand-alone office was compact, but well furnished. Two black leather armchairs sat on a tan Berber rug at one end. A sleek office desk and chair were at the other end, along with a small bookcase. There was no art on the walls—none was needed. The glass wall on the north side of the office provided a panoramic view of the woods beyond.

"What a great space!"

"Yes. It's like Claire, I think—warm, elegant, beautiful. It was my gift to her for her birthday this year. Well, early gift. I didn't want her to have to wait until September. I already had claims on the extra bedroom upstairs for use as my office, and she needs a space of her own, too. Please have a seat."

He pointed toward one of the chairs, then sat down in the other himself. I would have been perfectly content to sit alone, but it seemed that the hosting instinct was strong in William. I waded into the small talk pool again.

"So, how long have you and Claire been married?"

"Sixteen years next month."

"How did you meet?"

"I always tell people that God introduced us. I was serving as pastor at my first church. Claire had recently graduated from Robley College and was just starting her master's degree. I had no plans to marry until I was well established in my calling. But the first time I saw Claire, I'm afraid that idea fell by the wayside. I fell head over heels, as they say."

I found the idea of love-at-first-sight William surprising—and appealing.

"Did she feel the same about you?"

He smiled.

"Not quite. In fact, she did her best to discourage me. She planned to get her doctorate, become a therapist, and live in New York City. She spent her summers there as a child. It's where her maternal grandparents lived. She loved the excitement of the city. She wasn't interested in being a pastor's wife in Wisconsin. But I was persistent."

"It obviously paid off. Is that a picture of your kids?"

I pointed to one of the framed photos on Claire's desk.

"Yes," he answered, getting up and retrieving it to allow me a closer look. "Maeve is 14 and Billy is six."

Maeve looked out at the camera with Claire's dark eyes. Her features were fine, like Claire's, and her soft smile was the same. Billy looked a little small for his age. His eyes were blue and his hair blond like his father's, but I couldn't imagine the devilish grin on his face ever appearing on William's.

William's next words made me feel as though he'd been reading my mind.

"Billy has cystic fibrosis. It's why he's a bit behind other boys his age in size. He's as mischievous as they come, but he can't always do the things other boys his age do. Sometimes, he gets a little down, but he never gives up. And we're very optimistic. The doctors tell us there's a lot of hope for the future. Treatments are improving all the time."

His words were positive, but his expression was pained.

"I'm sorry, William. I didn't know. That must be hard to live with as a parent."

"It can be, at times. But of course, God is always there for us to lean on."

I've had mixed results with the trust-in-God thing, so I just nodded and moved on.

"Your daughter is very pretty. She looks a lot like Claire."

"Yes, she does. She has Claire's patience too. She's very good with her little brother."

A silence fell between us as he put the photo back on the desk.

Just then, we both heard footsteps coming down the path. As Claire opened the door she said, "Leah, I'm so sorry to keep you waiting."

"No problem, Claire. I've haven't been here very long, and William's been nice enough to keep me company."

"Thank you, William," she said, turning to her husband. "Maeve's inside with Billy. I asked her to keep him occupied so you can work on your sermon."

"Thank you. I'm having a little struggle with it this week."

He turned to me with a small nod. "Leah, it was good talking with you."

"You, too, William." A little to my surprise, I meant it.

47

"Well, Leah, how are you doing? I'm going to assume something isn't quite right, or you wouldn't be here," Claire said after we had each taken a chair and settled down.

"It doesn't have anything to do with my PTSD, but I'd like your help examining my motives. I thought I was pushing hard to help someone who needs it. But a friend made me wonder if I'm just an egomaniac who needs to be right all the time."

"That's an intriguing opening statement. I can't wait to hear the rest," she said.

"Okay, so, I'm involved in doing some work on the Rob Porter murder. Maybe I should say I *was* involved and now I'm not, but I want to be."

"I haven't followed the story very closely, I'm afraid. It's very distressing when something that seems like it should be on a true crime podcast happens to people you know. I'm aware that Erin Harper has been arrested for Rob's murder, but that's really all. Can you give me some context?"

"Sure, I—okay, wait a second. I'm thinking that this is a regular therapist/client session, even though you're kind of a friend. Whatever I say is confidential, right? Because I have to give you some information so you understand, but you can't give it to anyone else."

"Yes, it's confidential. 'Kind of a friend' isn't a bad description of a therapist's relationship with a client. In my profession, being friends with a client, or a former client, isn't forbidden—but it's definitely frowned upon."

"Really? Why's that?"

"Because there's an inherent imbalance in the relationship. A therapist knows a client's vulnerabilities and her secrets, some of them quite painful. That knowledge could be exploited if a therapist becomes friends with a client. Does that make sense to you?"

"Sure. Okay, we're therapist/client here."

Claire listened without comment as I walked her through an edited version of how I got involved in Erin's case and what had followed all the way through to my unhappy conversation with Gabe. But I didn't name Harley and Spencer as my current suspects.

"So, now Gabe says it's over, and it's time for me to stand down."

"And you don't want to."

"No, I don't."

"Why is that?"

"It's not because my ego won't let me say that I got it wrong, which is what Gabe seems to think. It's because I've got two suspects who fit the role of killer much better than Erin does. And their motives have nothing to do with scorned love."

"So, what's holding you back?"

"I guess it's respect for Gabe's judgment, and for Erin's right to make her own choices. Also, I'm mindful of the fact that I got it wrong twice before. If I keep going ahead with it, will I really save Erin, or will I just cause her more angst and still be wrong? In other words, does it make me an asshat if I keep digging for the truth? But wouldn't the real asshat behavior be just to walk away?"

"I understand your dilemma."

"I was hoping for some validation here, Claire. Like, 'No, Leah, that doesn't make you an asshat.'"

"No, Leah, that doesn't make you an asshat. But why are you so certain that Erin didn't kill Rob?"

"Well, for one thing I really can't see Erin falling for someone like Rob. I mean, maybe having a short—very short—fling, though even that's hard to imagine. But being so obsessed with him she can't let go? No. But there's an even stronger reason."

"What's that?"

"Nothing in Erin's confession is consistent with her personality or her normal behavior. I know how she approaches things. You must, too, after working with her. She organizes, she sticks to a plan, and she executes it. She says that she killed Rob on impulse. But I've never seen Erin do one impulsive thing in all the time I've known her. If she had killed Rob, she'd have a decent alibi. And she wouldn't let her movements be tracked by taking her phone with her. She'd be ready for the questions Owen asked, not stumble through them with obvious lies. And she would've searched Rob's office for the letter she wrote to him. She wouldn't have left it there for Owen to find."

As I finished, I noticed a bemused expression on Claire's face.

"Why are you looking at me like that?"

"Because the very things that you say the police are using to point to Erin's guilt—the letter she wrote, the tracking on her phone, the lie she told about being home all night—are the things you're using to point to her innocence. Let me ask you this: why didn't Erin confess as soon as she was arrested, if she wanted to protect her lover's identity?"

"When she reversed her story and confessed, she said she hadn't admitted it at first, because she didn't want to go to prison if she didn't have to."

"What made her change her mind?"

"I think she realized I'd keep digging after my first idea didn't work out. She wasn't worried about the police finding her secret lover because they think it was Rob. But she knew that I didn't believe that."

"So, are you going to pursue your investigation?"

Claire worked hard to keep her voice neutral, but I had the feeling she didn't think it was the greatest idea.

"That's what I'm trying to figure out. Do I have the right to if Erin's made the choice to confess? Is this about my ego or an actual quest for the truth? Gabe accused me of not wanting to let go just because I want to be right. Owen Fike said something similar. Actually, so did Coop."

"Do you think that's true?"

"Well, I do like to be right. But who doesn't? And I think what I have on my new suspects is solid. But maybe I'm wrong again. Am I really listening to my gut tell me to keep going, or am I just refusing to stop because I'm stubborn, and I can't bear to be wrong?"

"Those are important questions."

"A little more guidance would be helpful here, Claire."

"I can't tell you what your motives are or what you should do, Leah. My only advice is that you take a time out. Sit in your window seat, drink a Jameson, stream a favorite playlist, stare out the window, take a nap. Or perhaps do all of those things. I think your answer will come when you stop trying so hard."

"I'm having two thoughts about that advice," I said. "One is that you know way too much about my habits. The other is a nap sounds really good. I feel emotionally exhausted. But I also feel a little better, after having off-loaded on you. Thanks, Claire."

"You're welcome."

I turned back when I reached the door as a thought hit me. "Claire, William mentioned that your son Billy has been a little lonely. Gabe's son Dominic is about his age, and I think they might get along really well. If you want to set up a play date for Billy when Dominic gets back in the fall, let me know. Oh, and Dominic comes with a dog, so that might be a plus for Billy."

She smiled.

"Yes, it would. Billy loves dogs, but William is allergic. I'll take you up on that this fall. Thank you. You're a very thoughtful person, Leah."

"Don't give me too much credit. I'm a person who has a lot of thoughts, but that's not the same as being a thoughtful person. Thanks again, Claire," I said, then left quickly. I always feel like an imposter when someone says something nice about me, because I know that basically, I'm really not very nice at all.

48

On the drive home from Claire's, I changed my mind about waiting to talk to Coop about Spencer until I had everything sorted out.

"Hey, how about dinner tonight? We could go to McClain's for a Davey Burger Basket," I said without preamble when he answered his phone.

"That sounds good, but did you forget I've got a game at six? I'm on my way to the pre-game warm-up now."

Coop plays in a softball league. Not being a major sports head myself, it's hard for me to understand his devotion to the team, but it would take a major crime spree in progress for him to miss a game.

"Oh, that's right! Can you come by after?"

"Sorry, I can't do that either. My dad called and asked me to come help him cut up a tree. A big oak in his backyard came down in a storm last night and broke his fence. I said I'd drive up to his place after the game tonight so we can get at it first thing. I think I'm going to stay over on Saturday, too, and watch the Brewers game with him. We haven't done that in a while."

"That sounds like fun. Not the Paul Bunyan chopping trees part, but it'll be nice for you and Dan to have some time together."

Dan Cooper, Coop's dad, lives up north outside of Rhinelander. I was happy that he'd be able to spend some time with his father. But I was disappointed I wouldn't be able to talk to him until Sunday. He heard it in my voice.

"Hey, is anything wrong? I can come over after the game and let Dad know we'll have to start a little later tomorrow."

"No, there's nothing wrong. But you get the good boyfriend prize for asking, and for offering. I had kind of an eventful day, and kind of a disagreement with Gabe, and I wanted to talk to you about it. But it's better in person, and it's nothing that can't wait. You'll be back Sunday, right?"

"Yes. I thought you and I could drive out and see the property I'm thinking about buying if you don't have something else going on. But seriously, I can come over tonight after the game."

"No, don't worry about it. Really. A Sunday drive in the country with you will be fun. Have a good game and say hi to your dad."

"Okay, if you're sure."

"I'm sure."

Over the phone I could hear the sound of his car pulling into the parking lot at the softball field, and the shouted greetings of some of his teammates.

"You better go. I'll see you Sunday."

It was probably just as well that Coop was busy. It would give me more time to think through what I was going to do and prepare my case for his scrutiny. Now that my look into Spencer's background had the possibility of crossing over into his drug investigation, he'd have plenty of questions, and probably objections to my future involvement.

My phone pinged with a text from Miguel.

"What happened today with Cole?"

"Come up. I'll fill you in."

"So, Spencer is a killer!"

We were seated on my sofa, and I had just given Miguel the sum of what I learned from Cole.

"Maybe he's a killer. I want him to be a killer. And, in fact, all indications are that he *is* a killer. But there's work to be done, my son. I have to find out more about where Spencer was the night Rob was killed."

"How can I help?"

"You already did plenty digging up Spencer's background. Besides, hasn't Maggie got you filling in the blank pages in Rob's past? Be careful while you're doing that, by the way. If Harley gets wind of it, it might make him worried it could lead you in his direction. You don't want a worried Harley."

"I think Harley might not be around that much longer."

"Hey, are you talking about a drug bust? I can't get anything out of Coop. What do you know?"

"That you were right. My source said that a team with officers from three sheriff offices—Grantland, Olney, and Whitney counties—are working with Milwaukee cops on it. And it's happening soon."

"Do you know any details?"

"Just that it's going to happen in Milwaukee and here at the same time, so they can sweep up both ends of the operation. It's on for next week, but I don't know what day. I'm supposed to get a tip-off right after it goes down. I can't do anything with the information until after it happens. My source could get into big trouble if anyone found out."

"I take it your source is good? You've worked with him before?"

"Her," he said. "Yes. She is very reliable."

"Is it someone local, or someone in Milwaukee?"

Miguel was raised in Milwaukee and it's where most of his extended family live, so he still has a lot of connections there.

"Sorry. I promised, anonymous and off the record. Maggie knows, but that's it."

"Well, if you trust the source, and Maggie's satisfied, that's enough. This is a good sign that Cole's been telling the truth about Harley's drug operation. It makes me feel better about trusting his information on Spencer and Harley, too."

"Are you going to tell Coop about Spencer?"

"Yes. But he won't be back in town until Sunday. With what you just said, I can see that my investigation is moving pretty far into Coop's lane. I don't want to ask the wrong people the right questions and create a situation that jeopardizes the drug bust. Why are you staring at me like I'm speaking a foreign language?"

"A little bit, you are. It must be true love, if you're holding back so you don't make a problem for Coop."

"Hey, I never purposely cause a problem for him. And I'm not holding back. I'm just waiting until the time is right. Two things need to happen: First, Harley's drug enterprise needs to be stopped, and then Spencer and Harley both need to go down for murder."

"If they did it."

"Yes, if they did it. I'll hold off on my victory dance. Confirm first, dance second."

"I'm going shopping tomorrow in Madison. Do you want to come? It will be fun!"

"Tempting as shopping always is to me, which as you know is not at all, thank you, but no."

"Okay, if you won't go, I'll ask Hannah Johnson. She is very fun, and *she* won't whine that we should quit and go to The Old Fashioned for lunch. Besides, I want to ask her if she will go on the record with her story about her life with Rob. It will be better if she is feeling happy and relaxed and remembers that she can trust me. And if Hannah agrees, then it will be easier to get Bethany to talk to me."

"Have you approached her yet?"

"No. I want to get Hannah on the record first. I think it won't be so hard for her to say yes, because she doesn't live in Himmel, and she will be going back to California when her grandmother is better. But it's different for Bethany. She lives here."

"Right. Though I wouldn't be surprised if Bethany and Shane left, too. It's not fun to have the whole town know everything about your family tragedy. Trust me on that. Oh, and that reminds me. You're going to give Al Porter a heads up before the story on Rob's background runs, aren't you? The first time he learns the truth about his son shouldn't be in the paper."

"Yes. Maggie and I already talked about it."

"Of course you did. Sorry for my relapse into micromanaging. Poor Al."

"Not only Al. What about Paul, Spencer's father? He is a very nice man and to find out about Spencer—that will be very hard for him, too. I hate when a story hurts nice people."

"I do, too, Miguel. But remember, it's not the stories that are going to hurt Al and Paul. It's what their sons have done. I never met Rob's mother, so I can't speak to what she was like, but Rob wasn't anything like Al. And Spencer, well, Paul already suffers guilt because Spencer is such a horrible human being. I lay that at Marilyn's door. She's a terrible person, too. Although as far as I know she hasn't killed anyone. But give her time."

"It might be you, *chica*. When Spencer's story comes out."

"I can handle Marilyn, don't worry. Hey, are you hungry? Do you want to go to McClain's for dinner?"

"I can't. I'm going to Della Toomey's house to tape an interview with her."

"Della Toomey? The lady who lives in Delving? The one I met last spring, who thinks you're 'such a nice boy?'"

"Yes. And I am a nice boy."

"Why are you interviewing her?"

"Because she was a Rockette in New York City in 1955. I think it will be a fun story for my listeners to hear."

"She was a Rockette?"

I'd only spoken to the 87-year-old Della on the phone, but the image I had of her in my mind's eye was not that of a high-kicking precision dancer.

"Like you taught me, everybody has a story. When I had lunch with her a couple of weeks ago, she told me about when she lived in New York. She took a bus there when she graduated from high school, because she wanted to be a dancer. She had to audition three times for the Rockettes before she made it."

"Why did they come back?"

"You'll have to listen to my podcast next week to find out!"

"I will, even though you're throwing me overboard for a date with another woman. I'll talk to you later. Have fun."

49

After Miguel left, I ran downstairs to see if my mother was still there. It was nearly six o'clock, but she sometimes uses the hour after everyone else is gone to catch up on things in peace.

"Hi, hon," she said, looking up from her computer as I walked into her office. "I've barely seen you the last few days. How did your meeting with Nancy Frei go? Did you find out any more about financial problems at *GO News*? And what about Erin, how are you and Gabe doing on her case?"

"Come to dinner with me at McClain's and I'll tell you. Davey Burgers are on special tonight," I added by way of enticement. The burgers are named after the bartender at McClain's. He claims the ingredient that makes them so tasty is a secret from his grandmother that he will take to his grave. I hope not, because Davey doesn't take very good care of himself, and those burgers are really good.

"I'd love to, but Paul and I are meeting Marty and Noreen Angstrom for dinner at the new restaurant in Hailwell tonight."

"Okay, three strikes and I'm out. I guess it's just me and a bowl of Honey Nut Cheerios tonight."

"Oh, so I'm your third choice? Then I don't feel sorry for you," she said as she shut down her computer and began putting the file folders on her desk back into their proper drawers. As already noted, I do not belong to the clean desk club, but my mother is the president of it.

"Coop's got a game, and Miguel's got a hot date with an old lady from Delving. Don't think of yourself as third choice. Think of it as me saving the best for last."

Stealing a signature move of mine, she gave me some very good side eye.

"No. Don't even try. But despite your lack of daughterly devotion, I do want to know what you found out about *GO News* and what's happening with Erin. Can you give it to me in 10 minutes? I've only got that long before I have to go."

I gave her a stripped-down version of both. I told her about Spencer's apparent drug habit but included nothing about Spencer as hitman and most of Cole's other assertions. About Erin, I just said she wanted to change her plea to guilty, and that Gabe had cut me loose.

"Did you know Spencer had an addiction problem in the past?" I asked when I finished.

"I did. Paul told me. And don't even ask why I didn't tell you. It wasn't my story to tell. I've been wondering about Spencer a little myself."

"Really? Why?"

"He's so very thin, and he always seems to be agitated when I see him. The other day, his shirt looked like he'd picked it out of the bottom of the laundry basket, it was so wrinkled. That's not like him at all."

"Has Paul said anything about it?"

"No. Either he hasn't noticed, or he doesn't want to talk about it. He might be in denial. I can't blame him. He feels so guilty for the way Spencer behaves toward people. You, especially. The one bright spot for him, the thing that gives him hope, is Spencer's recovery from addiction."

"Well, he might not be able to ignore it for much longer."

"What do you mean?"

"I don't want to get into details because I don't know for sure. But it's possible Spencer is heading for some big trouble. I can't pretend I feel sorry for him, but I do for Paul."

"You can't just drop that on me and not tell me anything else," my mother said. "What kind of trouble? Why? Come on, now you have to tell me."

"No, I'm sorry. If it turns out to be real, I'll give you a heads up, but I can't say anything more."

She drew her eyebrows together in a frown and shot me a frustrated look.

"I wish I still had the power to send you to your room when you don't listen to me."

"I'm listening, Mom. I'm just not doing what you want me to do."

"Well, the next time you want apple bread, maybe I won't do what you want me to do, either."

"Oh, you're pulling out the big guns now. Luckily, I have options. I'll just ask Coop to ask you. You never say no to him."

She sighed.

"Fine. I respect your right to stay silent. But it's going to be hard to be around Paul, knowing he might have a world of hurt coming."

"He's got Spencer for a son. He's probably hurting all the time."

She didn't chide me for my uncharitable response because I know she agrees with me. She just doesn't say it out loud out of affection for Paul. She moved on.

"Are you really done with Erin? Who do you think she's protecting?"

"I'm not done, and I don't know. I'm leaving that alone for now, anyway, because I have a pretty good lead on someone with a very strong motive to kill Rob. But that's all you'll get out of me now. Even with apple bread."

"I'm glad Erin still has you in her corner."

"Thanks, Mom. I appreciate that. Erin's not too happy I won't just silently slip away, though. And Gabe doesn't want me involved, and Coop probably won't either. But I have to finish what I started."

"I know you do. You've always been that way. Nancy insists it's because you're a Scorpio."

"When did Aunt Nancy get into astrology?"

"She took a class online last spring. She did your horoscope and Coop's. She said Scorpio and Capricorn are a good match."

"Oh, well, then as long as the stars have spoken to Aunt Nancy, I think Coop and I are good for the long haul," I said.

"I hope so, Leah. Have I told you how glad I am that you two are finally together?"

"Yes. This makes the third time."

"I like to express my joy. Sue me."

"I won't sue you, Mom. In fact, I'll give you a bonus and tell you again that you were right, I'm glad I listened to you, and I owe my current state of delirious happiness to your advice that I should tell Coop how I feel."

She gave me a wide smile with no trace of I-told-you-so, just happiness because she knew I was happy, too. I hugged her and went upstairs, smiling myself. Not always, but often enough, we get this fraught and complicated mother-daughter thing just right.

Upstairs I poured myself a delicious bowl of Honey Nut Cheerios and sat down to stream a favorite classic film of mine. *Harvey* is the story of Elwood P. Dowd, played by Jimmy Stewart, and his imaginary (or is he?) friend Harvey, a six-foot rabbit. It's one of my go-to movies when I want to spend time with a sweet and wise friend but Father Lindstrom isn't around.

The next morning, I was lying in bed, thinking about the day ahead, when my phone rang. Jennifer.

"Hey, are you finally back?" I asked. I was unable to stifle the yawn that followed.

"I am. Did I wake you up? I'm sorry. What time is it?"

"It's almost seven. I was waking up, just not all the way there when the phone rang. Welcome home. What are you doing up so early? You're not usually an early riser on the weekend."

"I know, but I've been up since five. When I got home yesterday around six, I was so tired I just fell into bed and slept like a log. Then my eyes popped open at five and I got up. I've done two loads of laundry, sorted the mail, and I'm on my way to the grocery store now. I was calling to see if tonight was good for our girls' night out."

"Yes, sure. I've only been waiting since forever for us to get together so you can tell me the 'epic' news you taunted me with and then left town. What's the plan? What time are we going and where?"

"I was actually thinking of a girls' night in. If we go to McClain's, then Sherry will be giving you death stares all night and ignoring our drink requests because she's mad that you're with Coop and she's not, right? And if we go to Bonucci's there'll be a ton of people there. The wait staff will be hovering, waiting to clear our table for the next customers as soon as we take our last bite of pizza."

"I'm fine with a night in. Or we could go out of town. Mom and Paul said the new Chinese restaurant in Omico is good."

"If we do that, we'll have to make sure one of us stays sober enough to pass a breathalyzer, and I really feel it can't be me tonight. After this 'vacation' with my kids, my sister and brother-in-law, their kids, and my parents, I really need a little unrestricted wine consumption."

"Let's do a night in, then. Do you want to come here or me to go to your house?"

"Your place. Start at seven? I'm thinking Mexican instead of pizza for a change. How does that sound?"

"Great. Let's do nachos from Burrito Palace."

"I'll pick them up on my way over."

"Okay, I'll do something for dessert."

"By that you mean you'll raid your mother's freezer, I hope. I could really get into some of her brownies with fudge frosting."

"I'll check it out and see if she's got any in cold storage. If she doesn't, and I tell her they're for you, I'm sure she'll whip some up."

"Wonderful! I'll see you tonight with nachos in hand."

"Be prepared for a lengthy recital, every detail of the juicy story you promised. You've been teasing me with it for long enough."

"Will do. And trust me, it's worth the wait."

50

After we hung up, I took a quick shower and dressed in my favorite at-home summer attire, a vintage Maroon 5 T-shirt, shorts, and flip-flops. Then I ran across the street to the Wide Awake and Woke coffee shop for a large Chai. On impulse I picked up a raspberry scone to sustain me on what I had determined would be a hard day's work on the mystery novel I was supposed to be writing.

I broke for a peanut butter sandwich around one o'clock, and a quick run to my mother's to grab the promised brownies for Jennifer, but that was it. By the time Jennifer was at my door bearing nachos and two bottles of wine, I felt like I deserved both the nachos and a drink.

"Hey! You look great," I said as I gave her a hug. "Here, let me help you."

I took the carryout bag from her hand. "I do have wine here, you know."

"Yes, I know. But your reputation precedes you. I feel like something a little classier than wine in a box from the drug store."

"I can't believe you're dissing my skills as a *sommelier*. But also, do you even know how ecologically responsible boxed wine is?"

She rolled her eyes and followed me to the kitchen. We bustled around getting plates, wine glasses, and assembling the feast, which we then carried to the window seat. We each took a corner and leaned back, facing each other, our heavily laden plates on our laps.

"Now this is elegant dining," Jen said as she spoke around the nacho she had just scooped up and popped in her mouth. "I love that you still have that tray table," she said, pointing to the one I'd set up to hold our drinks.

"It's the only one left of the four seasons set we had at home. Autumn. It's my favorite. Remember how Annie and I used to fight over who got to use it when Mom would set up snacks for us on the porch in the summer?"

"I do. Those were fun days. I wonder what Annie and Lacey would be doing now?"

"I think Annie would be a veterinarian. You remember how she loved animals. I think Lacey would be starring on Broadway. What a great voice she had."

Then we both just sat there for a minute, thinking of those long-ago summers, and of my two younger sisters, both beautiful, both bright, both gone. Grief hits you like that sometimes. You can be laughing and remembering and suddenly you feel a jolt of pain as fierce as the first moment of loss. Usually when I think about them now, it makes me smile. Sometimes, though, the smile turns to tears.

Jennifer reached out and touched my hand.

"Hey, let's drink a toast to Annie, to Lacey, and to the kids you and I used to be," Jen said, lifting her glass of wine.

"Yes, let's. To the sisters I acquired by birth and lost. And to you, the sister I found in the kindergarten time-out corner," I said, clinking my glass with hers.

We laughed then, and I took a sip of wine, while Jennifer almost drained her glass.

"Slow your roll there, Jen. We've got a whole night ahead of us, right?"

"I can handle it. Like I said on the phone, I need it. I love my kids. I love my parents. I love my sister. I love her kids. I love my brother-in-law. Her kids and my kids had a blast, and Terri and I took some nice walks on the beach while Bruce and my parents managed the kids. It was good.

"But holy hell, 10 people—especially when five of them are under age eight—in a vacation rental is a lot. We also caught the tail end of that hurricane at the end of the week and were stuck inside the whole last day. Do not rain on my parade now."

"Your point is made. Drink away without judgment. So, tell me, is there anything new on the divorce front? Is John behaving any better?"

Jennifer's soon-to-be ex-husband, the only man she'd ever loved—practically the only one she'd ever dated—had recently taken a job in Green Bay, over three hours away. To date, their divorce had not been amicable, to put it mildly. John's affair was the cause, and it had been revealed in a fairly spectacular way. Jennifer had by turns been stunned, disbelieving, wounded, devastated, and angry. John's initial response had been to apologize and then say they should just put it behind them and move on.

But Jennifer was having none of it. So, he had gone on the offensive and fought her every step of the way over property settlement issues, custody of their five-year-old twins, and visitation rights.

"Actually, yes. Things are quite a bit better. My therapist helped me figure out that although John had done some really bad things, I was hurting myself and the kids by being so angry all the time. So, before the Florida trip, John and I sat down with a mediator to work the settlement out. It went pretty well. John has a new girlfriend, so he's motivated to wrap things up. I should be a fully divorced woman, not just a legally separated one, soon."

"You *sound* pretty Zen about it. Is it for real, or are you just trying to convince yourself?"

"No, it's for real. We were way too young to get married when we did. We both changed—or we both grew up. Maybe that's the same thing. Anyway, yes, I'm ready to let go and move on. Which is good, because as you know, John was ready to move on while we were still married."

She gave me a wry smile.

"Well, all right. Good, I'm glad."

She leaned over and picked up the bottle of wine and poured another glass for herself. "You?" she asked, tipping the bottle toward me.

"Not yet, I still have plenty."

She ignored me and reached over to top off my glass.

"I love it up here," she said, looking out the window. "It's practically a fairy tale tower. Like you're Rapunzel or something. And now you have a fairy tale prince, too. Time for another toast!"

As she spoke, she hoisted her glass high, and a little wine sloshed onto her wrist.

"I think you spent too much time in the Magic Kingdom. Coop's not a fairy tale prince, and I'm definitely not a princess. And happily ever after isn't the way every story ends."

"Whoa! You're in kind of a downer mood. What's the matter? Tell Aunt Jen all about it."

"Nothing is the matter. I'll drink to me and Coop," I said, "but let's hold on the happily ever after."

"Why? You guys are perfect together. Did something go wrong already?"

"No, no, it's not that. We're very happy. Well, I'm very happy, and I think Coop is. I just don't want the universe to know that yet, I guess."

"You mean because you're afraid it will be taken away?"

"Something like that."

"Leah, I get it. But that's not going to happen. Not this time. Not to you two. Trust me, I'm never wrong about these things. Except in my own case, of course. But it's the exception that proves the rule, right?"

She tapped her glass against mine and said, "To you and Coop!"

"Okay, to Coop and me."

We both drained our glasses that time. I set mine down and went to work on my plate of nachos until they were gone. Jennifer did the same, then poured herself another glass of wine. I held my hand over mine when she attempted to fill it.

"I don't have your stamina. Also, I'm not recovering from a family vacation. But before you drink yourself into a stupor, put the wine down and tell me the epic story you've been promising."

"I will, I will. Only first, you have got to tell me what's going on with Rob's murder. I checked the *Times* online while I was gone, but you guys didn't have much except that Erin was arrested—that was a shocker! Are you helping Gabe on this?"

"I was, but he fired me. Well, since he wasn't paying me, I guess he didn't really fire me, but he told me my services are no longer needed."

"What? Why?"

"Erin wants to change her plea. She says she did it, she was lying before, but now she wants to come clean."

"Wow! I can't believe it. Erin Harper killed Rob . . . So, everything else was true then, that they had a thing and when Rob dumped her, she couldn't let go? I never would have put Rob and Erin together in a million years."

"I don't think they were together."

"Then why did she kill him?"

"I don't think she did. I think she changed her plea to protect someone else."

"The real killer, you mean?"

"No, the man she was having an affair with—who isn't Rob. I think he's someone with a lot to lose and she loves him enough to go to prison for him so that he doesn't."

"Wow. I wish someone loved me that much. If that's true, who do you think the real killer is? Come on, you know I won't tell."

I gave her a skeptical stare.

"Hey, if it's really important to keep a secret, you know I can. You know I have. Many, many, many times—most of them for you. If you tell me to keep it quiet, I will."

"Okay, fine. But don't share it around. I haven't even had a chance to tell Coop what I think yet. I don't need him hearing about it through the sheriff's office grapevine."

"Oh, this must be really good. I swear what you tell me will not go further than this room. Now, who killed Rob?"

"I think it was Spencer."

Her eyes widened as she said, "Spencer! Why would he do it?"

"Just listen and I'll tell you."

I went through the story from the point where Miguel and I had stumbled across Spencer meeting with Harley through Cole's story about Spencer, Rob, and Harley. When I finished, Jennifer was staring at me with her mouth half-open.

"Hey, I know it's kind of a crazy story—Spencer as a hitman—but it makes sense. I just have to find out what Spencer was doing the night Rob was killed."

"I can help you there, Leah. Spencer was with me."

51

"I don't understand."

"I. Was. With. Spencer," Jennifer replied, coming to a full stop after each word.

"Jen, I heard what you said. My brain is refusing to process it. You were with Spencer the night Rob was killed? Why? For how long? Why didn't you say anything before?"

"I was with him all night—or most of it, anyway. That's the epic story I was going to tell you. I didn't know Spencer was connected to Harley or to Rob, or I would have said something sooner."

"Tell me everything from the moment you first saw him that night."

"All right. But don't judge me."

She took a large gulp of wine before starting.

"Okay, I want to give some background here, in my defense. So, you know that John and I were together for 15 years. Yes, he turned out to be a selfish bastard, but that doesn't mean our whole life together was bad. There were lots of good things. You get used to having someone around all the time—someone to talk to, to laugh with, to warm your feet up in bed when they're freezing. Just basically to *be* there, so you don't feel all alone. Don't say it. I know I have the boys, and my parents, and my friends, but it's not the same."

"I'm not saying anything. I'm still too dazed at the thought of you and Spencer together. Please, go on."

"The truth is, I'm lonely, Leah. And I just wanted to spend some time with an adult male who enjoyed being with me, talking, laughing, going out to dinner, normal things like that."

"So you chose Spencer?" I couldn't keep the incredulity out of my voice.

"God, no. That's not how it happened. I'm not telling this very well, am I? No, see, a few weeks ago, I signed up for an account on a dating app. I had no idea how many 'swipe left' guys are out there. That's when someone's profile picture comes up and you think 'uh-uh, no way.' You swipe to the left to clear their profile from your screen and move on. When you like someone, you swipe right. Then if they swipe right on your profile, you've got a match and you start texting and stuff."

"Jen, I know how the apps work, just get to the part about how you wound up with Spencer Karr."

"All right, all right. So, I had a lot of swipe lefts. And the swipe rights I connected with turned out to be weirdos, or gross, or scammers. It was pretty discouraging, not to mention demoralizing. But, I figured, why expect anything else? I'm an overweight, 30-something woman with two kids and not much else to say for my life."

"Jen, that's not tr—"

She held up her hand to stop me. "No, Leah. Don't tell me that's not true, or it's not how I should feel. I'm not asking for encouragement or sympathy. I'm just saying what is, okay?"

"Okay, I'm sorry. Keep talking. I'll shut up."

"So, I was just about to hang it up when this one guy, Jeff, matched with me. His picture was cute, he was my age, he said he was local, and I thought, what the heck? I'll give it one more try. We started texting and we hit it off. He said he was an amateur gourmet chef, and he wanted to cook dinner for me. No, don't even say it."

Again, she held up her hand to forestall my comment. I pressed my lips firmly together and ran my finger across them to show I knew I'd nearly violated my no-talk promise and wouldn't do it again. She picked up where she'd halted.

"I wasn't about to go to the house of some guy I'd never met for our first date. I suggested that instead of dinner, we just meet for a drink at the TRT."

The Tenney Road Tavern is in the village of Edgerton, population 986, on the far northeast corner of the county. It's the kind of small, local bar where the regulars all turn around when you walk through the door, give you the once-over, then turn back to their drinks if they don't know you. There's a little square of linoleum where people can dance to the music from the jukebox, though not many do.

The clientele is mostly area farmers and retired guys who don't care about fancy cocktails, or sticky tables, or that everything fried in the kitchen tastes like frog legs, the TRT's signature dish. They come to get away from the house, play some darts, drink some beer, and talk about the old days. It's not a place many would choose for a first date. All of that ran through my mind and must have shown on my face because Jen answered what I hadn't asked.

"It's kind of skeevy, I know. But it's not scary or anything. I just wanted to go someplace where we wouldn't run into a bunch of people from here. They'd all wonder who he was, and how we met, and come over to chat, and be introduced. I wasn't ready for that. I figured the TRT would be safe and anonymous."

I broke my promised silence because she was taking so long to get to the Spencer part.

"So how does Spencer come into this? You're not going to tell me he put up a fake dating profile and when 'Jeff' showed up, it was really Spencer, are you?"

"No, nothing like that. Jeff, whoever he is, never showed up at all. We were supposed to meet at eight. I sat at a table all by myself nursing a Diet Coke for over an hour. While I was waiting, Spencer Karr walked into the bar. He didn't notice me. It was just like high school. Or maybe not quite. Then he would've been high on weed. This time it looked like coke to me. He was really wired, talking fast to the bartender, putting on music, tossing back shots. He was starting to annoy the regulars.

"I'd texted Jeff to ask where he was, but he ghosted me. I finally gave up hope and went to the bar to get a beer to drown my sorrows. When I turned around, Spencer was right behind me. We bumped into each other, and beer went all over both of us."

"So that was your 'meet cute' moment? Spencer looked in your eyes and asked you where you'd been all his life, and then you two went off for a magical night together, and so he couldn't have killed Rob. Is that what you're telling me?"

I heard the snark in my voice, which wasn't fair to Jen, but I was grappling with the toppling of my last, best theory of the crime.

"No, it isn't. Let me finish. Also, I told you don't judge me, and you are sounding very judgy right now. It's not my fault the facts don't fit your theory."

"Sorry. Go ahead."

"I did look into Spencer's eyes. They were bloodshot and his pupils were dilated, so he looked kind of dazed. He had a smidge of white powder on his nose, too. He started apologizing for spilling the beer and grabbing napkins to wipe off my shirt. He ordered another beer for me, and one for himself. Then he took them over to my table without even asking me."

"That sounds like Spencer."

"The not asking part does, but the actually noticing me and apologizing part definitely doesn't. Spencer never talked to me in high school, except when he used to call me the DUFF. You know, the Designated Ugly Fat Friend."

"He called you that? What a rotten, untrue thing to say. Why didn't you tell me?"

I felt much angrier at the idea that Spencer had called Jennifer such a hurtful thing than I did at the idea that he had shot and killed Rob Porter.

"Because I didn't want you to make a big thing about it. It didn't bother me. Well, it did a little. But when I told John, he said he liked my curves and just forget about what Spencer said."

"That was it? John didn't say anything to Spencer?"

"He was trying to get the Women's Club scholarship for college. Spencer's mother was in charge of the committee reviewing applications. John didn't want to do anything that would make her mad. I understood. But Coop overheard Spencer call me that one day. He had a talk with him. Spencer stopped doing it."

"I still can't believe you didn't tell me. Or that Coop didn't."

"I made him promise. Anyway, do you want to hear the rest of the story?"

"Yes."

"So, we were back at the table, and Spencer kept telling me how great looking I was, and asking me to dance, and saying how he didn't know why he never asked me out in high school, stuff like that. I said, 'If I'm so gorgeous, why did you call me Leah's DUFF in high school?' He told me he was just a punk kid then. Now he was a man and he'd make it up to me, if I came home with him."

"And you did? You spent the night with him?"

"Yes, but not like you're thinking. He was wasted. I knew he shouldn't be driving. And he was near crashing. I've worked at the sheriff's office long enough to know the look. I said I'd go home with him, but he had to let me drive, because if he got stopped in the condition he was in, he could be in real trouble. He laughed and said he couldn't be in much worse trouble than he already was. But he gave me his keys."

"I would have left him at the bar."

"I couldn't. If he got in his car, he could kill someone. On the way to his place, he was coming down hard. He just sat in the passenger seat, kind of rocking back and forth. When we got to the house, I had to help him get to the front door. He was too shaky to get his key into the lock, so I took his key ring from him and opened the door. I told him to sit down, and I got him some water. When he drank it, he started choking and coughing and didn't get much down.

"He collapsed on his couch then, and he fell asleep pretty fast. But he was kind of snoring and snorting. I didn't dare leave. I was afraid he might throw up in his sleep and then he could asphyxiate."

"Yes. That would be so sad. So, when did you leave, Nurse Pilarski?"

"I stayed until he woke up around 6:30. He looked at me weird and I knew he couldn't figure out what I was doing there. I told him that I drove him home from the bar because between the coke and the shots of whiskey, he was out of it. He was kind of dazed and he didn't say much. He got up and went into the bathroom. I heard the shower go on, so I wrote him a note saying I was taking his SUV to the tavern to get my car. Then I left."

52

I reached for my wine and took a drink. I was dumbfounded. I had been so sure that not only was I going to save Erin without outing her secret lover, but I was also going to be the avenging angel who made Spencer pay for his crimes and shut down *GO News*. Cole had played me again. He suckered me into believing him.

"When I was trying to tell my story, my epic story, you couldn't stop interrupting me. Now that I'm finished, you've got nothing to say? Are you mad at me, or what?" Jen asked.

"I'm mad at myself, not you. I never should have believed Cole. He knew I wouldn't be able to resist dirt on Spencer. I set right to work building on what he told me. And you just collapsed my house of cards. That's on me for not laying a stronger foundation."

"I'm sorry, Leah. When I said I had an epic story to tell you, I thought it was going to be just strange and funny—you know, me and Spencer, and Spencer so high he didn't know which way was up. I didn't know it was going to be important. If I'd taken the time to tell you before I left, or called you while I was away, you would've known what Cole said wasn't true."

"It's my fault, not yours. I always jump too fast. Especially when I have a vested interest in being right—like I wanted to be about Spencer."

"Why did Cole lie to you?"

"I don't know. Maybe my Harley-had-a-hitman theory is right, but it was someone in the family who did it, and Cole was deflecting. Maybe it was even him. Or it could be Cole just enjoys pulling my strings and watching me do a little dance step with every tug of an appealing lie. I have no idea who did it."

"Maybe it really was Erin?"

She asked the question tentatively, as though she expected me to snarl at her.

Instead, I shrugged in defeat.

"Maybe it was, Jen. What the hell do I know?"

"You know a lot. Don't get so down on yourself. Let it go for now. We have a whole other bottle of wine to drink. You can tell me all the romantic details about you and Coop. Like what did he say to you? What did you say to him? After that, I'll tell you some of the truly bizarre things guys put on their dating profiles. And then we can just talk about people and say mean things about the ones we don't like."

"As long as we don't talk about Spencer, or Erin, or Rob Porter's murder, I'm in."

I held out my glass and she filled it and then her own. We repeated that process enough times that Jennifer wound up sleeping on my couch, and I had absolutely no trouble falling asleep when I dropped into bed.

"You're awfully quiet," Coop said on Sunday afternoon as we drove out to look at the property he was interested in. "Is that because you have a hangover after your girls' night with Jen?"

"We took down two bottles of wine between us—and I'm not lying when I say Jen was ahead of me the whole time. But I don't feel too bad. I'm just a little fuzzy, that's all."

"You had fun then?"

"We did, as soon as we stopped talking about who killed Rob."

He looked at me and raised an eyebrow as he turned off the paved road and onto a narrow track.

"It sounds like there's a story there."

"Oh, there is. I'll tell you while we walk the property," I said.

When we reached the end of the track, we parked next to a small cabin with broken windows, a sagging roof, a falling-down chimney, and a slight list to the right.

"What do you think?"

"Is it just as bad on the inside?"

"A little worse."

"Then I'd say you and your dad will be able to spend a lot of quality time together working on it."

"Yeah, that's what he said. He suggested we tear it down and start from scratch."

"Are you up for a tear-down and a new build? That's a lot of work."

"I'm not sure. Maybe. Come on, I'll show you the creek."

It was the perfect day to walk in the woods. Warm weather, bright sunlight, and just enough breeze to keep the bugs at bay. It wasn't long before we came to a fast-moving stream that created its own tiny rapids as it ran over and jumped down rocks in its path. Coop took a seat on a downed tree, and I sat next to him.

"Close your eyes and just listen," he said.

I did as he asked. After a minute, I said, "I don't hear anything except birds, squirrels, and water. What am I listening for?"

"That's it. No traffic, no sirens, no lawn mowers or leaf blowers. And no neighbors having a backyard barbecue where Uncle Arnie gets drunk and starts singing barbershop harmonies by himself."

"Come on, Coop. There's lots of quiet in town. I never hear lawn mowers or leaf blowers, or anyone's Uncle Arnie either, for that matter."

"That's because you live above it all in your tower."

I smiled thinking of Jennifer's comment the night before.

"What?"

"Jennifer told me last night that I live in a fairy tale tower and now I have a fairy tale prince. She meant you, by the way."

"Hardly," he said.

"That's what I told her."

"You did? I was just being modest. So, are you saying I'm not a prince?"

"No. If I were a fairy tale princess, I'd definitely pick you as my fairy tale prince. But neither of us live in fairy tale land. I will, however, grant you the title of Prince Among Men. How come you never told me what you did for Jennifer in high school?"

"What are you talking about?"

"Taking care of Spencer when you found out he was tormenting her by calling her the DUFF."

"She wasn't supposed to tell that story."

"The wine made her do it."

I felt a rush of affection for him and leaned over to kiss him.

"That was nice. But what was it for?" he said.

"Because you're a good person, and because I'm happy we're together, and I want you to know that. Because when I think about Jennifer and John, and Erin and her secret love, and my mother and my father, I realize it's not that easy to find the person you should be with. And even when you do, there's no telling how long it will last."

"I have a more optimistic spin. I think we'll last a very long time."

"Aunt Nancy told Mom that the stars are in alignment for us, or some astrology thing like that. I hope it's true. Let's not jinx it by talking about it. But there's something else I need to talk about. Rob Porter's murder."

"We've covered that already, haven't we? You don't think Erin did it. I think the investigation shows that she did. Erin confessing seems to give me the edge in that argument, you don't agree. Isn't that about it?"

"No. I'm starting to think you may be right after what Jennifer told me last night."

"Jen? What does she know about it?"

I launched into my tale of elation, triumph, and ultimate dejection, starting with Cole's fake news about Spencer and ending with Jennifer's unassailable alibi for him.

"I guess you were right, and so was Owen Fike, and so was Gabe when he told me to give it up. I know I don't always get to the truth of things in a straight line. Well, actually, I never do. But I'm not usually quite this wrong. I feel like I did way more harm than good this time around."

"Why do you say that? You believed in Erin. And you turned up some reasonable suspects. Owen didn't find out about Bethany and Shane, you did. He didn't know about Rob's history of domestic violence, either."

"Yeah, but those things turned out not to matter as far as who killed Rob. In fact, they took me in the wrong direction. I also managed to alienate Gabe along the way and did nothing to help Erin. This whole thing is definitely a big, fat fail for me."

"I disagree. Good investigating is always about turning over all the rocks. You did a good job because you looked at the whole picture. Owen missed some things that turned out not to matter, but they could have. Your process was better than his in this case."

"Isn't that sort of like that old joke? You know, where the doctor says, 'The operation was a success, but the patient died?' I did a whiz bang job of lifting up every stone, but I still didn't find the answer. Owen did."

"It's always better when the patient lives—or the right person is arrested. I'm just saying that Owen did a competent job, but you did a more thorough one. Part of the problem was that Cole's story was pretty plausible, so you went with it. You just forgot that you can't count on him."

"I didn't forget, really. I just wanted too bad for it to be Spencer."

"What are you going to do about Spencer now?"

"What do you mean?"

"Well, now you know that he has a coke habit, and that *GO News* is hanging on by a thread. Is the *Times* going to report that out? It's newsworthy, right?"

"Yes, it is. Maggie has Miguel digging in, but Spencer hasn't been charged with a crime and his business is still functioning. The *Times* will proceed with caution. I think Paul should get a heads up about Spencer's drug problem, though. From the story Jennifer told, I don't think Spencer is going to be able to hold it together much longer. He's going to wind up in trouble with the law, or with Harley, and either way it won't be good."

"I think you're right."

"Are you saying that because you know that Spencer's going to get caught up in the drug sweep along with Harley and his friends?"

"Leah, one of the things I love best about you is that you don't give up. Even though sometimes I wish you would. I'm not going to tell you anything about any drug investigation that may or may not be happening."

"Come on, Coop. You've just been super nice to me, and I feel a lot better. Don't you want to go the whole nine yards and restore me to my normal state of exuberant happiness? Just give me a little something on the investigation."

He shook his head, but then he said, "I'll go this far, and this is off the record. Yes, there is a multi-county drug investigation. It's coming to a head soon. You might want to have Troy or Miguel check in regularly if they want to be the first with the news."

"How regularly, daily, semi-daily, hourly?"

"Daily will be sufficient."

53

Later, back at Coop's, I texted Miguel while Coop pan-fried some trout a friend of his dad's had sent home with him.

"It's not Spencer. He was with Jennifer when Rob was killed."

"With Jennifer??!! I want to hear that story."

"Later. I'm at Coop's. Just wanted you to know."

"All set," Coop called from the kitchen. He had fried some potatoes to go with the fish and he set a grocery store container of coleslaw on the table.

"This looks great. You know, if you ever decide to give up law enforcement, I'd be willing to hire you as my personal chef. Though you'd have to take some lessons from my mom, so that you're up on all my favorites."

"I'll keep that in mind. So, what have you got going for the week?"

I pulled out my chair and sat down as I answered.

"Well, first off will be a visit to Cole Granger. I'm not going to let him get away with lying to me."

"I don't think you're going to get an apology from him, if that's what you're looking for."

"Oh, I know that. But I want the personal satisfaction of discussing it with him at maximum volume. I don't understand what his game is this time. Why did he tell me part of the truth—that Spencer has an addiction problem, and Harley is his dealer—and then lie his head off with the story that Spencer killed Rob?"

He shrugged and shook his head. "Cole's primary motivation in life is looking out for himself. I don't know why that involved lying to you about Spencer."

"How could I have been so stupid? Where was my head? Can you see Spencer doing anything as risky as confronting and killing Rob Porter? He likes to work behind the scenes, needle people, stab them in the back, stealth destroy their reputations. But a full-on frontal shooting in the chest while the person is looking right at you? No. He's too much of a coward for that."

"I agree. But you might have trouble finding Cole to ask him."

"Because of the drug bust going down this week?"

"Cole's pretty good at making himself scarce when consequences are being handed out. But you know what, let's declare a moratorium for the rest of the night on talking about investigations—yours or mine. How's the book coming?"

"I spent some productive hours on it yesterday before Jennifer and I got together. But I keep changing my mind about where the plot is going as I'm writing. Did you know there are two general schools of fiction writing—plotting and pantsing?"

"I've heard the terms. Pantsers write by the seat of their pants, right? And plotters use an outline."

"Yep. I'm a definite 'pantser.' I tried working with an outline, but I just can't stick to one."

"Somehow that doesn't surprise me."

"I'm thinking of taking a research trip to the Upper Peninsula. Do you want to come?"

"To the U.P.? Sure, if I can. When?"

"I'm not sure yet, but it will only be for a few days, maybe over a long weekend."

"Just give me enough notice to make sure things are squared away at work, and we'll do it. It'll be our first stay-away trip together," Coop said.

"Well, not really," I reminded him. "Don't you remember that camping trip we went on in high school?"

"I try to keep that deeply buried in my unconscious."

"Hey, how was I supposed to know that bears like donuts?"

"Okay, let's not get into that discussion again. I assume camping is a no this time?"

"You got that right," I said, standing to start clearing away the dishes. Coop joined me and we performed the familiar to and fro dance in his small kitchen. While we were loading the dishwasher, he started a different conversation.

"So, you didn't really say. What do you think of the property? Don't fixate on the cabin, there's a lot Dad and I can do with that. I mean the setting—the woods, the stream, the whole country life thing."

"Well, you're right, it's a beautiful spot. And the stream is big enough for you to fish for brooksies, right?"

"It's brookies. Brook trout. Yes, that's one of the attractions."

"And the woods are nice. I'm sure you'll like chopping wood and hunting coyotes and all that Daniel Boone stuff. As for me, I'm a townie through and through. I like the coffee shop across the street, the paper right downstairs, and more than anything I like my penthouse high atop Himmel's tallest building. Granted, it's only three stories, but on the plus side, if there's ever a fire, the ladder will reach high enough to rescue me. But it doesn't matter what I think. If it's what you want, go for it."

"It matters what you think. We're together, right? I care about your opinion."

"Well, sure, I care about yours, too. But we're in love, Coop, we're not joined at the hip. You do your thing, don't worry about if I like it or not. I'm sure I'll adjust to not having you only a few minutes away."

He started to say something, but his phone rang. He stepped into the living room to talk. When he came back, he said, "I'm sorry, Leah. Something's come up at work. I have to go."

"Something drug-related? Are things coming to a head tonight?"

"No, not tonight."

"But something happened with the investigation, right?"

"You're welcome to stay if you want."

He went on as though I hadn't asked the question, so I knew I was right.

"I might be home in a couple of hours, but it could be longer. This isn't the evening I had planned. I bought a double chaise lounge for us to lie on at night and watch the stars this summer. There's a strawberry moon tonight. I intended for us to go in the backyard and see it come up."

"Coop! That sounds very Hallmark movie and uncharacteristically romantic of you. I'm giving you full points for having the idea, even though you can't stick around to make it happen. We have a lot of summer ahead. In fact, let's do it tomorrow. A strawberry moon lasts for three days."

"Sorry, I can't tomorrow. It's going to be a long day, probably a long night. But how about Tuesday?"

"Yeah, sure. So, it's *tomorrow* the raid is happening, right? Never mind. I won't pressure you. I won't even use my feminine wiles on you. But I will make sure Maggie knows to keep Troy and Miguel on alert status," I said, pulling him in closer for a kiss.

When we moved apart, he said, "Thanks for dialing back those feminine wiles of yours, or I might have decided to stay home, to hell with work."

"That's a very nice thing to say to me. You know, I'm really enjoying the boyfriend side of you. Keep up the good work. Stay in touch tomorrow if you can, okay? I know you're a superhero sheriff, but I'd feel better with an occasional check-in to make sure you're all right."

"If I can, I will. But I'm going to be out of the county for a lot of the day, and I don't know how much time I'll have. Don't worry if you don't hear from me. If I *were* involved in a major drug bust tomorrow—and don't take this as confirmation or denial that I am— I would make sure everything was covered, so everything goes down right."

"I know, but stuff happens."

"Now what do you want to do?" Miguel asked.

We were sitting on the sofa at my place, and I had just given him a detailed recitation of Spencer's night with Jennifer.

"At the moment, nothing."

"You're giving up on Erin? But you were so sure she didn't do it."

"I know I was. A part of me still is, but I don't have any more suspects.

Well, there is one but it's pretty far out there. I don't know if I could even muster the energy to try and investigate it."

"Who is it?"

"Hannah, Rob's first wife."

"That's why you asked her if she was in town when Rob was killed, isn't it? But you don't really think that, do you? Why would she kill Rob after so many years?"

"Maybe because he beat the bejesus out of her, caused her to miscarry, and scared her so bad she's been too afraid to come back for the last eight years? Hannah told us that she was here the night Rob was killed. And that she spent the night alone at the motel instead of at the hospital with her grandmother. She knows how to use a gun. She could have shot Rob, then zipped back to the motel for a good night's sleep after a job well done."

"No. Her grandmother was on her mind, not Rob. She has a happy life now. Why would she risk that? I'm sorry, I think you're wrong. I cannot agree."

"Oh, that's okay. No need to be sorry that you don't agree. I don't even agree with myself, Miguel. I'm just running scenarios and that's the only one I could come up with. But it's the kind of thing that only happens in detective novels—usually not very good ones. I don't really think Hannah killed Rob. I'm feeling like I don't know much of anything."

"But you can find out. I know you can."

"I appreciate your faith in me, but it doesn't seem very warranted at the moment."

"What are you going to do about Cole lying to you?"

"I'm thinking about killing him, but I'm not sure how yet. If the drug bust wasn't coming down so soon, I'd rat him out to Harley and let him take care of it. But I don't want to do anything that could mess up the investigation. For now, I guess I'll content myself with writing 'Do Not Trust Cole Granger Under Any Circumstances' 500 times on the blackboard of my mind."

"What did Coop say?"

"That reminds me. It looks like tomorrow might be the day when the walls come tumbling down on Harley. I have some deep background cryptic information from an unnamed source that indicates it, anyway. So be sure you and Troy stay in touch with your sources."

"The drug bust? Oh, we'll be all over that. But I have something else to ask you. Is it true that Coop is buying a house in the country? If you're moving, I would love to rent this place from Miller when you leave."

"Where did you hear—wait, let me guess. A stylist at Making Waves heard it from a client, who heard it from her realtor, right?"

"Something like that. It's true, though?"

"He's looking, I'm not sure he's buying. And I'm definitely not moving. Why would I?"

"Because you are in love. Because people in love like to live together."

"Not these people in love."

"But why wouldn't you?"

"You know how I feel about my place. You can covet it, but you can't have it. Coop and I have never even talked about moving in together. We both like our own space."

"Both, or just you?"

"Both," I said firmly, speaking for Coop without ever having had a conversation about it with him. "If he buys a place, it'll be his. This is mine, and I'm not thinking about giving it up, so put that idea out of your head."

"Okay, okay. I was just asking."

54

I called it a night after Miguel left, but I had trouble sleeping. From my bedroom window I can see part of the night sky. I wished that Coop and I had been able to lie in his backyard as he had planned and watch the strawberry moon rise.

Then my thoughts turned to the conversation Miguel and I had about Coop's possible move.

Coop and I had been together for a few months, and we've known each other forever. It wasn't that odd for Miguel to think we'd be moving in together. But in truth, it had never crossed my mind.

Yes, I feel very at home at Coop's. And I think he does at my place, too. That doesn't mean I want to give up my space to move into his, or vice versa. For one thing, my loft is just perfect for one person. It works fine for the occasional overnight guest, but it's too small for two people to live comfortably in. Especially when one of the people is very expansive in her ideas of tidiness and organization, and the other has much stricter parameters.

The fact that Coop had started looking for a place but hadn't said anything about it to me first seemed to say he had similar feelings about maintaining his own space. Even when we were walking the property, the subject hadn't come up. And I didn't want it to. I've had enough changes in my life in the recent past. I'm not ready for any more.

I hadn't thought deeply about it, but I sort of assumed Coop and I would continue the way my mother and Paul did—together, but in our own spaces. It seemed both sensible and safer to me. I've seen a lot of couples split up after they started living together. Why mess with something that was working so well for Coop and me?

Sure, it was nice sometimes to wake up in the night and feel Coop's warmth beside me. Yes, it was pleasant to have a fun day together and know that we'd be spending the night together, too. Or to decide on impulse to stay at his house, or him at my place, because that was just how the evening flowed. But it was also nice, and fun, and important to me to have a place that was just my own. A space where I had control over who came and went, how things were done, whether or not I left the kitchen light on all night, or picked up my towels, or chose to sit in absolute silence and do nothing.

For me, the way things were between Coop and me was close to perfect on the emotional front. I felt safe, I felt loved, and I still felt like I was me. Why complicate things by moving in together? Why give more scope for tiny irritations to grow into big sore spots? Why risk the delicate balance of give and take, togetherness and independence, freedom and responsibility that we had by giving up the independence of our own spaces?

I was overcome by a yawn then, and I knew it was my body's way of telling me to stop thinking about it. The time had come to lie back and rest in the comfort of the Nash family rule for dealing with all emotionally fraught issues. Namely, a problem ignored is a problem solved. I thus fell into a deep and untroubled sleep, as Nashes before me had done for generations.

The call came mid-afternoon on Monday. I had just completed a satisfying chunk of writing and felt like I was really getting to know my lead character Jo Burke, a detective in a sheriff's office in Michigan's Upper Peninsula. I had managed to keep her moving in the direction I wanted the story to go and had the hubris to think that I was getting the hang of fiction writing. I credited it to a copious amount of caffeine and the determination to stay in my fictional world—and at my laptop—until I got something substantial done.

When my phone rang, I looked at the caller ID. Cole Granger. I'd just been deciding whether or not to reward myself by calling that manipulative weasel.

"Hello, Cole. I was just thinking about you."

"No time for romance this mornin', Leah. I'm callin' to warn you."

"About what?"

"Harley knows you and me was talkin' the other day. My sister Tabitha told him she saw you leavin'. I told you she don't like you. She don't like me much either, I guess, to put me in harm's way with Harley."

"And so?"

"And so he wasn't too happy about me talkin' to the sheriff's girl. I covered for you. I told him me and you was just havin' a quickie in the back, but I'm not sure he believed me. I'm just sayin' you might be gettin' a personal visit from him to corroborate. It'd be safest to admit to him that you can't stay away from me. Otherwise, he might think you and me was cookin' up something to his disadvantage."

"Cole, shut up. I don't care what your sister saw, or what you say Harley might do, or really about anything that comes out of your mouth. You lied to me about Spencer."

Okay, so much for care and caution. But once I started, I couldn't stop myself.

"Why did you lie? What was the point? Were you hoping I'd tell Coop and he'd make a fool of himself going after Spencer for killing Rob? Did you and Harley have a plan to punish Spencer by putting him in the middle of a murder investigation? What in the actual hell was the purpose of all that BS you gave me? Or don't you need a purpose? You just lie for fun?"

"Whoa, slow down there. What are you sayin'? Spencer didn't kill Rob Porter? What are you talking about? How do you know that?"

"I know it because he spent the entire night that Rob was killed with a friend of mine. He was high as hell on coke and whiskey at the Tenney Road Tavern from eight o'clock on that night. Until my friend drove him home and stayed with him the rest of the night to make sure he didn't vomit himself to death in his sleep."

"Hold on, hold on. You are 100 percent that Spencer didn't do the killing like he told Harley he did?"

"Cole, it's over. Don't act like you didn't make the whole thing up. Unlike you, my source is impeccable. I have no doubt that at least a few regulars at the TRT can confirm it, along with the fact that Spencer was in no shape to kill anybody. He could barely walk on his own. So you can take your warnings, and your inside information, and your fake tips, and shove them right—"

"You ain't seein' the picture, Leah. I was not lyin' to you. Oh, man, I wouldn't wanta be Spence when Harley finds out. I think you just got me out of a jam. When I tell Harley this, he's gonna forget all about bein' mad at me. I gotta go. But, a word of advice, keep your head down. When Harley gets mad, he's like a bull in a china shop. He's gonna be chargin' around in all directions knockin' things over and breakin' them. Be a shame if one of those broken things was you."

"Cole—"

But he was gone.

My first instinct was to call Coop and tell him about the conversation, but he'd said that he wouldn't be reachable for most of the day. And, really, what was he going to do about it? He had more pressing things on his mind at the moment. And, if all went well, Harley would no longer be a problem for anyone after today.

55

I tried to go back to work after talking to Cole, but instead I kept recalibrating my thinking about Cole lying to me. He hadn't been defensive. He hadn't made up a new lie to counter the truth I was telling him about Spencer. Instead, he had seemed genuinely and massively surprised to hear that Spencer didn't kill Rob. And why would he have called me at all if he'd just been setting me up with the Spencer story? One thing Cole wasn't lying about was Harley's temper. As Coop had warned me earlier, Harley was a mean kid in high school. Now he was a dangerous man.

It dawned on me then what I had done by telling Cole that Spencer had lied about killing Harley. Cole would take it right to Harley as a way of insulating and ingratiating himself. If Harley was having doubts about Cole's loyalty, he could make them go away by ratting out Spencer. A tiny part of me—no seriously, it was a very small part—said, *So what? Spencer did it to himself. Let him live—or die—with the situation.*

The rest of me said, *Holy hell, Harley's going to come after Spencer and fast.*

I didn't want to do it, but due to my mother's unflagging efforts to civilize me, I called Spencer's cell phone. He didn't pick up. I left a message. Then I texted him with an urgent message to call me. Then I called him again. Then I tried the front desk at *GO News*.

"Mr. Karr is on another line," the woman who answered the phone said. "I can put you through to leave a voicemail for him if you like."

"No, I need to talk to him. Could you break into his call? Or take a note to him that this is Leah Nash and I have urgent information for him?"

"No, I'm sorry. I couldn't do that. Thank you and have a good day." She spoke with the rote, soulless voice of someone doing a job that entails minimum wage and occasional verbal abuse.

I tried Spencer's phone again, and he ignored me again. I put my shoes on and headed for my car.

I hadn't visited the *GO News* offices in months. It's not a place I have much desire or need to go to. A silver-haired woman with the frustrated air of an ill-trained temp was at the front desk talking on the phone as I approached. She held up her index finger to indicate she saw me, but I'd need to wait. When she hung up after assuring the caller that Mr. Karr was unavailable, she looked up, but without the usual practiced smile of a well-trained receptionist.

"Yes?"

"Hi. I called a few minutes ago. I'm Leah Nash, and I really need to talk to Spencer. I'm sure you have orders not to disturb him, but this is very important."

"Mr. Karr has left for the day."

"Really? Because I can see his red SUV parked right out front."

"I wouldn't know about that. I'm just the temp here."

"I can appreciate that you were told not to put calls through or let visitors in, but I know Spencer is here, and this is urgent!"

I didn't give her time to repeat her refusal. Instead, I scooted around her desk and down the hall toward Spencer's office. His door was closed and when I knocked sharply, it brought one of the sales staff out from the back.

"He just left, Leah," she said.

"Do you know where he went, Lena?"

"No. He never says. And when it's this time of day, he usually doesn't come back."

"Okay, thanks."

I ran back to the reception area in time to see Spencer pulling out of his parking spot. I sprinted out the door and to my car. As I buckled my seatbelt, I saw him stopped at the light at the end of the block. His left blinker was on. When I got to the corner and turned myself, he was a block ahead of me, with several cars between us.

He was driving fast, and they were not. I tailgated the car in front of me, causing the driver to justifiably flip me off as she turned at the next street. Now there were only two cars between us, and one more stoplight on the route out of town that Spencer was obviously taking. If luck held, I'd be able to catch up with him. Of course, it did not.

He sped through as the light turned from yellow to red, and I was trapped behind a minivan and a pickup. Both were making left turns. By the time I got to the front of the line, the light had changed again. I peered down the road in front of me, and I could just make out Spencer driving toward the city limits. By the time the light turned green, he was out of sight.

I kept driving straight ahead, because I was pretty sure that I knew where he was going. Cole would have reached Harley with the story of Spencer's lie. Even if Harley was expecting a big delivery day from Milwaukee, he'd be too furious to just let that ride. My guess was that upon hearing the news from Cole, Harley had ordered Spencer to meet him at the sugar shack. Given the hold Harley had on him, Spencer would have hopped to it.

I sped up as I left town, trying to catch up with him. But my Ford crossover wasn't a match for the power of Spencer's Lexus SUV. He left me in the dust, literally. He got so far ahead of me that I couldn't see when or if he turned off at Sayer Road, which would take him to the Granger property.

I gambled and took the turn in time to see Spencer's SUV way down the road, almost to the turnoff that led to the Grangers' sugar shack. I slowed down for a minute to think. When Miguel and I had "visited" Harley, the gate into the property had been locked. Presumably Harley would have unlocked it for Spencer, but I couldn't exactly drive up to the front door of the shack, even if Harley hadn't relocked it. I wasn't sure exactly what I planned to do, but I knew it had to be done with stealth.

Instead of driving down the road, I turned into the parking lot where people leave their cars when they don't want to ride the whole length of the trail. Mine was the only one there when I parked. I grabbed my phone and set off down the trail at a run, heading for the break in the tree line that separated the trail from Granger land. When I burst through the other side, I stopped to assess the situation.

Harley's monster pickup truck was parked next to the shack. Spencer's vehicle was right next to it.

Now what?

I couldn't very well burst through the door and save Spencer from Harley with my rapier-like wit. Even though I'm fairly skilled at cutting remarks, I couldn't see that as an effective weapon with which to rescue Spencer. And there was the off chance that Spencer didn't need rescuing. I assumed Harley was intent on doing him harm, but without checking what was going on inside the shack, I didn't know for certain. I couldn't call 911 for emergency assistance when there might be no emergency. And I definitely couldn't call Coop for assistance when he was in the middle of executing a long-planned drug bust.

I hadn't formulated a plan when I jumped in my Ford and took off after Spencer, and now there was no time for planning. I needed to act.

56

I had to get up to the shack and see what was going on inside. That would determine what steps came next. I didn't like that it was broad daylight instead of the nearly dusk conditions of my first visit. It would be harder to hide. However, it was also easier to plot my path because I was able to see my surroundings better.

Tall grass and weeds in the open area had proliferated nicely in the weeks since Miguel and I had been there, as had the dappled willow on the side of the shack. There was also a downed tree in the field, and a cluster of small pines I could use for cover as I made my way to the building.

I darted forward like an action hero in a sniper scene and reached the building without incident. I could hear Harley's voice but couldn't make out what he was saying. There wasn't a sound from Spencer. I raised my head slowly, just high enough to peer through the dirty glass. Harley towered over Spencer, who was seated in a chair. His arms were tied to the back of it, and his legs to the chair legs. His head was bowed, and I could see what looked like a thin trail of blood running down his neck.

Harley lifted Spencer's head by the hair and whacked him so hard across the face that I instinctively recoiled myself. Spencer howled in pain —that came through loud and clear—and then his head dropped again. Help was obviously needed. If I called 911, deputies would come out with sirens blazing, Spencer would be saved, and Harley would be arrested. But it would be for something unrelated to the much bigger drug charges he was on the verge of going down for. With one phone call, I could ruin months of work. However, if I didn't call, Spencer could easily wind up dead.

Lucky for me and my immortal soul, I didn't have to make that choice. Before I could, Harley growled something at Spencer, hit him once more, and turned to leave.

I ducked down and made myself as small as my sturdy frame allowed, while mentally reconsidering my lack of interest in yoga. I stayed in that crouched position until the sound of Harley's truck faded away. Then I stood and scurried to the door.

When I stepped inside, Spencer's head was hanging down. He didn't look up, but I could see that he was breathing from the rise and fall of his chest. So far, so good, Harley hadn't killed him. Yet.

"Spencer?"

No answer.

A half-empty bottle of water sat on the table. I unscrewed the cap, stepped in closer, and tossed it in his face. Immediately he sputtered to life. Despite his dire situation, his first words were true to form. No "thank God!" no "I'm so glad to see you!"

"Why the hell did you do that? Untie me!"

"Hey, how are you? I was just taking a drive and thought I'd stop to see if you were dead yet. Since it's all good, I'll be on my way," I said, half-turning toward the door.

"Stop trying to be funny and get me out of here. Harley is going to kill me."

"Yes. I thought he might."

"What are you doing here?" he asked belatedly.

"Saving your life, I'd say. I wouldn't need to be here, and we both wouldn't need to be in danger if you had picked up your phone when I called about a hundred times, asshat! I was trying to tell you that Harley knows you lied. That you didn't kill Rob Porter, you faked it!"

He stared at me but didn't say anything.

"Are you still groggy? Or are you coming down from your most recent coke high and you're too messed up to take it in? I can throw some more water on you."

I made as if to do it.

"How do you know—wait, your fat friend Jennifer told you, didn't she? I don't care what you think you know, but Harley is coming back. If you don't untie me and we don't get out of here, we're both going to be in trouble!"

I almost did a Harley and smacked Spencer myself at the Jennifer comment.

"You win. Though there really wasn't any contest. You're the most detestable human being on earth. Jennifer stayed with you because she felt *sorry* for you. She didn't want you to asphyxiate on your own vomit. I'm not as compassionate as she is. So, see ya!"

This time, I walked all the way to the door.

"No, wait! You have to untie me! Don't you get it? Harley's going to kill me."

"I don't have to do anything," I said with a greater degree of calm than I felt. I was starting to get a little anxious about a possible return pop-in from Harley myself. But I wanted Spencer to believe that I'd abandon him. I had to push him hard enough to make him come clean about his relationship with Harley, drugs, and Rob.

"You won't leave me. You can't."

"Convince me."

"What do you want?"

"I want to know everything about your involvement with Harley, and the plan to kill Rob Porter."

"That's why he's going to kill me! Because I didn't kill Rob."

"Okay, now we're getting somewhere."

"Untie me and I'll tell you the rest."

"Let me think about that for a nanosecond. No. If you want out of those ropes, you've got some 'splainin to do, Lucy."

I worked hard not to show I was as worried about Harley's return as he was. If Spencer didn't confess now, he never would. I pulled out my phone, put it on record, then set it on the table in front of me.

"Start talking. We can skip the deep background. I know about Chicago, and rehab, and that you started in again with Harley as your local supplier.

Why don't you take it from the top of Act II, where you get caught by Rob with baggies full of cocaine."

"Do you promise to get me out of here?"

"If I'm satisfied with what you've got to say, yes. Start talking and we'll see."

57

Once Spencer started, he didn't need any prompts to keep going. His story matched Cole's, including him running into Rob when he had a big bunch of cocaine in his car and had already taken a considerable amount up his nose.

"So, you offered to kill Rob so Harley wouldn't kill you for being the dumbass that you are. Why didn't you do it?"

"I tried to. I knew Rob was going to be at his property that night. I went there earlier in the day to check it out. I had a gun I bought a while ago from a guy I know who doesn't keep records."

"You meet a lot of nice people in Cocaine World, I suppose."

He ignored me.

"But when it came time to do it, I just couldn't, not even jacked up on coke. I couldn't make myself go out there and shoot him. I went to the Trent Road Tavern to have a few drinks and do a few more lines to get myself in the right frame to do it. But I kept drinking and snorting lines until I ran into the DU—into Jennifer. I don't remember too much about it. She drove me home. I had to call my mother the next day to drive me back to the TRT to pick up my Lexus."

"You must have been doing some mad scrambling to think of an excuse you could give Harley for not killing Rob," I said.

"I was sweating it, yes. I turned my phone off so he couldn't reach me to see what had happened. But my mother likes to listen to the local radio station while she drives. When the news report came on, it led with the story that Rob was dead. I called *GO News* for more details. Andrea told me that Rob had been murdered and a source told her he'd been shot. I couldn't believe my luck!"

"Well, you know what they say, it's better to be born lucky than smart. And you sure didn't come wired with any smarts."

Spencer ignored my comment.

"I turned my phone back on and called Harley. He congratulated me. I felt pretty good. Later, when Erin Harper was arrested, he was really impressed. He thought I'd done something to throw suspicion on her as a way to take down two cops at once. I didn't tell him any different. I thought that would be the end of it. I'd paid my debt for getting caught by Rob. Only Harley found out I lied about killing Rob, apparently thanks to you. He is not going to let me go this time, no matter what I say. The only reason he didn't kill me just now is that he's got some big deal going down today. He had to check on something, but he's coming back. There. I told you every-thing, now untie me!"

"Give me a minute to think, Spence. Now, what should I do? I could stop recording and leave you here. It's not like you wouldn't do that in a heartbeat. And I could send someone back to check on you once I'm safe. Technically that meets my promise to get you out of here. I didn't promise when, or by whom your rescue would be carried out. Or I *could* risk life and limb by taking the time to untie you and get us both out of here. Hmm."

"Don't you get it? Harley told me he's going to make it look like I OD'd. He's coming back, he's gonna put me in my truck, drive it somewhere, and enjoy watching me die. When I'm found, it'll look like I shot up with a speedball and died accidentally."

"Well, that does sound pretty unpleasant. Though there's a little more finesse involved than I'd expect from Harley."

"Please! I have to get away. When I do, I'm not looking back. I'm leaving this stupid little town. Come on, Leah," he said, his voice changing from angry to wheedling. "Help me get out of here, and *GO News* goes away.

With me gone, you won't have any competition. It's the only way you're ever going to keep the *Times* alive."

"Aw, geez, Spence. I was just thinking maybe I should help out, and then you have to go and say something nasty like that. Well, thanks for the inside scoop on your downfall and imminent demise. I'll call someone to check on you later. Bye."

"Leah!"

The fear of abandonment was palpable in his voice.

"Do you want me to beg? All right, I'm begging you. Please don't leave me here."

Actual tears of fear were running down his cheeks, and unexpectedly, I felt sorry for him. I knelt down and began working at the knots that secured his feet together, and his legs to the chair.

"Hurry!"

"Sit still. I'm trying but Harley did a pretty serious job on these."

I finally picked the right end of the rope, and the knot began to loosen. When I'd freed his legs, I started to work on his arms. Either Harley had gotten careless, or I'd gotten the hang of things, because it didn't take long to free them from the chair.

"Okay, stand up. Let's go."

"You forgot my hands."

"No, I'm going to leave them tied behind your back. It will give me a little more control over the situation."

"I can't walk with my hands behind me. I don't have any balance!"

"I'm sure you can handle it. Or I can just leave you now. Have a good time trying to turn the doorknob with your hands tied behind your back. If a miracle happens and you get out, have even more fun driving with your hands tied."

"Okay, all right. Let's just go. You know, he'll kill you, too, if he comes back and finds you here."

"I'm aware. We'll take your SUV. It's bigger and faster. Are the keys in your pocket?"

"No, I left them in my Lexus."

"All right, let's go then," I said.

I helped Spencer into the passenger seat, then ran to the other side to get in. I slid into the driver's seat and reached for the key—which was not in the cupholder where I expected to find it.

Spencer was twisting around in his seat, leaning out the open window.

"Where's your secret hiding place for the key?" I asked, pulling down the visor but finding nothing.

"We have to go! We have to go now! Can't you hear it? Harley, he's coming back! Go! Go!"

I could hear it then, too, the revving, growling motor sound of Harley's pickup coming from a distance. I caught some of Spencer's nervous energy.

"I can't 'go, go!' because I can't find your flipping key! Where is it?"

"I left it on the dash. Harley must have taken it!"

The sound of the motor grew louder.

"Get out, now! Follow me!"

There was nothing for it but to make a dash across the field back to the bike trail and the parking lot where my car sat.

"Where? Where are we going to go? He's going to kill both of us now, thanks to you," Spencer shrieked.

"Go or stay. I'm going," I shouted as I jumped from the driver's seat and took off across the field toward the bike trail.

My heart was thumping loud from adrenalin and exertion. I was only about 10 feet from the break in the trees and brush that was our exit to the bike trail. I turned my head to look behind me. Spencer was a good 20 feet away. With his hands tied, he had trouble running. Beyond him, I saw Harley's truck pull up to the sugar shack.

"Hurry, man, he's getting out of the truck. He hasn't seen us yet, but he will!"

Spencer looked back, stumbled, and fell. Shit! I ran back and helped him to his feet.

"Get up. He's opening the door."

That was enough to motivate Spencer. I grabbed him by the arm and started running with him in tow. I heard a roar of rage. Harley had spotted us, but we were right at the trail. I lowered my head and led with my shoulder, heedless of the branches that tore at my shorts-clad legs and yanked pieces of hair from my head by the roots. In seconds we tumbled out on the paved bike trail. I heard the rumble of Harley's truck starting up again.

"This way! My car is in the lot. We've got a head start on him. We'll be at least a quarter mile away by the time he drives down the track and gets on the road to follow us."

That's when I realized the sound of Harley's engine wasn't receding as he drove down the track to the gravel road. It was getting louder as he drove straight across the field to catch us.

58

I pulled the key out of my pocket as we ran toward my car, clicking the button on the fob to open the doors. Spencer literally fell into the passenger's seat. I slid under the steering wheel, buckled myself and then him in before I started the engine. I threw the car in reverse and peeled out just as Harley's truck pushed through onto the bike trail.

"Go faster!" Spencer yelled.

"Shut up!" I shouted back as my Ford hit the loose gravel of the road and fishtailed. I righted it and looked in the rearview mirror as I pressed down on the accelerator. Harley's truck seemed to fill my whole back window. It felt like we were in that scene from *Jurassic Park*, with the T. rex barreling toward us.

If I went any faster, I'd lose control. If I didn't, Harley would ram me off the road anyway. I pushed down on the accelerator. Fishtailed again, straightened it again. The turn onto a blacktopped road was coming up. That meant more traffic, more witnesses, less chance for Harley to kill us. I stopped looking in the rearview mirror, grabbed the steering wheel tight, and floored the gas pedal.

Suddenly, there was a huge bump at the rear of the car. Harley's pickup. He began ramming us again and again, pushing me closer and closer to the edge of the road. I couldn't go any faster. We hit a pothole and my hands flew off the wheel. The car did a full 360 spinout. Harley hit us again.

This time, we went airborne, flying right over the ditch into a field. We landed with a thump and kept going. I fought to hold the steering wheel steady, but we hit a stump. The car bucked and we rolled over. Someone screamed. I don't know if it was Spencer or me.

Airbags went off, windows shattered, bits of glass and dust filled the air. I don't know how long it was before I realized that I was hanging upside down in my seatbelt. Spencer was, too. Where was Harley?

I started pulling at my seatbelt, but it wouldn't give. My body weight was pressing against the webbed fabric and forcing the belt to lock up. I tried pressing against the ceiling to take some of my weight off the belt and allow me to yank on it and loosen it. Spencer was motionless beside me.

"Spencer, are you okay?"

He didn't answer. I had to get out of there. I had to get help. I had to make sure Harley didn't come to finish us off.

I pulled desperately against the seatbelt, but it wouldn't budge. I heard the sound of shouting and footsteps running toward us. Harley!

I tried to reach the phone in my pocket, but the angle wasn't right, and I couldn't get to it. Suddenly, a hand reached through the window.

———

I shrank away, but when a man spoke, I realized it wasn't Harley.

"Hey, you all right? I saw that guy run you off the road. I called 911. Are you hurt?"

An older man with wire-rimmed glasses and a trim beard peered in at me with an anxious look on his face. I felt giddy with the wave of relief that rushed through me.

"No. I don't think so, anyway. But the man with me, he's unconscious. Can you get us out of here?"

"I can get you down, if you don't think there's anything broken. But I don't want to chance cutting him down in case there's something going on with him that could get worse if I move him."

"I'm all right," I said. I wasn't entirely sure that was true, but I felt more shaken than broken. Plus, I really didn't like hanging upside down.

"What's your name?" he asked as he opened the car door and leaned in to work on the seatbelt with his pocketknife.

"Leah Nash."

"I'm Walter Brewer, Leah. What in the world was that guy chasing you like that for?"

"It's a long story, Walter."

"I'll bet. I turned on Sayer Road and I saw him up ahead, bumping your car like he was trying to drive you into the ditch. Then when your car spun around and he came back at you, wow! I couldn't believe it when your little car flew up in the air and back down. I pulled over and called 911 right then. When I looked up again, you were here, flipped over, and the truck was tearing off."

"He must have seen you and gotten scared. Thanks, Walter. You might have just saved my life!"

"I don't know about that, but I'm mad at myself for not getting his license plate. I didn't even get a look at the driver. It was a Dodge Ram pickup, though. I know that much."

"It's all right, Walter. I know who it was."

He looked surprised. At least from my upside-down position he did, but before he could comment we both heard the wail of an ambulance in the distance, and then the sound of police and firetruck sirens.

"They'll be here in a minute. Now brace yourself because I'm just about to cut through this belt. You're going to drop fast. I don't want you to land on your head and crack it open after you survived a wreck like this."

As he made the final cut, the seatbelt gave way, and thanks to Walter, I had a fairly gentle landing. He helped me scramble out of the car. Spencer still hadn't moved, but I could see he was breathing.

The ambulance had pulled up and two EMTs came running over.

"I'm all right," I said. "But the man in the car, he's unconscious."

From that point on, the controlled chaos of an accident scene followed as EMTs and police did their jobs. Despite my protests, I was given an initial examination and ordered into the ambulance after they got Spencer in. I sat on the bench and made myself as small as I could while we sped to the hospital and the EMT monitored Spencer's vitals.

When we arrived, Spencer's stretcher was unloaded, and he was quickly wheeled inside and then whisked away by medical staff. I was taken to a small examination room to wait. Although it felt like it must be midnight at least, it was only seven o'clock.

I didn't call Coop because I didn't want to throw him off his game. I was sure that Harley would be keeping his drug delivery appointment, despite not managing to kill me and Spencer. He'd be more afraid of what his partners would do to him if he messed up on the drug distribution than he would be about a possible attempted murder charge. He could always deal with us later.

Instead, I called Jennifer.

"Leah! Hey, I was thinking of calling to see if you felt like having a beer at McClain's."

"Listen, Jen. I was just in a car accident and—"

"Oh my God! Are you okay? What happened?"

"Yes. I'm fine. I'm at the hospital getting checked out, but I'm fine. It's just a precaution. I don't know about Spencer, though. He—"

"Spencer was with you? What's going on? Why—"

"I promise, all will be revealed tomorrow. Right now, I just need a favor. I don't want to reach out to Coop when he's trying to hold up his end of the drug investigation he's working on. Yes, I know about it, but not the details. So you don't have to pretend it's not happening. Anyway, can you make sure word gets to him after everything breaks that I'm fine? I'll probably be at home by the time he's done anyway."

"Yeah, sure. But you're definitely all right?"

"Yes."

There was a knock on the examining room door and a nurse stepped in.

"I've got to go, Jen. The nurse just walked in. I'll talk to you later. Thanks."

59

I was sitting on the window seat, staring down at the empty street below and sipping slowly on a Jameson. I had fielded calls and visits from Miguel, Jennifer, my mother, and Maggie, and I was exhausted. I struggled to stay awake until Coop got there. Finally, a little after midnight the door opened. Coop was across the room in three strides, wrapping me in a hug.

"Leah, why didn't you call me?"

"Because I knew it was D-Day for your big drug bust. I wanted you to keep your head in the game. I'm fine. I've got the discharge papers to prove it. I'll be even finer, though, if you tell me you got Harley."

"We did. Things went off like clockwork. On the Milwaukee end, they rolled up the two leaders of the operation, as well as a nice assortment of lower-level traffickers and street-level dealers. Here we netted Harley and two other *Breaking Bad* wannabes at the level just below him, as well as a handful of assorted Grangers."

"Oh, that's great! I was afraid that me trying to rescue Spencer might have spooked Harley."

"About that. I've only got the barebones. Harley chased you and Spencer, ran you off the road, you got away with cuts and bruises, but Spencer's in the hospital with a concussion and a broken collarbone. How about filling in the blanks, starting with how you knew Spencer needed rescuing, and why you thought you were the one to do it."

I explained. When I finished, he was shaking his head.

"Don't say it. Remember, I just had a near death experience. I need comforting words and warm hugs, not yelling."

"I wasn't going to yell. I was going to say that I doubt Spencer would have done the same for you. You took a big chance trying to rescue him."

"I'm sure he wouldn't have. But you would, I would, anyone with a functioning conscience and a minimal sense of accountability would have. I'm the one who put Spencer in danger. I had to warn him. Also, I thought I was just going to warn him, not rescue him."

"I understand why you went to see Spencer at his office, but it was pretty crazy driving after him straight into the lion's den where Harley was waiting."

"That's not quite fair. I tried over and over to get Spencer on the phone, but he ignored me."

"And ignoring you is a cardinal sin. I think we all know."

"Hey, I'd like to make a motion for the return of boyfriend Coop, who has apparently been replaced in this conversation by your more judgy personality, best friend Coop."

"Sorry, lady, you've got them both. And when you do something that puts you in harm's way, I think the commonsense best friend side needs to be front and center, not the lovestruck boyfriend."

"I like the word lovestruck. It makes it sound like when you first saw me, you were hit in the head with the hammer of love."

"Now you sound like Miguel. Stop trying to get me off topic and explain to me how chasing down Harley wasn't taking a chance."

"I was chasing Spencer, not Harley. I didn't know where he was going when he took off. When I figured it out, I had to keep on because I thought a meeting between them had the potential of going very wrong."

"And you couldn't call me, or call Owen Fike?"

"And say what? That Spencer was going to the Grangers, and he *might* be meeting with Harley, and Harley *might* beat him up or worse? I didn't want to give you something else to think about when you were busy taking down Harley's would-be drug empire. Especially because it might have turned out to be nothing.

"And don't get me started on Owen. He is not my biggest fan. Now, if Ross weren't on vacation, I'd probably have called him. Things might not have escalated in quite the way they did. So, when you look at it that way, it's really Ross's fault for taking a vacation when I might need him. Let's just blame him and move on."

"I appreciate that you didn't want to jeopardize the work four agencies have put into the drug investigation, but I don't ever want you to think that anything is more important to me than you."

"Aw, hello, boyfriend, it's nice to see you back," I said, leaning over and giving him a kiss. "But I'm not some wimpy, simpy girlfriend who needs to be rescued by her big, strong boyfriend. Besides, I waited until Harley left. How could I know he'd come back so soon? But all's well that ends well, right? I'm thinking of having that chiseled on my headstone one day."

"You're incorrigible."

"But cute, right? And smart, and funny, and crazy in love with you, so really, you're coming out ahead on this relationship deal, aren't you?"

"I'd have to say yes," he said, smiling and pulling me closer.

"Thank you for that—but watch the ribs. I'm a little sore there."

"Really? Maybe I should give you another physical examination. Just to make sure the ER staff didn't miss anything. I am a certified first responder, remember. How does that sound?"

"Well, it's always good to get a second opinion, right? I think that sounds like just what I need."

And it was.

The next morning, I jumped out of bed without thinking and my sore muscles quickly reminded me of what I'd subjected them to the day before. I stood in a hot shower for a while and would have stayed longer if I hadn't been interrupted by the buzz of my intercom.

I threw on my robe and ran to the living room to answer it.

"Yes?"

"This is Owen Fike. I'd like to ask you a few questions about your accident yesterday. Can I come up?"

"Sure."

I hadn't interacted with Owen since he told me to back off investigating Rob's death and leave it to the professionals—or words to that effect. I wasn't looking forward to seeing him, but it had to be done.

Seated across from me at the kitchen island, he had refused my offer of coffee or water and was clearly anxious to get what he needed and leave.

"So, let's start with you telling me why Harley Granger tried to kill you yesterday afternoon."

"Isn't it in the report Marla Jarvis took down from me at the hospital yesterday? She's a pretty good deputy," I said.

"She is. But I'd like to hear it directly from you."

I gave him the background. He stopped me when I got to the part where Cole told me that Spencer had killed Rob, but Jennifer had debunked it with her alibi information.

"You didn't think you should've brought any of that to me?"

"After our last conversation, I was pretty sure you wouldn't be interested."

"Or did you not want to be embarrassed by how far off base you were? You thought you had something to crack the case and prove that I got it wrong again, didn't you?"

"I'm surprised you can walk around upright, given the size of the chip you're carrying on your shoulder. I wasn't trying to prove you wrong. I followed up on a lead I knew you wouldn't give any credence to, because it came from me. Also, I'm getting the feeling that you don't really need more from me than Marla's excellent notes will tell you about Harley's car chase with me."

"I told you, I like to hear witness accounts directly from them when possible."

"So, what do you want me to say, Owen? Erin Harper killed Rob Porter. Spencer and Harley were just incidental to the case. You're a brilliant detective who wrapped up the investigation and secured Erin's arrest in days. I've spent weeks stumbling around, coming up with dead end leads, and you were right all along. There, does that meet your needs?"

He flipped his notebook shut.

"Yes, I'd say that pretty much covers it," he said, standing. "We've had this conversation before, but maybe you didn't take me seriously. I don't want or need outsiders, especially journalists, involved in my work. I hope the Rob Porter case makes it clear that when it comes to investigating murder you don't have a part to play."

I didn't bother to argue with him. The funny thing is, I didn't actually dislike Owen. Not like I used to dislike Ross, or the way I didn't trust the old sheriff, Art Lamey. But the two of us just couldn't seem to find common ground.

"So, I take it we're done?"

"For now. I'll call you if I have any more questions. But there's something else I want to say. I don't have a beef with you personally. I'm sure you're a nice person in certain circumstances. But if you were good enough to be a cop, you'd be a cop. Civilians should stay out of police business, and if you don't, one of these days, your luck will run out. Just a word to the wise."

Okay, time to revise my assessment of Owen. Yes, I decided, I did actually dislike him.

"Noted. Great as this has been, Owen, I feel a headache coming on. I'm pretty sure it will go away when you do. So, goodbye."

60

Irritated as I was by Owen's visit, he was right about one thing. He had gotten to the truth about Rob's murder, not me. It was time to face the fact that Erin didn't want to be saved, because she had committed the crime. It wasn't the outcome I wanted, but it's the one I had to accept. In a case of life imitating art, my fake headache was actually materializing in real life. Served me right.

I took a couple of Tylenol, lay down on the sofa, and promptly fell asleep. I woke up with a start and bolted upright when I felt someone staring at me. My mother was leaning over the sofa, and Paul Karr was right beside her. Not for the first time I regretted that she had the key code for my apartment.

"Mom! Paul! What are you doing here? You scared the heck out of me."

"I'm sorry, hon. I knocked but you didn't answer and then I got worried that maybe you had a concussion after all and you were unconscious, so we came in to see."

"Mom, way to escalate. I'm fine. I had a—"

I'd started to say that I'd had a headache but decided not to give her something tangible to worry about, especially because it was gone.

"—late night and I was just catching a nap. What's going on?"

Paul answered instead.

"I'm sorry to barge in, Leah. But I had to thank you for saving Spencer's life. After talking to him and to the sheriff's office, I really believe that's what you did."

"It's all right, Paul. I was trying to save myself as much as him."

He went on as though I hadn't spoken.

"I just hope that finally he's ready to do something that says his life is worth saving. His attorney and I are talking to him this afternoon. We met with Cliff Timmins earlier. His mother was there, too. There's a chance that we can get a deal for Spencer that will keep him out of jail if he cooperates, and if he agrees to check into a rehab facility for his cocaine habit."

I had my doubts that Spencer would follow through on anything. I also didn't like the fact that without the Karr money, Cliff Timmins wouldn't be so willing to consider a deal. But when I looked at Paul's sad, tired eyes, I couldn't say any of that.

"I'm sorry, Paul. I hope Spencer is able to turn things around."

I even managed not to ask if that meant *GO News* would be going out of business.

After my mother and Paul left, I pretty much just lazed around the rest of the day. It was gray and rainy, making it perfect for dozing on and off and for convincing me that I really should rest instead of doing some writing. Miguel texted around five and I invited him to come up for some of the four-cheese macaroni casserole my mother had dropped off.

"This is my favorite hot dish," he said as he finished his last forkful. We had elected to eat sitting on the sofa so we could look out the windows at the thunderstorm that was rolling in.

"You say that about every casserole my mother makes."

"Because every one is my favorite. But now will you tell me why Owen Fike came to see you today? I saw him parking out front when I left for Hailwell this morning."

"His version of a 'come to Jesus' meeting, I guess. Only he wanted me to come to the conclusion that he's right, I'm wrong, and it's time for me to let Erin go."

I filled him in on my visit with Owen.

"It pains me to say this, but it looks like Owen's right, and Gabe's right, and Coop's right, and I'm wrong. Erin had an affair with Rob. I feel like I've exhausted every other possibility."

"You are giving up?"

"Let's say I'm letting go. That sounds better to me. But you know what? I don't want to talk about it anymore. Tell me about your day instead. What did you do in Hailwell?"

"I took some photos at the new bank office there, and then I interviewed a dairy farmer for the special Ag edition we're doing in August, and then I came back and used some of my comp time to work on my side hustle. Remember, I told you I was doing a big annual report for the Himmel Police Department? I got the hard proof for it today. Do you want to see it? I haven't showed it to Chief Riley yet, so you'll be the first."

I really didn't care about Mick Riley's swan song of praise to himself, but I care about Miguel, and I knew he'd put a lot of effort into the project.

"Of course I do. Hand it over."

He got his messenger bag from the hook next to the door.

"C'mere next to me so you can give commentary," I said, patting the space on the sofa beside me.

The cover was a great shot of the Himmel Police Department, which occupies the first floor of the Himmel City Hall. With careful lighting and the right angle, Miguel had managed to make it look classic and imposing, instead of outdated and in need of a makeover.

"This is a great cover, Miguel. Mick insisted on the inset of him in full dress uniform in the lower right, didn't he?"

"He did. I had a different idea, but he's the one who's paying, so there he is. But I like it anyway."

"I do, too," I said. I flipped through the hard proof of the report. The inside page featured another photo of Mick, this time in his office. There were also office-setting portraits of his next level command team, Rob Porter and Erin Harper.

"Oh-oh. Looks like you've got some tweaking to do. I know Mick set the layout with you before Rob died, but I think he's going to want to change his mind. He probably doesn't want his dead police captain and the lieu-tenant who killed him quite so front and center in his homage to himself."

"I know. I think he will want to forget about Erin, and maybe have a memorial page for Rob Porter."

"Maybe . . . But I think Mick will want to cut Rob out of the report, too. Featuring the police captain who was figuratively in bed with a local drug trafficker, and literally in bed with an officer under his command doesn't support the 'Hey, look at my great leadership' message Mick wants the report to convey."

"That is true."

Miguel saw my gaze shift to Erin's photo.

"I tried to get her to smile. Erin is very pretty when she smiles, but she was very serious that morning."

"Kind of like you would be if you just killed your ex-lover boss the night before?" I asked.

"I know, right? Look at her eyes, they are so sad," he said.

But as I looked more closely, it wasn't Erin's eyes that caught my attention.

"Miguel, you've got these photos stored in your Dropbox file, don't you?"

"Yes, of course."

I grabbed my laptop and handed it to him.

"Here, get into your file and find the photo of Erin," I said.

When Erin's photo came up, I leaned over and zoomed in so large that I could see the fine little hairs on her cheek. But it was what I saw on her ear —both ears—that made me shout.

"Erin is wearing her earrings!"

I shook Miguel's arm in excitement as he looked at me in bewilderment.

61

"This is the photo you took the day Rob's body was found, right? The one you took at Erin's office before you came into work that morning?"

He understood then. He nodded.

"Erin, she's wearing both her earrings! She had both of her earrings the morning *after* Rob was murdered."

"Exactly. She didn't lose her earring when she went out to kill him. She still had them after Rob was killed."

"So she didn't kill Rob? But then why did she confess to you and say that the earring the police have is hers?"

"Let's not get ahead of ourselves," I said, realizing the irony of the words as I spoke them. I'd spent the entire investigation getting ahead of myself and suffering the consequences.

"Right now," I continued, "the fact that Erin is wearing both her earrings after Rob's death only means that she lied when she told Owen she'd lost one weeks before."

"But she also lied to you when she confessed to the murder," Miguel said. "She told you she knew she lost the earring at Rob's. But she didn't. The earring the police found isn't hers at all. Why did she lie so much about her earrings?"

"Why indeed? Especially because she could have easily proved the earring found didn't belong to her. All she had to do was ask you for a copy of this photo showing she was wearing them both after Rob was murdered."

"*Chica,* it sounds like you are giving up on giving up."

"I think I am. Let's go back in time and flip things around."

"How do you mean?"

"When I started, I decided that Rob's murder was all about him and Harley and revenge and drugs—and I saw everything through that lens. Now I'm going to flip that lens, like your eye doctor does. 'Is it clearer this way, or that way? A, or B? Two, or three?'"

I said it in the singsong voice the optometrist uses when she's determining the strength a lens prescription should be.

"I'm not getting this."

"Sorry, I'm too excited to be articulate. I'm saying that I need to go back and look at things through the Erin lens, not the Rob lens."

"But how will you talk to her? She won't even see you. And Gabe won't help you see her."

"I'm not going to talk to Erin. You're right, she won't see me, and Gabe won't intervene—if she'd even listen to him. I don't need to talk to Erin yet. I need to go back to basics. First up is the earring the cops have. It's not Erin's. So, who does it belong to?"

"What can you find out that the police didn't? There's no DNA evidence on it. It's not Erin's, but you can find earrings that look like it in lots of stores. It could be anybody's."

"All true. But Erin herself said they were really good earrings. There might be a jeweler's mark and/or an ID number on the earring the police have. That could tell us where it was purchased and who bought it."

"But wouldn't the police have seen an ID number if it was there?"

"Not necessarily. First of all, remember that the reason there was no usable DNA from the earring is that Darmody coughed and sneezed and left grossness all over it. Would you want to examine the earring that closely after that?"

He wrinkled up his nose at the idea.

"If it's a good piece of jewelry—and we don't know yet if it is—there will be markings on it. I'm not dissing our fine police personnel, but it's not like we have a lot of high-end jewelry thefts around here. I'm not sure with everything going on plus Darmody's screw-up that whoever handled the earring as evidence would have known to look for the markings. Besides, they'd be very tiny, probably laser-etched on an earring post. They could even be too small to notice without a jeweler's loupe."

"How do you know so much about jewelry?"

"Are you implying that I'm not a connoisseur of fine jewels? Because you're right if you are. I did a story on a pawnbroker a few years ago. He showed me a lot. Realize that we're trafficking in the possible now, not necessarily the probable. But maybe we'll get a break for once. It's worth a look at the earring the cops have anyway."

"How will you get that? Owen will not agree. Or the prosecutor either, I think."

"No, but Gabe is still Erin's attorney. He has the right to see evidence. I'm going to call him right now and see if he'll look for identification marks on it for me."

I said it as though there was no question that Gabe would want to help me, but after our last conversation I really wasn't sure he'd even listen. He picked up on the first ring.

"Leah! Are you okay? I wanted to call yesterday after I heard about the car accident, but I wasn't sure if you'd want to talk to me. Our last conversation didn't end very well. I thought you might still be mad."

"Yes, I'm fine. Just bumps and bruises and a little stiffness. And no, our last talk didn't end well. But that was my fault, not yours. I'm sorry."

"Me, too. I said a few things I didn't really mean."

"That's all right. But on a scale of 1 to 10, how would you rank how sorry you are?"

"Why?"

"Because if you're north of a 5, then maybe you'll do me a favor."

"What is it?"

"Did you get a look—an actual physical look, I mean—at the earring that was found at Rob's place? Or did you just see a photo or get a description?"

"I saw a photo, but not the real thing. I was planning to go over to the sheriff's office to examine it and the original of the letter Erin wrote. But after she confessed, there wasn't any point."

"But you could still, right? I mean the case isn't settled yet, you're still her attorney, you still have discovery rights, correct? You could look at it in person."

"Yes, I could, but why would I?"

"Because I'd like to know if there's a maker's mark and an ID number on it. It would be on the earring post, super small, so you might need a jeweler's loupe to read it—maybe even to see it."

"Leah, I don't want to fight with you again, but I told you that Erin—"

"I know, I know. But listen, I'm not asking how Erin's case is going, or if you filed her plea change, or anything about her case at all, right? Telling me the number on an earring post isn't violating lawyer-client privilege. I'm not going to talk to her or even try to."

"Leah . . ."

"I just want to check out an idea I have. I promise you that I'm not going to spring it on Erin. If you don't want to know, I won't even tell you about it if what you find leads me anywhere. Gabe, please. If the help I've given you on other cases was worth anything, would you just do this one thing for me?"

A long sigh came across the phone.

"All right. I guess I can look for the markings and let you know."

"Tomorrow? First thing tomorrow?"

"Fine. First thing tomorrow."

"What about a jeweler's loupe? I can find someone who has one for you."

"No need. My neighbor does watch repair as a hobby. I'm sure he'll lend me his loupe."

"Thanks, Gabe. You're the best."

"I wish I were," he said, and hung up.

"Gabe will check the earring for you?" Miguel asked.

"Yes. First thing tomorrow."

"He's a good man. What do you think about Gabe and Jennifer? She's lonely and he's lonely. He's nice, and she's nice. He has a little boy, and she has two little boys. It could work," he said as he turned the possible match over in his head.

"It could also be a disaster. That's three little boys all age five. I can see a whole lot of chaos in that direction. Besides, I thought you were match-making Gabe with Kristin Norcross. You go ahead and work your magic if you must, but I want no part of that," I said, finishing with a surprise yawn.

"Sorry, Miguel. I don't know why I'm tired. I've been sleeping on and off all day."

"Because your body was traumatized yesterday. You should sleep some more. Call me tomorrow after you talk to Gabe."

"I will."

62

I was up and dressed early the next morning, thinking that Gabe would surely call me by nine. After all, he'd said he'd go look at the earring first thing. But nine o'clock went by with no call. I told myself that he was doing me a favor, and I had to be patient. But I'm never very good at that. So, I asked my mother for a ride to Nestor's Auto Sales to keep myself occupied while I waited. I needed a rental car until the insurance company decided whether or not to rule mine a total loss. When I got home at 10, I still hadn't heard from Gabe. Finally, at 10:30, I called him on his cell. He didn't pick up. I called his office and got Patty, the legal secretary who really runs the show at Miller Caldwell and Associates.

"Patty, this is Leah. I'm trying to find Gabe. He was going to call me this morning first thing, and—"

"Well, I don't know how he'd be able to do that, Leah. A very important, long-time client needed attention this morning. I told Gabe on Monday that he had to cover a breakfast meeting today with Helen Visser because Miller is away."

"Patty, I'm really anxious to talk to him. When do you think he'll be done?"

"I have no idea. But you do know, don't you, that Gabe works at Miller Caldwell and Associates? I don't believe your partnership arrangement with Miller at the *Times* puts the staff here at his legal office under your direction, does it?"

Ouch. Patty is a woman in late middle age who looks deceptively like Mrs. Santa Claus. But don't be lulled into expecting a twinkly-eyed grandma ready to ply you with sugar cookies. She is definitely that sometimes, but she also has full use of a very acerbic tongue that I feel she's used on me more often since I broke up with Gabe.

"You're right, Patty. It does not. Sorry. I'll wait for him to call me, I guess."

My apology mollified her somewhat, and she said, "I'll check with him when he gets in, and let him know you're anxious to talk to him."

When the call came at 10:45 it proved to be worth the wait.

I lunged for my phone and grabbed it on the first ring.

"Gabe! What did you find out?"

"There's a maker's mark on the earring, and an ID number, too. I checked the maker's mark online. The earring was made by John Grant and Sons out of New York. The ID number is JGS149323."

"Gabe, thank you so much! That's perfect."

"I'm sorry I didn't get it to you first thing. I forgot that I had to pick up a meeting for Miller today."

"No problem, Patty schooled me on that and reminded me that you work at Miller Caldwell and Associates, not at the *Times*. I don't think she likes me anymore."

"She does. She just likes me better. I'll have a chat and let her know she can stand down, that things are in a good place between us now. They are, right?"

"They are for me."

"Me, too."

"Okay, well, I'll see what I can find out. Thank you, Gabe. I owe you one."

I checked out the website for John Grant & Sons, and found it was a small, high-end jewelry business that had been creating "exquisite, handcrafted jewelry for clients who value beauty and quality" for over 100 years. I fixed my cover story in my mind and called the number listed.

"Thank you for calling John Grant & Sons. My name is Celia. How may I direct your call?"

I was so surprised that my first contact was an actual human, instead of an auto attendant phone service, that I stumbled a little in my answer.

"Um, oh, hi, Celia. My name is Alicia Huberman. I have a little problem I hope someone there can help me with. You see, I borrowed my mother's earrings, a favorite pair of hers. And I'm afraid that I lost one of them. I've searched everywhere, but I can't find it. The earrings were purchased at John Grant & Sons, and I have the ID number for the pair. I'd like to get another earring to replace the one I lost before she and my stepfather get back from France. Is that possible?"

"I'm going to put you through to Mr. Koenig, he's in charge of the design studio. I'm sure he'll be able to assist you, Miss Huberman. One moment, please."

Although I prefer a straight-on approach, occasionally I need to pretend to be someone else in order to get information. When I do, I sometimes use the name of a character in a favorite old movie. It helps me think of what I'm engaged in as "acting" as opposed to lying. Alicia Huberman is the character played by Ingrid Bergman in one of my all-time favorite movies, *Notorious*. The *Notorious* that Hitchcock made in the '40s, that is, not the one from 2009 about the rapper.

Celia had apparently explained my situation in detail because Mr. Koenig came on ready to help.

"Good afternoon, Miss Huberman. This is Julian Koenig. I can certainly help you get a replacement earring for the one you lost. As I'm sure you're aware, our jewelry is handcrafted by the finest artisans. You can be assured of the quality of the material and the work; however, I want to be sure you understand there could be a very small variation from the original piece."

"Please, call me Alicia. And that's fine, I'm sure Mother won't notice," I said breezily. "I just have to get it replaced before she and my stepfather get home next month. Otherwise, I'll be in serious trouble."

"Well, we can't have that, can we, Alicia? And you must call me Julian. If you give me the ID number, I'll look it up on our database."

I read off the number Gabe had given me. I could hear the tapping of keys as Julian called up the database.

"Yes, here it is. JGS149322. The pair of earrings was $850, but of course we can offer you a discount because you only need one."

"Oh, you're one number off, Julian. The ID on Mother's earring is JGS149323."

"I'm so sorry. I was reading the line above it. Yes, I—"

His voice broke off for a second, then he said, "That's a little odd. *Two* pairs of the same blue sapphire stud earrings in a gold setting, JGS149322 and JGS149323, were purchased at the same time, by Claire Montgomery last August. Is that your mother?"

I was so surprised at his answer that I didn't reply for a second.

"Alicia, are you there?"

"Oh, yes, Julian. I'm sorry. I've got a call coming in that I really must take. It's Mother! Can you believe it? Thank you so much. I'll be in touch."

"What in the actual hell?" I asked out loud.

As I tried to think through the ramifications of what Julian had told me, Miguel called.

"I just got back in the office. Are you home? What's going on? Did you find out about the earring?"

"Boy, did I. Can you come up? I need you to help me think."

"*Claire* bought the earring that was found at Rob's?"

"Not just that one, Miguel. According to my new friend Julian—or maybe I should say Alicia Huberman's friend Julian—she bought two pairs."

"But why?"

"I'm starting to have an idea. Hold on."

I closed my eyes for a minute as clues and missed cues came together, broke apart, and whirled around like dancers in a Busby Berkley musical. I could feel Miguel practically vibrating with impatience as he waited for me to explain.

Instead, I opened my laptop and called up the archive of the *Times'* photos we store in the cloud and typed Claire's name into the search bar. Miguel stood behind me and watched over my shoulder as I scanned the half dozen pictures that came up.

"I'm looking for a photo of Claire wearing the earrings."

"That one," he said, pointing to a picture of Claire that had run with a story we did when she gave a talk at the Women's Club. I zoomed in super close. Claire's ears were adorned with blue sapphire earrings in a gold setting.

"Can you get in your Dropbox file again, and bring up that photo of Erin you took for the annual report?"

I handed him my laptop and watched as he tapped in his password and pulled up Erin's photo. The wall behind her was hung with framed certificates and commendations.

"Go in close on that one," I said.

He enlarged it so we could both read it. Erin had received a Bachelor of Science Degree from Robley College in 2006.

"But what—"

"Hold on just another sec. I want to check a couple things. Then I'll tell you everything. Or not, if I'm wrong," I said.

I took the laptop back and found the story the paper had run when Claire first opened her practice. It corroborated what William had told me. Claire had graduated from Robley College. The article went a step further and gave me the year—2005.

Miguel, tired of waiting for me, put forth his own idea.

"So, Claire was Rob's lover? But we know he was such a bad man—he beat his wives, he was very bad to Erin, he took bribes from Harley Granger . . . Claire is so elegant, so beautiful. I can't see it."

"You don't need to try, Miguel. Claire wasn't having an affair with Rob. She was having an affair with Erin."

63

"Claire and Erin? Why do you think *that?*" he asked, his voice full of doubt.

"The breadcrumbs were there, Miguel. I just didn't follow them," I said.

He continued to look at me as though I had lost my mind.

"Hear me out. There's a cool framed print of the constellation Virgo in Claire's office. I asked her where she got it. She told me a college friend gave it to her, because they're both Virgos with the same September birthday. Erin and Claire both attended Robley College, at about the same time. Erin's birthday is in September. I know because I bought her a birthday drink at McClain's last year."

"And you think that Erin and Claire were in college together?"

"I know they were. The diploma on Erin's wall says she graduated from Robley College in 2006. Claire graduated from there in 2005. It's a small school, they were there at the same time, they had to know each other, but neither one of them ever mentioned it. Then we have the earrings. Claire bought two pairs of sapphire stud earrings. Sapphire is the birthstone for September. A gift for Erin and a pair for herself. They couldn't let the world know they were lovers, but when they wore the earrings, it was their private declaration. One of those earrings was found at the crime scene—now we know that it's Claire's, because Erin had both of her earrings the day after Rob died."

Miguel's eyes lit up as he followed my thinking, and it gave me a boost of confidence that finally I'd gotten it right.

"Let me add another layer. At the Players fundraiser, I was talking to William. Claire was off to the side. When I turned to bring her into the conversation, she was deep in discussion with Erin. They both looked up. I started to introduce Erin to William, but she cut me off. Said she was glad about me and Coop, that she already knew William, and she just left. It was pretty rude. I apologized for her, but Claire said she knew Erin and was used to her communication style. I thought she meant because they worked together on those workshops for the department. But now—"

"Now you know it meant more."

"Yes. And in hindsight, Erin's walkaway wasn't just her usual abruptness. She couldn't get out of there fast enough. Why? Because how awkward would it be to have a group chat with your lover and her husband? And then, there's the letter she wrote to her lover."

"Yes. She said that it wasn't to Rob, and she never sent it, she kept it in her desk where Rob found it. Then later she changed her story and said that it really was for Rob, and she had mailed it to him, but she thought he never got it," he said, nodding.

"Right. But let's think about what's in the letter. After I read it and Erin refused to say who she'd written it to, I thought that she was protecting her lover. I figured he was married, maybe had a career that an affair would damage, and a family he didn't want to hurt. My mistake was assuming that Erin was protecting a man. But if you look at the words closely you can see that Claire fits the part of Erin's lover better than Rob ever did."

I leafed through my legal pad to find the page with the wording of the letter.

"Erin wrote, 'There are other *people* who will be hurt.' But Rob didn't have 'people' in his life, he had just one person, his wife. If Erin was writing to him, she would have said 'your wife' will be hurt, not that other people would be hurt. Then she goes on to write that she'd do anything to 'lessen the pain for *them*.' Again, there is no 'them' in Rob's life, just his wife.

"But look at Claire. The letter describes her situation, not Rob's. Claire has a husband, and they both have careers that could be destroyed by the scandal if Claire's affair with Erin came to light. Claire has her kids to consider, too. Billy her son is only six, and he has a serious illness. Maeve her daughter is a teenager. Imagine the impact on her. Erin's letter is responding to Claire's decision that they can't be together. You can see that Erin understands how Claire feels, but she finds their separation impossible to bear."

"But if she wrote the letter to Claire, how did Rob get it? I'm getting very confused."

"That's because Erin made it super confusing by first denying an affair with Rob and then reversing everything she said by confessing. I don't believe either story she told was completely true, though parts of both were. That's what made it hard to see what had really happened."

"And what is that?"

"Erin told the truth when she said that she didn't have an affair with Rob, and she didn't write that letter to him. But she lied when she said she put it in her desk, and he found it. And she lied again in her confession when she said she'd written it to him but didn't think he'd received it. See, one of the reasons I had a hard time believing that Erin killed Rob is that her whole alibi was so half-assed. If Erin had done it, she'd have done a much better job of covering her tracks. The letter thing was a hot mess to begin with. Would Erin really have been sitting at her office desk writing this intensely personal, emotional, pleading letter to Rob when anyone could have wandered in? No. She wrote that letter at home. And she left it there until she needed it to set herself up to protect the real killer. Erin didn't shoot Rob. Claire did to protect her family."

Miguel's eyes had widened with shock, and I understood why.

"I know what you're thinking. Claire would never kill anyone. She's not that kind of person. But Miguel, we're all that kind of person if the circumstances are right. I'm proof positive of that. In everyday life, Claire is good, and kind, and in control, but in the complicated situation with her, and Erin, and Rob, she wasn't in control. She was in danger, and so were her family, her career, and her husband's career."

"But for Claire to kill Rob? I don't—"

"I know, I know. But let me paint the picture for you before you decide, okay?"

He nodded, but he looked very skeptical.

"So, going back to the beginning, Erin and Claire were together in college, but for whatever reason, they went their separate ways after Claire graduated. Claire married William, became a psychologist, had a family. Erin went into police work and made that the center of her life. Then years later, William and Claire moved to Himmel. Claire gets a contract to work with the Himmel Police Department. She and Erin meet again."

"Of all the gin joints, in all the towns, in all the world, she walks into mine," Miguel said, quoting the line from *Casablanca*.

"Exactly. Claire and Erin find each other again, but their situation isn't easy."

"A lot of things about being gay aren't easy," Miguel said.

It surprised me a little, though it shouldn't have. He doesn't talk about it much, but I know that he's run into bigotry and even physical violence before. It's just that he's so at home with who he is. And he walks in the world with such confidence and grace. It's easy for me to forget that he has to face intolerance and cruelty that I've never had to deal with.

"I know you're right, Miguel. That's probably why Erin's not out. Adding gay to female in a male-dominated field like law enforcement would be another obstacle for her to overcome. But when Claire and Erin meet again, they find they still feel the same love for each other that they did in college. They restart their relationship, only their situations are very different now. Especially Claire's.

"She loves Erin, but she's wracked with guilt about William and her kids. And there's the constant fear of discovery and what that would mean for William's career, for hers, for the life they've built together. She breaks it off. Erin understands, and she tries to accept it for Claire's sake, but she's dying inside. That's why she writes the letter to Claire. But she doesn't send it because she's trying to honor what Claire asked of her."

"That is very sad, for everybody."

"It gets a whole lot sadder. All the while Erin is feeling so much pain, she's also dealing with the pressure of Rob harassing and humiliating her at work and spreading lies about an affair they never had. And then every-thing gets worse. Rob finds out about her and Claire."

"Now we are back to the letter. How does Rob know, if he doesn't have the letter?"

"I'm not sure. Maybe he sees them in a private moment together. Maybe he overhears Erin talking to Claire on the phone. The point is, he knows, and he uses it to stop Erin's harassment complaint for good."

"How?"

"He tells her he knows about her affair with Claire, and so will everyone else if she doesn't drop the complaint and resign. If she does, it's all good. He'll still be on track to be police chief and Erin can start her career over somewhere else, while Claire keeps hers, and her family. Rob will keep their secret."

"But how can she trust Rob?" Miguel asked.

"I think Erin knew that she couldn't. But she has to capitulate and drop her complaint, as well as resign because Rob has all the power in the situa-tion. So, she agrees to his conditions, but she has to let Claire know both that she's leaving town and that Rob knows their secret. It's important that she warn Claire, so she can be prepared if Rob tries to use it against her in the future. She calls Claire to tell her that."

"Claire must have been very frightened by the news."

"Yes. I'm sure she was. I'm equally sure that Claire wouldn't just let the situation ride. She would want to talk to Rob herself, to make sure Rob understood that he held the lives not just of her and Erin, but also of her children and William, in his hands. Claire would try to reason with him, plead with him, do anything it took to secure Rob's promise that he wouldn't reveal what he knew."

"Even kill him?"

"I don't think she planned to. Rob was shot with his own gun. That says Claire didn't bring a weapon. But Rob would have really enjoyed the power he had over her in that moment. He enjoyed hurting people, physically and emotionally. He probably taunted her, dismissed her, laughed at her, provoked her in every way possible. Claire's human, like the rest of us. Her fear turned to fury, the gun was there, she picked it up, and she shot him."

"But then how did Erin get involved?"

"Remember, until she became a suspect, Erin was read in on everything Owen and his team were doing. She was told how Rob was killed and what the crime scene looked like. She knew Harley's alibi took him out of the running as chief suspect. And when she got the description on the earring that was found, she realized it had to be Claire's. And she knew she had to save her."

"Even though she would go to prison for a crime she didn't commit?"

"Yes. I think that without Claire, she feels like her life doesn't matter. She sees no way for herself to have a meaningful life without Claire. But Claire's situation is different. She has a husband, and children, and a career she loves. She has a chance at happiness that Erin doesn't. She decides to protect Claire by leading Owen toward herself. She gives him an alibi she knows won't hold up, she makes up a stupid story about her earring that no one believes, and she seals the deal by putting the letter she wrote to Claire in Rob's office. Rob has already set the stage by putting out the story that he and Erin had a fling, and she won't let go. Owen has what he needs to convince him that Erin is Rob's killer."

"But if Claire killed Rob, how can she let Erin take the blame?"

"That's the thing I don't understand. That's one of the things I'll ask her when I see her."

"You're going to see a killer?"

"Not a killer. Claire. I have to see her to verify what I just theorized."

"But you can't go alone."

"Yes. I can. This has to be one-on-one, me and Claire."

"Why don't you just tell Owen?"

"He wouldn't listen, and more importantly, I care about Claire. I want her to have a chance to talk to William before any police are involved."

"I know Claire is a good person, but if she killed Rob, she might think she needs to kill you to keep it secret."

"She won't. If it makes you feel any better, I'll let her know that you know everything I do. That way there's no point in her trying to kill me if she feels a homicidal urge."

He shook his head.

"Okay, listen. It's not like I'm going to meet her in a dark alley. I'll be at her office. Her secretary will be right outside the door."

"You are very stubborn."

"Thank you. But seriously, don't worry. This isn't a scary situation. It's a tragic one for everyone—Claire, William, their kids, Erin, Al Porter, too, when he finds out what Rob was really like. The truth is going to hurt so many people that I wish I'd never gotten involved."

64

When I walked into Claire's office, her secretary was at her desk in the reception area. She looked up from her computer and smiled at me.

"Hi, Barb. I don't have an appointment, but I was hoping Claire could see me. I'm happy to wait until she's free."

"I'm sorry, Leah. Claire is off all week. I'm just in to check the mail and catch up on some billing. Is it urgent? If not, I hate to disturb her."

"Oh. No, that's okay, Barb. I just wanted to touch base with her on something. No need for you to call her. Is she away with her family?"

"No, she's at home, catching up on things. I'm glad. I think she's been working too hard—she's seemed so tired and distracted to me lately. Some time away from the office is what she needs. I can schedule an appointment for you for next week if you like."

I knew that this was Barb's subtle way of telling me that if it wasn't urgent, I should leave Claire alone. Unfortunately, I couldn't do that.

"No need, Barb. Thanks."

I called Claire as I walked to my car.

"Hi, Claire. I know you're off this week, but do you have a little time to talk?"

"Leah, hello. I'm in the middle of painting my kitchen," she said, "but I can take a break if you need to see me. Come around the back of the house, the kitchen door is unlocked. I should warn you that it could get a little noisy. We've got the lawn care people coming today, but I don't know when. Their mower is very loud."

"That's okay."

Although I didn't relish the thought of shouting my way through the sad and awful things I was going to discuss with Claire, I also couldn't wait any longer. Then a potential problem popped into my head.

"Oh, Claire, are you alone at the house?"

"Yes. Billy's at day camp, Maeve is with a friend, and William is roaming the woods and won't be back for hours. His brother bought him a new hunting rifle for his birthday and he's sighting it in—I think that's what you call it. He took a lunch because he's planning to do some birdwatching, too. We won't be disturbed if you're worried about that."

"I'm not worried. I'd just rather no one walked in on our conversation."

"Is this related to the car accident you were in? When I read about it in the paper I wondered if it might trigger your PTSD."

"No, I'm fine. It's not that. I'll see you shortly."

I hung up before she asked me anything else.

When I reached Claire's house, an All Seasons Lawn Care truck and trailer was parked on the road. I pulled into the driveway as two men unloaded an industrial-size mower and equipment from the trailer. As I walked to the back of the house, I saw Claire on a ladder through one of the kitchen windows. I tapped lightly on the door and walked in.

Claire turned at the sound and smiled at me as she stepped down from the ladder. Just then the mower roared to life.

"I'm sorry. I was hoping the lawn service wouldn't show up until after we talked," she said. I helped her shut the kitchen windows and the sound receded to a dull growl.

"All alone still?" I asked, making sure.

"Yes. All clear. The children won't be home until after four, and I don't expect William to be much earlier than that. I'm going to have a cup of tea. Would you like one?"

"Sure, that would be nice."

I had no desire for tea, but at least holding a mug would give me something to twist in my hands as I began a conversation I had no desire for, either.

Claire poured us each a cup from a tea carafe and handed me mine before she sat down across from me at the big plank wood table. She leaned slightly forward in a listening position. Her hands were wrapped around a chipped mug that read World's Best Mom.

"What's going on, Leah?"

We were like two suburban mothers about to share our troubles. That is, if one of us was a murderer and the other was a hapless writer about to shatter her friend's life. On the way to Claire's, I had rehearsed what I'd say, how I'd lead into it, how I'd give Claire space to realize it was time for all the deception to end.

Instead, I blurted out, "Are you and Erin lovers?"

Claire's face paled and she jerked upright in straight-backed shock. Her eyes searched my face.

"Where is that coming from, Leah? I'm married to William, I have two children, we're a family. Of course Erin and I aren't lovers. I don't understand why you'd ask that."

Her voice was firm, but her hands gave her away. They were shaking and she sloshed a bit of tea on the table as she raised the cup to her lips.

"Claire, I'm sorry. That was a terrible way to start. But I can't think of any good way to do it either. So, I'll just be straight with you and get it all out there. I know you and Erin were in a relationship. I think that you killed Rob Porter because he discovered your secret somehow, and he threatened to ruin both your lives. I understand why you killed him. What I don't understand is why you let Erin take the blame."

"You think that *I* killed Rob? Did Erin tell you that?"

The astonishment in her voice was so genuine that I almost believed her.

"No, Erin hasn't said anything about you at all. But the things she's lied about have told me a lot."

I then went through a shortened version of the theory I'd shared with Miguel. Claire listened without saying a word. When I finished, she shook her head slowly—not in denial, but in the way of someone who knows all is lost.

"You're right, Leah. There's no point in lying to you. Erin and I were lovers. Rob found out somehow and he threatened to make it public. But I didn't kill him. I thought that Erin had, to protect me. I didn't know that my earring had been found during the search. There wasn't anything in the paper about that. It never occurred to me that Erin might be taking the blame because she thought that *I* had killed Rob."

Now I was the one who sat back in surprise.

"Claire, is this some kind of next-level, double-deception game the two of you are playing? How did your earring get there? And if you didn't kill him, are you saying Erin killed him after all?"

"I don't know if she did or not. I've only spoken to her twice since we ended things weeks ago. The first time was when she called to tell me that Rob knew about us. That was the day he was killed. The second time we spoke was after Rob died, but before she was arrested. It was at the Players fundraiser. She told me not to worry, that she'd taken care of everything. I didn't understand and there wasn't time to talk. When she was arrested a few days later, I thought that's what she'd meant. That she had killed Rob to protect me. You have to believe me."

"Before I can do that, Claire, I need the whole story from you, not just the pieces I was able to put together. I need you to tell me about you and Erin and Rob."

"Yes. All right. I'd really like to tell somebody. But I need to start at the beginning, so you can understand."

"Fine, that's what I want," I said.

She took a big breath in and let it out slowly. Then she began speaking and the words came quickly with the force of long pent-up emotion.

65

"I was an only child. My parents were very conservative. They raised me with love, but also with a clear awareness of the sinful condition of man. Our minister often preached against the sin of homosexuality and the danger it posed. When I was younger, I didn't understand. But by the time I was in high school, I was very frightened."

"Frightened? Why?"

"Because although I said I had crushes on different cute boys in our class, like my friends did, I was lying. I didn't feel the same way they did. My crushes were on other girls. I knew that was a sin and if I didn't conquer it, I would go to hell. I prayed to God every day to change the feelings I had, but I didn't dare tell anyone."

"That must have been very lonely for you."

"The guilt and the shame were terrible. But I thought that if my faith was strong enough, I could change. Then I went to college."

"And that's where you met Erin?"

She nodded.

"She was smart, and quick, and no one seemed to intimidate her. And she wasn't at all conflicted about her sexuality. She could tell that I was, I think. But she never asked me for anything beyond friendship. I was the one who gathered my courage and made the initial overture. And I was so glad that I had. For the very first time, I felt completely at ease with another person. I had nothing to hide, nothing to be ashamed of. I was so happy for a while that I didn't let myself feel guilty."

"Were you both out in college, then?"

"No. Erin was, but I wasn't ready for that. I suppose people might have guessed that we were more than friends, but no one seemed to care. It gave me hope that maybe in the outside world, I could be who I truly was."

"But you and Erin didn't stay together. What happened?"

"Just a few weeks before graduation I went home because my cousin Christopher was getting married. But the wedding was called off. My parents told me they had terrible news for me about Chris. I thought he'd been killed in an accident or something like that."

She stopped for so long that I finally gave her a prompt.

"But Christopher wasn't dead?"

"No. Though in a way he was to my parents and to his. He'd come out as gay. My mother said he had broken his parents' hearts. My father said he didn't know how my aunt and uncle were going to be able to go through life never seeing their child again. But Christopher had chosen to live in sin. All his parents—and we—could do was pray for his redemption."

"That makes it sound like he committed a crime."

"To them he had, a crime against God. I knew that's what would happen to me if I came out."

"Your parents would choose their faith over you, if they knew you were gay?"

"It wasn't just *their* faith, it was mine, too. I started sobbing, and my parents thought that it was in sympathy for my aunt and uncle. I cried off and on all weekend. All the buried guilt I felt about being in what my parents called 'an unnatural relationship' erupted and overwhelmed me. By the end of the weekend, I had decided to break up with Erin. I had to ask God's forgiveness and commit to a life lived in grace, not sin. When I went back to college, that's what I did."

"How did Erin take that?"

"She didn't understand. Her family wasn't like mine. They weren't religious at all. She'd never even been baptized, which I found shocking. She said my parents might be upset at first, but they'd come around, like hers had. I couldn't make her understand that they wouldn't. They couldn't. It was a violation of everything they believed . . . and of everything I believed, then, too. Then she said my parents didn't have to know. We didn't have to be out about our relationship. I told her that I'd know. I said I had to leave her and go back to the life and the faith that I was born into. I broke her heart. I didn't see Erin or speak to her again for more than 17 years."

"Claire, I'm so sorry."

"I met William when I was in graduate school. I didn't want to get married, but he was very kind, and very in love with me, and most of all he was very strong in his faith. I needed that, so I could stay strong as well. We married, we had our children, we built a family together. When he accepted the call to the church here, I had no idea that Erin was in Himmel. Then one day I was at a meeting with Rob. The department had just hired me to do some workshops for them. Rob had assigned Erin to work with me and he invited her into the meeting."

"You must have been shocked."

"I was, yes. But I also felt such a rush of joy at seeing her. Neither of us acknowledged that we knew each other. Rob had introduced me as Claire Montgomery, instead of Claire Collier, my maiden name. So, Erin knew that I was married. I didn't know if she was out in her professional life. When the meeting ended, she suggested that we get a coffee together."

"And then you started seeing each other again?"

"No. Not right away. We both had built other lives. I had made a choice years earlier to marry William and have a family with him. I love William, I want you to understand that. It's different from the way I feel about Erin, but it's very real and very important to me. So, I told myself that Erin and I could be friends, as we'd been when we first met."

"But things didn't stay that way," I said.

"No, they didn't. I'd like to say it just happened, but that's not honest. The attraction between us was strong. I knew things were building to a crisis point. I knew I should pull back, but I didn't. We came together because we grew tired of resisting something we both wanted, even though we both knew it was dangerous."

"What made you decide you had to break things off?"

"At first, I pretended to myself that I could live two lives. One as a woman with a husband and family, the other with Erin. It was as though I had my real life, and my life with Erin. Then one day, Erin said she couldn't go on like we were. I thought she wanted to stop seeing me."

"But she didn't?"

"No, she didn't want to end our relationship. She wanted me to tell William about us. She hated the deception. She said it wasn't fair to him or to either of us."

"You didn't want to be with her?"

"No, I did. But it was much more complicated than that. When we were in college, I didn't have the courage to be with Erin. Now I didn't have the right. I couldn't do that to my children, to William. He would be devastated, not just because I'd been unfaithful, but because I'd been with a woman. That's a grievous sin in the church. I was afraid, too, that if I left him, he might keep my children from me. Not because William is vindictive. He isn't. But he would want to keep them safe from my sin."

"How did Erin take it?"

"I broke her heart for the second time. It was truly the most awful I've ever felt in my life. It would have been easier if she'd been angry at me. Instead, she told me that she loved me enough to let me go. We agreed not to contact each other, and to take care not to be alone with each other at work. My contract with the city was almost up. After that we wouldn't need to see each other at all."

"That must have been very difficult for both of you."

"It was easier for me. I wasn't alone. I had a family. I had work that I loved. Erin had no one, and she was miserable at her job because of Rob. She was on her own. The guilt I felt over what I had done to her, and nearly done to my family, was very hard to bear."

"She called you the day Rob was killed to tell you that Rob knew about your affair, didn't she?"

Claire nodded. "She told me his condition for keeping it secret was that she drop her complaint and resign. She wanted me to know she was leaving town, but she wasn't sure that he'd keep his word."

"That must have been a terrible call to get."

"It was. I panicked. I thought if I could talk to him directly, I could make him understand the harm he'd be doing. Erin told me not to go. She begged me not to. She said it would make things worse. That he'd realize how much power he had over me. I knew she was right, but I couldn't let it go."

"You went to see Rob."

"I did. I called his office and found out that he was at his property for the night."

"What time did you go?"

"William had a finance committee meeting that night. He never gets back from those until after 10. At dinner I said that I'd had a call from a client in crisis. I was meeting her at the office at eight o'clock, and I wasn't sure when I'd be back. After William left, I drove to Rob's."

"What happened when you got there?"

"Rob was walking onto the dock with his fishing gear. I ran down to catch him before he got in his boat. When he saw me, he smiled. It was an ugly, knowing smile. He realized why I'd come."

"What did you say to him?"

"I begged him not to tell anyone about Erin and me. I talked about my children, about William. I said they didn't deserve to be hurt for something I had done. I pleaded with him. I even offered him money."

"What did he do?"

"He just stood there with a smirk on his face until I finished. Then he told me not to worry. As long as I was a 'good girl,' everything would be fine. It would be our little secret. Then he said that maybe we'd have some other little secrets to share, too. I knew it was hopeless. I put my hands over my ears to drown out the sound of his laughter, and I ran back to my car. That must have been when I lost my earring. When I got home, William was still at his meeting. I went right to bed. But I didn't sleep.

"I heard him come in. Then I heard the door to his den open. He has trouble sleeping and quite often he reads the Bible or works on church business until quite late. Luckily for me, that was one of those times. I wouldn't have been able to face him that night. By the time he came to bed I had finally fallen asleep."

"And the next morning?"

"William had an early meeting, and I had a full day with clients, so we didn't see each other until dinnertime. By then I knew that Rob was dead, that he'd been shot. God forgive me, I felt nothing but relief."

"But you thought that Erin killed him?"

"No, not then. I didn't know who had. I didn't care. But when she was arrested, I thought that's what she meant at the fundraiser, when she told me everything was taken care of—that she had killed Rob. I called the jail, but she wouldn't speak to me, and she wouldn't put me on her visitor list. I had no way to reach her."

"What did you think when I came to see you last week, and told you I didn't believe Erin's confession? That I had two suspects that I thought had killed Rob?"

"I hoped you were right. But it sounds like they didn't work out. Otherwise, you wouldn't be here thinking I killed him."

"Claire, I came here because I thought your earring found at the scene meant that you had done it. Now, I don't know what to believe. You had everything to lose. You just told me that you were out there that night. You've been lying for a long time. How do I know you're not lying now?"

"Leah, I swear that I'm not."

"Then who killed Rob?"

A shadow fell across the beam of light that had been streaming through the window onto the table where we sat. I glanced up to see if the weather was changing to match my dark and troubled mood. William was standing in the doorway.

66

"I did. I killed Rob Porter."

His words were so choked with pain that his voice sounded nothing like it usually did. He looked at Claire as he spoke, not at me. She stared at him in bewilderment.

"William?"

"I killed Rob Porter," he repeated.

"Why, William? Why would you do that?"

Claire's expression was both horrified and disbelieving.

"Because I thought you were having an affair with him. I was afraid you were going to leave me, Claire. I've been afraid of that since the day I met you. I knew you didn't love me the way that I love you. I tried not to think about it, but it was always there—the fear that you'd meet another man you truly loved, and you would leave me. I killed Rob because I thought he was that man. I couldn't bear it. But it wasn't a man you loved, Claire. It was another woman!"

"William, I don't know what you overheard but—"

"I forgot my binoculars. I left them in the den. You didn't hear me come in the front door because the lawn mower was so loud. I was walking to the kitchen to tell you I'd come back early. I heard you talking to someone. When I realized it was about Rob, I stopped and I listened."

"Oh, William," Claire said.

She walked toward him, holding out her hand, but he stepped away. She flinched as though he'd slapped her.

"Claire, I killed a man because of you. Taking a life is a terrible sin, but I listened to the devil, and I pushed that thought away. I told myself it was justified because Rob was going to destroy my family. I was defending it. But I wasn't, was I? There was no family to defend because there was no true marriage between us. How could there be? I killed a man to save something that was never real. But I committed an even greater sin than murder. I loved you more than I loved God. I put you before God, and this is my punishment."

"No, William. I'm the one who should be punished," she said.

He went on as though he hadn't heard her.

"I suspected you were having an affair. There were too many evening meetings, too many times you hung up the phone as soon as I walked into a room, too many times I called your office and you weren't there. And then one day, I read a text message that popped up on your phone. It said '*Can you get away tonight? I can't wait to see you.*' Then I knew for certain. You had a lover."

I noticed then that tears were starting to stream down his cheeks. Claire stood with her head bowed and her shoulders slumped as though she didn't dare to look directly at William. Neither of them seemed to know that I was in the room. I wished very hard that I wasn't. Then William spoke again. He didn't seem to realize that he was crying.

"I thought it was with Rob Porter. You worked with him. He was handsome, powerful, self-possessed, why wouldn't you be in love with him? And of course he wanted you, any man would. It never occurred to me that my real rival was a woman."

"Please, William, let me explain," Claire said, her voice barely above a whisper.

"You don't need to, Claire. I heard everything."

"What happened that night, William?" I asked.

He kept his eyes on Claire as he answered, as though she had asked him the question.

"When you told me you had to go to the office to meet with a client, I knew it wasn't true. I pretended to leave for my finance committee meeting, but I had cancelled it. I parked my car in the turnaround down the road and waited for you to leave the house. Then I followed you."

Claire kept her face in her hands as William spoke, not looking at him.

"I knew after a few minutes that you were going to Rob Porter's hunting land. I dropped back to make sure you didn't notice me. But I let you get too far ahead. You made it through the railroad crossing on Cleary Road before the crossing bar came down. I didn't. I waited there for 17 minutes. I know because I watched the numbers change on the dashboard clock as I thought of you with him. But when I finally got to Rob's, I saw you driving away."

"Oh, William. Why didn't you follow me home? Oh, why didn't you confront me then? Why did you go to Rob?" Claire asked, raising her tear-stained face.

"Because I was angry. Angrier than I've ever been in my life. I wanted to see Rob. I wanted him to know that he wasn't going to destroy my family. I wouldn't let him."

"What happened when you saw Rob?" I asked.

Again he responded as though Claire had asked him, looking directly at her.

"Rob had his back to me. He had set his gun on the dock. I picked it up. I wanted to scare him. I wanted him to be as afraid of losing his life as I was afraid of losing you. I wasn't going to kill him. But he just kept pretending he didn't know what I was talking about. As though he didn't have to answer me. As though he had the right to take anything he wanted. I shot once and it went wild. He came at me, and I killed him. It doesn't matter that I didn't plan to. I killed a man, Claire, to keep you. But now I know that I never had you. I loved you more than I loved God. And God forgive me, I still do."

Claire reached out to him again, this time succeeding in putting her hand on his arm. He didn't shake her off. For the first time he addressed me.

"Call the police, Leah. I'll be in my office waiting for them."

He turned then and walked away. Claire's body was wracked by sobs. I looked at the clock. It was 1:30. Maeve and Billy would be home in a little more than two hours. This needed to be over before then.

———————

I called Coop. Before he got there, we heard a shot. It came from the second floor. I followed Claire up the stairs. The door to William's office was closed. Claire burst in. He was slumped at his desk. But he didn't look like William anymore.

I tried to pull Claire away, but she wouldn't leave until the police got there and led her downstairs.

67

It took a week before Erin agreed to talk to me. She was home, packing up to move. I couldn't blame her. She'd been released from jail and cleared of all charges, although Cliff Timmins had made noises about charging her with obstructing a police investigation. His campaign manager talked him out of it because that would just keep the story on the front pages. It had gone statewide because of the sensational nature of the case. You can imagine what the headlines were like.

I was startled to see how gaunt Erin looked when she opened the door. Her face was drawn, and her eyes were flat and dull. She didn't say hello, she just stepped aside so I could enter. Her living room was filled with boxes—some taped and ready to go, some half-filled, some still flat and folded on a coffee table. A ginger cat with piercing green eyes jumped off a chair at the sight of me and dashed out of the room. Erin pointed at the empty spot to indicate I should sit down. She resumed her packing.

"Thanks for seeing me, Erin. I know this is—"

"Don't, Leah. Don't say you know this is hard, or you can imagine how I must feel, or you're sorry, or worse, please don't tell me there are better days ahead. I don't want to hear it. You said you needed to talk to me. You're here. Talk."

Her words were hostile, but her voice was monotone, as though every bit of life and feeling had been emptied out of her.

"I won't say any of the other things, but I have to say that I'm sorry, Erin. So deeply, profoundly sorry for everything that you went through. I'm sorry for the loss of your relationship with Claire, I'm sorry for the way Rob treated you, I'm sorry for the way this turned out."

"Are you? You should be. If you had stopped when I asked you—no, when I told you to—William would still be alive. No one would have ever known about me and Claire. She'd still have her husband, her children would be happy, her career would be thriving. She'd be living a good life. Instead, her husband is dead, her children are devastated, and her career is in ruins. That's on you."

The only good thing about Erin's harsh takedown was that at least some life had returned to her voice—even if only to excoriate me.

"I was trying to help you, Erin. I knew you didn't kill Rob. You didn't deserve to go to prison."

"Did you ever think that I might *want* to, Leah? I have nothing without Claire, but she had a chance at being happy. When you love someone, you want them to be happy, even if it isn't with you. I wasn't being a hero. I wasn't sacrificing. Without Claire, I don't care about my life. I'm never going to have her now. She doesn't want to see me or talk to me ever again. It would be too hard for her children, she said. I understand. They have enough to handle."

"Erin, you didn't kill Rob. You're innocent. You shouldn't go to prison for life for a crime you didn't commit."

"What does it matter who's innocent and who's guilty? A life was taken. Rob's. Someone had to pay. I was willing for it to be me. I didn't want your help in the first place, Leah. I should never have let Gabe talk me into it. But I didn't want to go to prison if I didn't have to. It wasn't until you came up with Rob's wife and Shane that it hit me. It was one thing for me to take the blame for Claire, but I couldn't let someone else become the scapegoat. And I realized that if you kept digging, you might find out about me and Claire. So, I changed my plea.

"But that wasn't enough. You just wouldn't stop. You ruined everything.

Now, thanks to you, when Claire thinks of me it won't be with love, it will be with hate, because I cost her everything that matters to her."

"I don't believe that, Erin. Claire has loved you since you were both in college. She won't think of what you cost her. She'll think about what you were willing to give up for her."

"I'll never know what she thinks. I'm never going to see or talk to her again. It's impossible. You've said your piece. What else do you want? My gratitude? Sorry, I don't have any. Please, just go."

As I stood and walked to the door, Erin said, "Wait."

I turned back to face her. She bent down and pulled an opaque green plastic ball out of a cat's toybox. It was the kind that dispenses treats when the cat rolls the ball around. She unscrewed the two halves, pulled out a small velvet jewelry bag, and handed it to me.

"What is this?"

"The earrings Claire gave me. I couldn't bear to throw them away, so I hid them where they wouldn't be found. Now they're just a reminder of what I've lost. You take them. A souvenir of how smart you are."

She shoved them into my hand and then opened the door for me to leave.

68

Father Lindstrom arrived home the next day. I had never needed the touchstone of his moral compass more. I barely gave him time to unpack before I showed up on his doorstep.

When he answered my knock on his apartment door, and I saw his fluff of white hair, and the gentle smile he always has for me, no matter what kind of stupid, mean-spirited, or ill-considered thing I've done, I couldn't help it. I started to cry. Without saying a word, he held out his arms and hugged me.

Some minutes later, sitting at his kitchen table, I refused the cup of tea he offered.

"I don't think so, Father. I just need to talk right now."

"I know, Leah. I'm here to listen."

And he did with his full attention all the way to the end of the rambling, repetitious, tragic story I told.

"So, nothing turned out the way I thought it would. Erin didn't go to prison, but she isn't happy. In fact, she's very angry at me. And she's leaving town. Claire put her house up for sale, and she and her kids have already gone. She asked me not to contact her again. It's too painful, she said. And of course, worst of all, William is dead. Claire told me not to blame myself, that the guilt and the burden are hers. But Erin said that none of this would have happened if I had just let things alone. And she's right, isn't she? Go ahead, you can say it."

"I won't say it because I don't believe it's true. There were things set in motion long before you came on the scene, Leah."

"Yes, but I'm the one who made them all collide, and look at the result."

"Do you know the lines by Sir Walter Scott, 'Oh what a tangled web we weave when first we practice to deceive?' "

"I didn't know who wrote it, but I've heard the quote, yes," I said.

"Everyone in this situation was involved in deceit—Claire, Erin, Rob, William, Spencer, the Grangers. They were lying to each other, to you, to the police, to themselves. The choices each of them made created a web of deception that entangled them all. And you, well, you walked into that spider's web of lies, and you did what people do. You hit at it, you brushed it away, and the strands of lies broke. The web fell apart and those entrapped in it fell. You are not to blame for what happened, Leah. All stories don't have a happy ending."

"That's not as comforting as you usually are, Father. I'm part of the reason the story didn't end well. A normal person would have stopped when Erin and Gabe said it was over."

"If you're making the argument that you're not a normal person, I won't counter that." He said it in a teasing tone, and I knew he was trying to make me smile. Which I couldn't help doing, a little.

"Hey, I don't come here for the burns, Father, I come here for the unconditional love," I said.

"You have it, Leah. I spoke in jest, but as with most joking, there's an element of truth in it. You were an unusual and original child. Although you're an adult now, I still see some of that young girl I first met so many years ago. You have a relentless need to find the truth. It pushes you further than most people would go. What you're struggling with now is what I've told you before. Finding the truth isn't the same as finding the answers."

"Maybe I should get that tattooed somewhere," I said with a heavy sigh. "I know that you're right. I just wish I was as good at finding answers as I can be at finding the unwanted, inconvenient, and in this case, devastating truth. Maybe it would help if I consulted with you *before* I start down a path, not after I've already carpet-bombed it."

"You do very well following your own path, Leah. And that reminds me. I'm so glad that you followed a path that led you to Coop."

"Thanks, Father. There's at least one part of my life I didn't mess up. I'm pretty happy about it myself. It's a little bit strange still, but it gets more normal feeling every day. The only thing I don't like is people sort of pushing us with questions."

"What kind of questions?"

"Oh, like when we're going to move in together, or get engaged, or married, or, in Miguel's case, if we'll name our first child after him. All of that is way, way outside of what I even want to think about now. I just want to be happy with where we are, and what we're doing. I don't want to jinx things. Let's just see what unfolds."

"Most people are only asking because they care about you, but you're well within your rights not to answer. And as long as you and Coop are in agreement about the direction of your relationship, that's all that matters."

"You're right, I know."

But there was this teeny, almost impossible to hear whisper in my head that said, *But are you and Coop on the same page?*

I shut it down.

"So, tell me about your fishing trip, Father. Have you got a story about the one that got away?"

"As a matter of fact, I do."

"This is really beautiful. What a good idea you had," I said to Coop.

We were lying on the double chaise lounge Coop had purchased specifically for the purpose of watching the night sky from his backyard. It was late, and most of the houses in the neighborhood were dark.

"When you look at that expanse of stars above you, it makes you think, doesn't it?" he asked.

"Is that a trick question? Because after a nice dinner and a shared bottle of wine, I'm really more in relaxing than thinking mode."

"No, I know, me, too. Maybe think isn't the right word. I should have said it makes you feel, doesn't it?"

"Feel like what?"

"Like we really are part of something much bigger than us. That most of the things we worry about aren't that important. That the universe was here before we were and will be here long after we're gone, and maybe we should just try to make life easier for one another while we're around and leave it at that."

"You mean like you shouldn't have yelled at me for going out to Claire's alone? Because I was right, and I wasn't in danger."

"I didn't yell. And I already said that you were right. But yes, that's along the lines of what I meant. Sometimes you can get so worn down by the daily grind that you forget there's more to life. When you look up at a big open sky like this, it helps your perspective."

"Agreed. But does your perspective need help? Is everything okay at the sheriff's office?"

"Yeah, I'd say so. We're not where I'd like us to be yet, but I think morale is improving. Except for Owen's. I think he's planning to leave."

"Wow. How do you feel about that?"

"Owen's a smart guy, but not as smart as he thinks he is. He let his ego and his temper get in the way of the investigation. He was really pissed that Darmody messed up handling the earring. When there was no way to get usable touch DNA from it, he didn't follow up with the old-school things he could've done—like getting a loupe and looking at the tiny markings on the earring post. He didn't like it when I pointed out that you ran circles around him on that."

"You think I ran circles around Owen? That makes me very happy. But to be fair, it was more like I was a pinball ricocheting off all the dead ends and bad ideas I came up with. I took a lot of wrong turns to get there."

"Maybe so, but you kept going and that's how you got there. Owen moved on too soon. And he didn't want to take responsibility for the things that went wrong on the investigation. He blamed the earring screw-up on one of the guys on the team. I don't like that. If you're in charge, you're responsible. I let him know. Now I think he's going to apply for the lieutenant position at HPD. Mick Reilly's got to be pretty desperate about now. Erin's gone, the guy they finally hired for my old position is just starting, and now the captain's spot is empty. I think there's a really good chance if Owen wants the job, it's his."

"What about you going back and taking Rob's job as captain? Or maybe even Mick's job when he retires in the fall?"

"No. No chance. I like the challenge in the sheriff's office. And I don't have to worry about a city council second-guessing me."

"If Owen leaves, that means you could hire a female officer. You've only got Marla Jarvis and she's only around for another year before she retires."

"I could, yes. And I'll make sure we get as many female candidates in the pool as possible. We'll see what happens."

"What are the requirements? Maybe I'll apply."

"I'd laugh if I was sure that you're joking."

"Well, I was, but since you say that, maybe I'm not. Think about it, Coop. We could be crime fighters together. I'm the cool detective who operates on gut instinct and amazing insights. You're the hard-working but unimaginative sheriff who hates to admit it but knows he couldn't crack the case without me."

He shook his head, then leaned over and kissed me.

"Sorry, no can do. I have a policy against nepotism in my office."

"Hey, come on. We'd be great together. Also, we're not related, so no nepotism."

"I think we're already great together. And my nepotism rule is very broad. It includes past, present, and future relatives. Listen, I've got an idea for you. How about you focus on that book you keep telling your agent you're working so hard on? Sooner or later, you're going to have to send him an actual draft, right?"

"You're killing my buzz. You're also right. I do have to get serious. Are you still willing to take a trip to the U.P. with me to do some research?"

"Absolutely. Are you still a hard no on camping when we do?"

"Absolutely. It's a motel all the way, baby, or possibly the spare room at my Aunt Nancy's. I—"

I broke off at the sight of an exceptionally bright object streaking across the night sky. "Coop, look, a shooting star! Make a wish!"

We watched in silence as the brilliant bit of heated dust and rock hurtled across the sky and out of sight.

"What did you wish for?" I asked.

"Can't tell, or it won't come true. But you'll be the first one to know if it does."

I didn't tell him my wish either, which was that we'd always have nights like this, that *GO News* would go away for good, and that I'd never get caught up in another investigation that hurt so many people I cared about. My wishes are always tightly packed. Two of them fell by the wayside pretty quickly. The jury's still out on the third.

DANGEROUS CHOICES: Leah Nash #10

Two can keep a secret...if one of them is dead.

Three children entered the woods; just two returned. And they are the only ones who know what happened to their friend. The secret they carry echoes down the years until it becomes too much for one of them to bear. But the attempt to set things right goes horribly wrong.

Exactly how wrong is what Leah Nash, a journalist with trust issues and a compulsion to find the truth, aims to discover. Leah is rocked by the seemingly senseless present-day murder of someone very close to her. Driven by her principles and fueled by personal grief, she follows a strange trail of clues that lead her to a dark past.

A past where the answer—and the killer—await.

ACKNOWLEDGMENTS

I'm lucky to have the support and encouragement of family, friends, and readers, and I appreciate you all. But I also have two people who deserve a specific shoutout not just for their help with this book, but with the entire series to date.

So, thank you, to my outdoorsman brother Jim Hunter who answers my queries about night fishing, the size of inland lakes, how thick river ice needs to be to walk on, and anything else I need to bolster my limited knowledge of outdoor pursuits.

And thank you to my favorite son-in-law Joe Sell, a Wisconsin native son who is always ready with any particulars I need about Wisconsin beer, sports, restaurants, slang, and more.

And of course, I could never have a section titled "Acknowledgements" that didn't acknowledge the unconditional support of my husband Gary Rayburn, who bears with my writing process—which can get a bit chaotic at times—and never complains or wavers in his belief that eventually it will all come together.

ABOUT THE AUTHOR

Susan Hunter is a charter member of Introverts International (which meets the 12th of Never at an undisclosed location). She has worked as a reporter and managing editor, during which time she received a first place UPI award for investigative reporting and a Michigan Press Association first place award for enterprise/feature reporting.

Susan has also taught composition at the college level, written advertising copy, newsletters, press releases, speeches, web copy, academic papers and memos. Lots and lots of memos. She lives in rural Michigan with her husband Gary, who is a man of action, not words.

During certain times of the day, she can also be found wandering the mean streets of small-town Himmel, Wisconsin, looking for clues, stopping for a meal at the Elite Cafe, dropping off a story lead at the *Himmel Times Weekly*, or meeting friends for a drink at McClain's Bar and Grill.

Sign up for Susan Hunter's reader list at
severnriverbooks.com/authors/susan-hunter

Printed in the United States
by Baker & Taylor Publisher Services